"At long... Grisham... dimensional to care about ... the book doesn't slow down for a second." —*Fortune*

"Compelling ... *Company Man* confirms what *Paranoia* made clear: [Finder] has unusually keen instincts for back-stabbing in the business world ... as much a novel about the chicanery of the business world as it is a mystery story ... Finder weaves these prospects menacingly throughout the story." —*The New York Times*

"Sharply created characters ... makes the workplace as duplicitous a world as any in the Cold War. *Company Man* resonates with anyone who has seen corporate politics at its worst." —Orlando *Sun-Sentinel*

"Finder skillfully places his story of corporate intrigue (who is trying to sell the company, and why?) in counterpoint to the unraveling of a family's secrets (why is Nick's son Lucas so disturbed?), and the plot, which also features rogue cops and at least one homicide, accelerates to a headlong finish." —*The New Yorker*

"It's everything a thriller should be: suspenseful, entertaining— and, above all, thrilling." —*Chicago Sun-Times*

"Finder (who last mined corporate culture in 2004's *Paranoia*) expertly keeps the pages turning as he ups the stakes chapter after chapter in Conover's professional and personal life. He is equally confident in portraying the small stuff involving family conflicts, marriages in turmoil and especially the telling details of corporate life ... it more than achieves its main goal of en- tertaining the reader—as a good thriller is supposed to do." —*Baltimore Sun*

ALSO BY JOSEPH FINDER

FICTION
Vanished
The Moscow Club
Extraordinary Powers
The Zero Hour
High Crimes
Paranoia

NONFICTION
Red Carpet: The Connection Between the Kremlin and America's Most Powerful Businessmen

COMPANY
MAN

JOSEPH FINDER

St. Martin's Paperbacks

This is a work of fiction. All of the characters, organizations, and events portrayed in this novel are either products of the author's imagination or are used fictitiously.

Published in the United States by St. Martin's Paperbacks, an imprint of St. Martin's Publishing Group.

COMPANY MAN

Copyright © 2005 by Joseph Finder.
Excerpt from *Killer Instinct* copyright © 2006 by Joseph Finder.

All rights reserved.

For information, address St. Martin's Publishing Group, 120 Broadway, New York, NY 10271.

www.stmartins.com

Library of Congress Catalog Card Number: 2004060155

ISBN: 978-0-312-99229-3

Our books may be purchased in bulk for promotional, educational, or business use. Please contact your local bookseller or the Macmillan Corporate and Premium Sales Department at 1-800-221-7945, ext. 5442, or by email at MacmillanSpecialMarkets@macmillan.com.

Printed in the United States of America

St. Martin's Press hardcover edition / April 2005
St. Martin's Paperbacks edition / March 2006

10 9 8 7 6 5 4 3 2 1

For my parents, Morris and Natalie Finder

And in loving memory of my in-laws,
Michel and Josephine Souda

That is the thankless position of the father in the family—the provider of all, and the enemy of all.

—AUGUST STRINDBERG, 1886

— PART ONE —

SECURITY

1

THE OFFICE OF the chief executive officer of the Stratton Corporation wasn't really an office at all. At a quick glance you'd call it a cubicle, but at the Stratton Corporation—which *made* the elegant silver-mesh fabric panels that served as the walls around the CEO's brushed-steel Stratton Ergon desk—"cubicle" was a dirty word. You didn't work in a cubicle in the middle of a cube farm; you multitasked at your "home base" in an "open-plan system."

Nicholas Conover, Stratton's CEO, leaned back in his top-of-the-line leather Stratton Symbiosis chair, trying to concentrate on the stream of figures spewing from the mouth of his chief financial officer, Scott McNally, a small, nerdy, self-deprecating guy who had a spooky affinity for numbers. Scott was sardonic and quick-witted, in a dark, sharp-edged way. He was also one of the smartest men Nick had ever met. But there was nothing Nick hated more than budget meetings.

"Am I boring you, Nick?"

"You gotta ask?"

Scott was standing by the giant plasma screen, touching it with the stylus to advance the PowerPoint slides. He was not much more than five feet tall, over a foot shorter than Nick. He was prone to nervous twitches, anxious shrugs, and his fingernails were all bitten to the quick. He was also rapidly going bald, though he wasn't even out of his thirties; his dome was fringed with wild curly hair. He had plenty of money, but he always seemed to wear the same blue button-down Oxford shirt, fraying at the collar, that he'd worn since Wharton. His brown eyes darted around as he spoke, sunken in deep lilac hollows.

As he rattled on about the layoffs and how much they were going to cost this year versus how much they'd save the next, he fidgeted, with his free hand, with what remained of his straggly hair.

Nick's desk was kept fastidiously clear by his terrific assistant, Marjorie Dykstra. The only things on it were his computer (wireless keyboard and mouse, no pesky rat's nest of wires, a flat-panel screen), a red model truck with the Stratton logo painted on the side, and framed pictures of his kids. He kept sneaking glances at the photos, hoping Scott would think he was just staring into space and concentrating on the interminable presentation.

What's the bottom line, dude? he wanted to say. *Are the guys in Boston going to be happy or not?*

But Scott kept droning on and on about cost savings, about outplacement costs, about metrics, about employees as "units," as bar graphs on a PowerPoint slide. "Current average employee age is 47.789 years, with a standard deviation of 6.92," Scott said. He noticed Nick's glazed expression as he touched the screen with the aluminum stylus, and a half smile tugged at the corner of his mouth. "But hey, age is just a number, right?"

"Is there any good news here?"

"Ahh, it's only money." Scott paused. "That was a joke."

Nick stared at the little display of silver frames. Since

Laura's death last year he cared about two things only: his job and his kids. Julia was ten, and she beamed with her thousand-watt smile in her school picture, her curly chestnut hair unruly, her enormous, liquid brown eyes sparkling, her big new teeth a little crooked, a smile so unself-conscious and dazzling she seemed to be bursting out of the photo. Lucas was sixteen, dark-haired like his little sister, and unnervingly handsome; he had his mother's cornflower-blue eyes, an angular jawline. A high school heartthrob. Lucas smiled for the camera, a smile that Nick hadn't actually seen in person since the accident.

There was just one photo of all four of them, sitting on the porch of the old house, Laura seated in the middle, everyone touching her, hands on her shoulder or her waist, the center of the family. The gaping hole, now. Her amused, twinkling blue eyes looked right at the camera, her expression frank and poised, seemingly tickled by some private joke. And of course Barney, their overweight, lumbering Golden/Lab mix, sat on his haunches in front of everyone, smiling his dog smile. Barney was in all the family pictures, even in last Christmas's family photo, the one with Lucas glowering like Charles Manson.

"Todd Muldaur's going to have a shit fit," Nick said, lifting his eyes to meet Scott's. Muldaur was a general partner in Fairfield Equity Partners in Boston, the private-equity firm that now owned the Stratton Corporation. Todd, not to put too fine a point on it, was Nick's boss.

"That's about the size of it," Scott agreed. He turned his head suddenly, and a second later Nick heard the shouts too.

"What the hell—?" Scott said. A deep male voice, somewhere nearby, yelling. A woman's voice, sounded like Marge's.

"You don't have an *appointment,* sir!" Marge was shouting, her voice high and frightened. An answering rumble, the words indistinct. "He isn't here, anyway, and if you don't leave right this *instant,* sir, I'm going to have to call Security."

A hulking figure crashed into one of the silver panels that outlined Nick's workstation, almost tipping it over. A bearded giant in his late thirties wearing a checked flannel shirt, unbuttoned, over a black Harley-Davidson T-shirt: barrel-chested, powerful-looking. The guy looked vaguely familiar. A factory worker? Someone who'd recently been laid off?

Immediately behind him followed Marge, her arms flailing. "You *cannot* come in here!" she shrilled. "Get out of here immediately, or I'll call Security."

The giant's foghorn voice boomed: "Well, whaddaya know, there he is. Boss man himself. The Slasher is in."

Nick felt a cold fear wash over him as he realized that the budget meeting might turn out to be the high point of his day.

THE GUY, PROBABLY a worker just laid off in the most recent round of cuts, was staring, wild-eyed.

Nick flashed on news stories he'd read about crazed employees—"disgruntled workers," they were always called—who'd been let go, and then showed up at work and started picking people off.

"I just remembered a phone conference I'm late for," Scott McNally muttered as he squeezed past the intruder. "If you'll excuse me."

Nick got up slowly, raised himself to his full six-two. The crazy bearded guy was considerably bigger.

"What can I do for you?" Nick asked politely, calmly, the way you might try to lull a rabid Doberman pinscher.

"What can you do for me? That's fucking hilarious.

There's nothing more you can do for me, or *to* me, asshole."

Marge, hovering directly behind him, her hands flailing, said: "Nick, I'll call Security."

Nick put up his hand to tell her to hold off. "I'm sure there's no need," he said.

Marge squinted at him to indicate her strong disagreement, but she nodded, backed away warily.

The bearded man took a step forward, puffing up his massive chest, but Nick didn't budge. There was something primal going on here: the interloper was a baboon baring his canines, screaming and strutting to scare off a predator. He smelled of rancid sweat and cigar smoke.

Nick fought the strong temptation to deck the guy but reminded himself that, as CEO of Stratton, he couldn't exactly do stuff like that. Plus, if this was one of the five thousand Stratton workers who'd been laid off within the last two years, he had a right to be angry. The thing to do was to talk the guy down, let him vent, let the air out of the balloon slowly.

Nick pointed to an empty chair, but the bearded man refused to sit. "What's your name?" Nick said, softening his voice a bit.

"Old Man Devries woulda never had to ask," the man retorted. "He knew everyone's name."

Nick shrugged. That was the myth, anyway. Folksy, paternal Milton Devries—Nick's predecessor—had been CEO of Stratton for almost four decades. The old man had been beloved, but there was no way he knew ten thousand names.

"I'm not as good with names as the old man was," Nick said. "So help me out here."

"Louis Goss."

Nick extended his hand to shake, but Goss didn't take it. Instead, Goss pointed a stubby forefinger at him. "When you sat down at your fancy computer at your fancy desk and made the decision to fire half the guys in the chair factory, did you even fucking *think* about who these people are?"

"More than you know," Nick said. "Listen, I'm sorry you lost your job—"

"I'm not here because I lost my job—see, I got seniority. I'm here to tell you that you deserve to lose yours. You think just because you waltz through this plant once a month that you know anything about these guys? These are human beings, buddy. Four hundred and fifty men and women who get up at four in the morning to do the early shift so they can feed their families and pay their rent or their mortgages and take care of their sick kids or their dying parents, okay? Do you realize that because of you some of these guys are going to lose their *houses?*"

Nick closed his eyes briefly. "Louis, are you just going to talk at me, or do you want to hear me out?"

"I'm here to give you a little free advice, Nick."

"I find you get what you pay for."

The man ignored him. "You better think seriously about whether you really want to go through with these layoffs. Because if you don't call them off by tomorrow morning, this place is going to grind to a halt."

"What are you trying to say?"

"I got half, maybe three-quarters of the factory floor with me on this. More, once we start. We're all sicking out tomorrow, Nick. And we're staying sick until my buddies get their jobs back." Goss was smiling with tobacco-darkened teeth, enjoying his moment. "You do the right thing, we do the right thing. Everyone's happy."

Nick stared at Goss. How much of this was bluster, how much on the level? A wildcat strike could paralyze the company, especially if it spread to the other plants.

"Why don't you think this over when you're driving home tonight in your Mercedes to your gated community?" Goss went on. "Ask yourself if you feel like taking your company down with you."

It's a Chevy Suburban, not a Mercedes, Nick wanted to say, but then he was struck by that phrase, "gated community." How did Goss know where he lived? There'd been nothing in the newspaper about that, though of course people talked . . . Was this a veiled threat?

Goss smiled, a mirthless, leering grin, saw the reaction on Nick's face. "Yeah, that's right. I know where you live."

Nick felt his rage flare up like a lit match tossed into a pool of gasoline. He sprang out of his seat, lunged forward, his face a few inches from Louis Goss's face. "What the hell are you trying to say?" It took all his self-restraint to keep from grabbing the collar of the guy's flannel shirt and twisting it tight around his fat neck. Up close he realized that Goss's bulk was all flab, not muscle.

Goss flinched, seemed to shrink back a bit, intimidated.

"You think everyone doesn't know you live in a fucking huge mansion in a gated community?" Goss said. "You think anyone else in this company can afford to live like that?"

Nick's anger subsided as quickly as it had surged. He felt a damp sort of relief; he'd misunderstood. The threat that Louis had actually made seemed suddenly tame by comparison. He leaned even closer, poked a finger against Goss's chest, jabbing the little white hyphen between "Harley" and "Davidson."

"Let me ask *you* something, Louis. Do you remember the 'town meeting' at the chair plant two years ago? When I told you guys the company was in a shitload of trouble and layoffs seemed likely but I wanted to avoid them if possible? You weren't sick that day, were you?"

"I was there," Goss muttered.

"Remember I asked if you'd all be willing to cut your hours back so everyone could stay on the job? Remember what everyone said?"

Goss was silent, looking off to one side, avoiding Nick's direct stare.

"You all said no, you couldn't do that. A pay cut was out of the question."

"Easy for you to—"

"And I asked whether you'd all be willing to cut back on your health plan, with your daycare and your health-club memberships. Now, how many people raised their hands to say yeah, okay, we'll cut back? Any recollection?"

Goss shook his head slowly, resentfully.

"Zero. Not a single goddamned hand went up. Nobody wanted to lose a goddamned hour of work; nobody wanted to lose a single perk." He could hear the blood rushing through his ears, felt a flush of indignation. "You think I slashed five thousand jobs, buddy? Well, the reality is, I *saved* five thousand jobs. Because the boys in Boston who own this company now don't fuck around. They're looking at our biggest competitor and seeing that the other guys aren't bending metal, they're not making their furniture in Michigan anymore. Everything's made in China now, Louis. *That's* why they can undercut us on price. You think the boys in Boston don't remind me of that every single goddamned chance they get?"

"I got no idea," Louis Goss muttered, shuffling his feet. It was all he could muster.

"So go right ahead, Louis. Have your strike. And they'll bring in a new CEO who'll make me look like Mister Rogers. Someone who'll shut down all of our plants the second he walks in this building. Then you wanna keep your job, Louis? I suggest you learn fucking *Mandarin*."

Louis was silent for a few seconds, and when he spoke, it was in a small, sullen voice. "You're going to fire me, aren't you?"

"You?" Nick snorted. "You're not worth the severance package. Now, get the fuck back on the line and get the hell out of my . . . work space."

A few seconds after Louis Goss had lumbered away, Marge appeared again. "You need to go home, Nick," she said. "Now."

"Home?"

"It's the police. There's a problem."

2

NICK BACKED HIS Chevy Suburban out of his space too fast, not bothering to check whether anyone was behind him, and careened through the parking lot that encircled the headquarters building. Even at the height of the workday, it stood half-empty as it had for the last two years, since the layoffs began. Gallows humor abounded among the employees these days, Nick knew. The upside of losing half the workforce was, you could always find a parking space.

His nerves felt stretched taught. Acres of empty black asphalt, surrounded by a great black field of charred buffalo grass, the remains of a prescribed fire. Buffalo grass never needed mowing, but every few years it had to be burned to the ground. The air smelled like a Weber grill.

Black against black against the black of the road, a desolate landscape. He wondered whether driving by the vast swath of scorched earth every day, staring at the charred field through the office windows, left a dark carbon smudge on your psyche.

You need to go home. Now.

When you have kids, they're the first thing you think of. Even a guy like Nick, hardly a worrywart, you get a

call from the cops and your imagination takes flight in
a bad direction.

But both kids were all right, the cops had assured
Marjorie. Julia was on her way back from school, and
Lucas—well, Lucas had been in classes today and was
doing whatever the hell he did after school these days,
which was another issue entirely.

That wasn't it.

Yes, it was another break-in, they'd said, but this
time he really needed to come by. What the hell could
that mean?

Over the past year or so, Nick had gotten used to
the periodic calls from the alarm company or the po-
lice. The burglar alarm would go off in the middle of
the day. There'd been a break-in. The alarm company
would verify that the alarm was genuine by calling home
or Nick's office and requesting a code. If no authorized
user said it was a false alarm, the company would im-
mediately dispatch the Fenwick police. A couple of
cops would then drive by the house, check it out.

Inevitably it happened when no one was there—
the crew working on the kitchen were taking one of
their frequent days off; the kids were at school; the
housekeeper, Marta, was out shopping or maybe pick-
ing up Julia.

Nothing was ever stolen. The intruder would force
a window or one of the French doors, get inside, and
leave a little message.

Literally, a message: words spray-painted in Day-
Glo orange, all capital letters formed with the precision
of an architect or mechanical engineer: NO HIDING
PLACE.

Three words, one on top of another.

Was there any doubt it was a deranged laid-off em-
ployee? The graffiti defaced the walls of the living
room, the dining room they never used, the freshly

plastered walls of the kitchen. In the beginning it had scared the shit out of him.

The real message, of course, was that they weren't safe. They could be gotten to.

The first graffiti had appeared on the heavy, ornate ash-wood front door, which Laura had deliberated over for weeks with the architect, a door that had cost a ridiculous three thousand dollars, a fucking *door,* for God's sake. Nick had made his feelings known but hadn't objected, because it was obviously important to her, for some reason. He'd been perfectly content with the flimsy paneled front door that came with the house they'd just bought. He didn't want to change anything about the house except maybe to shrink it to half its size. There was a saying that was popular at Stratton, which Old Man Devries was fond of repeating: the whale that spouts gets the harpoon. Sometimes he thought about having one of those bronze-looking estate wall plaques made for him by Frontgate, the kind you see on stone entrance pillars in front of McMansions, saying in raised copper letters, SPOUTING WHALE HOUSE.

But to Laura, the front door was symbolic: it was where you welcomed friends and family, and it was where you kept out those who weren't welcome. So it had to be both beautiful and substantial. "It's the *front door,* Nick," she'd insisted. "The first thing people see. That's the *one* place you don't cheap out."

Maybe, on some level, she thought a three-inch-thick front door would make them safer. Buying this insanely big house in the Fenwicke Estates: that was her idea too. She wanted the safety of the gated community. It took only a couple of anonymous threatening phone calls, as soon as the layoffs were announced.

"If you're a target, we're all targets," she said. There was a lot of anger out there, directed at him. He wasn't going to argue with her. He had a family to protect.

Now, with her gone, it felt as if he'd absorbed her neurosis, as if it had penetrated his bones. He felt, sometimes, that his family, what remained of it, was as fragile as an egg.

He also knew that the security of their gated community was little more than an illusion. It was a show, an elaborate charade, the fancy gatehouse and the guards, the private security, the high black iron fence with the spearhead finials.

The Suburban screeched to a stop before the ornately scrolled cast-iron gate beside the brick gatehouse built to resemble a miniature castle. A brass plaque on one of the piers said FENWICKE ESTATES.

That little "e" at the end of Fenwick—he'd always found it pretentious to the point of being irritating. Plus, he was so over the irony here, this posh enclosed neighborhood equipped with the priciest security you could get—the tall wrought-iron perimeter fence with the fiber-optic sensing cable concealed inside the top rail, the pan-tilt-zoom CCTV surveillance cameras, the motion-sensor intruder alarms—where you couldn't stop the loonies from scrambling in through the dense surrounding woods and climbing over the fence.

"Another break-in, Mr. Conover," said Jorge, the day guard. Nice guy, couldn't be nicer. The security guards were all professional in demeanor, all wore sharp uniforms.

Nick nodded grimly, waited for the motor-driven gate to open, ridiculously slow. The high-pitched electronic warning beep was annoying. Everything beeped these days: trucks backing up, dishwashers and clothes dryers, microwaves. It really could drive you crazy.

"Police are there now, you know," said Jorge. "Three cruisers, sir."

"Any idea what it is?"

"No, sir, I don't, I'm sorry."

The damned gate took forever to open. It was ridiculous. In the evening sometimes there was a line of cars waiting to get in. Something had to be done about it. For Christ's sake, what if his house caught fire—would the fire department trucks have to sit here while his house turned to toast?

He raced the engine in annoyance. Jorge shrugged a sheepish apology.

The second the gate was open far enough for the car to get through, he gunned it—the Suburban's pickup never ceased to amaze him—and barreled over the tiger-teeth tire-shredders that enforced one-way traffic, across the wide circular court paved in antique brick in a geometric pattern by old-world Italian stonemasons shipped over from Sicily, past the SPEED LIMIT 20 sign at twice that at least.

The brick pavement turned into glass-smooth macadam road, no street sign. He raced past the old-growth elms and firs, the mailboxes the size of doghouses, none of the houses visible. You had to be invited over to see what your neighbor's house looked like. And there sure as hell weren't any block parties here in Fenwicke Estates.

When he saw police squad cars parked on the street and at the entrance to his driveway, he felt something small and cold and hard forming at the base of his stomach, a little icicle of fear.

A uniformed policeman halted him a few hundred feet from the house, halfway up the drive. Nick jumped out and slammed the car door in one smooth, swift motion.

The cop was short and squat, powerful-looking, seemed to be perspiring heavily despite the cool weather. His badge said MANZI. A walkie-talkie hitched to his belt squawked unceasingly.

"You Mr. Conover?" He stood directly in front of

Nick's path, blocking his way. Nick felt a flash of annoyance. My house, my driveway, my burglar alarm: get the fuck out of my way.

"Yeah, that's me, what's going on?" Nick tried to keep the irritation, and the anxiety, out of his voice.

"Ask you some questions?" Dappled sunlight filtered through the tall birches that lined the asphalt lane, played on the cop's inscrutable face.

Nick shrugged. "Sure—what is it, the graffiti again?"

"What time did you leave the house this morning, sir?"

"Around seven-thirty, but the kids are normally out of there by eight, eight-fifteen at the latest."

"What about your wife?"

Nick gazed at the cop steadily. Most of the cops had to know who he was at least. He wondered if this guy was just trying to yank his chain. "I'm a single parent."

A pause. "Nice house."

"Thank you." Nick could sense the resentment, the envy rising off the man like swamp gas. "What happened?"

"House is okay, sir. It's brand-new, looks like. Not even finished yet, huh?"

"We're just having some work done," Nick said impatiently.

"I see. The workers, they're here every day?"

"I wish. Not yesterday or today."

"Your alarm company lists a work number for you at the Stratton Corporation," Officer Manzi said. He was looking down at an aluminum clipboard, his black eyes small and deeply inset like raisins in a butterscotch pudding. "You work there."

"Right."

"What do you do at Stratton?" There was a beat before the policeman looked up and let his eyes meet Nick's: the guy knew damned well what he did there.

"I'm the CEO."

Manzi nodded as if everything now made sense. "I see. You've had a number of break-ins over the last several months, is that correct, Mr. Conover?"

"Five or six times now."

"What kind of security system you have here, sir?"

"Burglar alarm on the doors and some of the windows and French doors. Basic system. Nothing too elaborate."

"Home like this, that's not much of a system. No cameras, right?"

"Well, we live in this, you know, gated community."

"Yes, sir, I can see that. Lot of good it does, keeping out the wing nuts."

"Point taken." Nick almost smiled.

"Sounds like the burglar alarm isn't on very often, sir, that right?"

"Officer, why so many cars here today for a routine—"

"Mind if I ask the questions?" Officer Manzi said. The guy seemed to be enjoying his authority, pushing around the boss man from Stratton. Let him, Nick thought. Let him have his fun. But—

Nick heard a car approaching, turned and saw the blue Chrysler Town & Country, Marta behind the wheel. He felt that little chemical surge of pleasure he always got when he saw his daughter, the way he used to feel with Lucas too, until that got complicated. The minivan pulled up alongside Nick and the engine was switched off. A car door opened and slammed, and Julia shouted, "What are *you* doing home, Daddy?"

She ran toward him, wearing a light-blue hooded Stratton sweatshirt and jeans, black sneakers. She wore some slight variant of the outfit every day, a sweatshirt or an athletic jersey. When Nick went to the same elementary school, more than thirty years before, you weren't allowed to wear jeans, and sweatshirts weren't considered appropriate school attire. But he didn't have time in the mornings to argue with her, and he was inclined to go easy on his little girl, given what she had to be going through since the death of her mother.

She hugged him tight around his abdomen. He no longer hoisted her up, since at almost five feet and ninety-something pounds, it wasn't so easy. In the last year she'd gotten tall and leggy, almost gangly, though there was still a pocket of baby fat at her tummy. She was starting to develop physically, little breast buds emerging, which Nick couldn't deal with. It was a constant reminder of his inadequacy as a parent: who the hell was going to talk to her, get her through adolescence?

The hug went on for several seconds until Nick released her, another thing that had changed since Laura was gone. His daughter's hugs: she didn't want to let him go.

Now she looked up at him, her meltingly beautiful brown eyes lively. "How come there's all these police?"

"They want to talk to me, baby doll. No big deal. Where's your backpack?"

"In the car. Did that crazy guy get in the house again and write bad stuff?"

Nick nodded, stroked her glossy brown hair. "What are you doing home now? Don't you have piano?"

She gave him a look of amused contempt. "That's not till four."

"I thought it was three."

"Mrs. Guarini changed it, like, *months* ago, don't you remember?"

He shook his head. "Oh, right. I forgot. Well, listen, I have to talk to this policeman here. Marta, you guys stay here until the police say it's okay to go in the house, okay?"

Marta Burrell was from Barbados, a mocha-skinned woman of thirty-eight, tall and slender as a fashion model with an air of sultry indifference, or maybe arrogance, her default mode. Her jeans were a little too tight, and she customarily wore high heels, and she was vocal about her disapproval of Julia's daily uniform. She expressed disapproval of just about everything in the household. She was ferociously devoted to the kids, though, and was able to make both of them do things Nick couldn't. Marta had been a superb nanny when the kids were little, was an excellent cook, and an indifferent housekeeper.

"Sure, Nick," she said. She reached for Julia, but the girl scampered off.

"You were saying," Nick said to the cop.

Manzi looked up, fixed Nick with a blank look, bordering on impertinence, but there was a gleam in his eyes; he seemed to be restraining a smile. "Do you have any enemies, Mr. Conover?"

"Only about five thousand people in town."

The policeman's eyebrows shot up. "Excuse me."

"We laid off half our workforce recently, as I'm sure you know. More than five thousand employees."

"Ah, yes," the cop said. "You're not a popular man around here, are you?"

"You could say that."

It wasn't that long ago, Nick reflected, that everyone loved him. People he didn't know in high school started sucking up to him. *Forbes* magazine even did a profile. After all, Nick was the youthful blue-collar guy, the son of a guy who'd spent a life bending metal in the chair factory—business reporters ate stuff up. Maybe Nick was never going to be beloved at the company like Old Man Devries, but for a while at least he'd been popular, admired, *liked*. A local hero in the small town of Fenwick, Michigan, sort of, a guy you'd point out at the Shop 'n Save and maybe, if you felt bold, walk up to and introduce yourself in the frozen-foods section.

But that was before—before the first layoffs were announced, two years ago, after Stratton's new owners had laid down the law at the quarterly board meeting in Fenwick. There was no choice. The Stratton Corporation was going down the crapper if they didn't cut costs, and fast. That meant losing half its workforce, five thousand people in a town of maybe forty thousand. It was the most painful thing he'd ever done, something he'd never imagined having to do. There'd been a series of smaller layoffs since the first ones were announced, two years ago. It was like Chinese water torture. The *Fenwick Free Press,* which used to publish puff pieces about Stratton, now ran banner headlines: THREE HUNDRED MORE STRATTON WORKERS FACE THE AXE. CANCER VICTIM SUFFERS LOSS OF STRATTON BEN-EFITS. The local columnists routinely referred to him as "the Slasher."

Nick Conover, local boy made good, had become the most hated man in town.

"Guy like you ought to have better security than that. You get the security you pay for, you know."

Nick was about to reply when he heard his daughter scream.

3

HE RAN TOWARD the source of the screaming and found Julia beside the pool. Her cries came in great ragged gulps. She knelt on the bluestone coping, her hands thrashing in the water, her small back torquing back and forth. Marta stood nearby, helpless and aghast, a hand to her mouth.

Then Nick saw what had made Julia scream, and he felt sick.

A dark shape floated in cranberry red water, splayed and distended, surrounded by slick white entrails. The blood was concentrated in a dark cloud around the carcass; the water got lighter, pinkish as it got farther away from the furry brown mass.

The corpse wasn't immediately recognizable as Barney, their old Lab/Golden Retriever. It took a second glance, a struggle with disbelief. On the bluestone not far from where Julia knelt, keening, was a blood-slick, carbon-steel Henckels knife from their kitchen set.

Many things immediately made sense, now: the unusual police presence, the questioning, even the absence of Barney's usual barked greeting when Nick arrived.

A couple of policemen were busy taking pictures,

talking to one another, their low conversations punctuated by static blasts from their radios. They seemed to be chatting casually, as if nothing unusual had happened. Business as usual to them. No one was expressing sympathy or concern. Nick felt a flash of rage, but the main thing now was to comfort his daughter.

He rushed to her, sank to his knees, put a hand on her back. "Baby," he said. "Baby."

She turned, flung her arms around his neck, let out a wail. Her gasping breath was hot and moist. He held her tight as if he could squeeze the trauma out of her little body, make everything normal again, make her feel safe.

"Oh, baby, I'm so sorry." Her gasps were like spasms, hiccups. He held her even tighter. The copious flow of her tears pooled in the hollow of his neck. He could feel it soak his shirt.

TEN MINUTES LATER, when Marta had taken Julia inside, Nick spoke to Officer Manzi. He made no effort this time to contain his fury. "What the *fuck* are you guys going to do about this?" Nick thundered. "What the hell are you waiting for? These break-ins have been going on for months already, and you haven't done a damned thing about it."

"Excuse me, sir," Manzi said blandly.

"You haven't assigned a detective to the case, you haven't done any investigation, you haven't gone through the lists of laid-off Stratton employees. You've had months to stop this fucking madman. What are you waiting for? Does this lunatic have to murder one of my *kids* before you take it seriously?"

Manzi's detachment—did Nick detect a smug sort of amusement, was that possible?—was infuriating. "Well, sir, as I said, you might want to think about upgrading your security—"

"*My* security? What about you guys? Isn't this your goddamned *job*?"

"You said it yourself, sir—you laid off five thousand Stratton employees. That's going to create more enemies than we can possibly protect you against. You should really upgrade your security system."

"Yeah, and what are *you* going to do? How are *you* going to protect my family?"

"I'll be honest with you, sir. Stalking cases are some of our hardest."

"Meaning you pretty much can't do shit, is that right?"

Manzi shrugged. "You said it. I didn't."

4

AFTER THE POLICE left, Nick tried for a long while to console his daughter. He called to cancel her piano lesson, then sat with her, talking a bit, mostly hugging. When she seemed stable, Nick left her in Marta's care and returned to the office for a largely unproductive afternoon.

By the time he returned home, Julia was asleep and Marta was in the family room, watching a movie about a baby who talks with Bruce Willis's voice.

"Where's Julia?" Nick asked.

"She's asleep," Marta said sadly. "She was okay by the time she went to bed. But she cried a lot, Nick."

Nick shook his head. "That poor baby. This is going to be hardest on her, I think. Barney was Laura's dog, really. To Julia, Barney . . ." He fell silent. "Is Lucas upstairs?"

"He called from a friend's house, said they're working on their history projects."

"Yeah, right. Working on a nickel bag, more like it. Which friend?"

"I think Ziegler? Um, listen—Nick? I'm kind of nervous being alone in the house—after today, I mean."

"I can't blame you. You lock the doors and windows, right?"

"I did, but this crazy person . . ."

"I know. I'm going to have a new system put in right away so you can put on the alarm while you're inside." Stratton's corporate security director had told Nick he'd drop by later, see what he could do. Anything for the boss. They'd gone too long with a rudimentary security system; it was time to put in something state-of-the-art, with cameras and motion detectors and all that. "You can go to sleep if you want."

"I want to see the rest of this movie."

"Sure."

Nick went upstairs and down the hall to Julia's bedroom, quietly opening the door and making his way through the darkness by memory. Enough moonlight filtered through the gaps in the curtains that, once his eyes adjusted, he could make out his daughter's sleeping body. Julia slept under, and with, an assortment of favorite blankets, each of which she'd given names to, as well as a rotating selection of stuffed animals and Beanie Babies from her vast menagerie. Tonight she was clutching Winnie the Pooh, who'd been given to her when she was a few days old, now frayed and matted and stained.

Her choice of sleeping partner was a pretty reliable indicator of her mental state: Elmo when she was feeling sprightly; Curious George when she was feeling mischievous; her little Beanie Baby koala, Eucalyptus, when she wanted to nurture someone needier than herself. But Pooh always meant she was feeling especially fragile and in need of the ultimate comfort of her longest-serving pal. For several months after her mommy's death, she slept with Pooh every night. Recently, she'd traded in Pooh for some of the other guys, which was a sign that she was starting to feel a little stronger.

Tonight, though, Pooh was back in her bed.

He touched her sweaty curls, breathed in the sweet baby-shampoo aroma mixed with the slightly sour smell of perspiration, and kissed her damp forehead. She murmured but did not stir.

A door opened and closed somewhere in the house, followed immediately by the thud of something being dropped to the floor. Nick was instantly alert. Heavy, bounding footsteps on the carpeted stairs told him it was Lucas.

Nick navigated a path through the minefield of books and toys and closed the door quietly behind him. The long hall was dark, but a stripe of yellow light glared through the crack under Lucas's bedroom door.

Nick knocked, waited, then knocked again.

"Yeah?"

The depth and timbre of his son's voice always startled him. That and the surly edge to it, in the last year. Nick opened the door and found Lucas lying back on his bed, boots still on, iPod earbuds in his ears.

"Where've you been?" Nick asked.

Lucas glanced at him, then found something in the middle distance that was more interesting. "Where's Barney?"

Nick paused. "I asked you where you've been, Luke. It's a school night."

"Ziggy's."

"You didn't ask me if you could go over there."

"You weren't around to ask."

"If you want to go over to a friend's house, you've got to clear it in advance with me or Marta."

Lucas shrugged in tacit acknowledgment. His eyes were red and glassy, and now Nick was fairly certain he'd been getting high. This was an alarming new development, but he hadn't yet confronted his son about it. He'd been putting it off simply because it was one more mountain to climb, a showdown that would require unwavering strength he didn't have. There was so much going on at work, and there was Julia, who was frankly a hell of a lot easier to console, and then there was his own sadness, which sapped his ability to be a good and understanding dad.

He looked at Lucas, could hear the tinny, percussive hiss coming from the earphones. He wondered what kind of crappy music Lucas was listening to now. He caught a whiff of stale smoke in the room, which smelled like regular cigarettes, though he wasn't sure.

There was a baffling disconnect between Lucas on the inside and Lucas on the outside. Externally, Lucas was a mature sixteen, a tall and handsome man. His almost feminine prettiness had taken on a sharp-featured masculinity. His eyebrows, above blue eyes with long lashes, were dark and thick. The Lucas inside, though, was five or six: petulant, easily wounded, expert at finding insult in the most unexpected places, capable of holding grudges to the end of time.

"You're not smoking, are you?"

Lucas cast his father a look of withering contempt. "Ever hear of second-hand smoke? I was around people who were smoking."

"Ziggy doesn't smoke." Kenny Ziegler was a big, strapping blond kid, a swimmer who was Lucas's best friend from when he was still on the swim team. But ever since Lucas had quit swimming, six months or so ago, he hadn't been hanging out with Ziggy nearly as much. Nick doubted that Lucas had actually spent the afternoon and evening at Ziggy's house. Somewhere else: some other friend, probably.

Lucas's stare was unwavering. His music squealed and hissed.

"You got homework?" Nick persisted.

"I don't need you to monitor me, Nick." Nick. That

was something else new, calling his father by his first name. Some of Lucas's friends had always called their own parents by their first names, but Nick and Laura had always insisted on the traditional "Mom" and "Dad." Lucas was just trying to push his buttons. He'd been calling him Nick for the last month or so.

"Can you please take those earphones out when I'm talking to you?"

"I can hear you just fine," Lucas said. "Where's Barney?"

"Take off the earphones, Luke."

Lucas yanked them out of his ears by the dangling wire, let them drop on his chest, the tinny sound now louder and more distinct.

"Something happened to Barney. Something pretty bad."

"What are you talking about?"

"We found him . . . Someone killed him, Luke."

Lucas whipped his legs around until he was perched on the edge of the bed, looking as if he were about to launch himself toward Nick.

"*Killed* him?"

"We found him in the pool today—some nut . . ." Nick couldn't continue, couldn't relive the gruesome scene.

"This is the same guy who keeps breaking in, isn't it? The spray-paint graffiti guy."

"Looks that way."

"It's because of *you*!" Lucas's eyes widened, gleaming with tears. "All those people you fired, the way everyone in town hates you."

Nick didn't know how to answer.

"Like half the kids in school, their parents got laid off by you. It's fucking embarrassing."

"Lucas, listen to me—"

Lucas gave him a ferocious look, eyes bulging, teeth

bared, as if Nick were the one who'd killed Barney. "Why don't you get the fuck out of my room," he said, his voice cracking.

Nick's reaction surprised himself. If he'd talked that way to his father, he'd have had the shit beaten out of him. But instead of flying into a fury, he was instead overcome by calm, patient sorrow—his heart ached for the kid, for what he'd had to go through. "Lucas," Nick said, so softly it was almost a whisper, "don't you ever talk to me like that again." He turned around and quietly closed the door behind him. His heart wasn't in it.

Standing in the hallway just outside her adored older brother's room was Julia, tears streaming down her face.

5

IT WASN'T LONG after Nick had finally gotten Julia back to sleep—picking her up, hugging her, snuggling with her in her bed—that there was a quick rap on the front door.

Eddie Rinaldi, Stratton's corporate security director, was wearing a tan fleece jacket and a pair of jeans, and smelled like beer and cigarettes. Nick wondered whether Eddie had just come over from his usual hangout, Victor's, on Division.

"Shit, man," Eddie said. "That sucks, about the dog."

Eddie was a tall, lanky guy, edgy and intense. His frizzy brown hair was run through with gray. He had pitted cheeks and forehead, the legacy of a nasty case of acne in high school. He had gray eyes, flared nostrils, a weak mouth.

They'd been high school teammates—Eddie was the right wing on the same hockey team on which Nick, the captain, played center—though they'd never been especially close. Nick was the star, of the team and of the high school, the big man on campus, the good-looking guy all the girls wanted to go out with. Eddie, not a bad hockey player, was a natural cut-up, half-crazy, and with a face full of zits, he wasn't exactly dating the prom queen. The joke about Eddie among some on the team was that he'd been left on the Tilt-A-Whirl a bit too long as a baby. That wasn't quite fair; he was a goofball who just scraped by in school, but he had a native cunning. He also looked up to Nick, almost hero-worshiped him, though his idolatry always seemed tinged with a little jealousy. After high school, when Nick went to Michigan State, in East Lansing, Eddie went to the police academy in Fraser and lucked out, got a job with the Grand Rapids PD, where after almost two decades he hit a bad patch. As he'd explained to Nick, he'd been accused of brutalizing a suspect—a bullshit charge, but there it was—banished to a desk job, busted down the ranks until the publicity blew over, or so he was assured by the police chief. But he knew his career was as good as done for.

Nick, by then CEO of Stratton, stepped in and saved his ass, offering Eddie a job he was maybe underqualified for, assistant director of corporate security, in charge of background checks, pilferage investigations, that sort of thing. Just as Nick had assured the longtime security director, a white-haired sergeant who'd retired from the Fenwick force, Eddie had poured himself into the job, deeply grateful to Nick and eager to redeem himself.

Two years later, when the security director took early retirement, Eddie moved into the top job. Sometimes Nick thought it was like the old hockey days: Nick, the star, the power forward as they called him, with his hundred-mile-an-hour slap shot, taking the face-offs, making a pass through nine sticks as if he were threading a needle; and Eddie, grinning wildly as he did wild stunts like kicking an opponent's skates out from under him, spearing guys in the gut, carving some other guy's face with his stick, skating up and down the wing with a jittery juking craziness.

"Thanks for coming over," Nick said.

"First I want to see the kitchen."

Nick shrugged, led him down the hall. He switched on the light and peeled back one of the heavy plastic sheets, taped to the doorjamb, which served as a dust barrier between the kitchen and the rest of the house.

Nick stepped through, followed by Eddie, who gave a low whistle, taking in the glass-fronted cabinets, the Wolf commercial range. He set down the little nylon gym bag he'd been carrying. "Jeez Louise, this gotta cost a fortune."

"It's ridiculous."

He switched one of the burners on. It *tick-ticked* and then ignited, a powerful roar of blue flame coming out. "Man, serious gas pressure. And you don't even cook."

"Had to bring in a new line for that. Tore up the lawn, had to reseed and everything."

"Shit, how many sinks you got?"

"I think they call that one a prep sink, and that one's for dishes."

"The dishwasher's gonna go in there?"

"Yeah." Fisher & Paykel, was that it? Another result of Laura's star-searches for the best appliances ever. *It's two drawers,* she'd told him, *so you can run smaller loads.* Okay, whatever.

Eddie tugged at a handle, releasing a slab of rock maple. "This a knife drawer?"

"Built-in cutting board."

"Sweet. Don't tell me you picked all this shit out."

"Laura designed the whole thing, picked out every appliance, the color scheme, the cabinets, everything."

"Tough to cook without a kitchen counter, you know."

"That's coming."

"Where do you keep the booze?"

Nick touched the front of a cabinet. It popped open, revealing an array of liquor bottles.

"Neat trick."

"Magnetic touch-latch. Also Laura's idea. Scotch?"

"Sure."

"Rocks, right?" Nick held a tumbler against the automatic icemaker on the door of the Sub-Zero and watched as the cubes *chink-chink-chinked* against the glass. Then he poured a healthy slug of Johnnie Walker, handed it to Eddie, and led the way out of the kitchen.

Eddie took a long sip, then gave a contented sigh. "Hey, Johnnie, Daddy's home. What are you drinking, buddy?"

"Better not. I've been taking a pill to sleep, not supposed to mix it with alcohol."

They left the kitchen, entered the dark back corridor, illuminated only by the orange glow from the switch plates. Nick switched on the lamp on the hall table, another of the millions of little details about this house that reminded him of Laura every single day. She'd spent months looking for the perfect alabaster lamp until she found it one day in an antiques store on the Upper East Side of Manhattan when she'd accompanied him on a business trip. The shop dealt only with the trade, decorators and interior designers, but she'd sweet-talked her way in, then spotted the lamp. The base was carved of alabaster quarried in Volterra, Italy, she'd explained, when Nick asked why it had cost so freaking much. To Nick it just looked like white rock.

"Aw, don't take pills, man. You know what you need to help you sleep?"

"Let me guess." The lights in his study came on automatically as they entered, pinpoints in the ceiling and little floods that washed the hand-plastered walls, the huge Sony flat-panel TV mounted on the facing wall, the French doors that opened onto the freshly seeded lawn.

"That's right, Nicky. Pussy. Look at this place. Incredible."

"Laura."

Eddie sank into one of the butter-soft leather Symbiosis chairs, took a swig of his Scotch, and placed it noisily down on the slate-topped side table. Nick sat in the one next to him.

"So I picked up this chick Saturday night at Victor's, right? I mean, I must've had my beer goggles on, because when I woke the next morning she—well, she had a great personality, know what I'm saying? I mean, the bitch must have fell off the ugly tree and hit every branch on the way down." He gave a dry, wheezing cackle.

"But you got a good night's sleep."

"Actually no, I was shit-faced, man. Point is, Nick, you gotta get out there and start dating. Get back on the trail of tail. But man, watch out, there's a lot of skanks out there."

"I don't feel like it yet."

Eddie tried to soften his voice, though it came out more as an insinuating rasp. "She died a year ago, Nicky. That's a long time."

"Not if you're married seventeen years."

"Hey, I'm not talking about getting *married* again. I'm the *last* one to tell you to get married. Look at me—I don't buy, I lease. Trade 'em in regularly for the latest model."

"Can we talk about my security system? It's late, and I've had a long day."

"All right, all right. My systems guy's a total fucking wizard. He put in my home system."

Nick's brows shot up.

"I mean, I paid for it out of my own pocket, come on. If he can get the equipment, I'll have him put one in tomorrow."

"Cameras and everything?"

"Shit. We're talking IP-based cameras at the perimeter and at all points of entry and egress, cameras inside, overt and covert."

"What's IP?"

"Internet-something. Means you can get the signal over the Internet. You can monitor your house from your computer at work—it's amazing shit."

"Back up to tape?"

"No tape. All the cameras record to a hard drive. Maybe put in motion sensors to save on disk space. We can do remote pan-and-tilt, real-time full-color streaming video at seven and a half frames per second or something. The technology's totally different these days."

"This going to keep my stalker out?"

"Put it this way, once he sees these robot cameras swiveling at him as he approaches the house, he'll turn and run, unless he's a total whack job. And at the very least, we get a bunch of high-quality images of him next time he tries to break in. Speaking of which, I saw some serious cameras around the guard booth down the road. Looks like you got cameras all around the perimeter fence, not just at the entrance. We mighta got lucky, got a picture of him. I'll talk to the security guys down there first thing in the morning."

"You don't think the cops already did that?"

Eddie made a *pfft* sound. "Those guys aren't going to do shit for you. They'll do the bare minimum, or less."

Nick nodded. "I think you're right."

"I know I'm right. They all hate your fucking guts. You're Nick the Slasher. You laid off their dads and their brothers and sisters and wives. I bet they love seeing you get some serious payback."

Nick exhaled noisily. "What do you mean, 'unless he's a total whack job'?"

"That's the thing about stalkers, man. They don't necessarily obey the rules of sanity. Only one thing can give you total peace of mind if he comes around again." He unzipped the black nylon gym bag and took out a small oilcloth bundle. He unwrapped it, revealing a blunt matte-black semi-automatic pistol, squarish and compact, ugly. Its plastic frame was scratched, the slide nicked. "Smith and Wesson Sigma .380," he announced.

"I don't want that," Nick said.

"I wouldn't rule anything out, I were you. Anyone who'd do that to your dog might well go after your kids, and you gonna tell me you're not going to protect your family? That's not the Nick *I* know."

6

NICK SLIPPED INTO the dark theater—the FutureLab, they called it—and took a seat at the back. The Film was still playing on the giant curved movie screen, a high-gain, rear-projection video screen that took up an entire curved front wall. The darkness of the theater was soothing to his bleary morning eyes.

Jangly techno music emanated in surround sound from dozens of speakers built into the walls, ceiling, and floor. Watching this beauty reel, you were careening through the Kalahari Desert, down a narrow street in Prague, flying over the Grand Canyon, close enough to the walls to be scraped by the jagged rocks. You were whizzing through molecules of DNA and emerging in a City of the Future, the images kaleidoscopic, futuristic. "In an interlinked world," a mellifluous baritone confided, "knowledge reigns supreme." The Film was about the future of work and life and technology; it was totally abstract and cerebral and very trippy. Not a stick of furniture was anywhere to be seen.

Only some customers were shown The Film. Some visitors, particularly Silicon Valley types, were blown away by it and, when the lights came up, wanted to chatter on and on about the "seamless integration" be-

tween office furniture and technology, about the Work-
place of the Future, ready to sign on the dotted line
right then and there.

Others found it pretentious and annoying, didn't get
it at all. Like this morning's audience, a delegation of
nine high-level executives from the Atlas McKenzie
Group. It was one of the world's largest financial ser-
vices companies, had its spindly tendrils in everything
from banking to credit cards to insurance, in more than
a hundred countries and territories. Nick watched them
squirm in their seats, whispering to each other. They
included the Senior VP of Real Estate and the VP for
Facilities Management and assorted minions. They'd
been flown up from Chicago the day before on the
Stratton corporate jet, been given the full-out tour by
Stratton's Guest Experience Team. Nick had had lunch
with them, shown them around the executive offices
himself, given them his standard pitch about the flat-
tening of the corporate pyramidal hierarchy and how
the work environment was moving from individual to
the collaborative community, all that stuff.

Atlas McKenzie was building an immense office
tower in Toronto. A million square feet, a third of which
would be their new corporate headquarters, which they
wanted outfitted from scratch. That meant at least ten
thousand workstations, at least fifty million bucks up
front, and then there was the ten-year maintenance
contract. If Stratton got the deal, it would be a huge
win. Beyond huge. Unbelievable. Then there were all
the Atlas McKenzie offices around the world, which
could well be standardized on Stratton—Nick couldn't
even calculate how much that could mean.

All right, so The Film was flopping. They might as
well have been watching some subtitled art house film
set in a small Bulgarian village.

At least yesterday afternoon they'd been totally

jazzed by the Workplace of the Future exhibit. Visitors always were, without exception. You couldn't help but be. It was a fully functional mock-up of a workstation, eight by ten, that looked a lot more like a network news anchor set than some cubicle out of Dilbertland. The visitors were given ID tags to wear that contained an embedded chip, which communicated with an electronic sensor so that when you entered the space, the overhead lights changed from blue to green. That way, co-workers could tell from way across the floor that you were at your desk. As soon as you sat down, an electronic message was flashed to your team members—in this case, the laptops provided to the visitors—telling them you were in. Amazing what Stratton's engineers came up with, he'd often marveled. In front of the worker's desk in the Workplace of the Future was a six-foot-long wraparound computer monitor, superhigh resolution, on which appeared a page of text, a video-conference window, and a PowerPoint slide. Clients saw this and coveted it, the way some guys drool over Lamborghinis.

They were running about ten minutes behind, so Nick had to sit through The Talk. The screen faded to black, and slowly, slowly, the lights in the Lab came up. Standing at the brushed-aluminum podium was Stratton's Senior Vice President for Workplace Research, a very tall, slender woman in her late thirties with long, straight blond hair cut into severe bangs and giant horn-rim glasses. She was Victoria Zander—never Vicky or Tori, only Victoria. She was dressed dramatically, in all black. She could have been a beatnik from the fifties, a pal of Jack Kerouac's on the road.

Victoria spoke in a mellifluous soprano. She said, "Your corporate headquarters is one of the most powerful branding tools you have. It's your opportunity to tell your employees and your visitors a story about *you*—who you are, what you stand for. It's your *brand-scape*. We call this the *narrative office*." As she talked, she jotted down key phrases—"smart workplace" and "heartbeat space" and "Knowledge Age"—on a digital whiteboard set into the wall in front of her, and her notes, zapped instantly into computer text, appeared on the laptops in front of the folks from Atlas McKenzie. She said, "Our model is *wagons around the campfire*. We live our private lives in our own wagon but come together at suppertime."

Even after hearing it a dozen times, Nick didn't understand all of her patter, but that was okay; he figured that no one else did either. Certainly not these guys from Chicago, who were probably rolling their eyes inwardly but didn't want to admit their lack of sophistication. Victoria's loopy little graduate seminar was intimidating and probably soared over their heads too.

What these guys understood was modular wiring infrastructure and pre-assembled components and data cables built into access floors. That was where they lived. They didn't want to hear about brandscapes.

He waited patiently for her to finish, increasingly aware of the visitors' restlessness. All he had to do was a quick meet-and-greet, make sure everyone was happy, chat them up a bit.

Nick didn't actually get involved in selling since he became CEO, not in any real hands-on way. That was handled on the national accounts level. He just helped close the deal, nudged things along, assured the really big customers that the guy at the top cared. It was remarkable how far a little face time with the CEO went with customers.

He was normally good at this, the firm handshake and the clap on the back, the no-bullshit straight answer that everyone always found so refreshing. This morning, though, he felt a steady pulse of anxiety, a dull stomachache. Maybe it was a rebound reaction to the Ambien he'd taken last night, that tiny sliver of a pill that lulled him to sleep. Maybe it was the three cups of coffee instead of his usual two. Or maybe it was the fact that Stratton really, *really* needed this deal.

AFTER VICTORIA FINISHED her presentation, the lights came up, and the two lead guys from Atlas McKenzie went right up to him. One, the Senior VP of Real Estate, was a slight, whey-faced man of around fifty with full, almost female lips, long lashes, a permanently bland expression. He didn't speak much. His colleague, the VP for Facilities Management, was a stubby man, all torso, with a heavy five-o'clock shadow, a beetle brow, obviously dyed jet-black hair. He reminded Nick of Richard Nixon.

"And I thought you guys just did chairs and filing cabinets," said Nixon, flashing bright white teeth with a prominent center gap.

"Far from it," Nick chuckled. They knew better; Stratton had been courting them for months, making their business case, running a long series of offsite meetings that Nick had thankfully been spared. "Listen, if you need to check your e-mail or your voice mail or whatever, we've got a wireless campsite down the hall."

The whey-faced man, whose name was Hardwick, sidled up to Nick and said silkily, "I hope you don't mind a rather direct question."

"Of course not." The delicate-featured, blank-faced Hardwick was a killer, a genuine corporate assassin; he could have been an apparatchik out of the old Soviet Politburo.

Hardwick unzipped a Gucci leather portfolio and pulled out a clipping. Nick recognized it; it was an article from *Business Week* headlined, "Has Midas Lost His Touch?" There was a picture of the legendary Willard Osgood, the crusty old founder of Fairfield Equity Partners—the man who'd bought Stratton—with his Coke-bottle glasses and leathery face. The article focused mostly on "the millions in pretax losses incurred by Stratton, once the fastest growing office-furniture company in the U.S." It talked about Osgood's "vaunted Midas touch for picking quality companies and growing them steadily over the long term" and asked, "What happened? Will Osgood stand idly by while one of his investments falls off a cliff? Not likely, say insiders."

Hardwick held the clipping up for a few seconds. "Is Stratton in trouble?" he asked, fixing Nick with a watery stare.

"Absolutely not," Nick replied. "Have we had a couple of lousy quarters? Hell, yeah—but so have Steelcase and Herman Miller and all the other players. We've been through two years of layoffs, as you know, and the severance costs are a bear. But we're doing what we've got to do to stay healthy in the long term."

Hardwick's voice was almost inaudible. "I understand that. But you're not a family-run company like you used to be. You're not running the whole show. I'm sure Willard Osgood's breathing down your neck."

"Osgood and his people pretty much leave us alone," Nick said. "They figure we know what we're doing—that's why they acquired us." His mouth was dry. "You know, they always like to give their companies enough rope."

Hardwick blinked, lizardlike. "We're not just buying a hell of a lot of workstations from you folks, Nick. We're buying a ten-year service contract. Are you going to be around a year or two from now?"

Nick placed a hand on Hardwick's bony shoulder.

"Stratton's been around for almost seventy-five years," he said, "and I can assure you, it's going to be here long after you and I are gone."

Hardwick gave a wan smile. "I wasn't asking about Stratton. I'm asking if *you're* going to be around."

"Count on it," Nick said. He gave Hardwick's shoulder a squeeze as, out of the corner of his eye, he saw Eddie Rinaldi leaning against the wall by the entrance to the Lab, arms folded.

"Excuse me for a second," Nick said. Eddie rarely dropped by, and when he did it was always something important. Plus, Nick didn't mind taking a break in this awkward exchange.

He went up to Eddie. "What's up?"

"I got something for you. Something you better take a look at."

"Can it wait?"

"It's about your stalker. You tell me if you want to wait."

7

EDDIE SAT DOWN in front of Nick's computer as if it were his own and pecked at the keyboard with two fingers. He was surprisingly adept for someone who'd never learned how to type. As he navigated through the corporate intranet to the Corporate Security area, he said, "The boys in the guard booth at your little concentration camp were more than happy to help out, of course."

"You're talking about Fenwicke Estates." Eddie smelled of cigarettes and Brut, the cologne he'd worn back in high school. Nick didn't even know they still made Brut.

"Now, *they've* got a nice setup there—high-definition, high-res Sony digital video cams positioned at the entrance and exit. Backlight compensation. Thirty frames a second. The cops didn't even ask to look at their hard-disk recorder, know that?"

"Like you said."

"Shit, they didn't even do the bare minimum, for appearances' sake. Okay." A color photo appeared on the monitor of a lanky, bespectacled figure. Eddie clicked the mouse a few times, zooming in on the figure. He was a man of around sixty with a deeply creased face, a small, tight mouth, close-cropped gray hair, eyes grotesquely magnified by the lenses of heavy-framed black glasses. Nick's heart began to thud. A few more mouse clicks, and the man's grim face took up most of the screen. The resolution wasn't bad. The man's face was clearly visible.

"Recognize him?" Eddie said.

"No."

"Well, he knows who you are."

"No doubt. What, did he just walk through? Some security."

"Climbed the fence in the wooded section, actually. Cameras there get triggered by motion sensors. No alarms there—they'd get way too many false alarms with all the animals and shit—but cameras up the wazoo."

"Great. Who is he?"

"His name is Andrew Stadler."

Nick shrugged. He'd never heard the name.

"I narrowed it down by laid-off male employees in their fifties or older, especially with outplacement irregularities. Man, I spent most of the morning looking at mug shots. My eyes are crossing. But hey, that's why I get the big bucks, right?"

Eddie double-clicked the mouse, and another photo appeared on a split screen beside the surveillance image. It was the same man, a little younger: the same heavy black glasses with the ogling eyes, the same slit of a mouth. Under this photograph was the name ANDREW M. STADLER and a Social Security number, a date of birth, a Stratton employee number, a date of hire.

Nick asked, "Laid off?"

"Yes and no. They sat him down for the layoff meeting and he quit. You know, said, 'After all I've done for this company?' and 'Fuck you,' and like that."

Nick shook his head. "Never even seen the guy before."

"Spend a lot of time at the model shop?"

The model shop was where a small crew of workers—metal-benders, solderers, woodworkers—built prototypes of new Stratton products, in editions of one or two or three, from specs drawn up by the designers. The model-shop employees tended to be odd sorts, Nick had always thought. They'd all done time on the factory floor, bending metal, and they were good with their hands. They also tended to be loners and perfectionists.

"Andrew Stadler," Nick said, listening to the sound of the name, scanning the data on the man's file. "He was with the company thirty-five, thirty-six years."

"Yep. Started as an assembler on the old vertical-file-cabinet line, became a welder. Then he became a specialist level two—worked by himself in the chair plant repairing the returns. Refused to work on any of the progressive build lines because, he said, he hated listening to other people's music. Kept getting into fights with his floor supervisor. They learned to leave him alone and let him do his work. When there was an opening in the model shop five years ago, he put in for it, and they were glad to get rid of him." With another couple of clicks, Eddie brought up Stadler's employee reviews. Nick leaned closer to read the small type. "What's this about hospitalization?"

Eddie swiveled around in Nick's chair and looked up, his half-wild eyes staring. "He's a fucking nutcase, buddy. A brainiac and a maniac. The guy's been in and out of the locked ward at County Medical."

"Jesus. For what?"

"Schizophrenia. Every couple of years he stops taking his meds."

Nick let his breath out slowly.

"Okay, Nick, now here's the scary part. I put in a call to the Fenwick PD. Something like fifteen years ago, Stadler was questioned in the possible murder of an entire family that lived across the street."

Nick felt a sudden chill. "What does that mean?"

"Family called Stroup, neighbors, used to hire this guy to do repairs, odd jobs. Mister Fix-It—guy's a mechanical genius, could fix anything. Maybe they got into some kinda fight, maybe they looked at him wrong, who knows, but one night there's a gas leak in their basement, something sets it off, whole house blows."

"Jesus."

"Never proven if the whole thing was an accident or this wacko did it, but the cops suspected he did. Never could prove it, though. Had to let him go—no evidence. Just strong suspicion. Nick, this guy Stadler is one dangerous motherfucker. And I'll tell you something else you're not going to want to hear. This fruit-cake's got a gun."

"What?"

"There's an old safety inspection certificate in his name—found it in the county records. Like twenty years old. And no record of sale, which means he's still got it."

"Jesus. Get a restraining order."

Eddie made a soft, dismissive *pfft* sound. "Come on, man, TROs are bullshit. Piece of paper."

"But if he tries to go on my property again—"

"You can get him arrested for *trespassing,* man. Not for stalking. Big fucking deal. You think that's going to stop a goddamned psychopath? Guy who eviscerated your goddamned dog? Guy who hears voices, wears a tinfoil hat?"

"Jesus Christ, Eddie. We got a time-stamped image of this nut climbing the fence right around the time my dog got killed. The cops got a knife that might have prints on it. They got enough to charge the guy with my dog's death."

"Yeah, and what have they done, right? They haven't done shit."

"So how do we make them take action?"

"I don't know, man. Got to apply some serious pressure. But they're going to be busy covering their big fat asses, so they're not exactly going to snap to. I say we scare the shit out of this loon first. Once the police get involved in any real way, we gotta keep hands off Stadler. But in the meantime, we got to make sure you and your family are safe."

Nick considered for a moment. "All right. But don't do anything that'll compromise me in any way. So no getting rough with him. I just want the fucker locked up somewhere."

"Fine with me. I'll track the guy down. Meantime, my man Freddie's going over to your house this afternoon to get started on the new system. I'm having him put a rush on it."

Nick glanced at his watch. He had to head over to the monthly meeting of the Compensation Committee. "Great."

"And hey, if all else fails, remember my little loaner."

Nick lowered his voice, aware that Marjorie was at her desk on the other side of the partition and might be able to hear their voices. "I don't have a permit, Eddie."

Eddie gave a slow shake of his head. "Permit? Come on, man. You know how long it takes to go through the hoops, do all the paperwork? You can't wait that long. Look, carrying an unlicensed weapon is a misdemeanor, okay? A hundred-buck fine. And that's if you get caught. Which you won't, because you won't have to use it. Isn't that worth it to protect your family from that sick fuck? A hundred bucks?"

"All right. Get out of here—I need to check my e-mail, and then I've got three meetings stacked up."

Eddie rose. "Man, you got some fancy computer equipment up here. I could use some monitors like this for my department."

"Not up to me," Nick said. "I'm just a figurehead."

8

SCOTT MCNALLY LIVED in a decent-sized, but perfectly ordinary, house in the Forest Hills section of Fenwick where many of the Stratton execs lived. A successful accountant could have lived here. It was a generic white colonial with green shutters, a two-car garage, a rec room, a finished basement. It was decorated generically too. Everything—the dining room set, the couches and chairs and rugs—seemed to have been bought all at once, at the same mid-priced home-furnishings store. Obviously Eden, Scott's trophy wife, didn't share Laura's interest in design.

Nick and Laura had talked about Scott's house once. He admired the fact that Scott, who was loaded from his McKinsey days, didn't try to show it off like so many financial types. Money to Scott wasn't something you spent. It was like frequent-flyer miles you never use. Still, Nick couldn't put his finger on what felt funny about Scott's house until Laura pointed out that it looked somehow *temporary,* like those short-term furnished corporate apartments.

As soon as they arrived, the kids dispersed, Julia to the bedroom of one of Scott's twin twelve-year-old daughters, and Lucas to the rec room to sit by himself and watch TV. Scott was manning the immense, stainless-steel charcoal grill, the only remotely expensive thing he seemed to own. He was wearing a black barbecue apron with a yellow hazard sign on the front of it that said DANGER MEN COOKING, and a matching DANGER MEN COOKING baseball cap.

"How's it going?" Nick said as they stood in the smoke.

"Can't complain," Scott said. "Who'd listen?"

"Think that grill's big enough?"

"A cooking surface of eight hundred and eighty square inches, big enough to burn sixty-four burgers at once. Because you just never know." He shook his head. "That's the last time I let Eden go shopping at Home Depot."

"How *is* Eden these days?"

"The same, only more so. She's become a real fitness nut. If it were up to her, we'd be feasting on texturized tofu, spirulina, and barley green juice. Her latest obsession is this Advanced Pilates course she's taking. I don't quite get how that works. Does it keep getting more advanced? Can you do graduate work in Pilates, end up with a doctorate?"

"Well, she looks great."

"Just don't call her arm candy. She'd rather be thought of as arm tempeh." Scott checked that all the knobs were set to high. "You know, I'm always kind of embarrassed when you come over. It's like the feudal lord leaving his castle to go visit the peasants in their hovels. We should be roasting a boar, really. Maybe a stag." He looked at Nick. "What would you like to drink? A flagon of mead, my liege?"

"A beer would do it."

Scott turned and began shouting to his portly nine-year-old son, who was sitting by himself on the back porch making immense bubbles using a strange gadget, a long pole with a cloth strap dangling off it. "Spencer! Spencer, will you get over here, please?"

"Aww!" Spencer whined.

"Right now!" Scott shouted. Lowering his voice a bit, he said, "Eden can't wait until he's old enough to send to Andover."

"Not you, though."

"I barely notice the kid," he said with a shrug. If Nick didn't know Scott better, he wouldn't realize Scott was kidding, doing his usual shtick. When his son was within speaking range, he said, "Spencer, could you please get Mr. Conover one of those brown bottles of beer?" To Nick he said, "You'll love this beer. It's a Belgian Abbey ale that's brewed in upstate New York."

"Got any Miller?"

"Ah, the Champagne of Beers. What I'd like to find is the beer of champagnes. I think Eden bought some Grolsch, if that'll work."

"Sure."

"Spencer, look for the green bottles that have the funny metal tops with the rubber stoppers on them, got it?"

"Dad, it's not supposed to be good for you to eat barbecued meats." Spencer folded his arms across his chest. "Do you know that barbecuing at high heat can create polycyclic aromatic hydrocarbons, which are known to be mutagens?"

Nick stared at the kid. How the hell do you learn to *pronounce* that stuff?

"Now, that's where you're wrong, son," said Scott. "They *used* to think that aromatic hydrocarbons were bad. Now they know that they're the best thing for you. What do they teach you in school, anyway?"

Spencer looked stymied, but only momentarily. "Don't say I didn't warn you if you get cancer later in life."

"I'll be dead by then, son."

"But Dad—"

"Okay, kid, so here's your burger," Scott said blithely, holding up one of the raw patties. "Go fetch yourself a bun and some ketchup, okay? So instead of cancer, you'll get salmonella and *E. coli* bacteria. Mad cow too, if you're really lucky."

Spencer seemed to get his father's sense of humor but wouldn't let on. "But I thought *E. coli* naturally colonizes the human intestine," he said.

"You don't stop, do you? Go play in traffic. But first get Mr. Conover his beer."

The boy trudged reluctantly away.

Scott chuckled. "Kids these days."

"Impressive," was all Nick could think to say.

"I'm sorry you don't want to try this Belgian ale," Scott said. "I discovered it at that dude ranch in Arizona I went to last month with my old college buddies, remember?"

"You didn't exactly rave about the place."

"Ever smell a horse up close? Anyway, I liked the beer."

"So, Spencer's a little scary, huh?"

"I guess. We first had an inkling of that when he was three and he started composing haiku using the letters from his alphabet soup."

"I don't think you appreciate how cooperative he is. If I'd asked Luke to go fetch me a beer he would have ripped my face off."

"Tough age. By the time Spencer turns sixteen we'll probably see him just once a year, at Christmas. But yeah, he's usually well behaved, and he's into math just like his dad. Of course, later, when he turns into Jeff Dahmer, we'll discover the dissected remains of dogs and cats in the backyard." He started to chuckle, and then his face fell. "Oh, shit, Nick, I forgot about your dog. I'm sorry."

"Don't worry about it."

"I can't believe I said that."

"You might want to turn the burgers. They're burning."

"Oh, right." He wrestled with a big metal spatula. "Nick, the cops have any idea who did it?"

Nick hesitated, then shook his head. "They're guessing it's a downsized employee. But I could've told 'em that."

"That narrows it down to five thousand and sixty-seven. You don't have a security system?"

"Not good enough, obviously. I mean, we're in a gated community."

"Jesus, that could happen to us too."

"Thanks for being so sensitive."

"No, I mean—sorry, but as the CFO I'm just as responsible as you are for the layoffs, and—God, you must be spooked as shit."

"Of course I am. But most of all I'm fucking pissed off."

"The cops aren't going to do anything, are they?"

"They all know someone we laid off. Alarm goes off at my house, they're not going to get off their stools at Dunkin' Donuts."

Spencer ran across the lawn with a bottle of beer in one hand and a glass in the other. "Here you go, Mr. Conover," he said, handing the beer and glass to Nick.

"Thanks, Spencer." Nick set down the glass and struggled with the complicated top of the Grolsch. He'd actually never had a bottle of the stuff outside of a bar, where they poured it for you.

Spencer circled his pudgy little arms around his dad's waist. Scott reached out his free hand and grabbed his son back, made a grunting sound. "Hey, sweetie," he said. His face was red from the heat, and he blinked the smoke out of his eyes.

"Hey, Dad."

Nick smiled. So Spencer was a little kid, too, not just a *Jeopardy* champ.

"Shit," Scott said, as one of his burgers slipped through the grate and into the fire.

"Do this often?"

"It's my only hobby. Understand, my idea of a good time is filling out my tax return using Roman numerals." He fiddled some more with the metal spatula. "Shit," he said again, as another burger dropped into the flames. "You like well done?"

9

THE ARCHITECT WHO was doing the renovations to the Conovers' kitchen was a stodgy but affable man named Jeremiah Claflin. He wore round black glasses of the sort that some of the famous architects affected—that Japanese guy, that Swiss guy, Nick forgot their names if he ever knew them—and his white hair contrasted pleasantly with his ruddy face and curled over his shirt collar. Laura had interviewed him and several other architects from Fenwick and the surrounding towns as intensively as she'd interviewed nanny candidates years ago. It was important to her that the architect she hired not only had a portfolio of projects she admired, but also wasn't too stubborn, too much of an *artiste* that he wouldn't do exactly what she wanted.

Nick got along with Claflin, as he got along with just about everyone, but he realized early on that the architect found Nick frustrating. Sure, he was pleased to be working on the house that belonged to Stratton's CEO—that gave him certain bragging rights—and since Laura had chosen nothing but the most high-end, most ridiculously expensive appliances and cabinets and all that, Claflin was making a boatload of money for not that much design work. But Nick wasn't all that interested in the fussy little details that Laura had had such patience for, and there sure as hell were a million fussy little details. The decisions never seemed to end. Did he want the kitchen counters to have a full bullnose or half bullnose or an ogee edge? How much of an overhang? How tall did he want the backsplash to be? A self-rimming sink or an undermount? What about the height of the countertop? Jesus, Nick had a company to run.

Claflin was forever faxing him drawings and lists of questions. Nick would inevitably tell the architect to just do whatever Laura had told him to do. He really didn't give a damn about what the kitchen looked like. What he cared about—was obsessed about, really— was that it be done precisely the way Laura wanted. The renovations had been Laura's last big project, pretty much all she thought about, talked about, in the months before the accident. Nick suspected that part of the reason she'd poured so much of herself into it was that the kids were getting older, and being a mom was no longer a full-time job. After Lucas was born, she'd quit her job teaching art history at St. Thomas More College. She tried to get her teaching position back when the kids were older, but she couldn't. She'd been mommy-tracked. She missed teaching, missed the intellectual engagement.

Laura was by far the smarter one in the marriage. Nick had gone to Michigan State on a full-boat hockey scholarship, busted his hump to get C's and B's, while Laura had breezed through Swarthmore *summa cum laude*. It was like she had a deep well of creative energy inside her that needed to be tapped or she'd go crazy, and the renovations filled a need for her.

But there was more to it: Laura had wanted to knock down the sterile old kitchen, which looked like no one ever used it, and turn it into a hearth, a great room where the whole family could gather. Laura, who was an excellent cook, could make dinner while the kids did their homework or hung out around the kitchen island. The whole family could be together comfortably.

The least Nick could do to honor her was to make sure the damned kitchen was done the way she wanted.

Their marriage had been far from perfect—hell, they'd been arguing the night she was killed, as he'd never forget—but Nick had learned you choose your battles. You made unspoken deals sometimes, ceded turf. Laura, who'd grown up in a shambling Victorian on the Hill, a pediatrician's kid, wanted to live a certain way, namely better than the way in which she'd been brought up. She wanted the elegance and style she never had growing up in a house that was always in some state of chaos and disrepair. She subscribed to *Architectural Digest* and *Elle Decor* and half a dozen other magazines that all looked the same, and she was always tearing out photos and two-page spreads and adding them to a steadily thickening file folder that she might as well have labeled DREAM HOUSE. To Nick, having a house with more than two bedrooms and a backyard and a kitchen you didn't eat in already bordered on unimaginable luxury.

Claflin was waiting for him in the kitchen when he arrived, twenty minutes late. From the family room Nick could hear Julia and her best friend, Emily, playing a computer game called *The Sims* in which they created their own creepily real-looking human beings and bent them to their will. Julia and Emily were shrieking with laughter over something.

"Busy day?" Claflin asked. His tone was jovial, but his eyes betrayed annoyance at being kept waiting.

Nick apologized as he shook the architect's hand, and then his eye was immediately caught by something. The countertops were in. He went up to the island and realized that, even to his untrained eye, something looked wrong.

"I see they've put a new alarm system in," Claflin said. "Fast work."

Nick nodded. He'd noticed the white touch pads on the wall as he entered. "The island," he said. "That's not what Laura wanted."

She'd designed a big island in the center of the kitchen around which the whole family could gather, sitting on stools, while she made dinner. But you sure as hell couldn't sit at this thing. It had walls of black granite that came up about two feet, no overhang, no place for stools.

Claflin beamed. "None of your guests will have to see the cooking mess from the dining table," he said. "Yet it works perfectly as a food-prep station. Clever, don't you think?"

Nick hesitated. "You can't sit at it," he said.

"True," Claflin conceded, his smile fading, "but there's no unsightly mess. That open-kitchen thing, that's the big problem with this great-room design that no one talks about. You have this stunning kitchen with all the best appliances, and this big farmhouse table where your guests eat their dinner, and what do they end up looking at? A mess of dirty pots and pans on the counters and island. This solves that problem."

"But the kids can't sit around it."

"Believe me, that's trivial compared to—"

"Laura wanted everyone to be able to sit around the kitchen island. She wanted to be able to see the kids hanging out here, doing their homework or reading or talking or whatever while she was making dinner."

"Nick," Claflin said slowly, "you don't cook, right? And Laura's—well, she's . . ."

"Laura wanted this big, open, hang-out kitchen,"

Nick said. "That's what she wanted, and that's what we're going to have."

Claflin looked at him for a few seconds. "Nick, I faxed you the specs, and you signed off on them."

"I probably didn't even look at them. I told you we're doing everything exactly according to Laura's wishes."

"This has already been cut. We can't . . . send it *back*. You own it."

"I really don't give a shit," Nick said. "You get the stone guy back here and have him recut it the way Laura wanted."

"Nick, there's a logic to this design that—"

"Just do it." Nick's voice was arctic. "Are we clear?"

10

AS SOON AS Claflin left, Julia entered the kitchen. She was wearing a gray sweatshirt emblazoned with the arch-shaped logo of the Michigan Wolverines. Her friend was still sitting at the computer in the family room, busily tyrannizing the lives of her Sims family like some high-tech Hitler.

"Daddy, are you the president of Stratton?"

"President and CEO, baby, don't you know that? Give me a hug."

She ran to him as if she'd been waiting for permission, threw her arms around him. Nick leaned over and gave her a kiss on her forehead, thought: *She's just figuring this out?*

"Emily says you fired half the people in Fenwick."

Emily looked up from the computer screen, stole a furtive glance at Nick.

"We had to lay a lot of really good people off," Nick said. "To save the company."

"She says you fired her uncle."

Ah, so that was it. Nick shook his head. "I didn't know that. I'm sorry to hear it, Emily."

Emily gave him an imperious, condescending look, almost withering, quite remarkable for a ten-year-old girl. "Uncle John's been unemployed for almost two years. He says he gave everything to Stratton and you ruined his life."

Nick wanted to respond—*It wasn't me, and anyway we provided extensive outplacement counseling, you know*—but once you start debating with ten-year-olds you might as well hang it up. He was saved by the honk of a car horn. "Okay, Em, you'd better get going. You don't want to keep your mom waiting."

EMILY'S MOM DROVE a brand-new gold Lexus LX 470 roughly half as long as a city block. She wore a white Fred Perry tennis shirt, white shorts, a Fenwick Country Club windbreaker, expensive-looking white tennis shoes. She had great, tanned legs, short auburn hair coiffed in a high-fashion cut, a giant glittering diamond engagement ring. Her husband was a plastic surgeon who was rumored to be having an affair with his receptionist, and if even Nick, who was completely out of the gossip stream, had heard it, it was probably true.

"Hello, Nick." Her cigarette-husky voice was chilly and bone-dry.

"Hi, Jacqueline. Emily should be out in a second. I had to tear her away from the computer."

Jacqueline smiled in an artful semblance of sociability. Nick knew her only enough to say hi: maintaining friendships among the school parents had been Laura's job. Not that long ago, Jacqueline Renfro would light up when she saw him at school plays and parents' nights, as if he were a long-lost friend. But people didn't suck up to him so much anymore.

"How's Jim?" he said.

"Oh, you know," she said airily. "When people lose their jobs they don't get Botox quite as often."

"Emily mentioned that her uncle got laid off from Stratton. Is he your brother or Jim's?"

She paused, then said sternly, "Mine, but Emily shouldn't have said that. Honestly, she has no manners. I'll talk to her."

"No, no—she was saying what was on her mind. Where'd your brother work?"

"I don't—" she faltered, then she called out, "Emily, what is *taking* you so long?"

They stood in awkward silence for a moment until her daughter emerged from the house, struggling under the weight of a backpack the size of a Sherpa's.

JULIA DIDN'T LOOK up from the computer monitor as Nick approached and asked, "Where's your brother?"

"I don't know."

"You finish your homework?"

Julia didn't answer.

"You heard me, right?"

"What?" What was it with the selective hearing? He could whisper "Krispy Kreme" in the kitchen and she'd come bounding.

"Your homework. We're eating dinner in half an hour—it's Marta's night off. Turn off the computer."

"But I'm in the middle—"

"Save it and shut down. Come on, sweetie."

He went to the foot of the stairs and shouted up for Lucas. No reply. The house was so unnecessarily big, though, that sound didn't carry far. Nick went upstairs, past Laura's study, its door unopened since her death, to Lucas's room.

He knocked. The door, slightly ajar, opened inward a few inches. He pushed it open the rest of the way, called, "Luke?" No answer; no Lucas here. His desk lamp was on, a textbook open. He walked over to see which textbook it was, inadvertently bumping against the desk. The iMac's flat panel screen came out of sleep mode, displaying a profusion of colorful flesh-tone photographs. Nick looked again and saw naked bodies in various sexual contortions. He came closer to get a closer look.

The entire screen was taken up with pop-up windows of slutty-looking women with huge boobs in garish shades of pink and orange. "Real Amateur Pussy," one window read, the word "real" flashing red like a neon sign.

Nick's first reaction was a very male one: he looked even closer, intrigued, felt a stirring he hadn't felt in months. Immediately after, though, he felt disgusted at the tawdriness of the images—who were these girls who were willing to do this stuff for all the heavy-breathing Internet world to see? And then the realization washed over him that this was Lucas's computer, that his son was looking at all this stuff. If Laura had discovered this, she would have freaked out, called him at work, demanded that he come home at once and have a Talk with his son.

Whereas Nick didn't know what to think, how to react. He was at a loss. The kid was sixteen, and developmentally a fairly advanced sixteen at that. Of course he was interested in sex. Nick remembered when he and a buddy, around the same age, had found a matted, waterlogged *Playboy* in the woods. They'd dried it out carefully, pored over it as if it were the Dead Sea Scrolls, hid it in Nick's garage. Looking back on it now, it was amazing how different smut was in those days, how innocent, though it sure didn't seem it at the time. The photos in *Playboy* were so heavily airbrushed that it was something of a shock when Nick first got an up-close glimpse of his first real-life tits not long afterward, in the finished basement of his first real girl-friend, Jody Catalfano. Jody, the cutest girl in the class, had been after him for months, was ready long before he was. Her breasts were far smaller than the voluptuous babes' in *Playboy,* her nipples larger and darker with a few stray hairs around the edges of the areolas.

But this stuff, garish and flashing, was way too *real,* somehow. It was more blatant, more perverted than anything from Nick's fevered adolescence. And here it was, a couple of mouse clicks away. It wasn't half-buried under dead leaves in the woods, didn't require conservation efforts or concealment in an empty Pennzoil box in a garage. On some level it was almost sickening. And what if Julia had wandered in here and seen it?

He picked up Lucas's desk phone and called his son's cell.

Lucas answered after five rings, fumbling with the phone a long time. "Yeah?" In the background was loud music, raucous voices.

"Luke, where the hell are you?"

A pause. "What's up?"

"What's *up*? It's suppertime."

"I ate already."

"We have dinner together, remember?" This "dinner together" thing had become one of Nick's recent obsessions, particularly since Laura was gone. He sometimes felt that if he didn't insist on it, the remains of his family could all fly away by centrifugal force.

Another pause. "Where are you, Luke?"

"All right," Lucas said and hung up.

AN HOUR LATER, Lucas still wasn't home. Julia was hungry, so the two of them sat down to dinner at the small round table that had been temporarily placed in one corner of the kitchen, away from most of the construction. Marta had set the table for the three of them before going out for the evening. In the warm oven was a roast chicken, tented with foil. Nick brought the chicken and rice and broccoli to the table, remembering to put trivets under the chicken pan so he didn't scorch the table. He expected a fight over the broccoli, and he got it. Julia would accept only rice and a chicken drumstick, and Nick was too wiped out to argue.

"I like Mommy's better," Julia said. "This is too dry."

"It's been in the oven for a couple of hours."

"Mommy made the best fried chicken."

"She sure did, baby," Nick said. "Eat."

"Where's Luke?"

"He's on his way back." *Taking his damned time of it too,* Nick thought.

Julia stared at the chicken leg on her plate as if it were a giant cockroach. Finally, she said, "I don't like it here."

Nick thought for a moment, unsure how to respond. "Like it where?"

"Here," she said unhelpfully.

"This house?"

"We don't have any neighbors."

"We do, but . . ."

"We don't know any of them. It's not a neighborhood. It's just . . . houses and trees."

"People do keep to themselves here," he conceded. "But your mommy wanted us to move here because she thought it would be safer than our last house."

"Well, it's not. Barney . . ." She stopped, her eyes welling up with tears, resting her chin in her hands.

"But we will be now, with this new security system in."

"Nothing like that ever happened in our old house," she pointed out.

The front door opened, setting off a high alert tone, and a few seconds later Lucas trundled noisily into the kitchen, threw his backpack down on the floor. He seemed to get taller and broader by the day. He wore a dark blue Old Navy sweatshirt, baggy cargo pants with the waistband of his boxer shorts showing, and some white scarflike thing under his backwards baseball cap.

"What's that on your head?" Nick asked anyway.

"Do-rag, why?"

"That like a hip-hop thing?"

Lucas shook his head, rolled his eyes. "I'm not hungry," he said. "I'm going upstairs."

"Sit with us anyway, Luke," Julia pleaded. "Come on."

"I've got a lot of homework," Lucas said as he left the kitchen without turning back.

11

NICK FOLLOWED HIS son upstairs. "We have to have a talk," he said.

Lucas groaned. "What now?" When he reached the open door to his room, he said, "You been in here?"

"Sit down, Luke."

Lucas noticed the computer monitor facing the door, and he leaped toward it, spun it away. "I don't want you going in my room."

"Sit down."

Lucas sat on the edge of his bed, hunched over with his elbows propped on his knees, his chin resting on his hands, a gesture that Julia had recently started imitating. He stared malevolently.

"You're not allowed to go to porn sites," Nick said.

Lucas blinked. His angry blue eyes were crystal clear, innocent and pure. He was trying to grow something under his chin, Nick noticed. For a moment Lucas seemed to be debating whether to own up to the evidence so prominently on display. Then he said: "There's nothing there I don't know about, Nick. I'm sixteen."

"Cut out the 'Nick' stuff."

"Okay, *Dad*," he said with a surly twist. "Hey, at least

I'm not going to snuff or torture sites. You should see the shit that's out there."

"You do that again and your Internet access gets cut off, understand?"

"You can't do that. I need e-mail for school. It's required."

"Then I'll leave you with just AOL with whatever those controls are."

"You can't *do* that! I got to do research on the Internet."

"I'll bet. Where were you this afternoon?"

"Friend's."

"Sounded like a bar or something."

Lucas stared as if he weren't going to dignify this with a response.

"What happened to Ziggy?"

"Ziggy's an asshole."

"He's your best friend."

"Look, you don't know him, all right?"

"Then who are these new kids you're hanging out with?"

"Just friends."

"What are their names?"

"Why do you care?"

Nick bit his lip, thought for a moment. "I want you to go back to Underberg." Lucas had seen a counselor for four months after Laura's death, until he quit, complaining that Underberg was "full of shit."

"I'm not going back there. No way."

"You've got to talk to someone. You won't talk to me."

"About what?"

"For God's sake, Lucas, you've just been through one of the most traumatic things a kid can go through. Of course you're having a hard time. You think it's any easier on your sister, or on me?"

"Forget it," Lucas said, raising his voice sharply. "Don't even go there."

"What's that supposed to mean?"

Lucas shot him a pitying look. "I got homework," he said, getting up from the bed and walking over to his desk.

NICK POURED HIMSELF a Scotch on the rocks, sat in the family room and watched TV for a while, but nothing held his interest. He started feeling a mild, pleasant buzz. Around midnight he went up to his room. Both Julia's and Lucas's lights were off. The newly installed alarm touch pad in his bedroom glowed green, announced READY in black letters. *Ready for what?* he thought. The installer had called him and given him the ten-minute lowdown that afternoon. If a door was open somewhere, it would say something like FAULT—LIVING ROOM DOOR. If someone moved downstairs it would say, FAULT—MOTION SENSOR, FAMILY ROOM or whatever.

He brushed his teeth, stripped down to his shorts, and climbed into the king-size bed. Next to Laura's side of the bed was the same stack of books that had been there since the night of the accident. Marta dusted them off but knew enough not to put them away. The effect was as if she were away on a business trip and might come back in, keys jingling, at any moment. One of the books, Nick always noticed with a pang, was an old course catalog from St. Thomas More College that had a listing for her art history class. She used to look at it sometimes at night, regretful.

The sheets were cool and smooth. He rolled over something lumpy: one of Julia's Beanie Babies. He smiled, tossed it out of the way. Lately she'd taken to leaving a different Beanie Baby in his bed each night, a little game of hers. He guessed it was her way of sleeping with Daddy, by proxy, since she hadn't been allowed to sleep in the parental bed for some time.

He closed his eyes, but his mind raced. The Scotch hadn't helped at all. A jerky, low-quality movie kept playing in his mind: The cop saying, *Do you have any enemies, Mr. Conover?* Julia's hot, wet tears soaking his shirt by the side of the pool.

Fifteen, twenty minutes later he gave up, switched on the bathroom light, and fished out an Ambien from the brown plastic pharmacy bottle and dry-swallowed it.

He turned on the bedside lamp and read for a while. Nick wasn't a reader, never read fiction, only enjoyed biographies but didn't have time to read anything anymore. He hated reading those books on business management that so many of his Leadership Team kept on their shelves.

After a while he began feeling drowsy, finally, and turned off the light.

He had no idea how much later it was when he was awakened by a rapid beeping tone. Eddie's installers had set the system to go off only in his bedroom or his study, and not too loud, when he was in the house.

He sat up, his heart pounding, his head filled with sludge. For a moment he didn't know where he was or what that strange insistent beeping was. When he realized where it was coming from, he leaped out of bed and squinted at the green touch pad's LED.

It was flashing: ALARM***PERIMETER***ALARM.

Keeping his footsteps light, in order not to wake the kids, he went downstairs to investigate.

12

NICK PADDED BAREFOOT downstairs, the house dark and silent. He glanced at one of the new touch pads at the foot of the stairs. It too was flashing: ***ALARM***PERIMETER***.

His brain felt viscous and slow. It was an effort to think clearly. Only the rapid beating of his heart, the adrenaline-fueled anxiety, kept him moving forward.

He paused for a moment, considering which way to go.

Then a light came on *inside* the house, flooding him with panic. He walked quickly toward the light—his study?—until he remembered that the software that ran the cameras had been programmed to detect pixel changes, shifts in light or movement. Not only did the cameras start recording when there was a change in light, but the software was connected to a relay that automatically switched on a couple of inside lights, to scare off potential intruders by making them think someone in the house had been awakened, even if no one was home.

He slowed his pace but kept going, trying to think. The motion-sensor software worked by zones. That meant that whoever or whatever was there was on the side of the lawn nearest his study. Eddie's guy had set up the system so that the alarm company wasn't alerted unless the house itself was broken into, since a large animal moving across the lawn was enough to set off the perimeter alarm. Otherwise there'd be too many false alarms. But if something did cross the lawn, the cameras started and the lights went on.

A deer. Probably that was all it was.

Still, he had to be sure.

He kept going through the family room, down the hall to his study. The lights were on.

He slowed as he entered the study, the sludge in his head starting to clear. No one was here, of course. The only sound was the faint hum from his computer. He looked at the French doors and the darkness beyond. Nothing there; nothing outside. A false alarm.

The room went dark, startling him momentarily, until he remembered that the lights were also programmed to go off after two minutes. He walked through the study, approaching the glass panes of the French doors, staring out.

He could see nothing.

Nothing out there but watery moonlight glinting on the trees and shrubbery.

He glanced back at the illuminated face of his desk clock. Ten minutes after two. The kids were asleep upstairs, Marta presumably back from her night out and asleep in her bedroom in the wing off the kitchen. He glanced back out through the windowpanes, checking again.

After a few seconds he turned to leave the study.

The lawn outside lit up. The floodlights came on, jolting Nick. He spun back around, looked outside, saw a figure approaching from a stand of trees.

He moved closer to the glass, squinted. A man in some kind of trench coat that flapped as he walked. He was crossing the lawn slowly, headed directly toward Nick.

Nick went to the touch pad and deactivated the alarm system. Then he reached for the French doors' lever handle, thought for a moment, and went to his desk. He took the key from the middle drawer and unlocked the bottom one, slid it open, took out the pistol.

He removed it from its oilcloth.

Blood rushed through his head; he could hear it in his ears.

Despite assuring him he'd never have to use the thing, Eddie had left it loaded. Now Nick gripped the weapon, pulled back the slide to chamber the first round, as Eddie had instructed, let the slide go.

He turned slowly, the weapon at his side, careful to keep his finger away from the trigger. With his left hand he turned the handle and opened the French doors. He stepped outside, the soil of the newly seeded lawn cold against his bare feet.

"Stop right there," he called.

The man kept advancing. Now Nick could make out his heavy black eyeglasses, his ogling eyes, his brushcut gray hair, his bent figure. The man, his name was Andrew Stadler, walked straight ahead, heedlessly.

Nick raised the gun, barked: *"Freeze!"*

Under the flapping trench coat, Stadler wore white pants, a white shirt. He was muttering to himself, all the while staring at Nick as he came closer and closer.

He's a fucking nutcase, buddy . . .

The guy kept coming, goggling eyes staring as if he didn't even see the gun, or if he did, he didn't give a shit.

Eddie's words. *A maniac. The guy's been in and out of the locked ward at County Medical.*

"Don't you fucking take another step!" Nick shouted.

Now the man's mutterings were starting to become

distinct. The man raised his hand, pointed a finger at Nick, his expression malevolent, enraged. "Never safe," the man croaked. He smiled, his hands fluttering to his sides, to his coat pockets. The smile was like a twitch: it came and disappeared several times in succession, no logic to it.

Stadler was questioned in the possible murder of an entire family that lived across the street.

"One more step, and I shoot!" Nick shouted, raising the weapon with both hands, aiming at the center of the lunatic's body.

"You're never going to be safe," the man in white said, one hand fumbling in his pocket, now *rushing* toward Nick, toward the open door.

Nick squeezed the trigger, and everything seemed to happen all at once. There was a popping sound, loud but not nearly as loud as he'd expected. The pistol bucked in his hands, flew backward at him. An empty shell casing flew off to one side. Nick could smell gunpowder, sulfuric and acrid.

The maniac stumbled, sank to his knees. A dark blotch appeared on his white shirt, a corona of blood. The bullet had entered his upper chest. Nick watched, his pulse racing, still gripping the pistol in both hands, leveling it at the man until he could be sure the man was down.

Suddenly, with surprising agility, the madman sprang to his feet with a throaty growl, shouting, "No!" in an aggrieved, almost offended voice. He propelled himself toward Nick, said, *"Never—safe!"*

The man was less than six feet away now, and Nick fired, aiming higher this time, wild with fear and resolve. He was able to stabilize the weapon better now, felt a spray of powder sting his face, and he saw the man tumble backward and to one side, mouth open, but this time he did not break his fall. He landed on his side, legs splayed at a funny angle, expelling a guttural, animallike sound.

Nick froze, watched in silence for a few seconds.

His ears rang. Gripping the weapon in both hands, he stepped to one side to see the man's face. The lunatic's mouth was gaping, blood seeping over his lips, his chin. The black glasses had fallen off somewhere; now the eyes, much smaller without the magnification of the lenses, stared straight ahead.

The man exhaled with a rattling noise and was silent.

Nick stood, dazed, flooded with adrenaline, even more terrified at this moment than he had been a minute earlier. He pointed the pistol, almost accusingly, at the man and walked slowly up to him. Nick thrust out his right foot, nudged the man's chest, testing.

The man rolled backward, his mouth open, a mouthful of silver fillings glinting, the eyes now staring into the night sky, blood seeping. The high metallic ringing in Nick's ears had begun to subside, and everything was strangely, eerily silent. From very far away, Nick thought he could hear a faint rustling of leaves. A dog now barked, far in the distance, then stopped.

The man's chest was not moving; he was not breathing. Nick leaned over him, the pistol now dangling in his left hand by his side. He placed his right forefinger on the man's throat and felt no pulse. This was no surprise; the staring eyes had already announced that the maniac lay dead.

He's dead, Nick thought. I've killed him.

I've killed a man.

He was suffused with terror. I killed this guy. Another voice in his head began to plead, defensive and frightened as a little boy.

I had to. I had no choice. I had no fucking choice.

I had to stop him.

Maybe he's just unconscious, Nick thought desperately. He felt the man's throat again, couldn't find the pulse. He grabbed one of the man's rough, dry hands, pressed against the inside of his wrist, felt nothing.

He let go of the hand. It dropped to the ground.

He poked again at the man's chest with his toes, but he knew the truth.

The man was dead.

The crazy man, this stalker, this man who would have dismembered my children the way he butchered my dog, lay dead on the freshly seeded lawn, surrounded by tiny sprouts of grass that poked out sparsely from the moist black earth.

Oh, Jesus God, Nick thought. I've just killed a man.

He stood up but felt his knees give way. He sank to the ground, felt tears running down his cheeks. Tears of relief? Of terror? Not, certainly not, of despair or of sadness.

Oh, please, Jesus, he thought. What do I do now?

What do I do now?

For a minute, maybe two, he remained on his knees, sunken in the soft ground. It was as if he were in a church, a place he hadn't been in decades, praying. That was what it felt like. He was praying on the soft, hydroseeded lawn, his back turned to the crumpled body. For a few seconds he wondered if he was going to lose consciousness, pass out on the soil. He waited for a sound, the sound of someone in the house, awakened by the gunshots, running out to see what had happened. The kids couldn't see this, mustn't be allowed to see it.

But not a sound. No one had awakened, not even Marta. Gathering his strength, he rose, dropping the weapon to the ground, moving back toward the study as if in a trance. The lights came on: the motion sensor software again.

He could barely stand. He sank into his desk chair, folding his arms on the desk, resting his head on his arms. His mind was racing, but to no purpose; he was not thinking clear thoughts. His brains felt scrambled.

He was terrified.

What do I do now?

Who can help me? Who do I call?

He lifted the handset on his desk phone, pressed the number nine.

Nine-one-one. The police.

No, I can't. Not yet. He hung up.

Must think. What do I tell them? Everything depends on this. Was it self-defense pure and simple?

The police, who despised him so much, would be looking to hang him. Once they showed up, they'd be asking all sorts of questions, and one wrong answer might put him in prison for years. Nick knew that, given how groggy and out of it he was, he might well be railroaded by the cops.

He needed help.

He picked up the handset again, punched the cell number of the one person who would know what to do now.

Dear God, he thought as the phone rang.

Help me.

Eddie's voice was sleep-thickened, clipped. "Yeah?"

"Eddie, it's Nick."

"Nick—Jesus, it's fucking—"

"Eddie, I need you to come over to my house. Right now." He swallowed. A cool breeze swept through the room from the open doors, making him shiver.

"Now? Nick, are you out of your—"

"Now, Eddie. Oh, God. Right now."

"What the hell is it?"

"The stalker," Nick said. His mouth was dry, and the words stuck in his throat.

"He's *there*?" For a few seconds, Nick couldn't answer. Eddie went on, "Christ, Nick, what *is* it? My God, don't tell me he got to your *kids*!"

"I—I gotta call nine-one-one, but—I need to know what to *tell* them, and—"

"What the fuck *happened,* Nick?" Eddie barked.

"I killed him," Nick heard himself say softly. He paused to think of how to explain it, blinked a few times, then fell silent. What was there to say, really? Eddie had to have figured it out.

"*Shit,* Nick—"

"When I call the cops, they're going to—"

"Nick, you listen to me," Eddie interrupted. "Do *not* pick up the phone again. I'll be there in ten minutes."

The phone slipped from Nick's hand as if his fingers were greased. He felt a sob welling up.

Please, dear God, Nick thought. Make this go away.

13

STANDING IN THE shadowed recesses of the front porch, Nick sipped from a mug of instant coffee and waited. Apart from physical sensations—the chill of the night air, the warmth of the mug against his palms, the gusts of wind—he felt nothing. He was beyond numb. He was a husk, an empty body standing on a porch at night while above him hovered Nick Conover, watching in disbelief. This hadn't happened. This was a nightmare that, even as he experienced it in real time, he told himself was merely a bad dream that he'd awaken from, soon enough, but not before he moved through the twisting, steadily more awful script. At the same time, he understood that it wasn't a dream. Any minute now, Eddie's car would pull into the driveway, and Nick, by telling another person, seeking his advice, would make it real.

As if on cue, Eddie's Pontiac GTO coasted quietly up the driveway, headlights extinguished. Eddie got out, shut the door quietly, jogged up to Nick. He was wearing sweatpants and a tan Carhartt jacket.

"Nicky, tell me exactly what happened?" Eddie's face was creased, unfamiliarly, with concern. His shoulders were hunched. His breath stank of stale booze; he looked like he'd been asleep.

Nick chewed the inside of his cheek, looking away.

Eddie twisted his head to one side. "All right. Where is he?"

"OKAY," EDDIE SAID. "Okay."

His hands made strange, resolute chopping motions in the air. "Okay." He stood over the crumpled body. The floodlights at his back cast a long, spindly shadow.

"Do you think anyone heard?" His first question. A strange one, it seemed to Nick. Not "What happened?"

Nick shook his head. He spoke in a low voice, hoping Eddie would do the same. "Marta or the kids would have gotten up if they did."

"Neighbors?"

"Hard to say. The security guys down at the booth normally drive up if they think there's a problem."

"No lights went on at any of the neighbors' houses?"

"Look for yourself. Our nearest neighbor is hundreds of feet away. Trees and everything between us. I can't see them, they can't see me."

Eddie nodded. "The Smith and Wesson's a .380. Makes kind of a loud popping noise." He leaned over to peer more closely at Stadler. "Did he enter the house?"

"No."

Eddie nodded again. Nick couldn't tell from his expression whether that was good or not.

"He see you?"

"Sure. I was standing right here."

"You told him to stop."

"Of course. Eddie, what the hell am I—"

"You did the right thing." His voice was low, soothing. "You had no fucking choice."

"He kept on going. He wouldn't stop."

"He would have attacked your kids if you didn't stop him."

"I know."

Eddie let out a long, slow breath, a little quaver in it. "Shit, man."

"What?"

"Shit."

"It was self-defense," Nick said.

Eddie drew closer to Stadler's corpse. "How many shots?"

"I think two."

"Chest and the head. The mouth."

Nick noticed that the bleeding had stopped. It looked black in the artificial light. The man's skin was white and waxen, his eyes staring.

"You must have a tarp here, all the construction."

"A tarp?"

"Canvas. Or plastic, better."

"A tarp?"

"A tarpaulin, Nick. You know. A big heavy plastic sheet. Or contractor bags if you have them. You must have those around."

"What for?"

"The hell do you think? Any idea how hard it is to carry a dead body?"

Nick felt a spasm of fear in his abdomen. "We got to call the cops, Eddie."

Eddie looked at Nick incredulously. "You are fucking kidding me. You think you even have a choice here?"

"What the hell else are we going to do?"

"Then what'd you call me for, Nick?"

"I—" He had a point, of course. "This is bad, Eddie. Really bad."

"You just used my fucking gun. To kill a guy, okay? Are you hearing me? My gun. We really don't have a choice."

14

NICK STARED, DIDN'T know what to say, went back into the study, Eddie right behind him. Nick sat in one of the side chairs, rubbed the heels of his hands into his eyes.

"It was self-defense," he repeated.

"Maybe."

"Maybe? What are you talking about, maybe? This guy was dangerous."

"Did he have a gun?"

"No. But how the hell could I have known that?"

"You couldn't," Eddie conceded. "Maybe you saw something glint, a knife or a gun or something, you couldn't be sure."

"I saw him reach in his pocket. You told me the guy has a gun—I figured he was reaching for a weapon."

Eddie nodded, turned grimly toward the doors, and stepped back into the inky blackness. He returned a minute or so later, some objects in his cupped hands. He dumped them onto the coffee table. "Wallet, key ring. No knife, no gun, no nothing on the guy."

"I didn't fucking *know* that," Nick said. "He kept saying, 'You're not safe.'"

"Nick, of *course* you didn't know. Jesus, I mean, you

were dealing with a fucking psycho, a guy's gotta do what a guy's gotta do. That's not it."

"The truth is, you lent me your gun as protection," Nick said. "Temporarily. You said it's a misdemeanor."

Eddie slammed his fist into his palm. "You still don't fucking get it, do you? You killed the dude outside the house, not inside."

"He was trying to get in, believe me."

"*I* know that. You're allowed to use physical force to terminate attempted commission of criminal trespass." The words sounded unnatural, halting, coming out of his mouth, as if he'd memorized them during his cop days. "But not deadly physical force. That's the premises law. See, Nick, the law says deadly physical force can only be used in the face of deadly physical force."

"But given the guy's record—"

"I'm not saying you wouldn't have a chance of beating this. But what the hell you think's going to happen to you, huh?"

Nick finished his mug of coffee. The caffeine only went so far in counteracting the sleeping pill; it was adrenaline and fear that were keeping him functioning. "I'm the CEO of a major corporation, Eddie. I'm a respected member of the community."

"You're fucking Nick the Slasher!" Eddie hissed. "What the fuck do you think's going to happen to you? And to your family? Think about it. You think the cops are going to cut you any slack?"

"The law's the law."

"Shit! Don't talk to me about the law, Nick. I know the law. I know how it gets twisted and bent if the cops want it to. I've done it, okay?"

"Not all cops," Nick said.

Eddie flashed him a look of barely concealed hostility. "Put it to you this way. The locals'll have no choice but to charge you, right?"

"Maybe."

"For absolute fucking sure. And when it comes to trial—and it will, you can be sure of that—yeah, you might beat it. Maybe. After ten months of a *nightmare*. Yeah, you could get lucky, get a reasonable prosecutor, but even they're going to face all sorts of pressure to string up Nick the Slasher. You're going to be facing a jury of twelve people who all hate your guts—man, the thought of locking you up . . . I mean, in a town this size, there isn't going to be a juror in the pool who doesn't know someone, a friend or a relative, that you fired, right? You saw what that jury did to Martha Stewart for a little insider trading. You fucking murdered an old man, are you with me yet? A sick old man."

"The bottom line is, I'm innocent." Nick was feeling ill again, thought he might throw up, looked around for his metal wastebasket in case he did.

"You don't get to say what the bottom line is, okay?"

"But it was fucking *self-defense*!"

"Hey, don't argue with *me*! I'm on *your* side. But it's homicide, Nick. Manslaughter at a minimum. You say it's self-defense, but you got no witnesses, you got no injuries, and you got a dead guy who was unarmed. I don't care how much money you spend on a lawyer— you get tried here, in Fenwick. And what the hell you think's going to happen to your kids during this god- damned media circus, huh? You have any fucking *idea* what this is going to do to them? You think it's hard for them, dealing with Laura and the layoffs and ev- erything? Imagine you on trial for murder. A fucking lynch mob, Nick. You want to put your kids through that?"

Nick didn't reply. He felt frozen in the chair, com- pletely at a loss.

"They're probably going to send you away, Nick. Five, ten years if you're lucky. Sentence like that, you're going to miss your kids' childhood. And they grow up with a jailbird father. They don't have a mom, Nick. All they got is you. You gonna play Russian roulette with your kids, Nick?"

Eddie's stare was unrelenting, furious.

Finally, Nick spoke. "What are you suggesting?"

— PART TWO —

TRACE EVIDENCE

15

AUDREY RHIMES'S PAGER shrilled in the semidarkness.

She jolted awake, out of a blissful dream of her childhood, a warm summer day, going down a Slip'N Slide that went on and on and on, in her family's steeply canted backyard. Ordinarily 6:30 A.M. wasn't early at all, but her shift had ended at midnight, and after that came the usual unpleasantness with Leon, so she'd gotten maybe four hours of sleep.

She felt raw, vulnerable like a freshly hatched chick.

Audrey was a woman who liked routine, schedule, regularity. This was a personality trait that didn't go well with her job as a detective with the Fenwick Police Major Case Team. Calls could come at any time of day or night. Though she could no longer remember why, this was a job she'd wanted, a job she fought for. She was not just the only African-American member of the Major Case Unit but the only woman—the real difficulty, it turned out.

Leon groaned, rolled over, buried his head beneath a pillow.

She slipped out of bed and moved silently through the dim bedroom, narrowly avoiding a cluster of empty beer cans that Leon had left there. From the kitchen phone she called Dispatch.

A body discovered in a Dumpster on the five hundred block of Hastings. A section of town where all of the town's vice seemed to be concentrated, all the prostitution and drugs and violence and shootings. A dead body there could mean any of a number of things, including drugs or gangs, but the odds were that it meant very little. Was this hard-hearted of her? She preferred not to think so. At first she'd been shocked at the reactions of the survivors, even the mothers, who seemed to be almost resigned to losing a son. They'd already lost their sons. Few of them pleaded their sons' innocence. They knew better.

When Audrey learned who'd be picking her up this morning, who she'd been partnered with on this case—the loathsome Roy Bugbee—she felt her body go rigid with annoyance. More than annoyance, she had to admit to herself. Something stronger. This was not a worthy feeling, not a generous impulse.

Silently, as she dressed—she kept a clean outfit in the parlor closet—she recited one of her favorite verses of scripture, from Romans 15: "Now the God of patience and consolation grant you to be likeminded one toward another, according to Christ Jesus." She loved this line, even as she realized she didn't yet fully understand it. But she knew it meant that the Lord first teaches us what is true consolation and true patience, and then He instills this in our hearts. Reciting this to herself got her through Leon's recent sulking fits, his drinking problem, lent her a much-needed serenity. Her goal had been to re-read the entire Bible by year's end, but the irregularity of her schedule made that impossible.

Roy Bugbee was a fellow detective in Major Cases who had an unaccountable loathing toward her. He didn't know her. He knew only her outward appearance, her sex, and the color of her skin. His words cut her, though never as deeply as Leon's.

She gathered her equipment, her Sig-Sauer and her handcuffs, rights cards and IBO request forms and her PT, her handheld radio. While she waited, she sat in Leon's favorite chair, the worn rust BarcaLounger, and opened her old leather-bound King James Bible, her mother's, but there was barely time to find her place before Detective Bugbee pulled up in his city car.

He was slovenly. The car, which he was lucky enough to have at his disposal—she hadn't been given one—was littered with pop cans and Styrofoam Quarter Pounder boxes. It smelled of old French fries and cigarette smoke.

He didn't say hello or good morning. Audrey said good morning to him, however, determined to rise above his pettiness. She sat in uncomfortable silence, amid the squalor, observing the scattering of ketchup packets on the floor around her feet and hoping that none of them was on the seat beneath her plum business suit. The stain would never come out.

After a few minutes he spoke as he flicked the turn signal at a red light. "You got lucky, huh?" Bugbee's blond hair was slicked back in a pompadour. His eyebrows were so pale they were almost invisible.

"Pardon me?"

His laugh was raucous. "I don't mean with your husband. If Owens wasn't drunk on his ass when Dispatch called, you'da been assigned to him. But lucky you, you get me."

"Mm hm," she said, her tone pleasant. When she first arrived at Major Cases, only two of the men would talk to her, Owens being one of them. The others acted as if she wasn't even there. She'd say, "Good morning," and they wouldn't answer. There was no women's bathroom, of course—not for one woman—so she had to share the men's. One of the guys kept urinating right on the toilet seat just to make it unpleasant for her. Her fellow detectives thought it was hilarious. She'd heard it was Bugbee, and she believed it. He'd done "practical jokes" on her she didn't like to think about. Finally she'd had to resort to using the bathroom downstairs in the warrant unit.

"Body found in a Dumpster on Hastings," Bugbee continued. "Wrapped up like a burrito in Hefty bags."

"How long has it been there?"

"No idea. You better not go blow your cookies on me."

"I'll do my best. Who found it, one of the homeless looking for food?"

"Trash guy. You lose it like you did with that little black girl, you'll get yanked off the case, I'll see to it."

Little Tiffany Akins, seven years old, had died in her arms a few months earlier. They'd got her father cuffed, but her mother and her mother's boyfriend had already died of their gunshot wounds by the time Major Cases showed up. Audrey could not keep herself from weeping. The beautiful little girl, wearing SpongeBob pajamas, could have been her own child if she'd been able to have kids. She didn't understand what kind of father would be so blinded by rage and jealousy that he'd kill not only his estranged wife and her lover but his own daughter too.

She recited to herself: *Now the God of patience and consolation grant you to be likeminded one toward another . . .*

"I'll do my best, Roy," Audrey said.

16

THE CRIME SCENE was a small blacktopped parking lot behind a ratty little diner called Lucky's. A yellow streamer of evidence tape secured the area, barricaded off a small gathering of the usuals. It was remarkable, Audrey thought, and not a little sad, that this unknown vagrant was getting in death the kind of attention that he surely never got when it could have made a difference. A man wanders through the streets alone and unnoticed and despairing. Now, with the life gone out of his body, a crowd gathers to pay him the respect he'd never received in life.

No TV cameras here, though. No Newschannel Six truck. Maybe not even a reporter from the *Fenwick Free Press*. No one wanted to come down to the five hundred block of Hastings at six in the morning to report on the discovery of some vagrant's body.

Roy Bugbee parked the city car on the street between two patrol cars. They got out without exchanging another word. She noticed the white van belonging to the Identification Bureau Office, meaning that the crime-scene techs were already there. Not the Medical Examiner yet. The uniformed first officer, who'd notified Dispatch, was swanning around self-importantly, warding off neighborhood gawkers, clearly enjoying the biggest thing that had happened to him all week. Maybe all month. He approached Audrey and Bugbee with a clipboard and demanded that they sign in.

Her eye was caught by a flash of light, then another. The IBO evidence tech on the scene was Bert Koopmans. She liked Koopmans. He was smart and thorough, obsessive-compulsive like the best crime-scene techs, but without being arrogant or difficult. Her kind of cop. Something of a gun nut, maintained his own personal Web site on firearms and forensics. He was a lean man in his fifties with a receding hairline and thick Polar Gray spectacles. He was snapping pictures, switching between Polaroid and digital and 35mm and video like some crazed paparazzi.

Her boss, Sergeant Jack Noyce, the head of the Major Case Team, was talking on his Nextel phone. He saw Audrey and Bugbee duck under the yellow tape, held up a finger to ask them to wait. Noyce was a round-faced, stout man with melancholy eyes, gentle and sweet natured. He'd been the one who'd talked her into putting in for Major Cases. He said he wanted a woman on the squad. Never had he admitted it might have been a mistake. He was her steadfast defender, and she did him the favor of never going to him with the petty insults of her colleagues. From time to time he'd hear about something and would take her aside, promise to talk to them. He never did, though. Noyce preferred to avoid confrontation, and who could blame him, really?

He ended the call and said, "Unknown older white male, sixties maybe, gunshot wounds to the head and chest. Waste Management guy spotted it after he loaded the Dumpster on his frontloader. First pickup too. What a way to start your day."

"Before or after he tipped the trash into the hopper, boss?" asked Audrey.

"He noticed it before. Left the contents intact, stopped a patrol car."

"Coulda been a lot worse," Bugbee said. "Coulda put it through the compactor, huh?" He chortled, winked at his boss. "'Stead of a burrito we'd have a quesadilla. Ever see a body like that, Audrey? You'd really blow lunch."

"You make a very good point there, Roy," Noyce said, smiling thinly. Audrey had always suspected that her boss shared her dislike of Roy Bugbee but was too polite to let on.

Bugbee put a comradely hand on Noyce's shoulder as he strutted past.

"I'm sorry about that," Noyce said under his breath.

Audrey didn't entirely understand what he was sorry about. "He's got a unique sense of humor," she said, taking a stab.

"Owens was intoxicated, according to Dispatch. Bugbee was next on the call list. I wouldn't have partnered you two, but . . ." He shrugged, his voice trailing off.

Noyce waved at someone. Audrey turned to look. Curtis Decker, the body mover, was getting out of his old black Ford Econoline van. Decker, a small man of ghostly pallor, had a funeral home in Fenwick and was also the town's conveyance specialist. He'd been transferring bodies from crime scenes to the morgue at Boswell Medical Center for twenty-seven years. Decker lit a cigarette, leaned back against his van, chatting idly to his assistant, waiting his turn.

Noyce's phone chirped. He picked it up, said, "Noyce," and Audrey silently excused herself.

Bert Koopmans was painstakingly brushing powder on the rim of the battered dark-blue Dumpster. Without turning his head from his work, he said, "Morning, Aud."

"Good morning, Bert." As she drew closer to the Dumpster, she caught a whiff of a ripe stench, which mingled with the odor of bacon that wafted from the open service entrance door.

The asphalt was littered with cigarette butts. This was where the busboys and short-order cooks smoked. There were a few jagged shards from a brown beer bottle. She knew there wasn't likely to be any evidence here, no shell casings or anything, since the body had been dumped.

"Partnered with Bugbee on this, I see."

"Mm-hmm."

"The Lord trieth the righteous."

She smiled, her eyes straying to the body in the Dumpster, wrapped tightly in black trash bags. It did look a little like a take-out burrito. The bundle lay atop a foul mound of slimy lettuce heads and banana peels, a discarded submarine sandwich, next to a giant empty tin of Kaola Gold All-Vegetable Solid Griddle Shortening.

"Was it right on top like that?" she asked.

"No. Buried under a bunch of trash."

"I assume you haven't found anything, shell casings or whatever."

"I didn't really look that hard. There's eight cubic yards of garbage in there. I figure that's a job for the uniformed guys."

"You already print the bags?"

"Huh," Koopmans said. "Hadn't thought of it." Meaning: Of course, what do you think?

"So what's your take, smart guy?"

"On what?"

"You unwrap that package up there, Bert?"

"First thing I did."

"And? A mugging? Did you find a wallet or anything?"

Koopmans finished dusting a patch, carefully replaced his brush in the kit. "Just this." He held up a plastic sandwich bag.

"Crack cocaine," she said.

"Off-white chunky material in a Baggie, to be precise."

"Which looks like crack. Like eighty dollars' worth."

He shrugged.

"A white guy in this part of town," she said, "has to be a drug deal."

"If the deal went bad, how come he got to keep the crack?"

"Good question."

"Where's your partner?"

She turned, saw Bugbee smoking, laughing raucously with one of the uniforms. "Hard at work interviewing witnesses, looks like. Bert, you'll get this stuff tested, right?"

"Standard procedure."

"How long does it take to get back results?"

"Few weeks, given the MSP's workload." The Michigan State Police lab did all the drug testing.

"You happen to have one of those field test kits with you?"

"Somewhere, sure."

"Can I have a pair of gloves? I left mine in the car."

Koopmans reached into a nylon rucksack beside him and pulled out a blue cardboard box, from which he yanked a pair of latex gloves. She snapped them on. "Could you hand me that Baggie?"

Koopmans gave her a questioning look but handed over the bag of crack. It was one of those Ziploc kinds.

She pulled it open, removed one of the individually wrapped chunks—five or six in there, she noticed—and peeled off the plastic wrap.

"Don't start doing my work," Koopmans said. "Leads to worse things. Pretty soon you'll be squinting into a microscope and bitching about detectives."

With one gloved index finger she scraped at an edge of the off-white rock. Strange, she thought. A little too round-looking, too perfect a formation. Only one side was jagged. Then she touched her forefinger to her tongue.

"What the hell are you doing?" Koopmans said, alarmed.

"Thought so," she said. "Didn't numb my tongue like it's supposed to. This isn't crack. These are lemon drops."

Koopmans gave a slow smile. "Still need me to get the test kit?"

"That's okay. Could you help me up the side of this Dumpster, Bert? Of all the days I picked to wear my good shoes."

17

ANOTHER ORDINARY MORNING at the office. Arrive at the Stratton parking lot at seven-thirty. Check e-mail, voice mail. Return a few calls, leave voice mails for people who won't be in their offices for at least another hour.

You have killed a man.

Just another ordinary day. Business as usual.

The day before, Sunday, he'd even fantasized about going to church, to confession, which he hadn't done since he was a kid. He'd never do it, he knew, but in his mind he rehearsed his confession, imagined the dark confessional booth, that musty cedar-vanilla smell, the scuffling footsteps outside. "Forgive me, Father, for I have sinned," he says. "It has been thirty-three years since my last confession. I have committed these sins. I have taken the Lord's name in vain. I have gazed lustfully upon other women. I have lost patience with my kids. And, oh yeah, I killed a man." What would Father Garrison say about that? What would his own father have made of it?

He heard Marge's voice, intercepting the early morning calls like the pro she was. "He *is* in the office, yes, but I'm afraid he's in conference just now . . ."

How much had he slept in the past two days? He was in one of those weird, wobbly all-nighter states poised between calm and despair, and despite the coffee he'd had, he felt a sudden surge of weariness. He would have been tempted to close his office door and lay his head on his desk, except there was no door.

And it wasn't an office, really, at all. Certainly not what he used to imagine a CEO's office would look like. Which wasn't to say he'd ever spent much time thinking about being CEO of Stratton, or CEO of anything for that matter. As a kid, sitting at supper at his parents' Formica kitchen table, inhaling the acrid must of machine oil that emanated from his dad's hair and skin even after his father had taken his post-shift shower, Nick used to imagine one day working alongside Dad on the Stratton shop floor, bending metal at the brake machine. His father's gnarled stubby fingers, with the crescents of black grime still lodged under his fingernails, fascinated him. These were the fingers of a man who knew how to fix anything, could open a Mason jar that had been rusted shut, could build a fort out of spare lumber, nestled securely in the oak in their tiny backyard, that was the envy of all the neighbor kids. They were the hands of a worker, a guy who came home from the factory exhausted but then went right to work again, after his shower, around the house, tumbler of whiskey in one hand: fixing the dripping sink, a wobbly table leg, a lamp whose socket had a short. Dad liked fixing things that were broken, liked restoring order, getting things to work right. But more than anything, he liked being left alone. Working around the house was his way to get what he really wanted: a cone of silence around him, his thoughts kept to himself, not having to talk to his wife or son. Nick Conover only realized this about his dad much later when he saw it in himself.

He never thought one day he'd be running the company his father spoke of, the rare times he did speak, with such awe and disgruntlement. They barely knew anyone who *didn't* work for Stratton. All the neighbor kids, all the grown-ups his parents ever saw or talked about, they all worked at Stratton. Dad always groused about fat old Arch Campbell, the nasty round-shouldered factory manager who tyrannized the day shift. Complaining about Stratton was like complaining about the weather: you were stuck with whatever you got. It was the big annoying extended family you could never escape from.

When he was around fourteen or fifteen, Nick's junior-high class took the obligatory tour of Stratton—as if any of the kids needed a close look at the company that dominated their parents' supper conversations, the company whose logo was sewn in red on their white baseball caps, on team uniforms, emblazoned in neon over the arched entrance to the high school stadium. Walking through the chair factory, cavernous and thundering, deafeningly loud, might have been fun if most of the kids hadn't already been taken there at one time or another by their dads. Instead, it was the headquarters building that fascinated the rambunctious eighth-graders, finally intimidated them into a respectful awed silence.

At the climax of the tour they were crowded into the anteroom of the immense office suite of the president and chief executive officer, Milton Devries. This was the inner sanctum, the beating heart of the company that they realized, even as kids, ruled their lives. It was like being taken into King Tut's tomb; it was that alien, that fascinating, that intimidating. There, Devries's frightening mastiff-faced secretary, Mildred Birkerts, gave them a grudging little memorized talk, punctuated by the occasional dyspeptic scowl, about the vital function of the chief executive officer at Stratton. Craning his neck, Nick caught an illicit glimpse of Devries's desk, an acre of burnished mahogany, bare except for a gold desk set and a perfectly neat pile of papers. Devries wasn't there: that would have been too much. He saw huge windows, a leafy private balcony.

When, years later, Milton Devries died, Nick— who'd become the old man's favorite vice president— was summoned by Milton's widow, Dorothy, to her dark mansion on Michigan Avenue, where she told him he was the next CEO. Her family owned Stratton, so she could do that.

With great discomfort, Nick had moved into the old man's Mussolini-size office, with the floor-to-ceiling windows, the Oriental rugs, the immense mahogany desk, the outer office where *his* executive assistant, Marjorie Dykstra, would guard his privacy. It was like living in a mausoleum. Of course, by then, Stratton had changed. Now everyone wanted to stuff as many employees as possible into a building, and Stratton had gone to the open-plan system, that fancy term for cubicles and all the furnishings that went with them. No one really liked the cube farm, but at least Stratton's designs were elegant, cool, and friendly, 120-degree angles, the panels not too tall, all the computer cables and electrical wires and stuff hidden in the floors and panels.

One day a visitor looked around Nick's office and made a crack. He was head of worldwide purchasing for IBM, a harried-looking guy with a sharp tongue, who'd surveyed Nick's mahogany chamber and muttered dryly, "Oh, *I* see—you get the fancy digs while everyone *else* gets the 'open plan.'"

The next day Nick had ordered the executive floor completely remodeled, switched to the open plan too, over the howls of protest from his entire executive management team. They'd busted their humps for years to finally land the big office with the private balcony and now they were all getting *cubicles*? This was a joke, right? You couldn't do this.

But he did. Of course, everyone on the fifth floor got the best of the best, the elegant, high-end Ambience Office System with its silver mesh fabric panels on brushed aluminum frames, sound-absorbing panel walls, and the top-of-the-line leather Stratton Symbiosis chairs, the harp-back beauties that had pretty much taken the place of the Aeron chair in fancy offices around the world, much coveted, just added to the permanent collection of the Museum of Modern Art.

Eventually people got used to the new arrangement. The complaints stopped. It got a little easier when *Fortune* did a big spread on the Stratton executive offices, on how they were walking the walk as well as talking the talk. It got easier still when delegations of design-school students started coming to gape at the executive offices, marvel at how *edgy* they were.

The new offices were pretty damned cool, it was true. If you had to work in cubicles, this was the best damned cube farm money could buy. So now, Nick had often reflected, you had guys sitting in cubicles thinking about . . . cubicles.

Of course, there really wasn't any privacy anymore. Everyone knew where you were, when you went out to lunch or to work out, who you were meeting with. If you yelled at someone on the phone, everyone heard it.

The bottom line was, when Steve Jobs from Apple Computer came in for a meeting, or Warren Buffett flew in from Omaha, they could see that the top executives of Stratton weren't hypocrites. They ate the same dog food they were selling. That was the best sales pitch of all.

So now Nick Conover's office was a "workstation"

or a "home base." The new arrangement was less gran-
diose, suited him more. It wasn't a big sacrifice. Most
days he liked it a lot more anyway.

Only this wasn't one of them.

"NICK, ARE YOU all right?"

Marjorie had come over to make sure he had the
stapled agenda for Nick's 8:30 meeting of his Executive
Management Team. She was dressed elegantly, as al-
ways; she was wearing a lavender suit, the short string
of pearls he'd bought as a gift for her a few years be-
fore. She wafted a faint cloud of Shalimar.

"Me? Oh, I'm fine, Marge, thanks."

She wasn't moving. She stood there, cocked her
head. "You don't look it. Have you been sleeping?"

Rough couple of nights, he almost said. Immediately
he could hear her repeating back the words in a court-
room. *He said he'd had a couple of rough nights, but
he didn't elaborate.* "Ah, Lucas is driving me crazy,"
he said.

A knowing smile. She'd raised two boys and a girl
pretty much by herself and rightly considered herself
an expert. "Poor kid's in a tough place."

"Yeah, called adolescence."

"Anything you want to talk about?"

"I'd love to, later on," Nick said, knowing that would
never happen; he'd make sure of it.

"Right, the EMT meeting. You all set for that, Nick?"

"I'm all set."

Was it possible to look like a murderer? Was it vis-
ible on his face? It was stupid, it made no sense, but
in his dazed, scrambled egg–brain state, he worried
about it. In the EMT meeting, he barely spoke, because
he could barely concentrate. He remembered the time
when the family was camping in Taos, and a snake got
into their cabin. Laura and the kids screamed, and she

begged Nick to get a shovel and kill the vile thing. But he couldn't. He couldn't bring himself to do it. It wasn't a venomous snake—it was a Western coachwhip— but Laura and the kids kept demanding that he get the shovel. Finally he reached down, picked it up, and threw it, twisting and wriggling, out into the desert.

Couldn't kill a snake, he thought.

Some irony in that.

He strode out of the room as soon as the meeting was over, avoiding the usual post-meeting entanglements.

Back at his desk, he went on the Stratton intranet and checked Eddie Rinaldi's online Meeting Maker to see what his schedule was. They hadn't talked since Eddie had driven away with the body in the trunk of his car. Every time the phone rang, all Saturday and Sunday, he flinched a little, dreading that it might be Eddie. But Eddie never called, and he never called Eddie. He assumed everything had gone okay, but now he wanted the assurance of knowing. He thought about e-mailing Eddie to tell him he wanted to talk, but then decided against it. E-mails, instant messages, voice mails—they were all recorded somewhere. They were all evidence.

18

THE ONLY REASON Audrey attended autopsies was that she had no choice. It was department policy. The Medical Examiner's office required that at least one detective on a case be present. She told herself she didn't see the need, since she knew she could ask the pathologist anything she wanted, anything that wasn't in the path report.

In truth, of course, it made perfect sense to have a detective there. There were all sorts of things you found out at an autopsy that didn't appear in the sterile lines of a report. Even so, they were the part of her job she most disliked. The dissection of bodies made her queasy. She was always afraid she might have to vomit, though she hadn't done so since her first one, and that was a terribly burned female.

But that wasn't what she hated most about autopsies. She found them deeply depressing. This was where you saw the human body devoid of its spirit, its soul, a carapace of flesh meted out in grams and liters. To her, on the other hand, homicide cases were about setting things right. Solving the crime didn't always heal the wounds of the victim's family—often it didn't—but it was her way of restoring some kind of moral order to a deeply messed-up world. She'd taped a sign to her computer at work, a quote from one Vernon Geberth, whose name was well known to all homicide investigators, the author of a classic text, *Practical Homicide Investigation*. It said, "Remember: We work for God." She believed this. She felt deeply that, as much as she was troubled by her work—and she was, most of the time—she really was doing God's work here on earth. She was looking for the one lost sheep. But autopsies required a detachment she preferred not to have.

So she uneasily entered this white-tiled room that stank of bleach and formaldehyde and disinfectant, while her partner got to make phone calls and do interviews, though she wondered just how hard Roy Bugbee was working to solve this case of what he called "a shitbird crackhead." Not too hard, she figured.

The morgue and autopsy room were located in the basement of Boswell Medical Center, concealed behind a door marked PATHOLOGY CONFERENCE ROOM. Everything about this place gave her the heebie-jeebies, from the stainless-steel gurney on which the victim's nude body had been placed, head a few inches higher than the feet to facilitate drainage of bodily fluids, to the handheld Stryker bone saw on the steel shelf, the garbage disposals in the stainless-steel sink, the organ tray whose plastic drainage tube, once clear, was now discolored brown.

The assistant medical examiner, one of three attached to the department, was a young doctor named Jordan Metzler, strikingly handsome and he knew it well. He had a head of dark curly hair, great brown eyes, a strong nose, full lips, a dazzling smile. Everyone knew he wasn't long for this job, or this town: he'd recently been offered a job in pathology at Mass General, in Boston. In a matter of months he'd be sitting at some fancy restaurant on Beacon Hill, regaling a beautiful nurse with tales of this backwater town in Michigan where he'd been stuck the last couple of years.

"Audrey's in the *house*!" he crowed as she entered. "'S'up, Detective?"

What was it with white guys who felt compelled to use black slang when African-Americans were around? Did they think it made them seem cool, instead of ridiculous? Did they think that made black folks connect with them better? Did Metzler even notice that she didn't talk that way?

She smiled sweetly. "Dr. Metzler," she said.

He found her attractive; Audrey could tell by the way he grinned at her. Her antennae still worked, even after eight years of marriage to Leon. Like most women, she was adept at reading males; sometimes she was convinced she knew them better than they knew themselves. Eight years of marriage to Leon hadn't knocked the self-esteem out of her, not even the terrible last couple of years. She knew that men had always been drawn to her, because of her looks. She didn't consider herself beautiful, far from it, but she knew she was pretty. She took care of herself, she exercised, she never went without makeup and she was adept at choosing the right lipstick for her skin tone. She liked to think that it was her deep abiding faith that kept her looking good, but she had seen enough women of equally deep abiding faith at church, women whose looks only God could love, to know better.

"Have you found any bullets?" she asked.

"Well, we've got two in there, X-ray shows. No exit wounds. I'll get 'em. You don't have an ID on this one yet, do you?"

She found herself avoiding looking at the body, the wrinkled flesh and the yellow-brown toenails, which meant she had to keep looking at Metzler, and she didn't want to send him the wrong signals. Not a horn-dog like him.

"Maybe we'll get lucky and score a hit on AFIS," she said. The crime scene techs had just finished fingerprinting the victim, having collected whatever trace evidence they could find on the body, scraping and clipping the fingernails and all that. Since the body was unidentified, they'd run the prints right away through the Michigan Automated Fingerprint Identification System in Lansing.

She asked, "Evidence of habitual drug use?"

"You mean needle marks or something? No, nothing like that. We'll see what tox finds on the blood."

"Look like a homeless guy to you?"

He jutted his jaw, frowned. "Not based on his clothes, which didn't smell unusually bad. Or grooming or dental care or hygiene. I'd guess no. In fact, the guy's pretty clean. I mean, he could take better care of his cuticles, but he looks more like a house case than a police case." That was what the pathologists called the autopsies they did on hospital patients, whose bodies were always clean and well scrubbed when they got here.

"Any signs of struggle?"

"None apparent."

"The mouth looks sort of bashed in," she said, forcing herself to look. "Broken teeth and all. Is it possible he got hit with, say, the butt of the gun?"

Metzler looked amused by her hypothesis. "Possible? Anything's *possible*." He probably sensed that he'd come off as too arrogant, so he softened his tone. "The teeth are chipped and cracked, not pushed in. That's consistent with a bullet. And there's no trauma to the lips—no swelling or bruising you'd find if there was a blunt-force injury. Also, there's the little matter of the bullet hole in his palate."

"I see." She let him enjoy his moment of superiority. The fragile male ego needed to be flattered. She had no problem with that; she'd been doing that all of her adult life. "Doctor, what do you estimate as the time of death? We found the body at six—"

"Call me Jordan." Another dazzling smile. He was working it. "We can't tell. It's in full rigor at this point."

"At the crime scene you said there was no rigor mortis, and since rigor doesn't really start setting in until three, four hours after death, I figured—"

"Nah, Audrey, there's too many other factors— physique, environment, cause of death, whether the guy was running or not. Doesn't really tell you anything."

"What about the body temperature?" she pointed out, careful to sound tentative. She wanted answers from the pathologist; she had no interest in showing him up.

"What about it?"

"Well, at the scene, didn't you take a body temperature reading of ninety-two? That means it dropped around six degrees, right? If the body temperature drops one point five to two degrees per hour after death, I estimate the victim had been killed three or four hours before the body was found. Does that sound about right to you?"

"In a perfect world, sure." Dr. Metzler smiled, but this time it was the look a parent might give a five-year-old asking if the moon was made of green cheese. "It's just not an accurate science. There are too many variables."

"I see."

"You seem more versed in forensics than a lot of the cops who come in here."

"It's an important part of my job, that's all."

"If you're interested, I'd be willing to teach you a

little, help you out. No sense me having all this infor-
mation in my head if I can't share it with someone who
so clearly wants to learn."

She nodded, smiled politely. The burdens of being
so smart, she wanted to say.

"I wonder whether they really appreciate you on the
Major Case Team." He pretended to adjust the perfo-
rated stainless-steel tubing around the perimeter of
the examination table, which washed the fluids off the
body during the autopsy.

"I've never felt unappreciated," she lied. For the first
time she noticed the toe tag on the body's left foot. It
said "Unknown John Doe #6." Wasn't that, what was
the word? A "John Doe" *was* unknown, wasn't it?

"Somehow I doubt your beauty helps you in your
line of work."

"That's very kind of you, Doctor," she said, casting
around desperately for a question in order to change
the subject, but her mind had gone blank.

"Not kind at all. Accurate. You're a fine-looking
woman, Audrey. Beauty *and* brains—not a bad com-
bination at all."

"Why, you sound just like my husband," she said
lightly. He'd never actually said anything remotely like
that, but she wanted the pathologist to get the message
without hammering him over the head about it, and
that was the first thing she thought of.

"I saw your ring, Audrey," he said, giving her a
smile that seemed more than playful.

The man was cutting up a dead body, for heaven's
sake. This wasn't exactly a singles bar.

"You're too kind," she said. "Doctor, do the gunshot
wounds give you any sense of the distance from the
shooter?"

Metzler smiled to himself awkwardly as he stud-
ied the body on the table before him. He took a steel

scalpel from the metal shelf attached to the table and, with maybe a little too much force, carved a large Y-shaped incision from the shoulders all the way down to the pubic bone. He was clearly trying his best to accept defeat gracefully. "There's no stippling, no powder burns, no tattooing, no soot," he said. His voice had changed; now he was all business.

"So they're not contact wounds?"

"Neither contact nor intermediate range." He began trimming back the skin and the muscle and tissue below.

"So what does that tell us distancewise?"

He was silent for a good thirty seconds as he worked. Then he said, "Actually, Detective, that tells us nothing except that the muzzle was more than three feet from the wound. Certainly not without determining the caliber of the bullet, the type of ammo, and then test-firing the gun. It could have been fired from three feet away, or a hundred feet. You can't tell."

The glistening rib cage exposed, he positioned the round jagged-toothed blade above the bone and flicked the switch to start it. Above the high-pitched mechanical whine, he said, "You might want to stand back, Detective. This can get a little messy."

19

AS BADLY AS he wanted to, Nick couldn't easily cancel the weekly number-crunching lunch with Scott McNally, not with the big quarterly board meeting coming up. He felt feverish, clammy, nauseated. He felt, unusually for him, antisocial. His normal ebullience had been tamped down. He felt the beginnings of a raging headache, and he hadn't had a headache in years. He felt hungover, his stomach roiling. Coffee upset his stomach now, even though he needed it to stay awake and alert.

A chef from the corporate cafeteria had set out lunch for the two of them at the small round table adjacent to his home base. It was the usual—an eggplant Parmesan sub and a salad for Scott, a tuna sandwich and a cup of tomato soup for Nick. Folded linen napkins, glasses of ice water and a glass pitcher, Diet Cokes for both of them. Nick normally just ate a sandwich at his desk unless he had to do a working lunch. And until Laura's death, she always packed his lunch—a tuna fish sandwich, a bag of Fritos, carrot sticks—and put it in his briefcase. It was a little tradition that went back to their earliest days, when they had no money, and he'd gotten used to it. It was one of those little things Laura liked to do for him, even when she was teaching college and barely had time in the morning before class to make his lunch. She always put a little mash note in the paper lunch bag, which always made him smile when he came upon it, like the prize in a Cracker Jack box. There'd been times when he'd been having an informal lunch with Scott or another of his executives and one of Laura's notes had fluttered out, to Nick's embarrassment and secret pride. He'd saved every single one of her notes, without telling her. After her death, he'd come very close to throwing them away or burning them or something, because it was just too excruciating to have them around. But he couldn't bring himself to do that. So a neat pile of yellow Post-it notes in Laura's beautiful handwriting lay in the bottom drawer of his desk at work, secured with a rubber band. Sometimes he'd been tempted to take them out and look through them, but in the end, he couldn't. It was too painful.

"You look wiped out," Scott said, tucking right in to his sub. "You getting sick?"

Nick shook his head, took a careful sip of ice water, its coldness making him shiver. "I'm fine."

"Well, this ought to help," Scott said. "I know how you feel about the numbers. You might want to grab a pillow." He produced a couple of Velo-bound documents, slid one in front of Nick, next to his lunch plate.

Nick glanced at it. Income statement, cash-flow statement, and balance sheet.

"Check it out," Scott said. "Man, I love the way they toast the bun. Grill it, maybe, I don't know." He took a slug of Diet Coke. "You're not eating?"

"Not hungry."

Nick skimmed through the statements without interest while Scott examined the Diet Coke can. "I hear the artificial sweetener in this stuff can cause mood disorders in rats," he said.

Nick grunted, not listening.

"Ever seen a depressed rat?" Scott went on. "Curled up in a ball and everything? Some days they just don't feel the maze is worth it, you know?" He took a large bite of his sub.

"What's Stratton Asia Ventures?" Nick asked.

"You read footnotes. Very good. It's a subsidiary corporation I've formed to invest in Stratton's Asia Pacific ops. We needed a local subsidiary for permitting and to take advantage of certain tax treaties with the U.S."

"Nice. Legal?"

"Picky, picky," Scott said. "Of course legal. Clever doesn't mean illegal, Nick."

Nick looked up. "I don't get it," he said. "Our earnings are *up*?"

Scott nodded, chewing his huge mouthful, made some grunting noises indicating he wanted to speak but couldn't. Then he said, mouth still half full of food, "So it appears."

"I thought—Jesus, Scott, you told me we were in the toilet."

Scott shrugged, gave an impish smile. "That's why you've got me around. You know I always come to play. I'm bringing my A game, huh?"

"Your 'A game'? Scott, did you ever play a competitive sport in your life?"

Scott tilted his head to one side. "What are you talking about? I was point guard on the Stuyvesant math team."

"Wait a second." Nick went back to the beginning of the booklet, began reading over the numbers more closely. "All right, hold on. You're telling me our *international* business is up twelve percent? What gives?"

"Read the numbers. The numbers don't lie. It's all there in black and white."

"I just talked with George Colesandro in London last week, and he was pissing and moaning all over the place. You telling me he was reading the numbers wrong? Guy's got a fucking microprocessor for a brain."

Scott shook his head. "Stratton UK reports in pounds, and the pound's way up against the dollar," he said with his Cheshire-cat smile. "Gotta use the latest exchange rate, right?"

"So this is all hocus-pocus. Foreign exchange crap." Nick's nerve endings were raw, and it felt good somehow to think about something besides Friday night. At the same time, though, what Scott seemed to be doing was unbelievable. It was smarmy. "We're not up at all— we're down. You're—you're juggling the numbers."

"According to GAAP, we're supposed to use the correct exchange rates." GAAP stood for Generally Accepted Accounting Principles, but bland and jargony as it sounded, it had the force of law.

"Look, Scott, it's not apples to apples. I mean, you're using a different exchange rate than the one you used last quarter. You're just making it *look* like we did better." Nick rubbed his eyes. "You did the same thing in Asia Pacific?"

"Everywhere, sure." Scott's eyes were narrowed, apprehensive.

"Scott, this is fucking *illegal*." Nick slammed the booklet down on the table. "What are you trying to do to me?"

"To *you*? This isn't *about* you." Red-faced, Scott was looking down at the table as he spoke. "First of all, there's nothing illegal about it. Call it pushing the envelope a little, maybe. But let me tell you something. If I don't pretty these numbers up a little, our friends from Boston are going to come down on you like Nazi storm troopers. They are going to parachute in and tear this place up. I'm telling you this is a perfectly legitimate way to spin the numbers."

"You're—you're putting lipstick on a pig, Scott."

"Well, a little lip *gloss,* maybe. Look, when company comes over for dinner, you clean house, right? Before you sell your car, you take it to the car wash. None of the board members are going to look this close."

"So you're saying we can get *away* with it," Nick said.

Scott shrugged again. "What I'm saying, Nick, is that everyone's job is at risk here, okay? Including yours and mine. This way, at least, we buy ourselves a little time."

"No. Uh-uh," Nick said, drumming his fingertips on the clear plastic cover. "We give it to 'em straight. You got me?"

Scott's face flushed, as if he were embarrassed or angry, or both. He was clearly straining hard to sound calm, like it was taking enormous effort to keep from raising his voice to his boss. "Gosh, and I was hoping to have a corporate tax loophole named after me," he said after a pause.

Nick nodded, dispensed a grudging smile. He thought of Hutch, the old CFO. Henry Hutchens was a brilliant accountant, in his green-eyeshade, bean-counting way—no one knew the intricacies of the good old-fashioned balance sheet the way he did—but he knew little about structured finance and derivatives and all the shiny new financial instruments you had to use these days to stay afloat.

Hutch would never have done anything like this. Then again, he probably wouldn't have known how.

"You told me we're having dinner tonight with Todd Muldaur, remember?"

"Eight o'clock," Nick said. He was dreading it. Todd had called just a few days ago to mention he was passing through Fenwick, as if anyone ever "passed through" Fenwick, and wanted to have dinner. It couldn't be a good thing.

"Well, I told him I'd get him the updated financials before dinner."

"Fine, but let's make sure we're on rock-solid foundations here, okay?"

"In accounting?" Scott shook his head. "No such thing. It's like that story about the famous scientist who's giving a lecture on astronomy, and afterward an old lady comes up to him and tells him he's got it all wrong—the world is really a big flat plate resting on the back of a giant turtle. And the scientist says, 'But what's *that* turtle standing on?' And the old lady says, 'You're very clever, young man, very clever, but it's no use—it's turtles all the way down.'"

"Is that meant to be reassuring?"

Scott shrugged.

"I want you to give Todd the real, unvarnished numbers, no matter how shitty they look."

"Okay," Scott said, looking down at the table. "You're the boss."

20

AUDREY'S DESK PHONE was ringing as she approached her cubicle. She glanced at the caller ID and was glad she did, because it was a call she didn't want to take.

She recognized the phone number. The woman called her every week, regular as clockwork, had done so for so many weeks Audrey had lost count. Once a week since the woman's son was found murdered.

The woman, whose name was Ethel Dorsey, was a sweet Christian woman, an African-American lady who'd raised four sons on her own and was justifiably proud of that, convinced herself she'd done a good job, had no idea that three of her boys were deep into the life of gangs and drugs and cheap guns. When her son Tyrone was found shot to death on Hastings, Audrey recognized right away that it was drug-related. And like a lot of drug-related murders, it went unsolved. Sometimes people talked. Sometimes they didn't. Audrey had an open file, one less clearance. Ethel Dorsey had one less son. But here was the thing: Audrey simply couldn't bring herself to tell poor devout Ethel Dorsey the truth, that her Tyrone had been killed in some bad drug deal. Audrey remembered Ethel's moist eyes, her warm direct gaze, during the interviews. The woman reminded Audrey of her grandmother. "He's a good boy," she kept saying. Audrey couldn't break it to her that her son had not only been murdered, but he'd been a small-time dealer. For what? Why did the woman need to have her illusions shattered?

So Ethel Dorsey called once a week and asked, politely and apologetically, was there any progress on Tyrone? And Audrey had to tell her the truth: No, I'm sorry, nothing yet. But we haven't given up. We're still working, ma'am.

Audrey couldn't bear it. Because she realized that they'd probably never find Tyrone Dorsey's killer, and even if they did, it would bring no peace to Ethel Dorsey. Yet even a lowlife drug dealer was someone's son. Everyone matters, or else no one matters. Jesus told of the shepherd who kept searching for the one lost lamb, leaving his flock behind. For this purpose, Christ said, I was born.

Today she couldn't even bring herself to pick up the phone and talk to the woman. She looked at the photo of Tyrone she'd taped to the side wall of the cubicle, alongside the pictures of all the other victims whose cases she was working or had worked. As she waited for the phone to stop ringing, she noticed a folded square of paper that had been placed on top of the brown accordion file at the center of her desk. "UNKNOWN WHITE MALE #03486," the file had been labeled in her neat capital letters.

The white square of paper, folded a little unevenly into a makeshift card. On the front a black-and-white image of some generic church, a cheesy graphic that looked like clip art downloaded off the Internet. Below it, in Gothic lettering done on someone's computer, the words "Jesus Loves You."

She opened it, knowing more or less what she'd find.

Inside it said, "But Everyone Else Thinks Your an Ass-hole."

She crumpled up Roy Bugbee's inane little prank, misspelling and all, and tossed it into the metal waste-basket. She glanced, for the five-hundred-thousandth time, at the index card taped to her computer monitor, the card starting to go sepia at the edges, her lettering neat and fervent: "Remember: We work for God." She wondered who Roy Bugbee thought he worked for.

BUGBEE SAUNTERED IN an hour or so later, and they sat in an empty interview room.

"Strikeout on AFIS," he announced, almost proudly. "Nada."

So the old man's prints didn't match any of the fingerprint records in Lansing, neither the Tenprint Database nor the unsolved ones in the Latent Database. No real surprise there. The victim's prints would only be in AFIS if he'd been arrested for something.

She said, "The rounds that were fired were .380s, according to Bert Koopmans. Brass-jacketed."

"Oh, that's helpful," said Bugbee, deadpan. "Narrows it down to about a thousand possible weapons."

"Well, not really." Audrey ignored his sarcasm, proceeded on the assumption that Roy just didn't know what he was talking about. "Once the MSP in Grand Rapids takes a look at it, they'll winnow it down a whole lot more for us." The Forensic Science Lab of the Michigan State Police, in Grand Rapids, handled the firearms investigations for the police in this part of the state. Their examiners were good, trained in identifying weapons and ammunition using all sorts of tools, including IBIS, the Integrated Ballistics Identification System database, which was managed by the Bureau of Alcohol, Tobacco and Firearms.

"That shouldn't take more than six months," said Bugbee.

"Actually, I was hoping that when you drive it over there, you could press them to speed it up."

"Me?" Bugbee laughed. "I think *you* ought to drive to Grand Rapids, Audrey. Pretty woman like you, bat your little eyes at them, ask 'em to put it on the top of the heap."

She breathed in. "I'll drive it over there," she said. "Now, what about informants?"

"None of the snitches know a damned thing about some old guy trying to buy crack down the dog pound," he said grudgingly, as if it annoyed him to part with the information. Why that section of town was called "the dog pound" Audrey didn't remember if she ever knew. It just was.

"But the crack in the guy's pocket was fake."

"Yeah, yeah," Bugbee said with a wave of his hand. "Oldest trick in the book. White guy, easy mark, goes down to the dog pound to buy rock, and some zoomer sells him flex made outta candle wax and baking soda."

"Horehound lemon drops broken up, actually." So Bert Koopmans had told her.

"Whatever, don't make no difference. White guy argues with the zoomer, who says, Who needs this shit? and wastes the guy. Takes his wallet while he's at it and takes off. Open and shut."

"And leaves the lemon drops."

Bugbee gave a "lay off" shrug. He leaned back in the steel chair until his head was resting against the wall.

"And then instead of leaving the body in an alley somewhere, he goes to the trouble of wrapping it in garbage bags and then lifting it into a Dumpster, which isn't easy."

"Coulda been two guys."

"Wearing surgical gloves."

"Hmm?" He looked annoyed.

"The lab found traces of surgical-grade cornstarch on the trash bags consistent with the use of latex gloves."

Bugbee probed a seam in the Sheetrock wall with a lazy forefinger. "Probably the lab's."

"I think they're more careful than that," she said, thinking: *Come on, Roy, did you even think this one through? Are you working this case?* She felt a pulse of annoyance, then willed herself back to serenity. "I kind of doubt many crackheads have surgical gloves lying around."

Bugbee exhaled showily. "Is Noyce in this room?"

"Excuse me?"

"I said, I don't see Sergeant Noyce standing here, so if you're trying to show off, no one's watching, okay?"

Audrey swallowed, heard her inner voice begin, *Now the God of patience and consolation grant you . . .* and then she interrupted that inward sensible voice and spoke in a voice even softer than usual: "Roy, I'm not here to impress you. I'm here to do my job."

Bugbee brought his chair forward, sat up straight, gave her a sleepy-eyed look.

She could hear her heart thudding. "Now, I know you don't like me, for whatever reason, but I'm not going to apologize to you for being who I am and what I am. I'm afraid you're just going to have to deal with it. I don't judge you, and you shouldn't judge me. You don't sign my paycheck on Fridays. If you want off of this case, talk to Noyce. Otherwise, let's both try to be professionals, okay?"

Bugbee looked as if he was debating shoving the table at her or getting up and slamming the door. A couple of seconds of silence passed. Then he said, "You don't judge me, huh? Christers like you, that's all you do. You're always ticking off everyone's little in-fractions like some hall monitor at school. It's all about feeling superior, isn't it, Audrey? Like you got the Big Guy on your side. All that praying you do, it's about sucking up to the Big Boss in the Sky. Ass-kissing your way to heaven, right?"

"That's enough, Roy," she said.

A pounding on the door, and it swung open. Ser-geant Noyce stood there, squaring his shoulders, looking from one to the other. "May I ask you two something?" he said. "Did either one of you check the missing persons database?"

"I called Family Services this morning," Audrey said, "but they had nothing."

"You've got to keep checking, you know," Noyce said. "These things sometimes take a day or more to get posted."

"You got a possibility?" Bugbee asked.

"It's a lead, a pretty decent one," Noyce replied. "I'd say it's worth a look."

21

NICK CALLED EDDIE, didn't IM him, still feeling para-
noid about what kind of records were stored on the cor-
porate server.

They met at the southwest building entrance, outside
of the Security offices, Eddie's idea. Eddie didn't want
to talk inside the building. What did that mean, Nick
wondered, if his own security chief didn't feel safe
talking in there?

They walked along the paved path that encircled one
of the parking lots. The air had a faint manure smell,
from all the surrounding farms, mixed with the charred
scent of the burnt buffalo grass.

"What's up?" Eddie said, lighting up a Marlboro.
"Dude, you look worried."

"Who, me?" Nick said, grimacing. "What's to worry
about?"

"Come on. Everything's under control."

Nick looked around, made sure no one was walking
remotely near. "What'd you do with . . . him?"

"You don't want to know."

Nick was silent, listened to the scuff of Eddie's shoes
on the pavement. "No, I do. I want to know."

"Nick, believe me, it's better this way."

"Did you get rid of the gun, or do you still have it, or what?"

Eddie shook his head. "The less you know, the better."

"All right, listen. I've been thinking a lot about it, and I think—I've got to go to the cops. There's just no other way. What happened was legally defensible. It'll be a goddamned mess, but with a smart enough attorney, I think I can tough it out."

Eddie gave a low, dry chuckle. "Oh, no, you don't," he said. "You can't put that toothpaste back in the tube."

"Meaning what?"

"Friday night you wanted it to go away. I made it go away." He seemed to be straining to keep his tone civil. "At this point, we've got a serious cover-up, involving both of us."

"A cover-up devised in a panic—"

"Look, Nick," Eddie said. "I don't swim in your toilet, you don't pee in my pool, understand?"

"Huh?"

"I don't tell you how to run Stratton. You don't tell me about crime and cops and all that shit. This is my area of expertise."

"I'm not telling you what to do," Nick said. "I'm telling you what *I'm* going to do."

"Any decision you make involves me too," Eddie said. "And I vote no. Which means you don't do a damned thing. What's done can't be undone. It's just too fucking late."

22

THEY PULLED UP in front of a modest house on West Sixteenth in Steepletown, Audrey feeling that jellyfish wriggling in her belly, the thing she always felt when she first met a survivor of a homicide. The spill of raw grief, disbelief, fathomless pain—she could hardly stand it. You had to distance yourself from all that, or you'd go crazy, Noyce had warned her early on. We all do. What looks to the outside world like cynicism, hardness, that's what it is. Protective insulation. You'll learn it.

She never did.

The investigative work, even the routine stuff that phone-it-in types like Roy Bugbee had no patience for, she enjoyed. Not this. Not feeling the hot spray of another human being's agony up close and being unable, fundamentally, to do anything about it. I'll find your dad's murderer, I'll track down the kids who killed your daughter, I'll uncover the guy who popped your father in the 7-Eleven—that was the most she could promise, and it helped, but it didn't heal.

So a missing persons report had been called in to the police by a woman whose father had never come home Friday night. The physical description—age, height, weight, clothing—matched the murder victim found in the Dumpster on Hastings. Audrey knew this was it. The Family Services Division had called the daughter, which was the protocol, to say in their most diplomatic, tender way—they were good at this—that a body had been found, and there was a chance, just a chance, that it was her father, would she be so kind as to come down to the police morgue at Boswell Medical Center and help them identify a body, rule it out?

The aluminum screen door slammed, the woman coming toward them, even before Audrey was out of the Crown Vic. She was a small woman, even tiny, and from twenty feet she looked like a little girl. She wore a white T-shirt, faded and paint-splotched jeans, a ragged jean jacket. Her brown hair was cut in a spiky sort of hairdo that Audrey associated with punk rockers and artists. Her hands flopped from side to side as she walked, making her look a little like some neglected rag doll.

"You must be from the police," she said. Her brown eyes were large and moist. Up close she was actually quite beautiful and even more fragile. She looked to be in her mid- to late twenties. She had that glazed look of disbelief that Audrey had seen dozens of times in the faces of victims' families. Her voice was deeper than Audrey had expected, its timbre oddly soothing.

"I'm Audrey Rhimes." She extended a hand, beamed a look of compassion. "That's my partner, Roy Bugbee."

Roy, standing beside the open driver's side door, did not come around to shake the daughter's hand, probably figuring that it would be overkill. He gave a quick wave, a tight smile. Move your butt over here, Audrey thought. The man had no manners, no compassion. He didn't even have the ability to fake it.

"Cassie Stadler." Her palm was warm and damp,

and her eye makeup was smudged. She got into the backseat of the cruiser. Bugbee drove.

The object here was to low-key it, to reduce the woman's anxiety if at all possible. She's being driven over to the city morgue to identify a body that might be her father's, for God's sake; probably nothing could diminish her anxiety. Cassie Stadler probably knew just as surely as Audrey knew. But Audrey kept speaking, turning around to face the passenger, who sat in the middle of the back seat, staring glassily ahead.

"Tell me about your father," she said. "Does he tend to go out at night?" She hoped the present tense would just slip in there unobserved, silently reassuring.

"No, not really," Cassie Stadler said, and fell silent.

"Does he get disoriented from time to time?"

She blinked. "What? I'm sorry. Disoriented? Yes, I guess he does, sometimes. His . . . his condition."

Audrey waited for more. But Bugbee, heedless, broke in, his voice booming. "Did your father go down to the Hastings Street area often, to your knowledge?"

A series of expressions flashed in this lovely woman's dark eyes, a slide show: puzzlement, hurt, annoyance, sorrow. Audrey, embarrassed, averted her gaze and turned back around in her seat, facing forward.

"It's him, isn't it?" was all the daughter finally said. "My daddy."

They pulled into the hospital parking garage in silence. Audrey had never done one of these before. Identifying a body in the morgue—it was not at all common, thank God, no matter what you saw on TV. There were no sliding drawers at the morgue either, none of those hokey gothic touches. But death was gruesome, unavoidably so.

The body lay on a steel gurney covered with a green surgical sheet, the room sterile and air-conditioned to a chill and smelling of formalin. Jordan Metzler, polite if distant, pulled back the green cloth as matter-of-factly as if he were turning down a bed, exposing the head and neck.

Beneath that spiky mane, Cassie Stadler's perfect little doll face crumpled, and no one had to say anything.

23

AUDREY FOUND AN empty room in the hospital base-
ment where the three of them could talk. It was an
employees' lounge: a collection of chairs upholstered
in different institutional fabrics, a short couch, a cof-
fee machine that looked as if no one ever used it, a TV.
She and Bugbee moved chairs into a cluster. A couple
of open soda cans were clustered on an end table. She
found an almost-empty box of Kleenex. Cassie Stadler's
narrow shoulders bobbed; she sobbed silently, with all
her body. Bugbee, who'd obviously learned how to
distance, sat impatiently with a clipboard on his lap.
Audrey couldn't take it anymore, put her arms around
the woman, murmuring, "Oh, it's so hard, I know it."

Cassie took in great gulps of air, her head bent.
Eventually she looked up, saw the Kleenex box and
pulled out a few tissues, blew her nose.

"I'm sorry," she said. "I didn't think . . ."

"Don't apologize, sweetheart," Audrey said. "What
a terrible time for you."

Cassie took out a pack of cigarettes and shook one
out. "Okay if I smoke?"

Audrey nodded, gave Bugbee a sidelong glance.

Smoking wasn't allowed in here, but she wasn't going to make a point of it, not with this poor woman at this time, and fortunately neither was Bugbee, who nodded as well.

Cassie took out a cheap plastic lighter and lit up, then exhaled a cloud of smoke. "He was shot in—in the mouth?"

A funeral home would have done some reconstruction, skillfully applied makeup. The face would have looked artificial in that way that all dead bodies look at funeral homes, but at least she'd have been spared the brutal sight.

"That's right," Bugbee said. He didn't elaborate, didn't say twice, didn't say Stadler had also been shot in the chest. He was following standard procedure, which was to give out as little information as possible, in case a withheld detail could help them, down the line, confirm the killer.

"God!" she erupted. "Why? Who'd *do* that to my daddy?" She took another puff, took an empty Coke can off the end table and tapped out the ash into its small opening.

"That's what we want to find out," Audrey said. *Daddy*: it stabbed her, hearing that from a grown woman. She thought of her own daddy, remembered his smell of tobacco and sweat and Vitalis. "We need your help. I know this is a painful time, and you probably don't want to talk at all, but anything you can think of will help."

"Miss Stadler," asked Bugbee, "was your father a drug user?"

"Drugs?" She looked puzzled. "What kind of drugs?"

"Such as crack?"

"Crack? My *dad*? Never."

"You'd be surprised at who uses drugs like crack cocaine," Audrey put in hastily. "People you'd never ever think of as users, people from all walks of life. Prominent citizens even."

"My dad didn't even know about that world. He was a simple guy."

"But it's possible he kept things from you," Audrey persisted.

"Sure, possible, but I mean—crack? I'd have noticed," Cassie said, expelling smoke through her nostrils like the twin plumes of a fire-breathing dragon. "I've been living with him for almost a year, I'd have seen something."

"Maybe not," Bugbee said.

"Look, I don't do drugs myself, but I sure know people who do. I mean, I'm an artist, I live in Chicago, it's not unheard of, you know? Dad had none of the signs. He—it's absurd, really."

"You're originally from here?" Audrey asked.

"I was born here, but my parents divorced when I was a kid, and I went to live with my mom in Chicago. I come . . . came back here to visit Dad pretty often."

"What made you come back to stay?"

"He called me and told me he'd just quit his job at Stratton, and I was worried about him. He's not well, and my mom passed away four or five years ago, and I knew he needed someone to take care of him. I was afraid he couldn't cope."

"When Detective Bugbee asked you about drugs just now, you hesitated," Audrey said. "Was he on any kind of medication?"

She nodded, passed a hand over her eyes. "A number of meds including Risperdal, an antipsychotic."

"Psychotic?" Bugbee blurted out. "Was he psychotic?"

Audrey briefly closed her eyes. The guy never failed to do or say the wrong thing.

Cassie turned slowly to look at Bugbee as she

snubbed out the cigarette on the top of the Coke can, then dropped it through the opening. "He suffered from schizophrenia," she said absently. "He suffered from it for most of my life." She turned to Audrey. "But it was more or less under control."

"Did he ever disappear for stretches of time?" asked Audrey.

"No, not really. He'd go out for walks once in a while. I was glad when he got out of the house. This last year has been hard for him."

"What did he do at Stratton?" Bugbee asked.

"He was a model builder."

"What's that mean?"

"He worked in their model shop making prototypes of products they were working on, the latest chairs or desks or whatever."

"He quit, didn't get laid off?" Bugbee said.

"They were about to lay him off, but he just sort of blew up and quit before they could do it."

"When did you last see him?" Audrey asked.

"At supper Friday night. I—I'd just made supper for us, and he usually watches TV after supper. I went to the room I've been using as a studio and painted."

"You're an artist?"

"Sort of. Not as serious as I used to be, but I still paint. I never got a gallery or anything. I support myself by teaching Kripalu yoga."

"Here?"

"In Chicago I did. I haven't worked since I got to Fenwick."

"Did you see him before you went to sleep?" Audrey asked.

"No," she said sadly. "I fell asleep on the couch in there—I do that fairly often, when a painting's not working and I want to think about it, sometimes I just fall asleep and wake up in the morning. That's what happened Saturday morning—I got up and had break-fast, and when he wasn't down by ten I started to worry about him, so I went to his room, but he was gone. I—will you excuse me? I'm thirsty—I need—"

"What can we get you, honey?" said Audrey.

"Anything, just—I'm so thirsty."

"Water? Pop?"

"Something with sugar in it." She smiled apologeti-cally. "I need a hit of sugar. Sprite, Seven-Up, anything. Just no caffeine. It makes me crazy."

"Roy," Audrey said, "there's a vending machine down the hall—could you . . . ?"

Bugbee's eyebrows went up, a nasty smile curling the corners of his mouth. He looked like he was about to say something unpleasant. But she wanted a little time alone with this woman. She had a feeling Cassie would open up more easily with her alone.

"Sure," Roy said after a long pause. "Happy to."

When the door closed, Audrey cleared her throat to speak, but Cassie spoke first.

"He has it in for you, doesn't he?"

Good God, was it that obvious? "Detective Bug-bee?" Audrey said, feigning surprise.

Cassie nodded. "It's like he can barely contain his contempt for you."

"Detective Bugbee and I have a very good working relationship."

"I'm surprised you put up with him."

Audrey smiled. "I'd prefer to talk about your father."

"Of course. I'm sorry. I just—noticed." She was weeping again, wiping a hand across her eyes. "Detec-tive, I—I have no idea in the world who might have killed my daddy. Or why. But I have a feeling that if anyone can find out, you can."

Audrey felt tears come into her eyes. "I'll do my best," she said. "That's all I can promise."

24

TERRA WAS THE finest restaurant in Fenwick, the place you went to celebrate special occasions like birthdays, promotions, a visit of a special old friend. It had the slightly forbidding air of an expensive place where it was assumed you didn't go often. Men were expected to wear ties. There was a maître d' and a sommelier who wore a big silver taste-vin on a ribbon around his neck like an Olympic medal. The waiters ground pepper for you in a mill the size of a Louisville Slugger. The tablecloths were heavily starched white linen. The menu was immense, leather-bound, and required two hands. The wine list itself, a separate leather-bound folio, was twenty pages long. Nick had taken Laura here for her birthday, a few weeks before the accident; it was her favorite place. She loved their signature dessert, a molten chocolate cake that oozed chocolate like lava when you spooned into it. Nick found Terra stuffy and nervous-making, but the food was always great. From time to time he'd take important clients here.

Dinner tonight was with his most important client: his boss, the managing partner from Fairfield Equity Partners in Boston. Nick hadn't particularly liked Todd Muldaur when he first met him, in the company of Fair-

field's founder, Willard Osgood. But Osgood always
placed one of his deputies in charge of the companies
his firm owned, and Todd was the man he picked.

Not long after Dorothy Devries had tapped Nick
as her husband's successor as CEO, she'd summoned
Nick back to her old dark mansion to announce that the
family was facing a huge tax bill and had to sell. It was
up to Nick to find the ideal buyer. There was no short-
age of interested bidders. The Stratton Corporation had
no debt, steady profits, a major market share, and a fa-
mous name. But plenty of the buyout firms wanted to
buy Stratton, gussy it up, then turn it around for a quick
sale to someone else. Spin it off, maybe take it public—
who the hell knew what those rape-and-pillage folks
might do? Then the call came from the famous Wil-
lard Osgood, who had a reputation for buying compa-
nies and holding on to them forever, letting them run
themselves. Willard Osgood: "the man with the Midas
Touch," as *Fortune* magazine called him. The perfect
solution. Osgood even flew in to Fenwick—well, he
flew in to Grand Rapids in his private jet and then was
driven out to Fenwick in a plain old Chrysler sedan—
and came a-courtin' on the widow Devries and Nick.
He charmed the pants off Dorothy Devries (she was
partial to pantsuits, actually), and won over Nick as
well. Willard Osgood was as plainspoken and unpre-
tentious in person as he was in all his interviews. He
was a lifelong Republican, an archconservative, just
like Dorothy. He told her his favorite holding period
was forever. Rule number one, he said, is never lose
money; rule number two is never forget rule number
one. He really won her over when he said it's better to
buy a great company at a fair price than a fair company
at a great price.

The deputy he brought with him, Todd Muldaur,
a straw-haired Yale football jock who'd done time at

the big management-consulting firm McKinsey, didn't say too much, but there was something about him Nick didn't like. He didn't like Todd's swagger. But hey, it was Osgood who ran the show, Nick figured. Not Muldaur.

Of course, now it was Todd who presided over the quarterly board meetings, Todd who read the monthly financial reports and asked all the questions, Todd who had to sign off on the major decisions. After that first meeting with Willard Osgood, Nick never saw the old guy again.

NICK ARRIVED A few minutes early. Scott McNally was already at the table, nursing a Diet Coke. He'd changed out of his frayed blue button-down shirt into a crisp blue-and-white broad-striped one, a red tie, a good dark suit. Nick was wearing his best suit too, which Laura had picked out for him at Brooks Brothers in Grand Rapids.

"Muldaur give you any sense of what he's here for?" Nick asked as he sat down. This was just about the last place he wanted to be, eating at a fancy restaurant when he had no appetite, being social with some strutting asshole when he just wanted to be home in bed.

"No idea. He didn't say."

"He told me he wanted to 'touch base' in advance of the board meeting."

"Gotta be the updated financials I just sent him. They can't be happy about our numbers either."

"Still, no need for a personal visit."

Scott lowered his head, muttered, "He just walked in." Nick looked up, saw the big blond man coming their way. Both he and Scott stood.

Scott stepped around the table, went up to Muldaur, gave him a hearty two-handed shake. "Hey, bud!"

"Scotty! My man!"

Muldaur extended his beefy hand to Nick and gave him one of those unnecessarily crushing handshakes, grabbing his fingers just below the knuckles in such a way that Nick couldn't shake back. Nick hated that. "Nice to see you," Todd said.

Todd Muldaur had a big square jaw, a button nose, and turquoise eyes that were bluer than they'd been last time Nick had seen him, in a glass-walled conference room at Fairfield's offices on Federal Street in Boston. Had to be colored contacts. He had the lean, drawn face of a guy who ate a lot of protein, worked out regularly. He wore a dove-gray suit that looked expensive. "So, this must be the one good restaurant in town, huh?"

"Nothing but the best for our friends from Boston," Nick said affably as they sat down.

Todd took the big white linen napkin, unfolded it, and put it in his lap. "Gotta be good," he said sardonically. "The American Automobile Association gives this place its 'prestigious Four Diamond Award,' it says out front."

Nick smiled and imagined punching Todd's face out. He noticed a couple being seated a few tables over and recognized them. The man had been a senior manager at Stratton until last year, when his division had been shut down in the layoffs. The guy was in his fifties, with two kids in college, and despite the best efforts of the outplacement service Stratton had hired, hadn't been able to find another job.

That familiar sinking feeling came over him. Nick excused himself, and went over to say hello.

It was the man's wife who saw him first. Her eyes widened briefly. She turned away, said something quickly to her husband, then stood up, but not to greet him.

"Bill," Nick said.

Now the man rose without saying anything, and he

and his wife turned and walked out of the dining room. For a few seconds, Nick stood there, his face burning. He wondered why he subjected himself to this kind of snub. It happened often enough for him to know better. Maybe, on some level, he felt he deserved it.

By the time he returned to his table, Todd and Scott were deep in conversation about the good old days at McKinsey. Nick hoped that neither man had seen what had just happened.

It had been Todd who'd insisted that Stratton replace their old CFO, Henry "Hutch" Hutchens, with Scott McNally. Nick had gone along quite happily, but it annoyed him sometimes that Scott was so friendly with Muldaur.

"Whatever happened to that guy Nolan Bennis?" Scott was saying. "Remember him?" He smiled at Nick. "Another McKinseyite. You wouldn't believe this dweeb." He turned back to Todd. "Remember that Shedd Island retreat?" He explained to Nick: "McKinsey always used to rent out this really posh hotel on this superexclusive island off the coast of South Carolina, for a retreat with top clients. So this guy Nolan Bennis is out there on the tennis court with some Carbide guys, and I swear to God, he's wearing black socks and penny loafers. Couldn't play for shit. Really stank up the place. We heard about that for months—what an embarrassment. I mean, the guy was a total loser. You couldn't take him out in public. He still at McKinsey?"

"You obviously didn't see the latest *Forbes* Four Hundred," Todd said.

"What are you talking about?" Scott said, a quizzical look on his face.

"Nolan Bennis is the CEO of ValueMetrics. Worth four billion dollars now. He bought the Shedd Island hotel a couple of years ago, along with about five hundred acres on the island."

"I always thought that guy would go places," Scott said.

"Gotta love this menu," Todd said. "Duck breast with raspberry coulis. I mean, how 1995 can you get? I'm getting nostalgic here."

The waitress approached their table. "May I tell you about our specials tonight?" she said. The woman looked familiar to Nick, though he couldn't quite place her. She glanced at Nick, looked away quickly. She knew him too. Not another one.

"We have a Chilean sea bass with roasted cauliflower, pancetta, and tangerine juice for twenty-nine dollars. There's a pistachio-crusted rack of lamb with celery root puree and wild mushrooms. And the catch of the day is a seared tuna—"

"Let me guess," Todd broke in. "It's 'sushi quality,' and it's served rare in the center."

"That's *right*!" she said.

"Where have I heard that before?"

"You look familiar," Nick said, feeling bad for the woman.

Her eyes flitted to him and then away. "Yes, Mr. Conover. I used to work for Stratton, in Travel."

"I'm sorry to hear that. You doing okay?"

She hesitated. "Waitressing pays less than half what I was making at Stratton, sir," she answered tightly.

"It's been tough all around," Nick said.

"I'll give you gentlemen a few more minutes to decide," she said, and moved quickly away.

"Is she going to spit in our salads?" Todd said.

"YOU GUYS DON'T need me to tell you we got a real problem here," Todd said.

"No question," Scott agreed quickly.

Nick nodded, waited.

"A bad quarter or two, blame it on a lousy economy,"

Todd said. "But it keeps happening, it begins to look like a death spiral. And we can't afford that."

"I understand your concern," Nick said, "and believe me, I share it. I want to assure you that we've got things under control. We've got a major customer coming in tomorrow—I mean *major*—and it looks good for signing them up. That contract alone will turn things around."

"Hey, we can always hope lightning strikes," Todd said. "Maybe you'll get lucky. But let me tell you something. Corporations may be based on continuity, but capital markets are all about *creative destruction*. If you're unwilling to change, you'll be drawn into that big slide toward mediocrity. As CEO, you've got to overcome the organizational inertia. Unclog those corporate arteries. Free the flow of fresh ideas. Even the best boats need rocking, man. That's the magic of capitalism. That's what Joseph Schumpeter said years ago."

"Didn't he used to play for the Bruins?" Nick said, deadpan.

"There's the quick, and there's the dead, Nick," Todd said.

"Well, I don't know about 'creative destruction,'" Nick said, "but I know we're all basically in sync. That's why we sold the company to Fairfield. You guys are value investors with the long view—that's the only reason I was able to convince Dorothy Devries to sell to you. I always remember what Willard said to Dorothy and me, in the parlor of her house on Michigan Avenue—'We want to be your partner, your sounding board. We don't want to run the business—we want you to run the business. We may have to go through some pain together, but we're all in this for the long haul.'"

Todd smiled slyly. He got what Nick was doing, invoking the words of the ultimate boss like Holy Scripture. "That sounds just like Willard. But you gotta understand something—the old man's been spending an awful lot of time fly-fishing in the Florida Keys these days. Guy loves fly-fishing—last year or so, he seems to think a lot more about tarpon and bonefish than P and Ls."

"He's retiring?"

"Not yet, but soon. All but. Which means he leaves the heavy lifting to us, the poor suckers who have to go to work every day and do the dirty work while he's standing in the bow of his Hell's Bay, casting his line. The world has changed, Nick. Used to be all the big institutional investors would write us a twenty-million-dollar check, maybe a hundred-million-dollar check, and let us do our job. At the end of six years, ten years, they cash out, everyone's happy. Not anymore. Now they're all looking over our shoulders, calling all the time. They don't want to see one of our major investments turn sour. They want to see results yesterday."

"They ought to go to your Web site," Nick said. Fairfield Equity Partners actually had an animated Flash movie on its Web site, the Aesop's fable of the tortoise and the hare, made to look like a storybook. It was beyond cornball. "Tell 'em to check out the tortoise-and-the-hare story. Remind 'em about the long view."

"These days, the tortoise gets made into turtle soup, buddy," Todd said.

Scott laughed a bit too loud.

"Don't worry," Nick said, "that's not on the menu."

Todd didn't smile. "The kind of companies we like are healthy companies that are growing. We don't believe in catching a falling knife."

"We're not a falling knife, Todd," Nick said calmly. "We're going through some adjustments, but we're on the right path."

"Nick, the quarterly board meeting is in a couple of

days, and I want to make sure the board sees a compre-
hensive plan to turn things around. I'm talking plant
consolidation, selling off real estate, whatever. Cre-
ative destruction. I don't want the board losing confi-
dence in you."

"Are you implying what I think you're implying?"

Todd cracked a victorious smile. "Hell no, Nick!
Don't take me the wrong way! When we bought Strat-
ton, we weren't just buying some outdated factories in
East Bumfuck, Michigan, with equipment out of 1954.
We were buying a *team*. That means you. We want you
to hang in there. We just need you to start thinking dif-
ferent. A balls-out, warp-speed effort to come up with
a way to change the trend line."

Scott nodded sagely, chewing his lower lip, twirling
a few strands of his hair behind his right ear. "I get
what you're saying, and I think I've got some interest-
ing ideas."

"What I like to hear. I mean, hell, there's no reason
for you to have all your components made in the U.S.
when you can get 'em at half the price from China, you
know?"

"Actually," Nick said, "we've considered and re-
jected that, Todd, because—"

Scott broke in, "I think it's worth taking up again."

Nick gave him a black look.

"I knew I could count on you guys. Well, who's up
for dessert? Let me guess—the dessert trend that swept
Manhattan in 1998 has finally made it to Fenwick:
molten chocolate cake?"

AFTER THEY SAID goodbye to Todd and watched him
drive away in his rented Lincoln Town Car, Nick
turned to Scott. "Whose side are you on, anyway?"

"What are you talking about? You've got to keep the
boss happy."

"I'm your boss, Scott. Not Todd Muldaur. Remember that."

Scott hesitated, seemingly debating whether to argue. "Anyway, who says there's sides? We're all in this together, Nick."

"There's always sides," Nick said quietly. "Inside or outside. Are you with me?"

"Of course, Nick. Jesus. Of course I'm on your side, what do you think?"

25

LEON WAS WATCHING TV and drinking a beer. That was pretty much all he did these days, when he wasn't sleeping. Audrey looked at her husband, slouched in the middle of the couch, wearing pajama bottoms and a white T-shirt that was too tight over his ever-expanding beer gut. The thirty or forty pounds he'd put on in the past year or so made him look ten years older. Once she would have said he was the hardest-working man she'd ever met, never missed a day of work on the line, never complaining. Now, with his work life taken away from him, he was lost. Without work, he retreated into a life of sloth; there was no in-between for him.

She went over to the couch and kissed him. He hadn't shaved, hadn't bathed either. He didn't turn his head to kiss her; he received her kiss, his eyes not even moving from the screen. After a while, Audrey standing there, hands on her hips, smiling, he said, "Hey, Shorty," in his whiskey-and-cigarettes voice. "Home late."

Shorty: his term of endearment almost since they'd started going out. He was well over six feet, she was barely five, and they did look funny walking together.

"I called and left you a message," she said. "You must have been in conference." He knew she meant asleep. That was how she dealt with Leon's newfound lifestyle. The idea of his sitting around watching TV and sleeping during the day, when they had a mortgage to pay—it was infuriating to her. She knew she wasn't being entirely reasonable about it. The poor guy had been laid off from his job, and there wasn't a company for hundreds of miles around that was looking to hire an electrostatic powder-coating technician. Still, half the town had been laid off, and plenty of people had managed to get jobs working for Home Depot or bagging groceries at the Foodtown. The pay was lousy, but it was better than nothing, and certainly better than sleeping on the couch all day.

He didn't answer. Leon had deep-set eyes, a large head, a powerful build, and once, not that long ago, he would have been considered a fine-looking man. Now he looked beaten down, defeated.

"You . . . get my message about dinner?" Meaning, of course, that she wanted him to make dinner. Nothing complicated. There was frozen hamburger he could defrost in the microwave. A package of romaine hearts he could wash for salad. Whatever. But she smelled nothing, no food cooking, and she knew the answer before he spoke.

"I ate already."

"Oh. Okay." She'd left him a message around four, as soon as she knew she'd be staying late, way before he ever ate supper. She suppressed her annoyance, went into the kitchen. The small counter was stacked so high—dirty plates, glasses, coffee mugs, beer bottles—that you couldn't even see the swirly rose Formica surface. How, she marveled, could one person create such a mess in a day? Why did he refuse to clean up after himself? Did he expect her to be breadwinner and wife and housekeeper all at the same time? In the plastic trash bucket was a discarded Hungry-Man box

and plastic compartmented tray, crusted with tomato
sauce goo. She reached down, felt it. It was still warm.
He'd just eaten. Not hours ago. He'd been hungry and
just made himself dinner, didn't make anything for her
even though she'd asked him to. Well, exactly *because*
she'd asked him to, probably.

Returning to the living room, she stood there, waiting
to get his attention, but he kept watching the baseball
game. She cleared her throat. Nothing.

She said, "Leon, honey, can I talk to you for a sec-
ond?"

"Sure."

"Could you look at me?"

He muted the TV, finally, and turned.

"Baby, I thought you were going to make us both
supper."

"I didn't know when you were getting back."

"But I said . . ." She bit her lip. She was not going to
yell at him. She was not going to be the one to start the
quarreling, not this time. She softened her voice a bit.
"I asked you to make dinner for us, right?"

"I figured you'd eat whenever you got home, Shorty.
Don't want to make something's gonna get cold."

She nodded. Paused. By now she knew the script by
heart. But our deal, our agreement, was that you make
dinner, clean up, you know I can't do everything. And
he says, How come you can't do what you did before?
You had time to do that stuff before. And she says, I
need help, Leon, that's the point. I get home exhausted.
And he says, How do you think I feel, sitting here like
a good-for-nothing piece of shit? At least you got a job.

That worked for a long time, that guilt thing. But
then he began to take it to another level, talking about
how cooking and cleaning, that was woman's work, and
how come all of a sudden he's expected to do woman's

work, was this all because he wasn't bringing home a paycheck? And by now she wants to scream, woman's work? Woman's work? What makes this woman's work? And can't you at least pick up after yourself? And so it would go, tedious and mind-numbing and pointless.

"Okay," she said.

SHE WAS WORKING six cases, three of them active, one a homicide. You couldn't really focus on more than one at a time; tonight was Andrew Stadler. She placed the accordion file on the couch next to her, and while Leon watched the Tigers and drank himself into a stupor, she read over the files. She liked to read case files just before she went to sleep. She believed that her unconscious kept working on things, poking and prodding, turning things over with its gimlet eye, saw things more clearly than she did awake.

How Andrew Stadler's body ended up in a Dumpster on the five hundred block of Hastings baffled her. So did the fake crack. His diagnosed schizophrenia— did that fit in anywhere? Obviously she'd have to talk to his boss at Stratton, and the Employee Relations director too. See if there'd been any indication of drug use.

She was tempted to ask Leon about Stratton, about the model shop, if he knew anything about it. Maybe he'd even run across Stadler in the factory some time, or knew someone who knew him. She was, in fact, just about to say something when she turned to look at him, saw his glazed eyes, his defeated face, and decided not to. Any little thing she mentioned about the job these days was like probing a bad tooth for him. It reminded him of how she had a job she was involved in, and how he didn't.

Not worth the pain, she decided.

When the game was over, he went to bed, and she followed. As she brushed her teeth and washed her face, she debated whether to put on her usual long T-shirt or a teddy. They hadn't had sex in more than six months, and not because she didn't want it. He'd lost all interest. But she needed it, needed to regain that physical closeness. Otherwise . . .

By the time she got into bed, Leon was snoring.

She slipped in beside him, clicked off her bedside lamp, and was soon asleep.

She dreamed of Tiffany Akins, dying in her arms. The little girl in the SpongeBob pajamas. The girl who could have been her own. Who could have been herself. She dreamed of her father, of that moment when Cassie Stadler called her father Daddy.

And then her gimlet-eyed subconscious kicked something upstairs, and her eyes came open. She sat up slowly.

It was all too clean. An *absence* of evidence.

Not just the daubs of pharmaceutical-grade starch on the plastic bags wrapped around the body. This indicated that the body had been moved by someone wearing surgical gloves, someone who was careful about not leaving fingerprints. That in itself revealed a degree of caution not often found in drug murder cases. But neither was there any particulate matter on the body, no fibers, none of the normal trace evidence you always found on the body of a victim. Even the treads on the victim's shoes, where you always found dirt, had been brushed clean.

She remembered, too, how clean the body was at the autopsy. She remembered the pathologist saying, "He looks more like a house case than a police case."

That was it; that was the anomaly. The body had been fastidiously cleaned, gone over by an expert. By someone who *knew* what the police looked for.

Andrew Stadler's body hadn't been disposed of by some crack dealer in a panic. It had been carefully, methodically placed in a Dumpster by someone who knew what he was doing.

It took her a long time to fall back asleep.

26

"THIS STUFF TASTES like twigs," Julia said.

Nick couldn't stop himself from laughing out loud. The front of the box had a photograph of two smiling people, a little Asian girl and a blond Nordic-looking boy. They weren't smiling about the cereal, that was for sure.

"It's good for you," he said.

"How come I always have to have healthy cereal? Everyone else in my class gets to have whatever they want for breakfast."

"I doubt that."

"Paige gets to have Froot Loops or Cap'n Crunch or Apple Jacks every morning."

"Paige . . ." Normally the parental responses came quickly to him, autopilot, but this morning he wasn't thinking very clearly. He worried about taking the sleeping pill so many days in a row. It was probably addictive. He wondered whether Julia or Lucas or Marta had heard anything two nights before. "Paige doesn't do well in school because she doesn't start off her day with a healthy breakfast." Sometimes he couldn't believe the crap he said aloud, the shameless propaganda. When he was a kid, he ate whatever the hell he wanted for breakfast, sugary shit like Quisp and Quake and Cocoa Puffs, and he did just fine in school. He didn't know, actually, if all kids were forced to eat healthy breakfasts by their parents these days, or if it was just Laura who'd insisted on it. Whatever, he observed the Law of Healthy Breakfast as if it were the Constitution.

"Paige is in my math group," Julia countered.

"Good for her. I don't care if she eats chocolate cake for breakfast." The TV had been set up on a table in this temporary corner of the kitchen. The *Today* show was on, but right now there was a local commercial for Pajot Ford, always an annoying ad. John Pajot, the owner, was also the pitchman—hell, he paid for the ads, he could star in them if he wanted to—and he always did them wearing a hunting outfit. He made puns about saving "bucks" and "racking up" savings.

"Where's your brother?" he asked.

She shrugged, staring balefully at the cereal. It actually did look like stuff gathered from the ground in a forest. "Asleep, probably."

"All right, just have some yogurt, then."

"But I don't like the kind we have. It doesn't taste good."

"It's what we have. That's your choice. Yogurt or . . . twigs."

"But I like strawberry."

"I'll ask Marta to get more strawberry. In the meantime we have vanilla. It's good." Marta was doing laundry. He'd have to remember to ask her to add strawberry yogurt to her shopping list. Also some healthy cereal that didn't taste like twigs.

"No, it's not. It's the organic kind. Their vanilla tastes funny."

"It's that or string cheese, take your choice."

Julia sighed with bottomless frustration. "String cheese," she said sullenly.

The local news segment came on, and the anchorman, a lean-faced, slick-looking guy with shoe-polish black hair, said something about "found brutally murdered."

"Where's the remote?" asked Nick. When Julia was in hearing range, he normally muted any TV stories about murders or gruesome crimes or child molestation. She reached for it between the carton of organic one-percent milk and the sugar bowl, handed it to her father. He grabbed it, searched for the tiny mute button—why didn't they make the damned mute button bigger, and a different color?—but as he was about to press it, he saw the graphic on the screen. A photograph of a horribly familiar face, the words "Andrew Stadler." He froze, stared, his heart pounding.

He heard: "Dumpster behind Lucky's Restaurant on Hastings Street."

He heard: "Thirty-six years at the Stratton Company until he was laid off last March."

"What's the matter, Daddy?" Julia asked.

He heard something about funeral arrangements. "Hmm? Oh, nothing. One of our Stratton employees died, baby. Come on, get yourself some string cheese."

"Was he old?" she asked, getting up.

"Yeah," Nick said. "He was old."

MARGE WAS ALREADY at her desk when he arrived, sipping coffee from a Stratton mug and reading a novel by Jane Austen. She flipped the paperback closed apologetically. "Oh, good morning," she said. "Sorry, I was hoping to finish this before my book group meets tonight."

"Don't let me stop you."

A copy of the *Fenwick Free Press* had been placed on his desk next to his keyboard. A front-page headline read: "Longtime Stratton Employee a Probable Homi-

cide." Marjorie must have placed it there, folded so that
the Stadler article faced up.

He hadn't bothered to look at the paper this morn-
ing before leaving the house; it had been too hectic.
Luke hadn't gotten up, so Nick had gone to his room
to awaken him. From under his mound of blankets and
sheet, Luke had said he had study hour first period and
was going to sleep in. Instead of arguing, Nick simply
closed Luke's bedroom door.

Now he picked up the article and read it closely.
Once again his heart was drumming. Not much here in
the way of details. ". . . body discovered in a Dumpster
behind a restaurant on Hastings Street." Nothing about
it being wrapped in plastic; Nick wondered whether
Eddie had, for some reason, removed the trash bags.
"Apparently shot several times," though it didn't say
where the man had been shot. Surely the police hadn't
released to the paper everything they knew about the
case. As nerve-wracking as it was to read, Nick found
it oddly reassuring. The details formed a convincing
picture of an unemployed man who'd been murdered in
a rough part of town, probably having been involved in
some street crime. There was a photo of Stadler taken
at least twenty years ago: the same glasses, the same
tight mouth. You'd read the article, shake your head
sadly over how the loss of a job had caused an already
troubled man to spiral into drugs or crime or some-
thing, and you'd move on to the sports.

Nick's eyes filled with tears. This is the man I killed.
A man who left behind one child—"a daughter, Cassie,
twenty-nine, of Chicago"—and an ex-wife who'd died
four years earlier. A modest, quiet-living man, worked
in a Stratton factory for his entire adult life.

He was suddenly aware of Marge standing there,
looking worriedly at him. She'd said something.

"Excuse me?"

"I said, it's sad, isn't it?"

"Terribly sad," Nick said.

"The funeral's this afternoon. You have a telcon with Sales, but that can be rescheduled."

He nodded, realizing what she was saying. Nick usually attended the funerals of all Stratton employees, just as old man Devries had done. It was a tradition, a ceremonial obligation of the CEO in this company town.

He'd have to go to Andrew Stadler's funeral. He didn't really have a choice.

27

"YOU'RE NOT HELPING me any," Audrey said.

Bert Koopmans, the evidence tech, turned at the sink where he was washing his hands. There was something birdlike about the way he inclined his head, gawked at her. He was tall, almost spindly, with small close-set eyes that always looked startled.

"Not my job," he said, dry but not unfriendly. "What's the problem?"

She hesitated. "Well, you really didn't find anything on the body, when it comes right down to it."

"What body are we talking about?"

"Stadler."

"Who?"

"The guy in the Dumpster. Down on Hastings."

"The tortilla."

"Burrito, really."

He allowed a hint of a smile. "You got everything I got."

"Did the body strike you as too . . . clean?"

"Clean? You talking hygiene? I mean, the guy's fingernails were filthy."

"That's not what I mean, Bert." She thought a

minute. "The dirt under his fingernails—that got tagged, right?"

"No, I lost it," Bert said, flashing her a look. "You forget who you're talking to? Like this was one of Wayne's cases?" Not all the techs were as meticulous, as obsessive-compulsive as Koopmans. He walked over to a black file cabinet, pulled it open, selected a folder. He scanned a sheet of paper. "Pubic hairs, head hairs, fingernails left hand, fingernails right hand. Fibers from shoe left, fibers from shoe right. Unidentified substance under fingernails right hand, unidentified substance under fingernails left hand. Want me to keep going?"

"No, thanks. What's the unidentified substance?"

Another look. "If I knew what it was, think I'd call it unidentified?"

"Are we talking skin or blood or dirt?"

"You try my patience, Detective. Skin and blood, these are substances I've seen before, believe it or not."

"Dirt you've seen before too."

He shrugged one shoulder. "But dirt isn't dirt. It's . . . stuff. It's anything. I made a note that it had a kind of greenish hue to it."

"Green paint? If Stadler scraped his fingernails against the side of a house, say . . . ?"

"Paint I would have recognized." He handed her the chain-of-custody sheet. "Here. Why don't you take a walk down to Property and get the shit? We can both take a look."

THE GUY WHO ran the Property room was a clock-puncher named Arthur something, a flabby white man with a toothbrush mustache who wore coveralls. She pushed the buzzer, and he took his time coming around to the window. She handed him the pink copy of the Property Receipt, explaining that she only wanted item number fifteen. All the evidence—the pulled head hair, pulled pubic hair, the two vials of blood—was kept in a big refrigerator. Arthur returned a few minutes later and could not have looked more bored. As he went through the ritual of scanning the bar code label on the five-by-seven evidence envelope marked "Nail Clippings From Autopsy," then the bar code on the wall chart to capture her name and number, Audrey heard Roy Bugbee's voice.

"That looks like the Stadler case," Bugbee said.

She nodded. "You working Jamal Wilson?"

Bugbee ignored her question. As the property guy slid the envelope under the window, Bugbee snatched it before Audrey could get to it. "Nail clippings, eh?"

"Just some more trace evidence I'm running past IBO again."

"Why do I get the crazy feeling we're not partnering on this, Audrey?"

"There's no end of things I'd appreciate your help on," she said uneasily.

"Right," Bugbee said. "You going over to IBO right now?"

KOOPMANS, WHO SEEMED surprised to see Roy Bugbee, placed two sheets of copy paper on the counter in the long narrow lab room where they fumed for fingerprints. He slit the bottom of each little envelope with a disposable scalpel and tapped out the contents onto the paper.

"Like I said, green dirt," Koopmans said. He and Audrey both wore surgical masks so that their breath wouldn't blow away the dirt. Bugbee did not.

Audrey peered closely. "Would it help to put it under a binocular microscope?"

"Happy to. But I've already done it, and there's nothing more to see." He sifted the tiny pile with a wooden applicator. "Sand, some kind of fine green powder, some fragments of what looks like pellets, maybe. Take it over to the state lab, if you want, but they're just going to tell you what I've just said. And it'll take 'em six weeks to tell you."

"Christ," said Bugbee, "you don't need a microscope for this shit."

"Oh, is that right," said Koopmans, giving Audrey a quick look.

"You don't have a lawn, obviously," Bugbee said. "That's hydroseed."

"Hydroseed," said Koopmans.

"Which is what, exactly?" Audrey asked.

"It's grass seed and, I don't know, ground-up newspaper and shit they spray. To start a new lawn. Hate the shit, myself—full of weed seed. I call it 'hydroweed.'"

"But it's green," Audrey said.

"That's the dye powder," Koopmans said. "And the pellets—that's the mulch." He pulled at his chin with his thumb and forefinger.

"Well, you saw the Stadler home," Audrey said. "I didn't see any hydroseed, did you?"

"Naw," said Bugbee, cocky. "A shitty lawn. All crabgrass and broadleaf weeds. Guys notice stuff like that."

"If you're lawn-obsessed," Koopmans said. "Is it possible your guy had some part-time job doing landscaping work or something?"

"No," Audrey said. "He could barely hold on to his job at Stratton. No, I suspect he got that stuff under his fingernails from wherever he went. Maybe—probably—the night he was killed."

28

THE MOUNT PLEASANT Cemetery was not the biggest
burial ground in Fenwick Township, nor especially
well tended. It sat on a high bluff above a busy high-
way and seemed forlorn, even for a cemetery. Nick had
never been here before. Then again, he hated cemeter-
ies and avoided them whenever possible. When he had
to attend a funeral, he went to the church or funeral
home and missed this part. Laura's death had made
burials harder, not easier.

But he was late. He'd missed the service at the fu-
neral home, having been unable to reschedule a major
teleconference with the CEOs of Steelcase and Her-
man Miller to discuss a lobbying effort against an idi-
otic bill before Congress.

He parked his Suburban along a curb near where a
ceremony was going on. There was a small clutch of
people in dark clothing, maybe ten or twelve people
in all. There was a pastor, a black woman, an elderly
couple, five or six guys who might have worked with
Stadler, a pretty young woman who had to be the man's
daughter. She was petite, with big eyes and short, sort
of chopped-looking punk hair. The paper had said she
was twenty-nine and lived in Chicago.

Nick approached tentatively, heard the pastor, standing beside the casket, say: "Bless this grave that the body of our brother Andrew may sleep here in peace until You awaken him to glory, when he will see You face to face and know the splendor of the eternal God, who lives and reigns, now and forever." The roaring traffic obliterated some of his words.

A couple of the mourners turned to look at him. The Stratton guys recognized him, their eyes lingering a moment longer. Nick thought he saw surprise, maybe a flash or two of indignation, though he wasn't sure. The beautiful daughter looked dazed, like a deer caught in the headlights. Near her stood the black woman, who was quite attractive as well. She looked at Nick, her glance piercing, tears running down her cheeks. Nick wondered who she was. There weren't that many blacks in town.

He wasn't prepared for the sight of the burnished mahogany casket, sitting atop the lowering device, Nick remembered from Laura's burial, which was hidden behind drapes of green crushed velvet. It jolted him. Somehow it was even more brutal, that tall, rounded mahogany coffin, than seeing Andrew Stadler's dead body crumpled on his lawn. It was more final, more *real*. This was a man with a family—a daughter, at least—and friends. He might have been a dangerous, unmedicated schizophrenic—but he was somebody's daddy too. This lovely young woman with the spiky hair and porcelain skin. Tears sprang to Nick's eyes. He was embarrassed.

The black woman glanced at him again. Who was she?

The Stratton guys looked at him again, no doubt noticing his tears and inwardly rolling their eyes at the hypocrisy. Slasher Nick weeping at the grave of a guy he laid off, they had to be thinking.

When it was over, and the coffin was lowered smoothly and silently into the grave, the mourners began tossing clods of earth and flowers onto the coffin. Some of them embraced the daughter, clutching her hand, murmuring condolences. When the moment seemed right, he approached her.

"Ms. Stadler, I'm Nick Conover. I'm the—"

"I know who you are," she replied coolly. She had the tiniest stud on the right side of her nose, a glint of light.

"I didn't know your father personally, but I wanted to tell you how sorry I am. He was a valued employee."

"So valued that you fired him." She spoke in a quiet tone, but her bitterness was obvious.

"The layoffs have been difficult for all of us. So many deserving people lost their jobs."

She sighed as if the subject wasn't worth discussing any further. "Yeah, well, everything started to fall apart for my dad when he got forced out."

He'd steeled himself against anger, given how often he met former Stratton employees, but this he wasn't quite prepared for, not here in a cemetery, from a woman who was burying her father. "It's a terrible thing he had to go through." He noticed the black woman watching the exchange with interest, though she was far enough away that she might not have been able to hear what they were saying.

Stadler's daughter smiled ruefully. "Let's get one thing straight, Mr. Conover. As far as I'm concerned, you killed my dad."

29

LEON'S OLDEST SISTER, LaTonya, was a very large woman with an imperious way about her, adamant in all her opinions, though maybe you had to be to raise six kids. Audrey liked being around her—she was everything Audrey wasn't, bawdy where Audrey was respectful, profane where Audrey was polite, stubborn where Audrey was compliant. Things might not have been so good with Leon, but that didn't affect their friendship. Sisterhood was stronger. LaTonya didn't have much respect for her younger brother anyway, it seemed.

Fairly often Audrey babysat the three younger Saunders kids. Most of the time she enjoyed it. They were good kids, a twelve-year-old girl and two boys, nine and eleven. No doubt they ran roughshod over her, took advantage of her good nature, got away with stuff their drill-sergeant mother would never let them. But that, she figured, was what aunts were for. It didn't escape her, either, that LaTonya herself took advantage of Audrey, asking her to sit way more than she should, because LaTonya understood what was never said aloud, that her kids were the only kids Audrey would ever have.

LaTonya arrived home an hour later this evening than she'd said she would. She was taking a motivational training seminar at the Days Inn on Winsted Avenue, learning to start a home business. Her husband, Paul, managed the service department of a GMC dealership and usually worked late, didn't get home until eight. Audrey didn't mind, really. She'd just come off a long shift, which included attending the Andrew Stadler funeral, and would rather spend a few hours with her niece and nephews than at home with Leon, to be honest. Or thinking about poor Cassie Stadler. You had to take a break sometimes.

LaTonya was lugging a huge cardboard box heaped with white plastic bottles. Her moon-shaped face was beaded with sweat. "This here," she announced as the screen door slammed behind her, "is going to liberate us from debt."

"What is it?" Audrey asked. Camille was practicing her piano in the den by now and the two boys were watching TV.

"Hey, what's this? What the *hell* is *this*?" LaTonya hollered at her sons as she dropped the box on the kitchen table. "I don't care how much of a pushover your Auntie Audrey is, we have a rule about the TV. Turn that goddamned set off, and get to your homework, right now!"

"But Audrey said we could!" protested Thomas, the younger son. Matthew, experienced enough to know never to argue with their mother, scampered upstairs.

"I don't give a shit what Audrey said, you know the rules!" she thundered. She turned to Audrey, her voice softening. "It's weight-loss supplements. In a year or two, I'm not going to *need* Paul's salary. Not that there's much of that."

"Weight-loss supplements?"

"Thermogenic," LaTonya said. It was clear she had just learned the word. "Burns the fat off. Stokes up your metabolism. Blocks carbs too. And it's all natural."

"Sistah, you got to be careful with those make-money-at-home schemes," Audrey said. It was funny, when she was around LaTonya she found herself talking black, the rhythms of her speech changing. She was acutely aware that LaTonya considered Audrey saditty, or conceited.

"Careful?" LaTonya gasped. "This is the wellness industry we're talking about. In five years it's going to be a *trillion*-dollar industry, and I'm getting on the elevator at the ground floor." She opened a new box of Ritz Crackers, offered it to Audrey, who shook her head. LaTonya tore open the wax paper on one of the cracker rolls and grabbed a handful.

"LaTonya, can I talk to you for a second?"

"Mmmph?" LaTonya replied through a mouthful of cracker.

"It's the way you talk to your kids. The language. I don't think children should hear that kind of language, particularly from a parent."

LaTonya's eyes widened in indignation. She put her hands on her hips. She chewed, swallowed, then said, "Audrey, baby, I love you, but they're my kids, you understand? Not yours. Mine."

"But still," Audrey said, regretting she'd said anything, wanting to take it back.

"Honey, these little buggers respect strong words. If you had kids, you'd understand." LaTonya saw the wounded look in Audrey's face. "I'm—I'm sorry, I didn't mean it the way it came out."

"That's okay," Audrey said with a dismissive shake of the head. "I shouldn't have said anything."

LaTonya was holding up one of the big white plastic bottles. "*This* you need," she said.

"*I* need?"

"For your no-good, lazy-ass husband. My brother. Least he can do while he's sitting on his butt is take some of these thermogenic supplements. Twenty-four ninety-five. You can afford it. Tell you what: I'll give you my discount. Sixteen fifty. Can't do better than that."

30

AUDREY DIDN'T MUCH like the security director of the Stratton Corporation, an ex-cop named Edward Rinaldi. For one thing, there was his initial unwillingness to meet her, which she found peculiar. She was investigating the death of a Stratton employee, after all. How packed could his schedule really be? On the phone, after she'd told him what she wanted, he'd said he was "raked."

Then there was his reputation, which was a little hinky. She always did her homework, of course, and before coming to Stratton headquarters, she called around, figuring that the security director of the biggest company in town had to be known to at least the uniform division of the police. She learned that he was a local boy, went to high school with Nicholas Conover, Stratton's CEO. That he'd joined the force in Grand Rapids. His dealings with the Fenwick police were limited to pilferage cases and vandalism at Stratton. "That guy?" a veteran patrol cop named Vogel told her. "He never woulda made it here. We'd have kicked him out on his ass."

"How come?"

"Smartass. Got his own rule book, know what I'm saying?"

"I don't think I do, no."

"I don't want to spread rumors. Ask around in GR."

"I will, but you've dealt with him yourself, haven't you?"

"Ah, he was all over us on some vandalism deal at the CEO's house like it was our fault, instead of some whacked laid-off employee."

"All over you how?"

"He wanted the priors on this employee."

"Who?"

Vogel seemed surprised. "What're you talking, your guy, of course, right? That Stadler guy, isn't that why you called me?"

Suddenly Edward Rinaldi was becoming more interesting.

When she called Grand Rapids, she had a harder time finding someone who'd talk to her about Edward Rinaldi, until a lieutenant there named Pettigrew confided that Rinaldi was not missed. "Put it this way," the lieutenant said cagily, "he lived pretty good."

"Meaning what?"

"Meaning his income wasn't necessarily limited to his salary."

"We talking bribes, Lieutenant?"

"Could be, but that's not what I mean. I'm just saying that not all the evidence from drug busts made it to the property room."

"He was a user?"

The lieutenant chuckled. "Not so far as I know. He seemed a lot more interested in the shoeboxes full of cash. But he was booted out without a formal IA investigation, so that's just rumor."

It was enough to make her wary of the man.

But most of all she didn't like Rinaldi's manner—the evasiveness, the shiftiness in his eyes, the quick and inappropriate grins, the intensity of his stare. There was something vulgar, something scammy about the man.

"Where's your partner?" he asked after they'd chatted a few minutes. "Don't you guys always work in teams?"

"Often." He and Bugbee would have hit it off just fine, she thought. Cut from the same bolt of polyester fabric.

"You're Detective Rhimes? As in LeAnn Rimes?"

"Spelled differently," she said. "Did Andrew Stadler vandalize your CEO's house, Mr. Rinaldi?" she asked, coming straight to the point.

Rinaldi looked away too quickly, searched the ceiling as if wracking his brain, furrowed his brow. "I have no idea, Detective."

"You wanted to know his priors, Mr. Rinaldi. You must have had some suspicion."

Now he looked straight at her. "I like to do a thorough job. I investigate all possibilities. Same as I'm sure you do."

"I'm sorry, I don't quite understand. You did suspect Mr. Stadler, or you didn't?"

"Look, Detective. My boss's house gets vandalized in a particularly sick and twisted way, first thing I'm gonna do is go through the rolls of people who got the ax here, right? Anyone who made any threats during their outplacement interviews, all that. I find out that one guy who got laid off has a mental history, I'm gonna look a little more closely. Make sense?"

"Absolutely. So what did you find when you looked closely?"

"What'd I find?"

"Right. Did he make any threats during his outplacement?"

"Wouldn't surprise me. People do, you know. People lose it, time like that."

"Not according to his boss at the model shop, the fellow who conducted the outplacement interview along with someone from HR. He said Stadler quit, but he wasn't violent."

Rinaldi guffawed. "You trying to trap me or something, Detective? Forget it. I'm telling you this guy was in and out of the loony bin."

"He was diagnosed with schizophrenia, is that right?"

"What do you want from me? You want to know if this guy Stadler was the sick fuck who went to my boss's home and killed his dog, I have no idea."

"Did you talk to him?"

Rinaldi waved his hand. "Nah."

"Did you ask the police to investigate him?"

"For what? Get the poor guy in trouble, for what?"

"You just said it wouldn't surprise you if he made threats during his outplacement interview."

Rinaldi spun his fancy chair around and looked at his computer screen, squinted his eyes. "Who's the head of Major Cases now? Is it Noyce?"

"Sergeant Noyce, that's right."

"Say hi for me. Nice guy. Good cop."

"I will." Was he threatening to pull strings? Wouldn't work if he did, she thought. Sergeant Noyce barely knew him. She'd asked her boss about Rinaldi. "But as to my question, Mr. Rinaldi—you never talked to Stadler, never pointed him out as a potential suspect in the incident at Mr. Conover's home?"

Rinaldi shook his head again, gave a thoughtful frown. "I had no reason to think he was the one," he said reasonably.

"So that situation is unresolved, what happened at Mr. Conover's home?"

"You tell me. Fenwick PD doesn't seem optimistic about solving it."

"Did you ever meet Andrew Stadler or talk with him?"

"Nope."

"Or Mr. Conover? Did he ever meet with Stadler or talk with him?"

"I doubt it. The CEO of a company this size doesn't usually meet most of his employees, except maybe in group settings."

"Then it was very kind of him to attend Mr. Stadler's funeral."

"Did he? Well, that sounds like Nick."

"How so?"

"He's very considerate about his employees. Probably goes to all funerals of Stratton workers. Town like this, he's a public figure, you know. Part of his job."

"I see." She thought for a moment. "But you must have run names by Mr. Conover, names of laid-off employees, to see if any of them rang a bell."

"I usually don't bother him at that level, Detective. Not unless I have a firm lead. I let him do his job, and I do mine. No, I wish I could help you. The guy worked for Stratton for, what, like thirty-five years. I just hate to see a loyal employee come to an end like that."

31

"YO," SCOTT SAID, appearing from behind Marge's side of the divider panel next to Nick's desk. "Looking for some exciting reading? The board books are ready."

Nick looked up from his screen, a testy e-mail exchange with his general counsel, Stephanie Alstrom, about some tedious and endless battle with the Environmental Protection Agency over the emissions of certain volatile organic compounds in an adhesive used in the manufacture of one of the Stratton chairs that they'd discontinued anyway.

"Fiction or nonfiction?" he said.

"Nonfiction, unfortunately. Sorry it's so last minute, but I had to redo all the numbers the way you wanted."

"Sorry to be so unreasonable," Nick said sardonically. "But I'm the guy on the hot seat."

"Muldaur and Eilers are arriving at the Grand Fenwick this afternoon," Scott said, "and I told them I'd get the board books over there before dinner tonight so they could look 'em over. You know those guys—there's going to be questions, the second they see you. Just so long as you're ready to face them."

The board of directors always had dinner in town the night before the quarterly board meeting. Dorothy

Devries, the founder's daughter and the only member of the Devries family on the board, usually hosted them at the Fenwick Country Club, which she more or less owned. It was always a stiff and awkward occasion, with no overt business transacted.

"Ah, Scott, I'm going to have to miss it tonight." He stood up, feeling rubbed raw, his headache full blown now.

"You're—you're kidding me."

"It's the fourth-grade school play tonight—they're doing *The Wizard of Oz,* and Julia's got a big part. I really can't miss it."

"Please tell me you're joking, Nick. The *fourth-grade play?*"

"I missed her school play last year, and I've missed the art exhibit and just about every school assembly. I can't miss this too."

"You can't get someone to videotape it?"

"Videotape it? What kind of dad are you?"

"Absentee and proud of it. My kids respect me more for being distant and unavailable."

"Now. Wait 'til they get into therapy. Anyway, you know as well as I do that nothing ever gets done at those dinners."

"It's called schmoozing. A Yiddish word that means saving your job."

"They're going to fire me because I didn't have dinner with them? If they do, Scott, they're just looking for an excuse anyway."

Scott shook his head. "Okay," he said, looking down at the floor. "You're the boss. But if you ask me—"

"Thanks, Scott. But I didn't ask you."

32

AUDREY SAT AT her desk, staring at her little gallery of photographs, and then phoned the Michigan State Police crime lab in Grand Rapids.

Yesterday she'd driven almost two hours to Grand Rapids and handed the bullets, in their little brown paper evidence envelopes, to a crime lab tech who looked barely old enough to be shaving. Trooper Halverson had been polite but all business. He asked her if there were any shell casings, as if she'd maybe forgotten. She told him they hadn't recovered any, found herself actually apologizing to the boy. She asked how long it would take, and he said their caseload was huge, they were badly understaffed, their backlog was running a good three or four months. Luckily, Sergeant Noyce knew one of the Ramp Rangers, as they called the Michigan Highway Patrolmen, and when she reminded him of that—subtly, delicately—Trooper Halverson had said he'd try to get right to it.

On the phone, Trooper Halverson sounded even younger. He didn't remember her name, but when she read off the lab file number, he pulled it up on the computer.

"Yes, Detective," he said, tentative. "Um, well, let's

see here. Okay. They're .380, brass-jacketed, like you said. The rifling looks to be six left. Gosh, you guys didn't turn up any casings?"

"The body was dumped. So, as I said, unfortunately, no."

"It's just that if you had a casing we could really learn a whole lot more," he said. He spoke as if she were holding the cartridge casings back and maybe just needed a little persuasion to hand them over. "The casings tend to take imprints so much better than the bullets."

"No such luck," she said. She waited patiently while he went through the measurements and specs from his microscope exam. "So, um, based on the land and groove widths, the GRC database spits out like twenty different possible models that might've been the weapon in question." The GRC, she recalled, was the General Rifling Characteristics database, put out by the FBI every year or so on a CD.

"Twenty," she said, disappointed. "That doesn't narrow it down too much."

"Mostly Colts and Davis Industries. A lot of street guns look like this. So I'd say you're looking for a Colt .380, a Davis .380, or a Smith and Wesson."

"There's no way to narrow it down any more? What about the ammunition?"

"Yes, ma'am, these are hollow-point brass-jacketed bullets. There are some indications that they're Remington Golden Sabers, but don't hold me to it. That's problematic."

"Okay."

"And also—well, I probably shouldn't say this."

"Yes?"

"No, I'm just saying. Personal observation here. The land width is between .0252 and .054. The groove measurement is between .124 and .128. So it's pretty tight.

That tells me the weapon that fired it is a pretty decent one, not just some Saturday night special. So I'm thinking maybe it's the Smith and Wesson, because they're a good manufacturer."

"How many possible Smith and Wesson models are we talking about?"

"Well, Smith and Wesson doesn't make any .380s anymore. The only one they ever made was the baby Sigma."

"Baby Sigma? That's the name of the gun?"

"No, ma'am. I mean, you know, they have a product line called the Sigma, and for a couple of years—like the mid- to late nineties—the bottom end of the Sigma line was a .380 pocket pistol that people sometimes called the 'baby' Sigma."

She wrote down "S&W Sigma .380."

"Okay, good," she said, "so we're looking for a Smith and Wesson Sigma .380."

"No, ma'am. I didn't say that. No suspect weapons should be overlooked."

"Of course, Trooper Halverson." The troops were supercareful about what they told you, because they knew that everything had to stand up in a court of law, everything had to be carefully documented, and there couldn't be any guesswork. "When do you think you might know more?"

"Well, after our IBIS technician enters it."

She didn't want to ask how long that would take. "Well, anything you can do to put wings on this, Trooper, would be much appreciated."

33

THE BRAND-NEW FENWICK Elementary School auditorium was fancier than a lot of college theaters: plush stadium seating, great acoustics, professional sound system and lighting. It was called the Devries Theater, a gift from Dorothy Stratton Devries, in honor of her late husband.

When Nick had gone to Fenwick Elementary, there hadn't even been an auditorium. School assemblies had been held in the gym, all the kids sitting on the splintery wooden bleachers. Now it seemed like the fourth-grade class was doing its annual play in a Broadway theater.

Looking around, Nick was glad he'd come. All the parents were here, grandparents too. Even parents who rarely came to any of their kids' school events, like Emily Renfro's plastic-surgeon dad, Jim. Jacqueline Renfro was a class mom or something, but her husband was usually too busy doing face-lifts or screwing his receptionist to show up. A number of the parents had mini videocams, ready to film the production on compact digital tape that no one would ever bother to watch.

He was late as usual. Everywhere he went, he

seemed to arrive late these days. Marta had dropped Julia off an hour ago so she and the rest of the fourth-graders could get into their handmade costumes, which they'd been working on in art class for months. Julia was excited about tonight because she got to play the Wicked Witch of the West—her choice, a role she'd auditioned for and then pleaded for. Not for her Dorothy, which all the other girls wanted. Nick's little tomboy had no interest in playing a wimpy character wearing a braided wig and a gingham dress. She knew that the witch part was the scene-stealer. He liked that about her.

She didn't expect him to be here. He'd already told her a couple of times that he had a work dinner he had to go to and couldn't get out of. She was disappointed, but resigned. So she'd be all the more excited when she saw her daddy here. In truth, of course, Nick considered sitting through the school play one of those unpleasant parental obligations like changing a poopy diaper, or going to "The Lion King On Ice" (or *anything* on ice, for that matter), or watching the *Teletubbies* or *The Wiggles* and not letting on how creepy they were.

The back sections of the theater had been cordoned off, and there didn't seem to be any available seats in the front. He peered around, saw a few spaces here and there, a sea of averted glances, a few unfriendly faces. Maybe he was being a little paranoid. Guilt burned on his face as visibly as a scarlet letter. He was convinced people knew what he'd done just by looking at him.

But that wasn't it, of course. They hated him for other reasons, for being Slasher Nick, for being the local hero who'd turned on them. He saw the Renfros, caught their icy glares before they looked away. Finally he saw one friendly face, a buddy of his from high school days whose son was in Julia's class.

"Hey, Bobby," he said, sitting down in the seat Bob

Casey had freed up by moving his jacket. Casey, a bald, red-faced guy with an enormous beer gut, was a stockbroker who'd tried to hit Nick up for business several times. He was a wisenheimer whose chief claim to fame since high school was his ability to memorize long stretches of dialogue from Monty Python or any of the *National Lampoon* or *Airplane* movies.

"There he is," Casey said heartily. "Big night, huh?"

"Oh, yeah. How's Gracie?"

"Doin' good. Doin' good."

A long, uncomfortable silence followed. Then Bob Casey said, "Ever see anything like this theater? We never had anything like this."

"We were lucky to use the gym."

"Luxury!" Casey said in his Monty Python voice. "Luxury! We had to walk thirty miles to school every morning in a blizzard—uphill, both ways. And we loved it!"

Nick smiled, amused but unable to laugh.

Casey noticed Nick's subdued response and said, "So, you've had a hard year, huh?"

"Not as hard as a lot of people here."

"Hey, come on, Nick. You lost your wife."

"Yeah, well."

"How's the house?"

"Almost done."

"It's been almost done for a year, right?" he gibed. "Kids okay? Julia seems to be doing good."

"She's great."

"I hear Luke's having a hard time of it."

Nick wondered how much Bob Casey knew about Luke's troubles—probably more than Nick did himself. "Well, you know. Sixteen, right?"

"Tough age. Plus, only one parent and all that."

The production was about what you'd expect for a fourth-grade play—an Emerald City set they'd all painted themselves, the talking apple tree made out of painted corrugated cardboard. The music teacher playing sloppily on the Yamaha digital piano. Julia, as the Witch, froze up, kept forgetting her lines. You could almost hear the parents in the audience *thinking* them out loud for her—"Poppies!" and "I'll get you, my pretty!"

When it was over, Jacqueline Renfro seemed to go out of her way to find Nick and say, "Poor Julia." She shook her head. "It can't be easy for her."

Nick furrowed his brow.

"Well, only one parent, and you hardly ever there."

"I'm there as much as I can," he replied.

Jacqueline shrugged, having made her point, and moved on. But her husband, Jim, lagged behind. He wore a brown tweed jacket and a blue button-down shirt, looking like he was still a Princeton undergrad. He pointed a finger at Nick and winked. "Can't imagine how I'd get by without Jackie," he said in a confiding tone. "I don't know how you get by. Still, Julia's a great kid—you're very lucky."

"Thanks."

Jim Renfro was smiling too hard. "Of course, the thing about family is, when they get to be too much, you can't exactly downsize them." A cheery, self-satisfied wink. "Am I right?"

Any number of responses occurred to Nick—too many. None of them nonviolent. He had this strange feeling of a lid coming off, the bleed valves blowing.

At that point, Julia came running up, still wearing her pointed black construction-paper hat and her green face makeup. "You came!" she said.

He threw his arms around her. "I couldn't miss this."

"How was I?" she asked. There wasn't a drop of concern in her voice, no awareness that she'd messed up. She was bursting with pride. He loved this little girl.

"You were great," he said.

34

IN THE CAR on the way home, Nick's cell phone went off, a weird synthesized, symphonic fanfare that he'd never bothered to reprogram.

He glanced at the caller ID, saw that it was Eddie Rinaldi. He picked it up from the cradle, not wanting Julia to hear whatever Eddie had to say over the speakers. She was sitting in the backseat of the Suburban, poring over the *Wizard of Oz* program in the darkness. She still had the green zinc-oxide face makeup on, and Nick could see a bedtime struggle ahead when he made her clean it off.

"Hey, Eddie," he said.

"There you are. You had the phone off?"

"I was watching Julia's school play."

"Okay," he said. Eddie, who had no kids, no plans to have any, and no interest in them, never asked about his kids beyond the bare minimum required. "I was thinking of dropping by."

"Can't it wait?"

A pause. "I think not. We should talk. Only take five minutes, maybe."

"There a problem?" Nick was suddenly on edge.

"No, no. No problem. Just, we should talk."

* * *

EDDIE SPRAWLED IN the easy chair in Nick's study, legs splayed wide as if he owned the place.

"A homicide detective came to talk to me," he said casually.

Nick felt his insides go cold. He leaned forward in his desk chair. Here they sat, just a few feet from where it had happened. "What the fuck?" he said.

Eddie shrugged, no big deal. "Standard operating procedure. Routine shit."

"Routine?"

"She's just covering all the bases. Got to, sloppy if she didn't."

"It's a woman." Nick focused on the anomaly, avoiding the main issue: *a homicide detective was on the case, already?*

"Negro lady." Eddie could have put it much more crudely. His racism was no secret to anyone, but maybe he'd learned over the years that it wasn't socially acceptable, not even around his old buddies. Or maybe he didn't want to antagonize Nick at the moment.

"I didn't know the Fenwick police had any."

"I didn't either."

A long silence in which Nick could hear the ticking of the clock. A silver clock, engraved FENWICK CITIZEN OF THE YEAR, awarded to him three years ago. When everything was going great. "What'd she want?"

"What do you think? She wanted to ask about Stadler."

"What *about* Stadler?"

"You know, what you'd expect. Did he make any threats, whatever."

Eddie was being evasive, and Nick didn't like it. Something didn't sit right. "Why was she talking to you?"

"Hey, man, I'm the security director, remember?"

"No. There has to be some more specific reason she went to talk to you. What are you leaving out, Eddie?"

"Leaving out? I'm leaving nothing out, buddy. I mean, look, she knew I asked some guys on the job about Stadler."

So that was it. By doing his background check on Stadler, he'd in effect tipped his hand to the police. "Shit."

"Come on. I never talked to the guy."

"No," Nick said, one hand cupping his chin. "You call the cops, asking about some downsized employee who slaughtered your boss's dog, then the guy turns up dead a couple days later. This doesn't look good."

Eddie shook his head, rolling his eyes in contempt. "Like this is, what, the Mafia or something? Get real. The guy goes off the deep end, doing sick shit, matter of time before he pisses off the wrong guy."

"Yeah."

"In the dog pound, I mean, come on. Look, they got nothing tying Stadler to me—or to you."

"Then what was she asking about?"

"Ah, she wanted to know if you'd ever talked to Stadler, had any contact with the guy. Told her you probably didn't even know who the guy was. Pretty much true."

Nick inhaled slowly, tried to calm himself, held his breath. "And if I did? What's the assumption here, that I went after the guy, *killed* him?" Nick heard the aggrieved tone in his own voice, as if he were actually starting to believe himself innocent.

"Nah, she's just looking for scraps. Anyway, don't worry, I handled her fine. Believe me, she left knowing she's barking up the wrong tree."

"How do you know?"

"I can tell, come on. Get serious here, Nick. The CEO of Stratton murdered one of his employees? I don't *think* so. No one's going to believe that for a second."

Nick was silent for a long while. "I hope so."

"I just wanted to keep you in the loop. In case she comes to talk to you."

Nick, his chest tightening, said, "She said she was going to?"

"No, but she might. Wouldn't surprise me."

"I'd never even heard the name," Nick said. "Right? You tell her otherwise?"

"Exactly. Told her you're a busy guy, I do my job, you don't get involved."

"Right."

"So you figured maybe some downsized employee went wacko, killed your dog, but you called the cops, figured they'd handle it, you had no idea who it mighta been."

"Right."

"Guy turns up dead, mighta been the same guy, mighta been different, you have no idea. Like that."

Nick nodded, rehearsing the answer in his mind, turning it over and over, poking at the soft spots. "There's nothing tying me to this thing?" he said after a few moments.

A long silence. Eddie replied with a kind of smoldering indignation. "I did my job, Nick, you clear?"

"I don't doubt it. I'm asking you to think like a cop. Like a homicide cop."

"That's how I think, man. Like a cop."

"No prints, nothing like that, on the . . . body? Fibers, DNA, whatever?"

"Nick, I told you, we're not going to talk about this."

"We are now. I want to know."

"The body was clean, Nick," Eddie said. "Okay? Clean as a whistle. Clean as I could get it in the time we had."

"What about the gun?"

"What about it?"

"What'd you do with it? You don't still have it, do you?"

"Like I'm a stupid fuck? Come on, man."

"Then where is it?"

Eddie let out a puff of air, made a sound like *pah*. "Bottom of the river, you really want to know." Fenwick, like so many towns in Michigan, was built on the shores of one of the many waterways leading into Lake Michigan.

"Shell casings too?"

"Yup."

"And if it turns up?"

"You realize how unlikely that is?"

"I'm saying."

"Even if they do find it, they got no way to connect it to me."

"Why not? It's your gun."

"It's a goddamned drop gun, Nick."

"A what?"

"A throw-down. A piece I picked up at a scene in GR. Some crack dealer, who the hell knows where he got it? Point is, there's no record anywhere. No paperwork, no purchase permit, nothing. Clean."

Nick had heard of cops picking up guns they found at crime scenes, keeping them, but he knew you weren't supposed to do that, and it made him nervous to hear Eddie admit to it. If he did that, what else did he do?

"You sure?" Nick said.

"Sure as shit."

"What about the security cameras?"

Eddie nodded. "Hey, I'm a pro, right? Took care of that too."

"How?"

"Why do you need to know?"

"I need to know. My own fucking security cameras recorded me killing the guy."

Eddie closed his eyes, shook his head in irritation. "I reformatted the hard drive on the digital video recorder. That night's gone. Never happened. System started recording next day—makes sense, right? Since we just put it in the day before."

"Not a trace?"

"Nada. Hey, don't worry about it. The lady comes to talk to you, you cooperate, tell her everything you know, which is a big fat zero, right?" Eddie gave his dry cackle.

"Right. I know she talked to you?"

Eddie shrugged. "Play it either way. Let's say, no, I didn't get around to it. Got nothing to do with you, right?"

"Right."

Eddie got up. "Nothing to worry about, man. Get some sleep. You look like shit."

"Thanks." Nick got up, to walk Eddie out, then thought of something. "Eddie," he said. "That night. You said it was your gun, tied everything to you, right? That's why I didn't have a choice."

Eddie's eyes were dead. "Yeah?"

"Now you tell me the gun was clean. No connection to you at all. I don't get it."

A long silence.

"Can't take chances, Nicky," Eddie finally said. "Never take chances."

Nick walked Eddie out of his study, heard footfalls

on the carpeting. Saw a jeans-clad leg, a sneaker, disappear up the stairs.

Lucas.

Just getting home? Was it possible that he'd overheard their conversation? Nah, he'd have had to have stood outside the study door, listening. Lucas didn't do that, the main reason being that he had no interest in what his dad was up to.

Still.

Nick wondered, a tiny wriggle of worry.

35

DRIVING TO WORK the next morning, Nick was in a foul mood. The news that a homicide detective was poking around the corporation had sent him spiraling into a tense, sleepless night. He thrashed around in the big bed, got up repeatedly, obsessed about that night.

What Happened That Night—that was how he thought of it now. The memory had receded to attenuated, kaleidoscopic images: Stadler's leering face, the gunfire, the body sprawled on the ground, Eddie's face, carrying the body wrapped in black trash bags.

He was out of pills, which was just as well; any more of them, he figured, and he was headed for the Betty Ford clinic. He tried to think about work stuff, anything but that night. But that just meant the board meeting in the morning. Board meetings always made him tense, but this time he knew that the shit was about to rain down.

On the way into work he stopped at a light next to a gleaming silver S Class Mercedes. He turned to admire it and saw that the driver was Stratton's VP of sales, Ken Coleman. Nick rolled down his passenger's side window, tapped on his horn until he got Coleman's attention. When Coleman—forty-one, a good seventy pounds overweight, a bad hairpiece—rolled down his window, his face lit up.

"Hey, Nick! Looking pretty slick."

"Board meeting. New car, Kenny?"

Coleman's grin got even wider. "Got it yesterday. You like?"

"Must list for a hundred grand, right?"

Coleman, always hyper, nodded fast, up and down and up and down like some bobble-head doll. "Over. Fully loaded. Like, AMG sports package and, I mean, heated *steering wheel,* you know?" The top sales guys at Stratton made more than Nick did. He didn't resent it; someone had to do the soul-destroying shit they did.

The light turned green, but Nick didn't move. "Buy or lease?" he asked.

"Well, lease. I always lease, you know?"

"Good. Because it's going back to the dealer."

Coleman cocked his bobble head, a movement like a terrier, almost comic. "What?"

Behind him, someone honked a horn. Nick ignored it. "We laid off five thousand workers, Ken. Half the company. To cut costs, save Stratton. Pretty much wiped out the town. So I don't want a member of my executive management team driving around town in a fucking hundred-thousand-dollar Mercedes, understand?"

Coleman stared in disbelief.

Nick went on, "You take that back to the dealership by close of business today and tell 'em you want a fucking Subaru or something. But I don't want to see you behind that heated steering wheel again, you understand?"

Nick gunned the engine and took off.

THE FIVE MEMBERS of the board of directors of the Stratton Corporation, and their guests, were gathered in the anteroom to the boardroom. Coffee was being served from vacuum carafes, and not the institutional food-service blend that was served in the Stratton employee cafeteria, either. It was brewed from Sulawesi Peaberry beans fresh-roasted by Town Grounds, Fenwick's best coffee place. Todd Muldaur had complained about the coffee at the first board meeting after the buyout, poked fun at the Bunn-O-Matic. Nick thought Todd was being ridiculous, but he ordered the change. That, and little cold bottles of Evian water, melon slices, raspberries and strawberries, fancy pastries trucked in from a famous bakery in Ann Arbor.

Todd Muldaur, in another of his expensive suits, was at the tail end of a joke when Nick arrived, holding forth to Scott, the other guy from Fairfield Partners, Davis Eilers, and someone Nick had never seen before. "I told him the best way to see Fenwick is in your rearview mirror," Todd was saying. Eilers and the other guy laughed raucously. Scott, who'd noticed Nick's approach, just smiled politely.

Davis Eilers was the other deal partner, a guy who had a lot of operational experience. He'd done his time at McKinsey like Todd and Scott, only he'd played football at Dartmouth, not Yale. He later ran a number of companies, sort of a CEO-for-hire.

Todd turned, saw Nick. "There he is." He tipped his cup at Nick. "Great coffee!" he said expansively and gave a wink. "Sorry to miss you last night. Busy being a dad, huh?"

Nick shook Todd's hand, then Scott's, then Eilers's. "Yeah, couldn't get out of it. My daughter's school play, you know, and given—"

"Hey, you got your priorities straight," Todd said with an excess of sincerity. "I respect that."

Nick wanted to toss the cup of hot Sulawesi Peaberry in the guy's face, but he just looked straight in Todd's too-blue eyes and smiled appreciatively.

"Nick, I want you to meet our new board member, Dan Finegold." A tall, handsome guy, athletic-looking. A thatch of dark brown hair starting to silver over. What was it with Fairfield Equity Partners? It was a fucking frat.

Dan Finegold's handshake was a crusher.

"Don't tell me Yale football too," Nick said cordially. Thinking: *Our new board member? Like, were they going to tell me? Just spring it on me?*

"Yale baseball, actually," said Todd, clapping both men on their shoulders, bringing them together. "Dan was a legendary pitcher."

"Legendary, my ass," said Finegold.

"Hey, man, you *were,*" Todd said. He looked at Nick. "Dan's got twenty years' experience in the office-supply space, with all the scar tissue. I'm sure you know OfficeSource—that was his baby. When Willard bought it, he grabbed Dan for Fairfield."

"You like Boston?" Nick asked. He couldn't think of anything else to say. He couldn't say what he was really thinking, which was: Why are you here, and who invited you onto the board, and what's really going on here? Fairfield had the right to put whomever they wanted on the board, but it wasn't exactly cool for them to just show up with a new board member in tow. They hadn't done it before. It wasn't a good precedent, or maybe that was the point.

"It's great. Especially for a foodie like me. Lot of happening restaurants in Boston these days."

"Dan's part owner of an artisanal brewery in upstate New York," said Todd. "They make the best Belgian beer outside of Belgium. Abbey ale, right?"

"That's right."

"Welcome to the board," Nick said. "I'm sure your expertise in Belgian beer's going to come in handy."

Something about Belgian beer and Abbey ale sounded familiar, but he couldn't place it.

Todd took Nick by the elbow as they walked to the boardroom. He spoke in a low voice. "Bummer about Atlas McKenzie."

"Huh?"

"Scott told me last night."

"What are you talking about?"

Todd gave him a quick, curious glance. "The deal," he said under his breath. "How it fell through."

"What?" What the hell was he talking about? The Atlas McKenzie deal was all but inked. This made no sense!

"Don't worry, it's not going to come up this morning. But still, a *major* bummer, huh?" In a louder voice, he called out, "Mrs. Devries!"

Todd turned away and strode up to Dorothy Devries, who had just entered the boardroom. Todd clasped her small hand in both of his large ones and waited until she turned her cheek toward him before he kissed it.

Dorothy was wearing a Nancy Reagan burgundy pantsuit with white piping around the lapels. Her white hair was a perfect cumulus cloud with just a hint of blue rinse in it, which brought out the steely blue of her eyes. Fairfield Partners had left Dorothy Stratton Devries a small piece of the company and a seat on the board, which was a condition of hers that Willard Osgood had no quibble with. It looked good to have the founder's family still connected to Stratton. It told the world that Fairfield still respected the old ways. Of course, Dorothy had no power. She was there for window dressing, mostly. Fairfield owned ninety percent of Stratton, controlled the board, ran the show. Dorothy, a sharp cookie, understood that, but she also understood that, outside the boardroom at least, she still possessed some moral authority.

Her dad, Harold Stratton, had been a machinist for the Wabash Railroad, a tinsmith's apprentice, a steeplejack. He worked as a machinist at Steelcase, in Grand Rapids, before he started his own company with money provided by his rich father-in-law. His big innovation had been to develop a better roller suspension for metal file cabinets—progressive roller bearings in a suspension-file drawer. His only son had died in childhood, leaving Dorothy, but women didn't run companies in those days, so eventually he turned it over to Dorothy's husband, Milton Devries. She'd spent her later years in her big, dark mansion in East Fenwick as the town matriarch, a social arbiter as fearsome as only a small-town society queen can be. She was on every board in town, chairwoman of most of them. Even though she liked Nick, and made him the CEO, she still looked down on him as being from a lower social class. Nick's dad, after all, had worked on the shop floor. Never mind that Dorothy was but one generation away from having machinist's grease on her own fingers.

Nick, reeling from Todd's casual revelation, saw Scott sitting down at his customary place at the oval mahogany board table. As Nick approached him, put a hand on his shoulder, he heard Todd saying, "Dorothy, I'd like you to meet Dan Finegold."

"Hey," Nick whispered, standing immediately behind Scott, "what's this about Atlas McKenzie?"

Scott craned his neck around, eyes wide. "Yeah, I just got the call on my cell at dinner last night—Todd happened to be there, you know . . ." His voice trailed off. Nick remained silent. Scott went on: "They went with Steelcase—you know, that joint venture Steelcase has with Gale and Wentworth—"

"They called *you*?"

"I guess I was on Hardwick's speed-dial, all those negotiations at the end—"

"You get bad news, you tell me first, understand?"

Nick could see Scott's pale face flush instantly. "I— of course, Nick, it was just that Todd was right there, you know, and—"

"We'll talk later," Nick said, giving Scott a shoulder squeeze too hard to be merely companionable.

He heard Dorothy Devries's brittle laugh from across the room, and he took his place at the head of the table.

The Stratton boardroom was the most conservative place in the headquarters—the immense mahogany table with places for fifteen, even though there hadn't been fifteen board members since the takeover; the top-of-the-line black leather Stratton Symbiosis chairs, the slim monitors at each place that could be raised and lowered with the touch of a button. It looked like a boardroom in any big corporation in the world.

Nick cleared his throat, looked around at the board, and knew he was not among friends anymore. "Well, why don't we get started with the CFO's report?" he said.

36

SOMETHING ABOUT THE way Scott went through his depressing presentation—his dry, monotone, doom-and-gloom voice-over to the PowerPoint slides projected on the little plasma screens in front of everyone—was almost defiant, Nick thought. As if he knew full well he was hurling carrion to the hyenas.

Of course, they didn't need his little dog-and-pony show, since they'd all gotten the charts in their black loose-leaf board books, FedExed to everyone yesterday, or couriered over to their hotel. But it was a board ritual, it had to go into the minutes, and besides, you couldn't assume that any of them had actually read through the materials.

Nick knew, however, that Todd Muldaur had read the financials closely, the instant he got them in Boston, the way some guys grab the sports section and devour the baseball box scores. Todd probably didn't wait even for the printouts; he'd surely gone through the Adobe PDF files and Excel spreadsheets as soon as Scott had e-mailed them.

Because his questions sounded awfully rehearsed. They weren't even questions, really. They were frontal assaults.

"I don't believe what I'm seeing here," he said. He looked around at the other board members—Dorothy, Davis Eilers, Dan Finegold—and the two "invited guests" who always attended the first half of the board meeting: Scott, and the Stratton general counsel who was here in her capacity as board secretary. Stephanie Alstrom was a small, serious woman with prematurely gray hair and a small, pruned mouth that seldom smiled. There was something juiceless, almost desiccated about Stephanie. Scott had once described her as a "raisin of anxiety," and the description had stuck in Nick's mind.

"This is a train wreck," Todd went on.

"Todd, there's no question these numbers look bad," Nick tried to put in.

"*Look* bad?" Todd shot back. "They *are* bad."

"My point is, this has been a challenging quarter— hell, a challenging year—for the entire sector," Nick said. "Office furniture is economically sensitive, we all know that. Companies stop buying stuff practically overnight when the economy slows."

Todd was staring at him, rattling Nick momentarily. "I mean, look, new office installations have plummeted, business startups and expansions have slowed to almost nothing," Nick went on. "Last couple of years, there's been serious overcapacity in the office furniture sector, and that, combined with weaker demand across the board, has put serious downward pressure on prices and profit margins."

"Nick," Todd said. "When I hear the word 'sector,' I reach for my barf bag."

Nick smiled involuntarily. "It's the reality," he said. He folded his arms, felt something crinkle in one of the breast pockets of his suit.

"If I may quote Willard Osgood," Todd went on, "'Explanations aren't excuses.' There's an *explanation* for everything."

"Uh, in all fairness to Nick," Scott put in, "he's just seeing these numbers for the first time."

"*What?*" said Todd. "Today? You mean, *I* saw these numbers before the CEO?" He turned to Nick. "You got something more important on your mind? Like, your daughter's *ballet recital* or something?"

Nick gave Scott a furious look. Yeah, it's the first time seeing the *real* numbers, he thought. Not the fudged ones you wanted to fob off on them. Nick was sorely tempted to let loose, but who knew where that might lead? Nervously, he fished inside the breast pocket of his suit and found a scrap of paper, pulled it out. It was a yellow Post-it note. Laura's handwriting: "Love you, babe. You're the best." A little heart and three X's. Tears immediately sprang to his eyes. He so rarely wore this suit that he must not have had it dry-cleaned last time he wore it, before Laura's death. He slipped the note carefully back where he'd found it.

"Come on, now, Todd," said Davis Eilers. "We're all dads here." Noticing Dorothy, he said, "Or moms." He ignored Stephanie Alstrom, who had no kids and wasn't married and seemed to shrink into herself as she tapped away at her laptop.

Calm, Nick told himself, blinking away the tears. *Stay calm.* The room revolved slowly around him. "Scott means the final figures, Todd, but believe me, there's no surprise here. I take heart from the fact that our profit margins are still positive."

"No surprise?" Todd said. "No *surprise*? Let me tell you something, I don't really care how the rest of the sector's doing. We didn't buy Stratton because you're like everyone else, because you're *average*. We bought you because you were marquee. Same reason we use Stratton chairs and work panels and all that in our own offices in Boston, when we could have bought anything. Because you were the best in your space.

Not just good enough. As Willard's so fond of saying, "'Good enough' is *not* good enough.'"

"We're still the best," Nick said. "Bear in mind that we did our layoffs early—at your insistence, let me remind you. Everyone else waited. We got ahead of the curve."

"Fine, but you're still not delivering on your plan."

"To be fair," Scott pointed out, "Nick's plan didn't assume the economy was going to get worse."

"Scott," Todd said in a deadly quiet voice, "Nick's the CEO. He should have anticipated turns in the economy. Look, Nick, we always like to give our CEOs a lot of rope." He gave Nick a steady blue stare. What did that mean, anyway? Give a man enough rope and he'll hang himself—was that it? "We don't want to run your business—we want *you* to run your business," Todd went on. "But not if you're going to run it into the ground. At the end of the day, you work for us. That means that your job is to protect our investors' capital."

"And the way to protect your capital," Nick said, straining to remain civil, "is to invest in the business now, during the downturn. Now's the time to invest in new technology. That way, when the economy comes back, we kick butt." He looked at Dorothy. "Sorry." She didn't respond, her icy blue eyes focused on the middle distance.

Todd, leafing through his board book, looked up. "Like spending thirty million dollars in the last three years in development costs for a new *chair*?"

"A bargain," Nick said. "Design and retooling costs, twenty-six patents, two separate design teams. And that's actually less than Steelcase spent on their Leap chair, which turned out to be a great investment. Or Herman Miller spent on developing the Aeron chair. I mean, don't forget, product design and development is a core value at Stratton." Todd was silent for a moment.

Score one for the defense. Before he could reply, Nick went on: "Now, if you want to continue this discussion, I'd like to move that we go into executive session." The motion was seconded and approved by voice vote. This was the point when Scott, as an invited guest but not a board member, normally got up to leave. Nick caught his eye, but Scott's expression was opaque, unreadable. He wasn't gathering his things, wasn't getting up.

"Listen, Nick, we're going to ask Scott to stay," Todd said.

"Really?" was all Nick could think to say. "That's—that's not the protocol."

Now Davis Eilers, who'd barely said a word, spoke up. "Nick, we've decided that it's time that Scott join the board formally. We really feel that Scott's become an important enough part of the management team that we'd like his official participation on the board. We think he can add a lot of value."

Nick, stunned, swallowed hard as he racked his brain for something to say. He tried to catch Scott's eye again, but Scott was avoiding his glance. He nodded, thought. The Dan Finegold thing was outrageous. But now, adding Scott as a board member without even telling him in advance, let alone pretending to seek his opinion? He wanted to call them on it, bring it all out into the open, but all he said was, "Well, he can certainly add value."

"Thanks for understanding," Eilers said.

"Uh, Nick, we're going to be making a few changes going forward," Todd said.

As opposed to what? Nick thought. *Going backward?* He said, "Oh?"

"We think this board should be meeting every month instead of quarterly."

Nick nodded. "That's a lot of travel to Fenwick," he said.

"Well, we can alternate between Boston and Fenwick," Todd said. "And we'll be looking to see the financials weekly instead of monthly."

"I'm sure that can be arranged," Nick said slowly. "As long as Scott doesn't mind." Scott was examining his board book closely and didn't look up.

"Nick," said Davis Eilers, "we've also been thinking that, if and when you decide to fire any of your direct reports—any of the executive managers—that's going to require board approval."

"Well, that's not what my contract says." He could feel his face start to prickle.

"No, but it's an amendment we'd be in favor of. Sort of making sure we're all on the same page, personnel-wise. Like they say, the only constant is change."

"You guys are hiring me to do the best job I can," Nick said. "Enough rope, like you always say. And you just said you want me to run the company—you don't want to run it yourself."

"Of course," Eilers said.

Todd said, "We just don't want any surprises. You know, keep things running smoothly." He'd adopted a reasonable tone, no longer combative. He knew he'd won. "We've got an almost-two-billion-dollar company to run. That's a big job for anyone, even someone who's paying full attention. Hey, it's like football, you know? You may be the quarterback, but you're not going to have a winning team without linesmen and receivers and running backs—and coaches. Think of us as your coaches, right?"

Nick gave a slow, faint smile. "Coaches," he said. "Right."

WHEN THE BOARD meeting came to an end an hour and a half later, Nick was the first to leave the room. He needed to get the hell out of there before he lost it.

That wouldn't be good. I'm not going to quit, he told himself. Make them fire me. Quit and you get nothing. Get fired without cause, and the payoff was considerable. Five million bucks. That was in the contract he'd negotiated when he sold to Fairfield, when the idea of getting fired seemed like science fiction. He was a rock star then; they'd never dump him.

As he left, he noticed two people seated just outside the boardroom, a thuggy-looking blond man in a bad suit and a well-dressed, attractive black woman.

The woman Rinaldi had told him about.

The homicide detective.

The woman he'd seen at Stadler's funeral.

"Mr. Conover," she called out. "Could we talk to you for a few minutes?"

— PART THREE —

GUILT

37

NICK TOOK THEM into one of the conference rooms. Talking at his home base was out of the question, given the way anyone, including Marjorie, could listen in.

He took the lead. He sat at the head of the table. The moment the two homicide detectives sat, he began speaking. He adopted a calm, authoritative tone, brisk but cordial. He was the head of a major corporation with a million things going on, and these two cops were here without an appointment, without even giving him the courtesy of a heads-up call. Yet he didn't want to diminish the importance of what they were doing. They were investigating the murder of a Stratton employee. He wanted them to feel that he took this seriously. It was a delicate balancing act.

He was scared shitless. He didn't like the fact that they'd just shown up at his workplace. There was something aggressive, almost accusatory about that. He wanted to let them know, through his tone and his attitude, that he didn't appreciate this, while at the same time communicating his respect for their mission.

"Detectives," he said, "I can spare maybe five minutes. You've caught me on my busiest day."

"Thanks for seeing us," said the black woman. The

blond man blinked a few times, like a Komodo dragon admiring a delicious-looking goat, but said nothing. Nick could tell that he was going to be trouble. The black woman was sweetly apologetic, an obvious push-over. The blond man—Busbee? Bugbee?—was the one to watch.

"I wish you'd called my office and made an appoint-ment. I'd be happy to talk to you at greater length an-other time."

"This shouldn't take that long," said the blond man.

"Tell me what I can do for you," Nick said.

"Mr. Conover, as you know, an employee of the Stratton Company was found dead last week," said the black woman. She was quite pretty, and there was something serene about her.

"Yes," Nick said. "Andrew Stadler. A terrible tragedy."

"Did you know Mr. Stadler?" she went on.

Nick shook his head. "No, unfortunately. We have five thousand employees—as many as ten thousand two years ago, before we had to let so many people go—and I can't possibly get to know everyone. Though I wish I could." He smiled wistfully.

"Yet you went to his funeral," she pointed out.

"Of course."

"You always go to the funerals of Stratton employ-ees?" said the blond detective.

"Not always. When I can, though. I don't always feel welcome, not anymore. But I feel it's the least I can do."

"You never met Mr. Stadler, is that right?" the black woman said.

"Right."

"You were aware of his . . . situation, though, isn't that right?" she continued.

"His situation?"

"His personal troubles."

"I heard later that he'd been hospitalized, but plenty of people have mental illness and aren't violent."

"Oh?" the black detective said quickly. "How did you know he'd been hospitalized? Did you see his personnel file?"

"Didn't I read it in the newspaper?"

"There wasn't anything in the paper about that," said the blond man.

"Must've been," Nick said. There *had* been something in the paper, hadn't there? "Said something about a 'troubled emotional history' or something, right?"

"Nothing about hospitalization," the blond man said firmly.

"Someone must have mentioned it to me, then."

"Your corporate security director, Edward Rinaldi?"

"Possibly. But I don't recall."

"I see," the black woman said, jotting something down.

"Mr. Conover, did Edward Rinaldi tell you he thought Andrew Stadler was the guy who killed your dog?" the blond cop asked.

Nick squinted, as if trying to recall. He remembered asking Eddie about this.

Told her you didn't even know who the guy was. Pretty much true.

"*I never even heard the name,*" Nick had said. "*Right? You tell her otherwise?*"

"*Exactly. Told her you're a busy guy, I do my job, you don't get involved.*"

"Eddie didn't mention any names to me," Nick said.

"Is that right?" the woman said, sounding surprised.

Nick nodded. "To be honest, it's been a rough year. I'm the head of a company that's had to let half its employees go. There's a lot of anger out there, understandably."

"You're not the most popular man in town," she suggested.

"That's putting it mildly. I've gotten angry letters from downsized employees, really heartbreaking letters."

"Threats?" she asked.

"Could be, but I wouldn't know about them."

"How could you not know about threats?" the male cop said.

"I'm not the first to open my mail here. If I get a threatening letter, it goes right to Security—I never see it."

"You don't want to know?" he said. "Me, I'd want to know."

"Not me. Not unless I need to know for some reason. The less I know, the better."

"Really?" said the blond man.

"Really. I don't like to go around feeling paranoid. There's no point in it."

"Did Mr. Rinaldi tell you why he was looking into Mr. Stadler's background?" the black woman persisted.

"No. I didn't even know he was."

"He didn't tell you later he'd been looking into Stadler?" she persisted.

"Nope. He never told me anything about Stadler. I mean, I had no idea—*have* no idea—what Eddie was looking into. He does his job and I do mine."

"Mr. Rinaldi never even mentioned Stadler's name to you?" the woman said.

"Not that I recall, no."

"I'm confused," she said. "I thought you just said Mr. Rinaldi might have told you about Andrew Stadler's hospitalization. Which would sort of require him to mention Stadler's name, right?"

Nick felt the tiniest trickle of sweat run slowly down his earlobe. "After the news of Stadler's death came out, Eddie may have mentioned his name to me in passing. But I really don't recall."

"Hmm," the woman said. A few seconds of silence went by.

Nick ignored the sweat trickle, not wanting to call attention to it by brushing it away.

"Mr. Conover," said the blond man, "your house has been broken into a bunch of times in the last year, right? Since the layoffs began?"

"Several times, yes."

"By the same person?"

"It's hard to say. But I'd guess, yeah, the same person."

"There was graffiti and such?"

"Graffiti spray-painted inside my house, on the walls."

"What kind of graffiti?" the black detective asked.

"'No hiding place.'"

"That's what they wrote?"

"Right."

"Did you receive any death threats?"

"No. Ever since the layoffs started, two years ago, I've gotten occasional threatening phone calls, but nothing quite that specific."

"Well, your family dog was killed," said the blond detective. "That's sort of a death threat, wouldn't you say?"

Nick considered for a moment. "Possibly. Whatever it was, it was a sick, depraved thing to do." He worried that he'd just gone too far: had be just betrayed his anger? Yet how else would he be expected to react? He noticed that the black woman wrote something down in her notebook.

"The Fenwick police have any idea who did this?" the guy said.

"No idea."

"Does Mr. Rinaldi get involved in your personal security, outside the corporation?" the black detective asked.

"Informally, yeah," Nick said. "Sometimes. After this last incident, I asked him to put in a new security system."

"So you must have discussed the incident with him," she said.

Nick hesitated, a beat too long. What did Eddie tell them, exactly? Did Eddie tell them he came over to the house after Barney was slaughtered? He wished he'd talked to Eddie longer, found out everything he'd said. Shit. "A bit. I asked his advice, sure." He waited for the inevitable next question—inevitable to him, at least: did Eddie Rinaldi come to his house after Barney had been discovered in the pool? And what was the right answer?

Instead, the black detective said, "Mr. Conover, how long ago did you move into Fenwicke Estates?"

"About a year ago."

"After all the layoffs were announced?" she went on.

"About a year after."

"Why?"

Nick paused. "My wife insisted."

"Why was that?"

"She was concerned."

"About what?"

"That our family might be threatened."

"What made her so concerned?"

"Instinct, mostly. She knew there were a few people who might want to do us harm."

"So you did hear about threats," the black woman said. "But you just said you didn't know about any— you didn't *want* to know about them."

Nick folded his hands on the table. He was feeling increasingly frantic, trapped like some cornered animal, and he knew the only way to respond was to sound both reasonable and blunt. "Did I hear about specific threats? No. Did I hear that there *were* threats—that a few isolated fringe cases might have it in for me and my family? Sure. People talk. Rumors spread. I wasn't going to wait to see if there was any basis in these rumors. And I can tell you my wife sure as hell wasn't going to wait."

The two detectives seemed to accept his answer. "Before you moved to your new house, Mr. Conover, did you have any break-ins?"

"Not till we moved to Fenwicke Estates."

The blond detective smiled. "Guess the . . . *gated community* . . . didn't give you much protection, huh?" He put a surly spin on the words "gated community," made no attempt to conceal a note of smugness.

"Just takes longer to get in and out of," Nick admitted.

The blond guy chuckled, shook his head. "Costs a lot more, though, I bet."

"There you go."

"But you can afford it."

Nick shrugged. "Wasn't my idea to move there. It was my wife's."

"Your wife," said the black woman. "She—she passed away last year, isn't that right?"

"That's right."

"Nothing suspicious about her death, was there?"

A pause. "No, nothing suspicious," Nick said slowly. "She was killed in a car accident."

"You were driving?" she asked.

"She was driving."

"Nothing—was alcohol involved?"

"The other driver, yeah," Nick said. "A semi. He'd been drinking."

"But not you."

"No," he said. "Not me." He compressed his lips, then looked at his watch. "I'm afraid—"

The blond guy stood up. "Thanks for taking the time."

But the black woman remained seated. "Just a couple more things, sir?"

"Can we continue this some other time?" Nick said.

"Just—just another minute, if you don't mind. We don't want to leave any stone unturned. Do you own any guns, Mr. Conover?"

"Guns?" Nick shook his head. He hoped his face hadn't reddened.

"No handguns at all?"

"Nope. Sorry."

"Thank you. And last Tuesday night, where were you?"

"At home. I haven't traveled anywhere in ten days or so."

"What time did you go to sleep, do you remember?"

"Last Tuesday?"

"A week ago."

Nick thought a moment. "I went out for dinner Wednesday night. Tuesday I was at home."

"Do you remember what time you went to sleep?"

"I can't—well, I'm normally asleep by eleven, eleven-thirty."

"So you'd say by eleven-thirty you were in bed?"

"That sounds about right." She was smart, Nick realized. Smarter, he saw now, than the blond guy, who was all posture and attitude.

"Sleep through the night?"

"Sure." *Jesus,* he thought. What was she implying?

"Okay, great," she said. She got up. "That's all we need. We appreciate your taking the time to talk to us."

Nick rose, shook their hands. "Anytime," he said. "Just next time, give me some notice."

"We will," the black woman said. She stopped, appeared to hesitate. "I'm sorry to take up your time,

Mr. Conover. But you know, our victims aren't just victims—they're human beings. Whatever their problems, whatever their difficulties, a man is dead. Someone who mattered to someone. We're all beloved by someone, you know."

"I'd like to think so," Nick said.

38

AS SOON AS Nick showed the two homicide cops to the elevator, he returned to the boardroom, hoping to catch Todd Muldaur, but the room was empty. Todd and the others had left. He returned to his office area—hell, his *cubicle*—taking an indirect route, past Scott's area.

"Afternoon, Gloria," he said to Scott's admin, a small, hypercompetent woman with a broad face and blond hair cut in bangs. "Scott in?"

"Good afternoon, Mr. Conover. Scott's right—"

"Hey, Nick," Scott said, emerging from behind his panel. "Man, that was a rough ride today, huh?"

"Tell me about it," Nick said blandly. He kept on going, toward Scott's desk, to the round table where Scott held his conferences.

"That put root canals in a whole new perspective," Scott said. He began lifting piles of papers off the round table, moving them to a credenza next to his desk. "So what'd you think of that new guy, Finegold?"

"Seems nice enough," Nick said guardedly, standing at the table, waiting for Scott to finish clearing away the papers.

"That guy's rolling in it, you know. I mean, totally loaded. You know he hired that boy band 'N Sync to play at his daughter's bat mitzvah a couple of years back, when they were still hot?"

"He's a hot spare," Nick said.

"A what?"

"A hot spare. Disk drive fails, you swap it with a spare, all ready to go. Plug-'n'-play. Ready to go."

"Dan? Oh—no, I'm sure they're just trying to strengthen the bench. Is that the right sports term? He's a great guy, actually—tell you a funny story, when he was at—"

"I had to learn about Atlas McKenzie from *Todd*?" Nick broke in. "What the hell's up with that?"

Scott's face colored; he examined the tabletop. "I told you, I got the call from Hardwick on my way over to dinner," he said. "I tried you on your cell, but I guess it was off."

"You didn't leave a message."

"Well, it's—it wasn't the sort of thing you want to leave in a voice mail, you know—"

"And you didn't e-mail me? You didn't call me this morning before the board meeting? You let me find out from *Todd* fucking *Muldaur*?"

Scott's hands flew up, palms out. "I didn't have a chance—"

"And you didn't have a *chance* to tell me they wanted to put you on the board?" Nick said.

Scott stared at the white Formica tabletop as if he'd just seen something alarming there. "I didn't," he began, falteringly.

"*Don't* tell me you didn't know that was going to happen. Why the hell didn't you mention it to me? You couldn't reach me on my cell, that it?"

"It—it wasn't my place, Nick," Scott said. He looked up at last, face gone burgundy, eyes watering. His voice was meek but his expression was fierce.

"Not your place? The fuck are you telling me? You

knew they were going to put you on the board and it
wasn't your place to tell me that? You kept their little
secret, embarrassed me in front of the board?"

"Hey, come on, Nick, calm down," Scott said. "All
right? It was complicated—I mean, maybe I should
have said something, in retrospect, but Todd wanted
me to keep it—Nick, you should take it up with Todd."

Nick got up. "Yeah," he said. "I just might do that."

Don't fuck with me, he thought. Almost said it, but
at the last second something stopped him.

AS HE RETURNED to his desk, Marge stopped him,
holding up an envelope.

"This just came in from HR," she said. "That check
you requested."

"Thanks," he said, taking the envelope as he re-
sumed walking.

"Nick," she said.

He stopped, turned around.

"That check—for Cassie Stadler?"

"Yeah?"

"That's a lot of money. It's for her dad's severance
pay, isn't it? Which he lost when he quit?"

Nick nodded.

"The company isn't obligated to pay that, right?"

"No, it's not."

"But it's the right thing to do. It's—that's nice,
Nick." There were tears in her eyes.

Nick nodded again, returned to his desk. He imme-
diately picked up his handset and called Todd Muld-
aur's cell phone. It rang three times, four, and just as
Nick was about to hang up, Todd's voice came on.
"This is Todd."

It sounded like a prerecorded voice-mail message,
so Nick waited a second before saying, "Todd, it's Nick
Conover."

"Oh, hey, Nick, there you are. You bolted before I had a chance to say goodbye, dude."

"Todd, are you trying to squeeze me out?"

A beat. "What makes you say that?"

"Come on, man. What happened in there, in the board meeting. Bring in Finegold, your hot spare, putting Scott on the board without giving me a heads-up. The monthly board meetings, the weekly financials. Changing the rules of the game like that. Taking away my ability to change my team the way I see fit. What, you think I'm an idiot?"

"Nick, we don't need to squeeze you out," Todd said, his voice gone steely. "If we wanted you gone, you'd be gone."

"Not without a pretty damned huge payday."

"A rounding error at Fairfield Partners, buddy."

"Five million bucks is a rounding error to you guys?"

"Nick, I meant what I said. We want to bring more to the table. Strengthen the team."

"You don't trust me to run the company, you should just come out with it."

Todd said something, but the signal started to break up ". . . the way," he was saying.

"Say again?" Nick said. "I lost you there."

"I said, we trust you, Nick. We just don't want you getting in the way."

"In the *way*?"

"We need to make sure you're responsive, Nick. That's all. We want to make sure you're on board."

"Oh, *I'm* on board," Nick said, deliberately ambiguous, insinuating. He didn't know what that was supposed to mean, exactly, except that he hoped it sounded vaguely threatening.

"Excellent," Todd said. His voice got all crackly again as the signal weakened. A fragment: ". . . to hear."

"Say again?" Nick said.

"Man, do you guys have, like, one cell tower out here in cow town? I swear, the reception *sucks*. All right, I better go. I'm losing you." Then the line went dead.

For a long time, Nick stared at the long blue Stratton check he'd had the treasurer's office cut for Cassie Stadler: a payoff, pure and simple. Andrew Stadler had quit before being laid off; legally, he wasn't entitled to any severance. But what was legal, and what the courts might decide—if Cassie Stadler decided to press the issue—were two separate things. Better to pre-empt, he'd decided. Be generous. Show her that her father's employer meant well, that Stratton was willing to go above and beyond what it was required to do.

That was all there was to it, he told himself.

Keep the woman happy. No one wanted a lawsuit.

And he remembered what that black woman detective had said as she left. "We're all beloved by someone," she'd said. She had a point. As crazy, as deranged as Andrew Stadler was, he'd been loved by his daughter.

He hit the intercom button. "Marge," he said. "I need you to call Cassie Stadler for me."

"I believe she's living in her father's house," came Marge's voice over the speakerphone.

"Right. Tell her I want to stop by. I have something for her."

39

SERGEANT JACK NOYCE pulled Audrey into his glass-walled office, which was not much bigger than Audrey's cubicle. He had it outfitted with an expensive-looking sound system, though, a top-of-the-line DVD player and speakers. Noyce loved his audio equipment, and he loved music. Sometimes Audrey would see him with his headphones on, enjoying music, or listening to the speakers with the office door closed.

As head of the Major Case Team, he had all sorts of administrative responsibilities and more than a dozen cops to supervise, and he spent much of his day in meetings. Music—Keith Jarrett, Bill Evans, Art Tatum, Charlie Mingus, Thelonious Monk, all the jazz piano greats—seemed to be his only escape.

A piece was playing quietly on Noyce's stereo, a beautiful and soulful rendition of the ballad "You Go to My Head," a pianist doing the melody.

"Tommy Flanagan?" Audrey said.

Noyce nodded. "You close your eyes, and you're back in the Village Vanguard."

"It's lovely."

"Audrey, you haven't said anything about Bugbee."

His sad eyes, behind thick aviator-framed glasses, shone with concern.

"It's okay," she said.

"You'd tell me if it wasn't, right?"

She laughed. "Only if I couldn't take it anymore."

"The practical jokes seem to have stopped."

"Maybe he got tired of them."

"Or maybe he's learned to respect you."

"You give him way too much credit," she said with a laugh.

"And you're the one who's supposed to believe in the possibility of redemption. Listen, Audrey—you guys went over to Stratton?"

"Now don't tell me he's filling you in on every step we take."

"No. I got a call from the security director at Stratton."

"Rinaldi."

"Right. You talked to him, and then you both went over to talk to Nicholas Conover."

"What'd he call you for?"

"He says you just showed up and waited for Conover outside a board meeting? That true?"

She felt a prickle of defensiveness. "That was my decision. I wanted to avoid any prepared answers, any coordination."

"I'm not following." Noyce took off his glasses and began rubbing at them with a little cleaning cloth.

"I'd already talked to Rinaldi, and something didn't sit right with me. I can't explain it."

"You don't need to. Gut instinct."

"Right."

"Which ninety percent of the time doesn't pan out. But hey." He smiled. "You take what you get."

"I didn't want Rinaldi talking to his boss and getting his story straight."

"So you just ambushed the CEO outside the board-room?" Noyce laughed quietly.

"I just thought if we set up a meeting with him in advance, he'd call his security director and say, What's this about?"

"Still not following. You telling me you think the CEO of Stratton's got something to do with this case?"

She shook her head. "No, of course not. But there may be some connection. A couple of days before Stadler's death, there was an incident at Nicholas Conover's house. Someone slaughtered the family dog and dumped it in the swimming pool."

Noyce winced. "My God. Was it Stadler?"

"We don't know. But this was just the latest of a long series of incidents at the Conover house since they moved in, about a year ago. Up till now it's been graf-fiti, nothing stolen, no violence. But each time, our uni-formed division was notified—and we haven't done a thing. They didn't even print the knife that was used to kill the dog. From what I hear, there wasn't a lot of mo-tivation to do anything about it, given the way people feel about Conover."

"Well, yeah, but that's not right."

"So just before Stadler's death, Rinaldi got in touch with our uniformed division to ask about this guy An-drew Stadler and find out if he had any priors."

"And were there any?"

"A long time ago Stadler was questioned in connec-tion to the death of a neighbor family, but nothing ever came of it."

"What got Rinaldi interested in Andrew Stadler?"

"Rinaldi said he went through the list of people they laid off—and it's a long list, like five thousand people—to see who might have exhibited signs of vio-lence."

"Stadler did?"

"Rinaldi was evasive on that point. When I interviewed Stadler's supervisor, at the model shop where he worked, the guy said Stadler wasn't violent at all. Though he did quit in anger, which meant he lost the severance package. But Rinaldi said he found that Stadler had a history of mental illness."

"So he suspected Stadler of being Conover's stalker."

"He denies it, but that's the feeling I got."

"So you think Conover or Rinaldi had something to do with Stadler's murder?"

"I don't know. But I do wonder about this Rinaldi fellow."

"Oh, I know about Rinaldi."

"He said you're friends, you two."

Noyce chuckled. "Did he, now."

"He didn't exactly play by the rules on the GRPD. He was squeezed out on suspicions of holding on to cash in a drug bust."

"How do you know that?" Noyce was suddenly intrigued.

"I called Grand Rapids, asked around until I found someone who knew him."

Noyce frowned, shook his head. "I'd rather you didn't call GR."

"Why not?"

"People talk. Rumors spread like wildfire. Things could get back to Rinaldi, and I don't want him knowing that we've been asking around about him. That way we're more likely to catch him in a lie."

"Okay, makes sense."

"You saying you like Rinaldi for the Stadler homicide?"

"That's not what I'm saying. Edward Rinaldi's an ex-cop, and a guy like that may know people, you know?"

"Who might have done a hit on some loony ex-employee?" Noyce replaced his glasses, raised one brow.

"Far-fetched, right?"

"Just a little."

"But no more unlikely than a crack-related murder involving a guy who doesn't fit the profile of a crack-head, had no crack in his bloodstream, and had fake crack in his pocket. A setup, in other words."

"You make a good point."

"Also, no fingerprints anywhere on the plastic wrapped over the body. Traces of talc indicating that surgical gloves were used to move the body. It's all very strange. I'd like to get Rinaldi's phone records."

Noyce gave a long sigh. "Man, you're opening a can of worms with Stratton."

"What about Rinaldi's personal phone records—home, cell, whatever?"

"Easier."

"Could you sign off on that?"

Noyce bit his lip. "Sure. I'll do it. You got an instinct, I like to go with it. But Audrey, listen. The Stratton Corporation has a lot of enemies in this town."

"Tell me about it."

"That's why I want to be fair. I don't want it to look like we're going after them arbitrarily, trying to embarrass them. Bowing to public pressure, pandering. Nothing like that. I want us to play fair, but just as important, I want the *appearance* of fairness, okay?"

"Of course."

"Just so long as we're on the same page here."

40

CASSIE STADLER'S HOUSE was on West Sixteenth Street, in the part of Fenwick still known as Steepletown because of all the churches that used to be there. It was an area Nick knew well; he'd grown up here, in a tiny brown split-level with a little scrubby lawn, a chain-link fence keeping out the neighbors. When Nick was a kid, Steepletown was blue-collar, most of the men factory workers employed at Stratton. Mostly Polish Catholic, too, though the Conovers were neither Polish nor members of Sacred Heart. This was a place where people kept their money in mattresses.

He was overcome by a strange, wistful nostalgia driving through these streets. It all looked and smelled so familiar, the American Legion hall, the bowling alley, the pool hall. The triple-deckers, the aluminum siding, Corky's Bottled Liquors. Even the cars were still big and American. Unlike the rest of Fenwick, which had gone upscale and fancy, vegan and latte, with all the galleries and the SUVs and the BMWs, something uncomfortable and ill fitting about it, like a little girl playing dress-up in her mother's high heels. Just before he parked the car at the curb in front of the house, a song came on the radio: Billy Joel's "She's

Always a Woman." One of Laura's favorites. She'd
taught herself to play it on the piano, not badly at all.
She'd sing it in the shower—*"Oh, she takes care of
herself . . ."*—badly, off-key, in a thin, wobbly voice.
Hearing it caused a lump to rise in Nick's throat. He
switched the radio off, couldn't take it, and had to sit
there in the car for a few minutes before he got out.

He rang the doorbell: six melodious tones sounding
like a carillon. The door opened, a small figure emerg-
ing from the gloom behind the dusty screen door.

What the hell am I doing? he thought. Jesus, this is
insane. The daughter of the man I killed.

Everyone is beloved by someone, the cop had said.
This is that someone.

"Mr. Conover," she said. She wore a black T-shirt
and worn jeans. She was slim, even tinier than he re-
membered from the funeral, and her expression was
hard, wary.

"May I come in for a second?"

Her eyes were red-rimmed, raccoon smudges be-
neath. "Why?"

"I have something for you."

She stared some more, then shrugged. "Okay." The
bare minimum of politeness, nothing more. She pushed
open the screen door.

Nick entered a small, dark foyer that smelled of mil-
dew and damp carpeting. Mail lay in heaps on a trestle
table. There were a few homey touches—a painting
in an ornate gold frame, a bad seascape, looked like a
reproduction. A vase of dried flowers. A lamp with a
fringed shade. A sampler in a severe black frame, done
in needlepoint or whatever, that said LET ME LIVE IN
THE HOUSE BY THE SIDE OF THE ROAD AND BE A FRIEND
TO MAN, over a stitched image of a house that looked
a good deal nicer than the one it hung in. It seemed as
if nothing had been moved, or dusted, in a decade. He

caught a glimpse of a small kitchen, a big old white round-shouldered refrigerator.

She backed up a few steps, standing in a cone of light from a torchere. "What's this all about?"

Nick produced the envelope from his jacket pocket and handed it to her. She took it, gave a puzzled look, examined the envelope as if she'd never seen one before. Then she slid out the pale blue check. When she saw the amount, she betrayed no surprise, no reaction at all. "I don't get it."

"The least we can do," Nick said.

"What's it for?"

"The severance pay your father should have gotten."

Realization dawned in her eyes. "My dad quit."

"He was a troubled man."

She flashed a smile, bright white teeth, that in another context would have been sexy. Now it seemed just unsettling. "This is so interesting," she said. Her voice was velvety smooth, pleasingly deep. There was something about her mouth, the way it curled up at the ends even when she wasn't smiling, giving her a kind of knowing look.

"Hmm?"

"This," she said.

"The check? I don't understand."

"No. You. What you're doing here."

"Oh?"

"It's like you're making a payoff."

"A payoff? No. Your father should have been counseled better at his outplacement interview. We shouldn't have let him walk out without the same severance package everyone else got, whether he quit or not. He was angry, and rightly so. But he was a longtime employee who deserved better than that."

"It's a hell of a lot of money."

"He worked for Stratton for thirty-six years. It's

what he was entitled to. Maybe not legally, but morally."

"It's guilt money. *Schuldgeld,* in German, right?" Those corners of her mouth turned all the way up in a canny smile. Closer to a smirk, maybe. "The word guilt has the same root as the German word for money, *Geld.*"

"I wouldn't know." He felt his insides clutch tight. "I just didn't think you should be left high and dry."

"God, I don't know how you can stand doing what you do."

She has the right to go after me, Nick thought. *Let her. Let her rant, do her whole anti-corporate thing. Trash Stratton, and me. Make her feel better. Maybe that's why you're here: masochism.*

"Ah, right," he said. "'Slasher Nick' and all that."

"I mean, it can't be easy. Being hated by just about everyone in town."

"Part of my job," he said.

"Must be nice to have one."

"Sometimes yes, sometimes no."

"Life must have been a lot easier a couple of years ago when everyone loved you, I bet. You must have felt you were really in the groove, hitting on all cylinders. Then all of a sudden you're the bad guy."

"It's not a popularity contest." *The hell was this?*

A mysterious smile. "A man like you wants to be liked. *Needs* to be liked."

"I should be going."

"I'm making you uncomfortable," she said. "You're not the introspective type." A beat. "Why are you really here? Don't trust the messenger service?"

Nick shook his head vaguely. "I'm not sure. Maybe I feel really bad for you. I lost my wife last year. I know how hard this can be."

When she looked up at him, there seemed to be a kind of pain in the depths of her hazel eyes. "Kids?"

"Two. Girl and a boy."

"How old?"

"Julia's ten. Lucas is sixteen."

"God, to lose your mother at that age. I guess there's always enough pain to go around at the banquet of life. Plenty of seconds, right?" She sounded as if the wind had suddenly gone out of her.

"I've got to get back. I'm sorry if it bothered you, me coming by like this."

Suddenly she sank to the floor, collapsing into a seated position on the wall-to-wall carpet, canting to one side. Her legs folded up under her. She supported herself with one arm. "Jesus," she said.

"You okay?" Nick came up to her, leaned over.

Her other hand was against her forehead. Her eyes were closed. Her translucent skin was ashen.

"Jesus, I'm sorry. All the blood just left my head, and I . . ."

"What can I get you?"

She shook her head. "I just need to sit down. Light-headed."

"Glass of water or something?" He kneeled beside her. She looked like she was on the verge of toppling over, passing out. "Food, maybe?"

She shook her head again. "I'm fine."

"I don't think so. Stay there, I'll get you something."

"I'm not going anywhere," she said, her eyes unfo-cused. "Forget it, don't worry about it. I'm fine."

Nick got up, went into the kitchen. Dirty dishes were piled up in the sink and on the counter next to it, a bunch of Chinese takeout cartons. He looked around, found the electric stove, a kettle sitting on one burner. He picked it up, felt it was empty. He filled it in the sink, shoving aside some of the stacked plates to make room for the kettle. It took him a couple of seconds to figure out which knob on the stove turned on which burner. The burner took a long time to go from black to orange.

"You like Szechuan Garden?" he called out.

Silence.

"You okay?" he said.

"It's pretty gross, actually," she said after another pause, voice weak. "There's like two, maybe three Chinese restaurants in this whole town, one worse than the next." Another pause. "There's more than that on my *block* in Chicago."

"Looks like you get a lot of takeout from there anyway."

"I can walk to it. I haven't felt much like cooking, since . . ."

She was standing at the threshold to the kitchen, entered slowly and unsteadily. She sank down in one of the kitchen chairs, chrome with a red vinyl seat back, the table red Formica with a cracked ice pattern and chrome banding around the edge.

The teakettle was making a hollow roaring sound. Nick opened the refrigerator—"Frigidaire" on the front in that great old squat script, raised metal lettering, reminding Nick of the refrigerator in his childhood home—and found it pretty much empty. A quart of skim milk, an opened bottle of Australian chardonnay with a cork in it; a carton of eggs, half gone.

He found a rind of Parmesan cheese, a salvageable bunch of scallions.

"You got a grater?"

"You serious?"

41

HE SET THE omelet on the table before her, a fork and a paper napkin, a mug for tea. The mug, he noticed too late, had the old 1970s Stratton logo on one side.

She dug into it, eating ravenously.

"When's the last time you ate today?" Nick asked.

"Right now," she said. "I forgot to eat."

"Forgot?"

"I've had other things on my mind. Hey, this isn't bad."

"Thank you."

"I wouldn't have figured you for a chef."

"That's about the extent of my cooking ability."

"I feel way better already. Thank you. I thought I was going to pass out."

"You're welcome. I saw some salami in there, but I thought you might be a vegan or something."

"Vegans don't eat eggs," she said. "Yum. God, you know, there's some kinds of ribbon worms that actually eat themselves if they don't find any food."

"Glad I got here in time."

"The head of Stratton makes a mean omelet. Wait till the newspapers get hold of that."

"So how did you end up in Chicago?"

"Long story. I grew up here. But my mom grew tired of my dad's craziness, when I was like nine or ten. That was before he was diagnosed as schizophrenic. She moved to the Windy City and left me here with Dad. A couple of years later, I went to live with her and her new husband. Hey, this is my house, and I'm not being much of a hostess."

She got up, went over to one of the lower cabinets, opened the door. It held a collection of dusty bottles, vermouth and Baileys Irish Cream and such. "Let me guess—you're a Scotch kinda guy."

"I've got to get home to the kids."

"Oh," she said. "Right. Sure." Something waiflike and needy in her face got to him. He'd told Marta an hour or so; another hour wouldn't be a big deal.

"But maybe a little Scotch would be okay."

She seemed to light up, leaned over and pulled out a bottle of Jameson. "Irish, not Scotch—okay?"

"Fine with me."

She pulled out a cut-glass tumbler from the same cabinet. "Whoo boy," she said, blowing a cloud of dust out of it. She held it under the running tap in the sink. "I'm going to say rocks."

"Hmm?"

"Ice cubes. You drink your whiskey on the rocks." She went to the antique Frigidaire, opened the freezer, took out the kind of ice tray Nick hadn't seen in decades, aluminum with the lever you pull up to break the ice into cubes. She yanked back the handle, making a scrunching sound that sounded like his childhood. Reminded him of his dad, who liked his Scotch on the rocks, every night and too much of it.

She plopped a handful of jagged cubes into the glass, glugged in a few inches of whiskey, came over and handed it to him. She looked directly into his eyes, the first time she'd done that. Her eyes were big and gray-green and lucid, and Nick felt a tug in his groin. He immediately felt a flush of shame. *Jesus,* he thought.

"Thanks," he said. The glass had FAMOUS GROUSE etched into it. It was the kind of thing you get at a liquor store packed with the bottle, a promotional deal.

"How about you?"

"I hate whiskey," she said. The kettle began whistling shrilly. She pulled it off the burner, found a carton of teabags in a drawer, and poured herself a mug of herbal tea.

"How does it feel being home?" The whiskey had a pleasant bite to it, and he felt its effect immediately. He didn't recall when he'd last eaten anything himself, actually.

"Strange," she said, sitting down at the table. "Brings a lot of things back. Some good things, some not good things." She looked at him. "I don't expect you to understand."

"Try me."

"Do you know what it's like to have a parent with severe mental illness? The whole point is, you're a child, so you don't grasp what's going on."

"Right. How could you?"

Cassie closed her eyes, and it was as if she were in some other place. "So you're his beloved daughter, and he hugs you like nobody can hug you and he puts his forehead to yours and you feel so safe, and so loved, and everything's right with the world. And then, one day, he's different—except, as far as he's concerned, *you're* different."

"Because of the disease."

"He looks at you and you're a stranger to him. You're not his beloved daughter now. Maybe you resemble her, but he's not fooled, he knows you've been replaced by someone or something else. He looks at you and he sees

a Fembot, you know? And you say, 'Daddy!' You're three
or four or five and you throw your arms open, waiting
for your super-special hug. And he says, 'Who are you?
Who are you *really*?' and he says, 'Get away! Get away!
Get away!'" Her mimicry was uncanny; Nick was be-
ginning to glimpse the nightmare she had endured.
"You realize that he's *terrified* of you. And it's differ-
ent from anything you've ever experienced. Because it
isn't what happens when, you know, you misbehave,
and Mommy or Daddy turns red and you get yelled at.
Every kid knows what that's like. They're mad. But you
know they still love you, and they're still aware of your
existence. They don't think you're an alien. They're
not frightened of you. It's different when a parent has
schizophrenia. It steals over them, and suddenly you
don't exist to them any longer. You're not a daugh-
ter anymore. Just some impostor. Just some intruder.
Some . . . outsider. Someone who doesn't belong." She
smiled sadly.

"He was ill."

"He was ill," Cassie repeated. "But a child doesn't
understand that. A child *can't* understand it. Even if
anybody had explained to me, I probably wouldn't
have understood." She sniffed, her eyes flooded with
tears. She frowned, turned away, wiped her eyes with
her T-shirt, exposing her flat belly, a tiny pouting navel.
Nick tried not to look.

"Nobody ever told you what was going on?"

"When I was maybe thirteen, I finally figured it
out. My mother didn't want to deal, and her way of not
dealing meant you didn't talk about it. Which is pretty
crazy, too, when you think about it."

"I can't imagine what you had to go through." And
he couldn't—not what she'd had to go through, nor
what her father's death was causing her to relive. He
ached to do something for her.

"No, you can't imagine. But it messes with your head. I mean, it messed with mine."

She tucked her chin in close to her chest, ran her fingers through her spiky hair, and when she looked up, her cheeks were wet. "You don't need this," she said, her voice thick with tears. "I think you should go."

"Cassie," he said. It came out in a whisper, sounded far more intimate than he'd intended.

For a while, her breaths came in short little puffs. When she spoke again, her voice was strained. "You need to be there for your kids," she said. "There's nothing more important than family, okay?"

"Not much of a family these days."

"Don't say that," Cassie said. She looked up at him, eyes fierce. "You don't *fucking* talk that way, *ever*." Something had flared up inside her, like a whole book of matches, and then subsided almost as quickly. But who could blame the woman, having so recently put her father in the ground? And then he remembered why.

"Sorry," he said. "It hasn't been easy for the kids, and I'm not exactly doing my job."

"How'd she die?" Her voice was soft. "Their mother."

He took another sip. A quick scene played in his head, jittery, badly spliced film. The pebbles of glass strewn throughout Laura's hair. The spiderwebbed windshield. "I don't like to talk about it."

"Oh, I'm sorry."

"Don't apologize. Natural question."

"No, you're—crying."

He realized that he was, and as he turned his face, embarrassed, cursing the booze, she got up from her chair, came up to him. She put a small warm hand on his face, leaned close to him, and put her lips on his.

Startled, he backed away, but she moved in closer, pressed her lips against his, harder, her other hand pressed against his chest.

He turned his head away. "Cassie, I've got to get home."

Cassie smiled uncomfortably. "Go," she said. "Your kids are waiting."

"It's the babysitter, actually. She hates it when I come home later than I promised."

"Your daughter—what's her name, again?"

"Julia."

"Julia. Sweet name. Go home to Julia and Luke. They need you. Go back to your gated community."

"How'd you know?"

"People talk. It's perfect."

"What?"

"You living in a gated community."

"I'm not really the gated-community type."

"Oh, I think you are," she said. "More than you know."

42

LATONYA'S TWELVE-YEAR-OLD DAUGHTER, Camille, was practicing piano in the next room, which made it hard for Audrey to concentrate on what her sister-in-law was saying. LaTonya was speaking in a low voice, uncharacteristically for her, while she removed a sweet-potato casserole from the oven.

"Let me tell you," LaTonya said, "if Paul didn't have a steady income, I don't know how we'd get by with three kids still in the house."

Audrey, who'd noticed the kitchen piled high with cartons of thermogenic fat-burning supplements, said, "But what about the vitamins?"

"Shit!" LaTonya shouted, dropping the casserole to the open oven door. "These damned oven mitts have a hole in them—what the hell good are they?"

Thomas, who was nine, ran in from the dining room where he and Matthew, eleven, were allegedly setting the table, though mostly just clattering the dishes and giggling. "You okay, Mom?"

"I'm fine," LaTonya said, picking up the casserole again and putting it on the stovetop. "You get back out there and finish setting the table, and you tell Matthew to go tell your father and Uncle Leon to get off their lazy butts and come in to dinner." She turned to Audrey, a disgusted look on her face. "Once again, I'm ahead of the curve."

"How so?"

"These thermogenic supplements. Fenwick is a backward, fearful community," she said gravely. "They do *not* want to try new things."

"And now you're stuck with all these bottles."

"If they think I'm paying for them, they've got another think coming. I'm going to ask you to read the small print on my agreement, because I don't think they can get away with it."

"Sure," Audrey said without enthusiasm. The last thing she wanted to do was get involved in extricating LaTonya from another mess she'd created. "You know, the money isn't the worst part," Audrey said. "I mean, it's not easy, but we can get by."

"Not having kids," LaTonya pointed out.

"Right. It's dealing with Leon."

"What the *hell* does he do all day?" LaTonya demanded, one hand on her left hip, waggling the other hand to cool it off.

"He watches a lot of TV and he drinks," Audrey said.

"You see, I knew this would happen. We spoiled him growing up. The baby of the family. Anything he wanted, he got. My momma and me, we waited on him hand and foot, and now you're paying the price. You hear what I hear?"

"I don't hear anything."

"Exactly." She shouted, earsplittingly loud, "Camille, you've got twenty more minutes of practicing, so don't stop now!"

An anguished, garbled protest came from the next room.

"And you don't get any supper until you're done, so

move it!" She glowered at Audrey. "Honestly, I don't know what's wrong with her ownself. She pays me no mind at all."

DINNER WAS MEAT loaf, macaroni and cheese, collards, and sweet-potato casserole, everything heavy and greasy but delicious. Leon sat next to his sister at one end of the table, LaTonya's husband at the other, the two squirming boys on one side facing Audrey and Camille's empty place.

The sound of the piano came from the living room, sporadic, sullen. Brahms, Audrey recognized. A pretty piece. A waltz, maybe? Her niece was struggling with it.

Thomas squawked with laughter over something, and Matthew said, "Fuck you!"

LaTonya exploded: "Don't you *ever* use language like that in this house, you hear me?"

The two boys fell instantly silent. Matthew, looking like a whipped puppy, said, "Yes, ma'am."

"That's right," LaTonya said.

Audrey caught the younger boy's eye and gave him a mildly disapproving look that was still, she hoped, filled with aunty love.

Leon was stuffing his face meanwhile. He said, "I wish I could eat supper here every night, LaTonya."

She beamed, then caught herself. "Is there any reason you can't get yourself a job?"

"Doing what?" Leon said, dropping his fork dramatically. "Operating an electrostatic spray gun at the Seven-Eleven, maybe?"

"Doing something," LaTonya said.

"Doing something?" Leon said. "Like what? Like what do you think a guy with my skills can do here?"

"Your skills," LaTonya scoffed.

"How do you think it feels getting laid off?" Leon

said, his voice rising. "Do you have any idea? How do you think I feel about myself?"

"I'll tell you how I feel about you sitting around doing absolutely nothing," LaTonya said. She cocked her head. "Camille," she shouted, "what are you doing?"

Another muffled cry.

"We're all eating in here," LaTonya yelled. "We're likely to finish dinner without you, rate you're practicing."

Camille screamed back, "I can't stand it!"

"You can yell all you want," LaTonya bellowed. "Won't make any difference. You're not getting over on me."

"Let me talk to her," Audrey said. She excused herself from the table, went into the next room.

Camille was weeping at the piano, her head resting on her elbows atop the keys. Audrey sat down at the bench next to her. She stroked her niece's hair, lingering on the kitchen, that kinky hair at the nape of her neck. "What is it, honey?"

"I can't stand it," Camille said. She sat up. Her face was streaked with tears. She looked genuinely upset; it was no act. "I don't understand this. This is torture."

Audrey looked at the sheet music. Brahms's Waltz in A Minor. "What don't you get, baby?"

Camille touched the music with a pudgy, tear-damp finger, making a tiny pucker.

"The trill, is that it?"

"I guess."

Audrey nudged Camille over a bit and played a few measures. "Like that?"

"Yeah, but I can't do that."

"Try this." Audrey played the trill slowly. "Down an octave."

Camille placed her fingers on the keyboard and tried.

"Like this," Audrey said, playing again.

Camille imitated her. Close enough. "That's it, baby. You got it. Try it again."

Camille played it, got it right.

"Now go back a couple of measures. To here. Let me hear it."

Camille played the first two lines of the second page.

"Boy, are you a fast learner," Audrey marveled. "You don't even need me anymore."

Camille smiled faintly.

"When's your recital?"

"Next week."

"What are you doing besides this?"

"Little Prelude."

"Beethoven?"

Camille nodded.

"Can I come?"

Camille smiled again, this time a happy grin. "You think you have time?"

"I'll make time, baby. I'd love to. Now, hurry up and finish. I'm getting lonely at the table without you."

PAUL LOOKED UP as Audrey entered the dining room. He was a pigeon-chested man with sunken cheeks, a recessive gene but a sweet-natured guy. Camille was back at the Brahms, strong and enthusiastic. "I don't know what you threatened her with, but sounds like it worked," he said.

"She probably pulled out her handcuffs," said LaTonya.

"Probably her gun," Leon mumbled. He seemed to have calmed down in the meantime, retreated back into his old, monosyllabic self.

"No," Audrey said, sitting down. "She just needed a little help figuring something out."

"I want an ice cream sundae for dessert," the younger boy said.

"I'll be the judge of that," said LaTonya. "Right now it's looking awful grim for you."

"How come?"

"You got more than half your meat loaf left. Now Audrey, what are you working on these days?"

"It's not dinner-table conversation," Audrey said.

"I don't mean the gory details."

"I'm afraid it's all gory details," Audrey said.

"She's working on that murder of the Stratton worker got murdered down on Hastings," Leon said.

Audrey was amazed he even knew what she was working on. "People aren't supposed to know what I'm doing," she told him.

"We're all family here," said LaTonya.

"Right, but still," said Audrey.

"No one's going to say anything, my saditty sister," LaTonya said. "You think we know anybody? This guy fell off the edge, that right? Get into crack and other poisons like that?" She cast an evil eye at her two sons.

"I met the guy," Leon said.

"Who?" said Audrey. "Andrew Stadler?"

Leon nodded. "Sure. He kept to himself, but I talked to him in the break room once or twice." Leon reached for the macaroni and cheese and shoveled a huge lump onto his plate, a third helping. "Couldn't meet a nicer guy."

"A troubled man," Audrey said.

"Troubled?" said Leon. "I don't know. Gentle as a lamb, I'll tell you that."

"Really?" said Audrey.

"Gentle as a lamb," Leon said again.

"I'm done," Camille announced, entering the room and sitting down next to Audrey. She found Audrey's hand under the table and gave it a little secret squeeze. Audrey's heart fluttered for a moment.

"Took you long enough," said LaTonya. "I hope you learned your lesson."

"You sounded great," Audrey said.

43

NICK GOT IN a little earlier than usual, got a cup of coffee from the executive lounge, and checked his e-mail. As usual, his inbox was cluttered with offers for Viagra and penis enlargement and low-interest mortgages, the subject headings inventively misspelled. The putative wives and sons of various deceased African heads of state urgently sought his assistance in transferring millions of dollars out of their country.

He thought about this woman, Cassie Stadler. She was not only seriously attractive, but she was unlike any woman he'd ever met before. And she—who, of course, had no idea what he'd done—was clearly as attracted to him as he was to her.

No message from the Atlas McKenzie guys—the mammoth deal that had unaccountably fallen through—but that didn't surprise him. He was going to have to confront them on it, find out what the reason was, see if there was a way to sweet-talk them back on board.

Marjorie wasn't in yet, so Nick placed the calls himself. It was 7:10 A.M. The Atlas McKenzie guys were usually in by then. Ten digits away. Not a lot of work to press those ten digits on the telephone keypad. How many calories did this take? Nick imagined a tiny scrap of the twiggy cereal Julia wouldn't eat: *that* many calories. Why wouldn't he place his own calls?

The woman on the other line was really sorry. Mr. Hardwick was still in conference. Nick imagined Hardwick making throat-cut, I'm-not-in gestures.

There it was. *That* was a reason not to place your own calls. To spare yourself the humiliation of dissembling secretaries. The smile in the voice that accompanied the singsongy formula *I'm sorry.* The micro–power trip of putting one over on a CEO. Fun for the whole family. He wondered whether the waitress at Terra really had spit in his arugula salad. She'd brightened a little when she brought it out, hadn't she?

Nick felt a little acid come up his gullet as he stared at the silver-mesh fabric panels in front of him. There were certain things that money and position protected you from. There were certain things that it didn't. When his driver's license needed renewing a couple of years ago, he didn't stand in line at the DMV, the way he once had to. The CEO of a major corporation didn't wait in line at the DMV. Some young staffer from the corporate counsel's office did, and it got taken care of. Nick couldn't remember the last time he'd waited in line for a taxi at an airport. Senior execs had cars; you looked for the guy holding a sign that said CONOVER. And senior execs of major corporations didn't haul their own baggage. That got taken care of, too, even when Nick was flying commercial. But when the weather was bad, it was bad for you too. When your car was stuck in traffic, it didn't matter what your company's valuation was; traffic was traffic. Those things were the Levelers. The things that reminded you that you lived in the same world and were going to end up in the same place as everybody else. You thought you were a master of the universe, but you were just lording it over a little box of dirt, the tyrant of a terrarium.

Having a kid who hated you—that had to be a Leveler too. And so was sickness.

And so was death.

Next he tried MacFarland—that was the name of the Nixon look-alike. But his assistant apologized: Mr. MacFarland was traveling. "I'll be sure to let him know that you called," MacFarland's assistant told him, with the bright artificiality of someone from a casting director's office. Don't call us, we'll call you.

Twenty minutes later came the faint settling-in noises, the heavy vanilla smell of Shalimar: Marjorie was in.

Nick got up, stretched, stepped around the partition. "How's the novel coming?" He tried to remember the title. "*Manchester Abbey,* was it?"

She smiled. "We did *Northanger Abbey* a few weeks ago. This week is *Mansfield Park.*"

"Got it," Nick said.

"I think Jane Austen wrote *Northanger Abbey* first, but it didn't come out until after her death," Marjorie said, turning on her computer. She said distantly, "Amazing what comes out after people die."

Nick felt as if someone had touched his neck with an ice cube. His smile faded.

"*Persuasion* did too," she went on. "And *Billy Budd,* which we read last year. I didn't know you had such an interest, Nick. You ought to come to our book club."

"Let me know when you decide to do the Chevrolet Suburban Owner's Manual—that's what *I* call a book," he said. "Listen, I'm expecting a call from those Atlas McKenzie guys. Hardwick, MacFarland. Let me know when they're on the line. Wherever I am, I'll take the call."

Nick spent the next couple of hours in conference rooms, two back-to-back, bun-numbing meetings. There was the supply-chain-management team, whose seven members had reached an important conclusion: Stratton needed to diversify its suppliers of metallic paint. They were bubbling with excitement as they reviewed the considerations they had taken into account, like they'd discovered penicillin. Then there was the industrial-safety team, which always had more lawyers than engineers, more concerned about lawsuits than limbs. Nobody came to spring him. No message from Marjorie.

He gave Marjorie a questioning look as he made his way back to his desk.

"The Atlas McKenzie people—they were supposed to get back this morning?" she asked.

Nick sighed. "I'm beginning to feel like I'm getting the bum's rush. I phoned first thing today, you know, and they said Hardwick's in conference, MacFarland's on the road, they'll get back to me." Then again, they were supposed to return his call from yesterday too. Apparently they had other priorities.

"You think they're trying to dodge you."

"Could be."

"Want to get them on line?" Marjorie looked sunny but sly. It was a good look.

"Yup."

"Let me have a go."

Nick took a few more steps toward his desk as Marjorie made a couple of phone calls. He couldn't hear everything. "That's right," she was saying. "United Airlines. We've located the lost baggage, and he gave us a cell number to call him at. James MacFarland, yes. He seemed frantic. But the clerk must have written it down wrong . . ."

A minute later, an intercom tone told Nick to pick up his Line 1.

"Jim MacFarland?" Nick said as he answered the phone.

Cautiously: "Yes?"

"Nick Conover here."

"Nick. Hey." Friendly, but with a tremor of unease.

Nick wanted to say, *Do you realize the amount of money and man-hours we've spent designing your goddamn prototypes? And you can't be bothered to return my calls?* Instead he tried to sound breezy. "Just wanted to touch base," he said. "About where things stood."

"Yeah," MacFarland said. "Yeah. I meant to give you a call about that. About the current thinking."

"Lay it on me."

A deep breath. "Thing is, Nick—well, we hadn't realized that Stratton's on the block. Which kind of changes the picture for us."

"On the block? Meaning what?" Nick struggled to keep his voice calm. At the start of his career, Nick figured that being the boss meant not having to kiss ass. A nice thought, anyway. Turned out there was always somebody whose ass you had to kiss. The commander in chief of the free world had to suck up to farmers in Iowa. *It's good to be the boss*—wasn't that what they said? But every boss had a boss. Turtles all the way down. Asses all the way up.

That was how it felt sometimes, anyway. That was how it felt just now.

"It's just that Hardwick's always real concerned about stability when it comes to sourcing and support," MacFarland was saying. "We hadn't realized things were in flux that way. It's not like you had a big 'For Sale' sign over the front door, right?"

Nick was dumbfounded. "Stratton's not for sale," he said simply.

There was a moment of silence on the other end. "Huh." Not the sound of agreement. "Look, Nick, you didn't hear this from me. We use the same law firm in Hong Kong that Fairfield Partners does. And, you know, people talk."

"That's *bullshit*," Nick said.

"What it is, is water under the bridge."

"Come on. I'm the CEO of the company. If Stratton was being sold, you'd think I'd know, right?"

"You said it." The chilling thing was that MacFarland sounded kindly, sympathetic, like an oncologist breaking the news of a bad diagnosis to a favorite patient.

44

MARJORIE POKED HER head around at ten thirty.

"Remember, you've got a lunch at half past with Roderick Douglass, the Chamber of Commerce guy," she said. "He'll be wanting to hit you up again. Then there's the meeting with the business development execs right after."

Nick swiveled around and looked out the window. "Right, thanks," he said, distracted.

It was a beautiful day. The sky was blue, deepened a little by the tint of the glass. There was enough of a breeze to flutter the leaves of the trees. A jet was making its way across the sky, its double contrails quickly turning into smudgy fluff.

It was also the seventh day in a row that Andrew Stadler hadn't been alive to see.

Nick shivered, as if a gust of cool air had somehow made it through the building's glass membrane. Cassie Stadler's fragile, china-doll face now filled his mind. *What did I do to you?* He remembered the look of infinite hurt in her eyes, and he found himself dialing her number before he was even conscious of having decided to.

"Hello." Cassie's voice, deep and sleepy-sounding.

"It's Nick Conover," he said. "Hope I'm not calling you too early."

"Me? No—it's—what time is it?"

"I woke you up. I'm sorry. It's ten thirty. Go back to sleep."

"No," she said hastily. "I'm glad you called. Listen, about yesterday—"

"Cassie, I'm just calling to make sure you're okay. When I left, you didn't look so great."

"Thanks."

"You know what I mean."

"I—it helped, talking to you. Really helped."

"I'm glad."

"Would you like to come over for lunch?"

"You mean today?"

"Oh, God, that's ridiculous, I can't believe I just said that. You're this big CEO, you've probably got lunch meetings scheduled every day until you're sixty-five."

"Not at all," he said. "My lunch meeting just canceled, in fact. Which means a sandwich at my desk. So, yeah, I'd love to get out of the office, sure."

"Really? Hey, great. Oh—just one little thing."

"You don't have any food in your refrigerator."

"Sad but true. What kind of host am I?"

"I'll pick something up. See you at noon."

When he hung up, he stopped by his assistant's desk. "Marge," he said, "could you cancel my lunch meetings?"

"Both of them?"

"Right."

Marjorie smiled. "Going to play hooky? It's a beautiful day."

"Hooky? Does that sound like me?"

"Hope springs eternal."

"Nah," he said. "I just need to run a couple of errands."

45

THE HOUSE ON West Sixteenth, in Steepletown, was even smaller than he remembered it. A dollhouse, a miniature, almost.

Two stories. White sidings that could have been aluminum or vinyl, you'd have to tap to be sure. Black shutters that weren't big enough to pretend to be shutters.

Nick, holding a couple of brown bags from the Family Fare supermarket he'd stopped at on the way over, rang the bell, heard the carillon tones.

It was almost half a minute before Cassie came to the door. She was in a black knitted top and black stretchy pants. Her face was pale, and sad, and perfect. She was wearing glossy orange lipstick, which was a little strange, but it looked right on her. She also looked better, more rested, than she had yesterday.

"Hey, you actually came." Cassie opened the door, and walked him past the vase with the dried flowers and the framed embroidered sampler to the small living room. He could hear "One Is the Loneliest Number" come from the small speakers of a portable CD player. Not the old Three Dog Night version.

A modern cover. A woman with a voice like clove cigarettes. Cassie switched it off.

Nick unloaded the stuff he'd bought—bread, eggs, juice, milk, bottled water, fruit, a couple of bottles of iced tea. "Toss whatever you don't like," he said. Then he unwrapped a couple of sandwiches, placing them ceremoniously on paper plates. "Turkey or roast beef?"

She looked doubtfully at the roast beef. "Too bloody," she said. "I like my meat burned to a crisp, basically."

"I'll have it," Nick said. "You have the turkey."

They ate together in silence. He folded up the Boar's Head delicatessen wrappers into neat squares, a form of fidgeting. She finished most of her iced tea and toyed with the cap. It was a little awkward, and Nick wondered why she'd invited him over. He tried to think of something to say, but before he could, she said, "Hey, you never know what you're going to learn from a bottle cap. It says here, 'Real Fact—the last letter added to the English-language alphabet was the "J." ' "

Nick tried to think of something to say, but before he could, she went on: "Aren't you supposed to be running a Fortune Five Hundred company or something?"

"We're not a public company. Anyway, I had a boring lunch I canceled."

"Now I feel guilty."

"Not at all. I was happy to have an excuse to miss it."

"You know, you really surprised me yesterday."

"Why?"

"It wasn't very 'Nick the Slasher.' I guess people are never what you expect. Like they say, still waters—"

"Get clogged with algae?"

"Something like that. You know how it is—you see someone who seems so desperate, and you just have to reach out and help."

"You don't seem desperate."

"I'm talking about you."

Nick reddened. "Excuse me?"

She got up and put the kettle on. Standing at the stove, she said, "We've both suffered a loss. It's like Rilke says—when we lose something, it circles around us. 'It draws around us its unbroken curve.'"

"Huh. I used to have a Spirograph set when I was a kid."

"I guess I figured you for the typical company man. Until I met you. But you know what I think now?" Her gaze was calm but intent. "I think you're actually a real family man."

He cleared his throat. "Yeah, well, tell that to my son. Tell that to Lucas."

"It's a bad age for a boy to lose his mom," Cassie said quietly. She took a teapot down from a cabinet, then some mugs.

"Like there's a good one?"

"The kid probably needs you badly."

"I don't think that's how he sees it," Nick said, a little bitterly.

Cassie looked away. "You're saying that because he's isolated and he's angry, and he turns on you. Am I right? Because you're safe. But you'll get through it. You love each other. You're a family."

"We were."

"You know how lucky your kids are?"

"Yeah, well."

She turned to face him. "I'll bet being a CEO is sort of like being head of a family too."

"Yeah," Nick said acerbically. "Maybe one of those Eskimo families. The kind that puts Grandma on the ice floe when she's not bringing in the whale blubber anymore."

"I bet the layoffs were hard on you."

"Harder on the people who got laid off."

"My dad had a lot of problems, but I think having a job helped him keep it together. Then when he found out they didn't want him anymore, he fell apart."

Nick felt as if there was a metal strap around his chest and it was steadily tightening. He nodded.

"I was mad at Stratton," Cassie said. "Mad at you, is the truth. Maybe because I'm a girl, I take these things too personally. But it might have had a bad effect on him. Someone with a thought disorder, it's hard to know."

"Cassie," Nick started, but whatever he was going to say died in his throat.

"That was before I met you, though. You didn't want to do this. The people in Boston made you. Because, end of the day, Stratton is a business."

"Right."

"But it's never just a business to you, is it? See, I just realized something. Being a Stratton employee in the past couple of years must have been like being the daughter of a schizophrenic. One day you're a beloved family member, the next you're a unit, a cost center, something to be slashed." She leaned against the counter, her arms folded.

"I'm sorry about your dad," Nick said. "More sorry than I can tell you." *With more to be sorry about than I can tell you.*

"My daddy . . ." Cassie's voice was hushed, halting. "He didn't—he didn't want to be the way he was. It would just take over him. He wanted to be a good father like you. He wanted . . ." Cassie's breathing started to become ragged, and Nick realized that she was weeping. Her face was red, bowed, and she put a hand over her eyes. Tears rolled copiously down her cheeks.

Nick got up suddenly, his chair scraping against the linoleum floor, and put his arms around her.

"Oh, Cassie," he said softly. "I'm sorry."

She was tiny, birdlike, and her shoulders were

narrow and bony. She made a sound like she was hiccupping. She smelled like something spicy and New-Agey—patchouli, was that it? Nick was ashamed to realize he was getting aroused.

"I'm sorry," he said again.

"Stop saying that." Cassie looked up at him and smiled wanly through her tears. "It's got nothing to do with you."

Nick remembered a time when he was trying to fix a lamp socket he'd thought was switched off. An eerie, hair-erecting, tingling feeling had swept through his arm, and it had taken him a second to identify the sensation as house current that was leaking through the screwdriver. He felt something like that now, guilt washing through his body like an electrical flux. He didn't know how to respond.

But Cassie said, "I think you're a good man, Nicholas Conover."

"You don't know me," he said.

"I know you better than you think," she said, and he felt her arms squeezing against his back, pulling him toward her. Then she seemed to be standing on tiptoes, her face close to his, her lips pressing against his.

The moment for refusing, for backing out, came and went. Nick's response was almost reflexive. This time he kissed her back, her tears sticky against his face, and his hands moved downward from her shoulders.

"Mmm," she said.

The teakettle started whistling.

FOR A LONG time afterward, she lay on top of him in the slick of their perspiration, her mouth pressed against his chest. He could feel her heartbeat, fast as a bird's, slowing gradually. He stroked her hair, nuzzled her porcelain neck, smelling her hair, a conditioner or whatever. He felt her breasts against his stomach.

"I don't know what to say," Nick began.

"Then keep silent." She smiled, lifted herself up on her elbows until she was sitting upright on him. She lightly scratched her fingernails across his upper chest, tangling them in his chest hair.

Nick shifted his butt against the coarse-textured couch in the living room. He rocked upward, enfolded her in an embrace, leaned forward until he was sitting up too.

"Strong guy," she said.

Her breasts were small and round, the nipples pink and still erect like little upturned thumbs. Her waist was tiny. She reached across him to the table next to the couch, and as she did, her breasts brushed against his face. He gave them a quick kiss. She retrieved a pack of Marlboros and a Bic lighter, took one out of the pack and waved it at him, offering.

"No, thanks," Nick said.

She shrugged, lighted the cigarette, took in a lungful of air and spewed out a thin stream of smoke.

"'Let me live in a house by the side of the road and be a friend to man,'" Nick quoted.

"Yep."

"Needlepoint by Grandma?"

"Mom got it in some junk store. She liked what it said."

"So how long has it been since you left this place?"

"I just turned twenty-nine. Left when I was around twelve. So, a long time. But I came back to visit Dad a bunch of times."

"School in Chicago, then."

"You're trying to piece together the Cassie Stadler saga? Good luck."

"Just wondering."

"My mom remarried when I was eleven. An orthodontist. Had a couple of kids of his own, my age, a little older. Let's just say it wasn't the Brady Bunch. Dr. Reese didn't exactly take to me. Neither did the little Reese's pieces, Bret and Justin. Finally shipped me off to Lake Forest Academy, basically to get me out of the way."

"Must have been tough on you."

She inhaled, held a lungful of smoke for several seconds. Then, as she let it out, she said, "Yes and no. In some ways, they did me a favor. I actually flourished at the academy. I was a precocious kid. Got a Headmaster scholarship, graduated top of the class. Should have seen me when I was seventeen. A real promising young citizen. Not the head case you see before you."

"You don't seem like a head case to me."

"Because I don't drool and wear bad glasses?" She crossed her eyes. "Fools them every time."

"You talk about it like it's a big joke."

"Probably it *is* a joke. Some cosmic joke that's just a little over our heads. God's joke. Nothing to do but to smile and nod and try to pretend that we get it."

"You can go pretty far in life doing that," Nick said. He sneaked a glimpse at his wristwatch, saw it was after two already. With a jolt, he realized he had to get back to the office.

She noticed. "Time to go."

"Cassie, I—"

"Just go, Nick. You've got a company to run."

46

DR. AARON LANDIS, the clinical director of mental
health services for County Medical, seemed to wear a
permanent sneer. Audrey realized, though, that there
was something not quite right about the man's face, a
crookedness to the mouth, a congenital deformity that
made him look that way. His gray hair resembled a
Brillo pad, and he had a receding chin that he tried to
disguise, not very successfully, with a neatly trimmed
gray beard. At first Audrey felt a bit sorry for the psy-
chiatrist because of his homeliness, but her compassion
quickly faded.

His office was small and messy, so heaped with
books and papers that there was scarcely room for the
two of them to sit. The only decoration was a photo-
graph of a plain-looking wife and an even plainer son,
and a series of colorful scans of a human brain, purple
with yellow-orange highlights, on curling slick paper,
thumbtacked along one wall.

"I don't think I understand what you're asking, De-
tective," he said.

She had been as clear as day. "I'm asking whether
Andrew Stadler exhibited violent tendencies."

"You're asking me to breach doctor–patient confidentiality."

"Your patient is dead," she said gently.

"And the confidentiality of his medical records survives his death, Detective. As does physician–patient confidentiality. You know that, or if you don't, you should. The Supreme Court upheld that privilege a decade ago. More important, it's part of the Hippocratic oath I took when I became a doctor."

"Mr. Stadler was murdered, Doctor. I want to find his killer or killers."

"An effort I certainly applaud. But I don't see how it concerns me."

"You see, there are a number of unanswered questions about his death that might help us determine what really happened. I'm sure you want to help us do our job."

"I'm happy to help in any way I can. Just so long as you don't ask me to violate Mr. Stadler's rights."

"Thank you, Doctor. Then let me restate my question. Speaking generally. Do most schizophrenics tend to be violent?"

The psychiatrist looked upward for a moment, as if consulting the heavens. He exhaled noisily. Then he fixed her with a sorrowful look. "That, Detective, is one of the most pernicious myths about schizophrenia."

"Then maybe you can enlighten me, Doctor."

"Schizophrenia is a chronic recurring psychotic illness that begins in early adulthood, as a rule, and lasts until death. We don't even know if it's a single disease or a syndrome. Myself, I prefer to call it SSD, or schizophrenia spectrum disorder, though I'm in the minority on this. Now, the defining symptoms of schizophrenia are thought disorder, a failure of logic, reality distortion, and hallucinations."

"And paranoia?"

"Often, yes. And a psychosocial disability. So let me ask *you* something, Detective. You see a good deal of violence in your work, I'm sure."

"Yes, I do."

"Is most of it inflicted by schizophrenics?"

"No."

"My point. Most violent crimes are not committed by persons with schizophrenia, and most persons with schizophrenia don't commit violent crimes."

"But there's a—"

"Let me finish, please. The vast majority of patients with schizophrenia have never been violent. They're a hundred times more likely to commit *suicide* than homicide."

"So are you saying that Andrew Stadler was not a violent man?"

"Detective, I admire your persistence, but the back-door approach won't work either. I will not discuss the particulars of his case. But let me tell you what the real correlation is between schizophrenia and violence: schizophrenia increases the likelihood of being the *victim* of a crime."

"Exactly. Mr. Stadler was the victim of a terrible crime. Which is why I need to know whether he might have provoked his own death by killing an animal, a family pet."

"If I knew that, I wouldn't tell you."

"I'm asking whether he was capable of such an act."

"I won't tell you that either."

"Are you saying that schizophrenics are never violent?"

After a long pause, he said: "Obviously there are the exceptions."

"Was Andrew Stadler one of those exceptions, Doctor?"

"Please, Detective. I won't discuss the particulars of Mr. Stadler's medical records. I don't know how much more clear I can be."

Audrey sighed in exasperation. "Then let me ask you a purely hypothetical question, all right?"

"Purely hypothetical," Dr. Landis repeated.

"Let's take a . . . *hypothetical* case in which an individual repeatedly breaks into a family's house in order to write threatening graffiti. Is able to do so, cleverly and without leaving any evidence, despite the security provided by the gated community in which this family lives. And has even slaughtered the family's pet. What sort of person might do this, would you say?"

"What sort of *hypothetical* individual?" He attempted a smile, which twisted unpleasantly. "Someone, I would say, who's extremely intelligent, high-functioning, capable of higher-order thinking and goal-governed behavior, and yet has pervasive impulse-control problems, marked mood swings, and is highly sensitive to rejection. There may be, say, a great fear of abandonment, derived from difficulties in childhood feeling connected to important persons in one's life. He might have absolutely black-and-white views of others— might tend to idealize people and then suddenly despise them."

"And then?"

"And then he might be subject to sudden and unpredictable rages, brief psychotic episodes, with suicidal impulses."

"What might set him off?"

"A situation of great stress. The loss of someone or something important to him."

"Or the loss of a job?"

"Certainly."

"Can a schizophrenic exhibit this pattern of behavior you're describing?"

Dr. Landis paused for a long moment. "Conceivably. It's not impossible." Then he gave a creepy sort of smile. "But what does all this have to do with Andrew Stadler?"

47

"GROVER HERRICK," MARJORIE said over the intercom the next morning.

Grover Herrick was a senior procurement manager at the U.S. General Services Administration, which did purchasing for federal agencies. He was also the point man for an enormous contract Stratton had negotiated for the Department of Homeland Security. DHS now encompassed the Coast Guard, Customs, Immigration and Naturalization Service, and the Transportation Security Administration—thousands of offices, a hundred and eighty thousand employees, and a major infusion of federal cash. The contract was second in value only to the Atlas McKenzie deal, and had been in the works almost as long.

You didn't keep a GSA procurement manager on hold for long. That was one rule. Another was that anytime Grover Herrick wanted to talk to the CEO, Grover Herrick talked to the CEO. On half a dozen occasions in the past year, Nick fulfilled his duties as Stratton's chief executive by feigning interest as Grover talked about the sailboat he was going to buy as soon as he retired, and pretending to care about the difference between a ketch and a yawl. If Herrick had wanted to talk about hemorrhoids, Nick would have boned up on that topic too.

This time, though, there were no preliminaries.

"Nick," the GSA man said, "Gotta tell you, it looks like we're going with Haworth."

Nick felt gut-punched. It was all he could do not to double over. "You're *kidding*."

"I think you know by now when I'm kidding." There was a pause. "Remember when I told you the story about dropping the Thanksgiving turkey in front of all the guests, and how my wife had the presence of mind to say, 'Never mind, just bring out the other bird'? *That* I was kidding about."

"Fucking *Haworth*?"

"Well, what the hell did you *think* would happen?" Herrick's voice was a squawk of indignation. "You were going to have us ink the deal, move the company to *Shenzhen*, and then what? Have us outfit Homeland Security offices with desks from *China*?"

"What—?" Nick managed to choke out.

"When were you planning on telling us? I can think of some Senators who'd have a ball with that—but politics aside, it's completely against GSA procurement guidelines. Can't happen. Don't pretend you've forgotten about 41 USC 10. You guys oughta have the Buy American Act tattooed on your forehead."

"Wait a minute—who told you Stratton's going offshore?"

"What does it matter? Where there's smoke, there's fire. We liked Stratton. Great American company. I can see the temptation to cash in, put everything on a fast boat to China. Still think it's a mistake, though. My personal opinion."

"What you're saying doesn't make any sense. We're not going anywhere. I don't care what you've heard."

Herrick ignored him. "What was the game plan—

inflate revenues with a hefty GSA prepayment, jack up the purchase price, figure the Heathen Chinese wouldn't figure out the game? Strategic vision, huh? I guess that's why you get the big bucks."

"*No*, Grover. This is bullshit."

"I told you before. We really liked you guys. We liked Haworth, too, but the Stratton price points looked better, all in. We just didn't realize your price points came courtesy of cheap Chinese labor."

"Listen to me, Grover." Nick tried to cut him off, to no avail.

"Thing that chafes my ass is, you guys wasted a *hell* of a lot of my time. Got half a mind to bill you for it."

"Grover, *no*."

"Happy sailing, Nick," the GSA man said, and he hung up.

Nick cursed loudly. He wanted to fling the phone across the room—across *a* room—but the Ambience system didn't really lend itself to boss-man theatrics.

Marjorie came over. "Something going on that I should know about?"

"That's pretty much *my* question, Marge," Nick said, struggling to regain his composure.

He walked across the executive floor to Scott's area, taking a back way in order to bypass Gloria, Scott's admin. As he approached, he heard Scott talking on the phone.

"Well, sure," Scott was saying. "We'll give it a try, Todd man, why not?"

Nick advanced until he was in Scott's line of sight.

Scott noticed him now, seemed to flinch just a bit, but instantly recovered: widening his eyes and smiling, raising his chin by way of greeting. "Right," he said, more loudly. "Sounds like a great trip. Gotta go." He hung up and said to Nick, "Hey, my liege, welcome to the low-rent district."

"How's Todd?" Nick said.

"Ah, he's trying to set up a golf trip to Hilton Head."

"I didn't know you golf."

"I don't." He laughed uncomfortably. "Well, badly. But that's why they love having me around. Makes them look like Tiger Woods."

"'They' being Todd and the other Fairfield boys?"

"Todd and his wife and Eden and another couple. Anyway."

"I had an interesting talk with MacFarland at Atlas McKenzie."

"Oh, yeah?" Scott's expression seemed wary.

"Yeah. Learn something new every day. You know why they decided not to go with us?"

"Gotta be price, what else? Not quality, that's for sure. But you get what you pay for."

"MacFarland seems to think we're on the block. Now, why would he think that?"

Scott spread out his palms.

"Atlas McKenzie uses the same Hong Kong law firm as Fairfield, which is how they heard."

"That's *crazy*."

"Funny thing is, I heard something sort of similar from the guy at GSA just now."

"GSA?" Scott said, swallowing.

"The Homeland Security deal? That just fell apart too."

"Shit."

"And you know why? They need Made-in-America, and they heard a rumor we're going to be offshoring our manufacturing to China. Isn't that the craziest thing?"

Scott, picking up on Nick's bitter sarcasm, sat up straight in his chair and said solemnly, "If Todd and those guys were planning a move like that, don't you think they'd at least mention it to me?"

"Yeah, I do, actually. Have they?"

"Obviously not—I would have told you right away."

"Would you?"

"Of course—Jesus, Nick, I can't believe people listen to stupid rumors like that. I mean, it's no different from those idiotic rumors about the deep-fried chicken head in the box of Chicken McNuggets, or the bonsai kittens, or how the moon walk was a fraud—"

"Scott."

"Look, I'll make some calls, look into it for you, okay? But I'm sure there's nothing to it."

"I hope you're right," Nick said. "I really hope you're right."

48

EDDIE DIDN'T STAND up when Nick came to his office that afternoon. Just gave him a mock salute, as he leaned back in his Symbiosis chair with his feet on his desk. On the silver-mesh fabric wall behind him was a poster with the words "MEDIOCRITY. It Takes a Lot Less Time and Most People Won't Notice the Difference Until It's Too Late." Above the slogan was a photograph of the Leaning Tower of Pisa. It was one of those wiseass spoofs of corporate workplace propaganda, but Nick sometimes wondered how much irony Eddie really meant.

"I get a promotion?" Eddie asked. "I mean, with you coming down here instead of making me come up."

Nick pulled up a small, wheeled stool. "They call it Management by Walking Around. MBWA."

"Lot to be said for MBSOYA. Management by Sitting on Your Ass."

Nick forced a smile, and told him about what Mac-Farland and Grover Herrick had said, skipping the incidentals.

"Fuck me," Eddie said. "Gotta be bullshit, right? You talk to Scott McNally about this?"

"He says there's nothing to it. But he knows more than he's telling me. I'm sure of it."

Eddie nodded slowly. "If you're out, I'm out, right?"

"Who said anything about my being out? I just want you to see what Scott's up to, that's all."

Eddie grinned slowly. "You want an assist, I'll fire you the puck and cross-check the assholes. I'll even break the fucking stick over their heads."

"A little e-mail surveillance should do it, Eddie."

"I'll get one of the techs to pull his e-mail records off the server, right? Just get me a few keywords."

"That sounds like a start."

"Oh, sure. Phone records, all that stuff. Easy peasy. But boy, you sure do have a knack for stepping in the shit." Eddie's skin formed webbing around his eyes as he smiled. "Good thing you got a friend who doesn't mind cleaning your shoes."

"You'll let me know if you find anything."

"That's what friends are for."

Nick didn't meet his eyes. "And not a word to anyone."

"Back at ya, buddy."

Nick hesitated for a moment, then wheeled the stool close to Eddie's desk. "Eddie, did you tell the cops you went over to my house after we found my dog?"

Eddie peered at him for a while. "They didn't ask me. I don't volunteer information. That's cop interview lesson number one."

Nick nodded. "They didn't ask me either. Not yet. But in case it comes up, I want to make sure we have a consistent story, okay? I asked you to come over, and you did. Only natural that I'd give you a call. You're my security director."

"Only natural," Eddie repeated. "Makes sense. But you got to calm down, buddy. You worry too much."

49

WHEN HE RETURNED to the executive floor, Marjorie stopped him and handed him a slip of paper, a concerned look in her face. "I think you need to return this call right away," she said.

Principal J. Sundquist, she had written in her clear, elegant script, and then the telephone number.

Jerome Sundquist. Twenty-five years ago, he'd been Nick's high school math teacher. Nick remembered him as a rangy guy—a former tennis pro—who bounced around the classroom and was pretty good at keeping up the Math Is Fun act. To his students, he was Mr. Sundquist, not "Jerome" or "Jerry," and though he was reasonably laid back, he didn't pretend to be pals with the kids in their chair desks. Nick half-smiled as he remembered those chair desks, with the little steel basket for books under the seat, and a "tablet arm" supported by a continuous piece of steel tube that ran from the back supports to the crossover legs. They were manufactured, back then as they were now, right in town, at Stratton's chair plant, a few miles down the road. Nick hadn't seen the numbers recently, but they listed for about a hundred and fifty, on a unit cost of maybe forty. Basically, it was the same design today.

Jerome Sundquist hadn't changed that much, either. Now he was the school principal, not a young teacher, and allowed himself a little more sententiousness than he used to, but if you were a high school principal, that was pretty much part of the job description.

"Nick, glad you called," Jerome Sundquist said, in a tone that was both cordial and distant. "It's about your son."

FENWICK REGIONAL HIGH was a big brick-and-glass complex with a long traffic oval and the kind of juniper-and-mulch landscaping you found at shopping centers and office parks—nothing fancy, but somebody had to keep it up. Nick remembered when he came home after his first semester at Michigan State, remembered how *small* everything seemed. That's how it should have felt when he visited his old high school, but it didn't. The place was *bigger*—lots of add-ons, new structures, new brick facings on the old ones—and somehow plusher than it was in the old days. Plenty of it had to do with how Stratton had grown over the past couple of decades, with a valuation that broke two billion dollars three years ago. Then again, the higher you got, the longer the fall to the bottom. If Stratton collapsed, it would bring a lot of things down with it.

He stepped through the glass double doors and inhaled. As much as the place had changed, it somehow *smelled* the same. That grapefruit-scented disinfectant they still used: maybe they'd ordered a vat in 1970 and were still working through it. Some sort of faint burnt-pea-soup odor wafting from the cafeteria, as ineradicable as cat piss. It was the kind of thing you only noticed when you were away from it. Like the first day of homeroom after summer vacation, when you realized that the air was heavy with hair-styling products and eggy breakfasts and cinnamon Dentyne and underarm deodorant and farts—the smell of Fenwick's future.

But the place had changed dramatically. In the old days everyone came to school on the bus; now the kids were either dropped off in vans or SUVs or drove to school themselves. The old Fenwick Regional had no blacks, or maybe one or two a year; now the social leaders of the school seemed to be black kids who looked like rappers and the white kids who tried to. They'd added a sleek new wing that looked like something out of a private school. In the old days there used to be a smoking area, where longhaired kids in Black Sabbath T-shirts hung out and puffed and jeered at the jocks like Nick. Now smoking was outlawed and the Black Sabbath kids had become Goths with nose rings.

Nick hadn't spent much time in the principal's office when he was a student, but the oatmeal curtains and carpeting looked new, and the multicultural photographs of tennis champs on the court—the Williams sisters, Sania Mirza, Martina Hingis, Boris Becker—was very Jerome Sundquist.

Sundquist stepped around from his desk and shook Nick's hand somberly. They sat down together on two camel-colored chairs. Sundquist glanced at a manila file he had left on his desk, but he already knew what was in it.

"Love what you've done with the place," Nick said.

"My office, or the school?"

"Both."

Sundquist smiled. "You'd be surprised how many two-generation families the school has now, which is a nice thing. And obviously the district has been very lucky in a lot of ways. When the parents prosper, the schools prosper. We're all hoping the downturn isn't permanent. I appreciate you've got a lot on your shoulders right now."

Nick shrugged.

"You were a pretty good student, as I recall," Sundquist said.

"Not especially."

Sundquist looked amused, tilted his head. "Okay, maybe 'indifferent' would be closer to the mark. I don't think I ever persuaded you about the glories of polar coordinates. Your interest in trig was more practical. All about what angle you could use to slap a puck between the goalie's legs."

"I remember your trying to sell me on that at the time. Nice try, though."

"But you always did okay on the exams. And, Christ, you were a popular kid. The school's blue-eyed boy. Brought Fenwick Regional to the state semifinals, twice, isn't that right?"

"Semifinals one year. Finals the next."

"That's one area where we haven't kept up. Caldicott has kicked our ass for the past four years."

"Maybe you need a new coach."

"Mallon is supposed to be good. Gets paid more than me, anyway. It's always hard to know when to blame the coach and when to blame the players." Sundquist broke off. "I know how busy you are, so let me get right to the point."

"Luke's been having problems," Nick said with a twinge of defensiveness. "I realize that. I want to do whatever I can."

"Of course," Sundquist said, sounding unconvinced. "Well, as I told you, Lucas is being suspended. A three-day suspension. He was caught smoking, and that's what happens."

So Lucas would have even more time to light up. That was really going to make things better. "I remember when there used to be a smoking area."

"Not anymore. Smoking is forbidden on the entire

campus. We've got very tough rules on that. All the kids know it."

Campus was new. When Nick was at school, the school only had *grounds*. Campuses were for colleges.

"Obviously I don't want him smoking at all," Nick put in. "I'm just saying."

"Second offense, Lucas gets thrown out of school. Expelled."

"He's a good kid. It's just been a rough time for him."

Sundquist looked at him hard. "How well do you know your son?"

"What are you saying? He's my kid."

"Nick, I don't want to overstate the situation, but I don't want to understate it, either. It's pretty serious. I spent some time this morning talking to our crisis counselor. We don't think this is just about smoking, okay? You need to appreciate that we have the right to search his locker, and we may do some surprise searches, with the police."

"The police?"

"And if drugs are found, we will let the police prosecute. That's the way we do it these days. I want to warn you about that. Lucas is a troubled kid. Our crisis counselor is very concerned about him. Lucas isn't like you, okay?"

"Not everybody has to be a jock."

"That isn't what I meant," Sundquist said, not elaborating. Another glance back at the manila folder on his desk. "Besides which, his grades are going to hell. He used to be an honor student. With the grades he's been getting, he's not going to stay in that track. You understand what that means?"

"I understand," Nick said. "I do. He needs help."

"He needs help," Sundquist agreed, tight-lipped. "And he hasn't been receiving it."

Nick felt as if he were being graded as a father, and getting an *F*. "Jerry, I just don't see how suspending him or—God forbid—expelling him is the right thing to do. How is that *helping* him?" he asked. Then he wondered how many times those words had been spoken in that office.

"We have these rules for a reason," Sundquist said smoothly, leaning back a little in his chair. "There are almost fifteen hundred kids in this high school, and we have to do what's in the best interests of all of them."

Nick took a deep breath. "It's been hard for him, what happened. I get that he's a troubled kid. Believe me, this is something that's very much on my mind. I just think that he's been hanging out with a bad crowd."

"One way to look at it." Sundquist's gaze was unwavering. "Of course, there's another way to look at it."

"How do you mean?" Nick asked blankly.

"You could say that he *is* the bad crowd."

"LUKE."

"What?" He'd picked up his cell phone on the first ring. The deal was that if he failed to answer a call from his father, he'd lose the phone.

"Where are you?"

"Home. Why?"

"What the hell happened at school?"

"What do you mean?"

"What do I *mean*? Three guesses. Mr. Sundquist called me in."

"What'd he tell you?"

"Don't play this game, Luke." Nick tried to stay calm. Talking to Lucas was like dousing a fire with lighter fluid. "You were smoking, and you got caught. Forget about what *I* think about smoking—you know the rules on smoking at school. You just got a three-day suspension."

"So? It's all bullshit anyway."

"Suspension from school is bullshit?"

"Yeah." His voice shook a bit. "Because school is bullshit."

An instant message popped up on his monitor from Marge:

Compensation Committee meeting right now, remember?

"Luke, I'm furious about this," he said. "You and I are going to have a talk about this later."

Yeah, Nick thought. *That's telling him.*

"And, Luke—?"

But Lucas had hung up.

50

NO SOONER HAD Audrey returned to the squad room than Bugbee found her. He approached her desk holding a mug of coffee in one hand, a sheaf of papers in the other, looking pleased about something.

"Don't tell me," he said. "The shrink spilled it all about his looney-tunes patient."

Now she understood his self-satisfied look. He was gloating, yes, but it was something more. It was the told-you-so look she'd seen LaTonya give the boys when they got in trouble for doing something she'd told them not to.

"He gave me some useful background on schizophrenia and violence," she said.

"Stuff you could have read in a textbook, I'm figuring. But he wouldn't talk about Stadler, would he? Doctor–patient confidentiality, right?"

"There has to be a way to get access to Stadler's medical records." She couldn't bring herself to tell Bugbee he was right any more directly than that.

"What would Jesus do, Audrey? Get a search warrant."

She ignored the crack. "That won't do it. The most we can get out of a search warrant is dates of admission to the hospital and such. The medical records are still protected. Maybe a Freedom of Information request."

"How many years you got?"

"Right."

"Speaking of search warrants," Bugbee said, waving the sheaf of papers in his left hand, "when were you planning on telling me you requested the phone records of the Stratton security guy?"

"They came in already?"

"Not my point. What'd you want 'em for?"

Bugbee must have picked them up from the fax machine, or maybe he'd seen them in her in-box. "Let me see," she said.

"Why are you so interested in Edward Rinaldi's phone records?"

Audrey gave him a long cold look, the sort of look LaTonya was so skilled at. "Are you holding them back from me, Roy?"

Bugbee handed the papers right over.

Boy, she thought, I'm going to have to take LaTonya Assertiveness Training. She felt a pulse of triumph and wondered whether this was a worthy feeling. She thought not, but she enjoyed it guiltily all the same. "Thank you, Roy. Now, in answer to your question, I wanted them because I'm curious as to whether Rinaldi ever made any phone calls to Andrew Stadler."

"How come?"

"Well, now, think about it. He called our records division to find out if Stadler had any priors, right? Stadler's the *only* former Stratton employee he called about. That tells me he was suspicious of Stadler—that he must have suspected Stadler of being the stalker who kept breaking into Nicholas Conover's home."

"Yeah, and maybe he was right. There haven't been any more break-ins at Conover's house since Stadler's murder."

"None that he's reported," she conceded. "But it's only been a week or so."

"So maybe Stadler was the guy. Maybe Rinaldi was on to something."

"Maybe. Maybe not. Either way, it wouldn't surprise me if the security director called Stadler and warned him to stay away from Nicholas Conover's house. You know, said, 'We know it's you, and if you do anything again you'll regret it.'"

The computer-generated phone record faxed over by Rinaldi's cell-phone provider was dense and thick, maybe ten or twenty pages long. She gave it a quick glance, saw that most of the information she'd requested was there, but not all. Dates and times of all telephone calls he'd placed and received—all those seemed to be there. But only some of the phone numbers also listed names. Some did not.

"I assume you already looked through this," Audrey said.

"Quick scan, yeah. Guy has a pretty active social life, looks like. Lot of women's names there."

"Did you come across Andrew Stadler's name?"

Bugbee shook his head.

"You looked closely at the day and night when the murder took place?"

Bugbee gave her his deadeye look. "Phone numbers don't all have names."

"I noticed that. There doesn't seem to be a logic to it."

"I figure if a number's unlisted, the name doesn't pop up automatically."

"Makes sense," she said. She hesitated, tempted to be as stingy with praise as Bugbee always was. But wasn't it written in Proverbs somewhere that a word fitly spoken is like apples of gold in settings of silver? "I think you're right. Very good point."

Bugbee shrugged, a gesture not of modesty but of

dismissiveness, his way of letting her know that clever thinking was second nature to him. "That means a hell of a lot of cross-referencing," he said.

"Would you be able to take a crack at that?"

Bugbee snorted. "Yeah, like I got free time."

"Well, someone's got to."

A beat of silence: a standoff. "Did you get any more on that hydroseed stuff?"

Bugbee gave a lazy smile, pulled from his pants pocket a crumpled pink lab request sheet. "It's Penn Mulch."

"Penn Mulch? What's that?"

"Penn Mulch is a proprietary formula marketed by the Lebanon Seaboard Corporation in Pennsylvania, a fertilizer and lawn products company." He was reading from notes prepared by someone else, probably a lab tech. "The distinctive characteristic is small, regular pellets half an inch long by an eighth of an inch wide. Looks kinda like hamster shit. Cellulose pellets made up of freeze-dried recycled newspaper, one-three-one starter fertilizer, and super-absorbent polymer crystals. And green dye."

"And grass seed."

"Not part of the Penn Mulch. The lawn company mixes in the grass seed with the mulch and a tackifier and makes a kind of slurry they can spray on the ground. Kind of like a pea soup, only thinner. The grass seed in this case is a mixture of Kentucky Bluegrass and Creeping Red Fescue, with a little Saturn Perennial Ryegrass and Buccaneer Perennial Ryegrass thrown in."

"Nice work," she said. "But that doesn't really mean much to me—is this a pretty common formula for hydroseed?"

"The grass seed, that varies a lot. There's like nine hundred different varieties to choose from. Some of it's cheap shit."

"The lawn companies don't all use the same mix, then?"

"Nah. The shit they use along the highway, the contractor mix, you don't want to use on your lawn. The better the mulch, the better results you get."

"The Penn Mulch—"

"Expensive. Way better than the crap they normally use—ground-up wood mulch or newspaper, comes in fifty-pound bags. This is pricey stuff. Doubt it's very common. It's what you might use on some rich guy's lawn—rich guy who knows the difference, I mean."

"So we need to find out what lawn companies in the area use Penn Mulch."

"That's a lot of phone calls."

"How many lawn companies in Fenwick? Two or three, maybe?"

"Not my point," Bugbee said. "So you find the one company that sometimes uses Penn Mulch in its hydroseed mix. Then what?"

"Then you find out whose lawns they used Penn Mulch on. If you're saying it's so expensive, there can't be all that many."

"So what do you get? Our dead guy walked over someone's lawn that had Penn Mulch on it. So?"

"I don't imagine there are too many fancy lawns down in the dog pound, Roy," she said. "Do you?"

51

DURING THE DRIVE from the high school back to Stratton, Nick found himself thinking about Cassie Stadler.

She was not only gorgeous—he'd had more than his share of gorgeous women over the years, especially during college, when Laura had wanted them to "take a break" and "see other people"—but she was so smart it was scary, eerily perceptive. She seemed to understand him fully, to see through him, almost. She knew him better than he knew himself.

And he couldn't deny the physical attraction: for the first time in over a year he'd had sex, and he felt like a sexual being again. This was a sensation he'd almost forgotten about. The pump had been primed. He felt horny. He thought about yesterday afternoon and got hard.

Then he remembered who she was, how he'd come to know her, and his mood collapsed. The guilt came surging back, worse than ever.

A voice in his head: *Are you kidding me? You're screwing the daughter of the man you murdered?*

What's wrong with you?

He didn't understand what he was doing. If he allowed himself to get close to her . . . Well, what if she found out, somehow? Could he keep up this crazy balancing act?

What the hell am I doing?

But he badly wanted to see her again. That was the craziest thing of all.

It was late afternoon by now, and he didn't have to return to the office. He pulled over to the side of the road and fished a scrap of paper out of his jacket pocket. On it he'd scrawled Cassie Stadler's phone number. Impulsively—without heeding that chiding voice in his head—he called her on his cell.

"Hello," he said when she answered. His voice sounded small. "It's Nick."

A beat. "Nick," she said, and stopped.

"I just wanted to . . ." His voice actually cracked. Just wanted to—what? Turn back the clock? Reverse what happened That Night? Make everything *all better*? And since that wasn't possible, then what? He just wanted to talk to her. That was the truth. "I was just calling . . ."

"I know," she said quickly.

"You okay?"

"Are *you*?"

"I'd like to see you," he said.

"Nick," she said. "You should stay away from me. I'm trouble. Really."

Nick almost smiled. Cassie didn't know what trouble was. *You think you're trouble? You should see me when I've got a Smith & Wesson in my hands.* Acid splashed the back of his throat.

"I don't think so," Nick said.

"Don't you think you've done enough?"

He felt something like an electric jolt. Hadn't he done enough? That was one way of looking at it. "Excuse me?"

"Not that I didn't appreciate it. I did. *All* of it. But we need to leave it there. You've got a company to run. A family to hold together. I don't fit into that."

"I'm just leaving an appointment," he said. "I can be there in about five minutes."

"HEY," CASSIE SAID, opening the dusty screen door. Carpenter-style jeans, white T-shirt, flecks of paint. Then she smiled, a smile that crinkled her eyes. She looked better, sounded better. "I didn't think you'd come back."

"Why?"

"Well, you know, buyer's remorse. Regret over what you'd done. The usual male stuff."

"Maybe I'm not your usual male."

"I'm getting that idea. Bring me anything today?"

Nick shrugged. "Sorry. There's a bottle of windshield-wiper fluid in the trunk."

"Forget it," Cassie said. "That stuff always gives me a hangover."

"Might have a can of WD-40 around, too."

"Now that's more promising. I'm really digging the idea of having the CEO of Stratton as my personal grocery boy."

"Point of pride with me. Nick Conover buys a mean turkey sandwich."

"But should I take it personally that you got me non-fat yogurt?" She brought him inside. "Let me make you some of the tea you bought."

She disappeared into the kitchen for a moment. She had a CD on, a woman singing something about, "I'm brave but I'm chicken shit."

When she came back, Nick said, "You look good."

"I'm beginning to feel more like myself again," she said. "You caught me at a low point the other day. I'm sure you know how it goes."

"Well, you look a lot better."

"And you look like shit," she said, matter of fact.

"Well," Nick said. "Long day."

She stretched herself out on the nubby brown sofa, with the gold thread woven through the upholstery like something out of the 1950s.

"Long day, or long story?"

"Trust me, you don't want to hear a grown man bitch and moan about troubles at the shop."

"Trust me, I could use the distraction."

Nick leaned back in the ancient green La-Z-Boy. After a few moments, he began to tell her about the Rumor, leaving out a few details. He didn't mention Scott by name, didn't go into Scott's disloyalty. That was too painful a subject right now.

Cassie hugged her knees, gathering herself into some tight yoga-like ball, and listened intently as he explained.

"And if that weren't enough, I get a call from Lucas's school," he went on. He stopped. He wasn't accustomed to talking about his life that way. Not since Laura's death. Somehow he'd gotten out of practice.

"Tell me," she said.

He did, telling her, too, about how he'd called Lucas at home, confronted him, and how Luke had hung up. When he finally checked his watch, he realized he'd been talking for more than five minutes.

"I never understood that," Cassie said.

"Understood what?"

"Kid gets suspended for three days, meaning what? They don't have to go to school for three days? They stay home?"

"Right."

"And get into more trouble? That's supposed to be a punishment? I mean, a baseball player gets suspended for five games for fighting with the umpire, that's a punishment. But telling a kid he can't go to school, which he hates, for three days?"

"Maybe it's like social humiliation."

"For a teenager? Isn't that more like a badge of honor?"

Nick shrugged. "Wouldn't have been for me."

"No, you were probably Mr. Perfect."

"No way. I got into the usual trouble. I was just careful about it. I didn't want to get kicked off the hockey team. Hey, where's that tea?" he asked.

"That stove takes forever. Electric, and underpowered. Dad wouldn't allow gas in the house. One of his many 'things.' But we won't go there." She craned her head, listening. "I'm sure it's ready now."

"Just that all this talking makes a man thirsty," Nick said.

Cassie came back with two steaming mugs. "English Breakfast," she said. "Though I saw that you also bought me a box of Blue Moon Kava Kava and Chamomile mix. I'm guessing that's not Nick Conover's usual cup."

"Maybe not."

"Why do I get the feeling you've got me figured for some sort of New Age nut?" She shrugged. "Possibly because I am one. How can I deny it? You make chairs, I teach asanas. Hey, when it comes down to it, we're both in the sitting industry, right?"

"So you're not going to tell me about my aura."

"You can take the girl out of Carnegie Mellon—and believe me, they did." A smile hovered around her lips. "But you can't take the Carnegie Mellon out of the girl. Never really got into chakras and shit. There's a lot of my dad in me. I've got an empirical streak a mile wide."

"And I took you for a nineteen waist."

"Thanks." She took a careful sip of her tea. "So you've got problems. You'll deal, because that's the kind of person you are. When life gives you lemons, you make lemon Pledge."

"I was expecting something more Zen, somehow."

"I see you haven't touched your English Breakfast. So what kind of tea do you like?"

"Any kind. So long as it's coffee."

She found a bottle of Four Roses bourbon on a low table beside the sofa, handed it to him. "Put a slug of this in it. It'll cut the tannins."

He sloshed a little into his cup. It definitely improved the taste.

Cassie was looking at him with cat eyes. "So are you here for me or for you?"

"Both."

She nodded, amused. "You're my caseworker?"

"Come on," Nick said. "You're not exactly a charity case."

"I'm doing okay."

"Well, I want you to know that if you're ever not doing okay, you've got me here to help."

"This is starting to sound like adios."

"No. Not at all."

"Good." She got up, tugged at the cord on the venetian blinds, closing them and darkening the room. "That's a relief."

He came up to her from behind, slipped his hands under her knit top, and felt the silky warmth of her belly.

"Why don't we go upstairs?" Nick said.

"We don't go upstairs," she said at once.

"We don't, huh? Okay." Slowly he began moving his hands upward until he found her breasts, teased her nipples as he kissed and licked the back of her neck.

"Yeah," she said throatily.

Still with her back to his, she brought her hands around to his butt and squeezed each cheek, hard.

He entered her from behind this time.

"JESUS," HE SAID, and she looked up at him, her eyes gleaming.

It took him several minutes to catch his breath.

"Wow," he said. "Thank you."

"My pleasure."

"Well, mine, I think."

She took a sip of tea, curled up next to him on the sofa. She began singing along with the CD, which must have been set on repeat mode, something about "best friend with benefits."

"You've got a nice voice."

"Sang in the church choir. Mom was a real holy roller, used to drag me there. It was the only thing that got me through. So, boss man, you can't give up the fight, you know." An odd sort of vehemence had entered Cassie's voice. "You've got to play the game balls out, with all your heart. *Everything* matters."

"That's the way I always played hockey. Gave it my all—you have to."

"Always kept your head up while you skated?"

He smiled. She obviously got hockey too. "Oh yeah. Put your head down for a second, and you're signed, sealed, and delivered. The game's fast."

"You been keeping your head up at Stratton?"

"Not enough," he admitted.

"I suspect people maybe underestimate you sometimes, because they sense you're eager to be liked. My guess is that people who push you too far live to regret it."

"Maybe." Memories swirled in Nick's head, dark ones that he didn't want to reexamine.

"You've already surprised a lot of people, is my bet.

Dorothy Devries—she's cooled toward you in the past several years. Am I right?"

Nick blinked. It wasn't a conscious realization he'd had, but it was true. "Yes," he said. "How did you know?"

Cassie looked away. "Don't take this the wrong way. But when Old Man Devries's widow appoints a successor, there are a lot of things going on in her head. One thing she's *not* looking to do is to bring in someone who's going to show up her beloved Milton. A reliable hand on the tiller, sure. The kind of reliable guy about whom you could say, 'He's no Milton Devries, of course, but who is?' They could have poached some hotshot from the competition—I bet that would have been the usual thing. But it wasn't what she wanted. You were meant to be Milton's mini-me. Then you came in, and you kicked ass. You weren't Milton's protégé anymore. And even if she benefited from that financially, the whole Nick Conover show had to bother her too."

Nick just shook his head.

"You don't believe me, do you?"

"The trouble is," Nick said slowly, "I do believe you. What you say never really occurred to me before, and it's sure not doing anything for my ego, but when I listen to you talk, I'm thinking, Yeah, that's probably what went down. The old lady wasn't expecting what she got. Truth is, I wasn't either. I got in there, made three or four critical hires, let them do their thing. It could have played differently. I'm not that smart, but I know what I don't know. What I'm good at, maybe, is bringing in smarts."

"And so long as they're loyal to you, you're going to be okay. But if they aren't family-first people, you could have problems."

"Family-first?"

"The Stratton family."

"You really are the woman with X-ray eyes," Nick said. "You see right through people." Suddenly he shivered. How much *did* she see? Did she see the blood on his hands? He swallowed hard. It wasn't a good time to start losing it.

"You know what they say."

"Who?"

"They. Anaïs Nin, maybe, I forget. 'We don't see things as they are. We see things as *we* are.'"

"Not sure I get that."

"And the hardest people to see, sometimes, are the people we love. Like your son."

"A complete mystery to me these days."

"What time did you say your kids would be home?"

"Less than an hour."

"I'd like to meet them," she said.

"Uh, I'm not sure that's a good idea," Nick said.

Cassie got to her feet, ran her fingers through her hair. "Jesus, what am I saying, it's a *terrible* idea," she said. The change in her was abrupt, startling. "What was I thinking? I'm not part of your life. I don't make *sense* in your life. Listen, I'd probably be ashamed of me too." She tugged at her paint-flecked jeans. "So let's leave things here. After all, we'll always have Steepletown. Goodbye, Nick. Have a good life."

"Cassie," Nick said. "That's not what I meant."

Cassie was silent. When Nick turned to look at her, her eyes were wells of sorrow. He felt a wave of guilt, and longing.

"Would you like to come by for dinner?" he asked.

52

CASSIE WAS SUBDUED as the Chevy Suburban waited in a queue in front of the Fenwicke Estates gatehouse. Nick suppressed the urge to drum his fingers on the steering wheel.

"Evening, Jorge," Nick said, as they slowly passed the gatehouse.

Cassie leaned over so she could see him. "Hi, Jorge, I'm Cassie." She smiled and gave him a little wave.

"Evening," Jorge said, more animatedly than usual.

Okay, Nick thought. Chalk one up for the girl's humanity. She noticed the guys in uniform. So long as it wasn't the start of some big worker's solidarity trip, that was probably a good sign.

He wondered how the kids would react to his bringing a woman home. More than wondered: he was, he had to admit, nervous about it. She was the first woman he'd been involved with in any way since Laura's death, and he had no idea how they'd react. Lucas, he could safely predict, would be hostile. Hostility was his default mode. Julia? Now, that was a question. There was the Freudian thing where the girl wants Daddy all to herself, and there was that powerful strain of unthinking loyalty to her mom: how dare Daddy date someone other than Mommy?

It could be ugly. But the one who'd really suffer the brunt of it was Cassie. He felt bad for her, for what she was about to experience. As he drove to the house, he began to regret his impulsive invitation. He should have introduced her to the kids more gradually.

As they approached the driveway to the house, Cassie gave a low whistle.

"Sweet," she said. "Wouldn't have guessed it was your style, I have to admit."

"Maybe it isn't," Nick admitted, but he felt self-conscious about saying it. Like he was putting the blame on Laura.

She squinted at the yellow Dumpster that was stationed underneath a basketball hoop. "Construction?"

"Always."

"Portoncini dei morti," she said.

"You're in America now," Nick said lightly. "About time you learned to speak English."

"I take it you've never been to Gubbio."

"If they don't manufacture casters there, I've probably never been."

"It's in Umbria. Amazing place. I spent a whole year there—painting, busking, you name it. Great place, but spooky too. You go through the old part of town, and you start to notice that a lot of the houses have these areas that look oddly bricked up. Turns out that they had this old custom, like a sacrament. They bricked up the doorway where a dead person was taken out of a house. They're called *portoncini dei morti*. Doors of the dead. Ghost doors."

"Must have kept a lot of masons busy," Nick said. *It's the front door, Nick. That's the one place you don't cheap out.* Doors of the dead.

"This was Laura's house, wasn't it?" Cassie asked.

That wasn't how Nick would have put it, but it was more or less true. It was Laura's house.

"Sort of," he said.

Marta was at the door when they came in. "I told you we'd be having company," Nick said. "Well, she's the company."

Marta didn't shake Cassie's hand, he noticed, just said, "Nice to meet you," and none too cordially. Same expression she reserved for telephone solicitors.

"Where's Julia?" Nick asked Marta.

"Watching TV in the family room. Emily just left a little while ago."

"And Luke?"

"In his room. On the computer, maybe. He said he can't stay for dinner."

"Oh, that right? Well, he's *going* to stay for dinner," Nick said, icily. Christ. The whole suspension thing— they would have to have a Very Serious Talk. Which probably meant a Perfect Storm of an argument.

Just not tonight.

Nick took Cassie over to the family room, where Julia was engrossed in *Slime Time Live* on Nickelodeon.

"Hey, baby," Nick said. "I want you to meet my friend Cassie."

"Hi," Julia said, and turned back to the show. Not rude, but not exactly friendly. A little cool, maybe.

"Cassie is going to be joining us for dinner."

Julia turned around again. "Okay," she said, warily. To Cassie, she said, "We usually don't have company for dinner."

Then she turned back to the flickering screen. Someone was getting doused with green slime.

"Don't worry," Cassie said. "I eat like a bird."

Julia nodded.

"Two and half times my body weight in earthworms," Cassie said.

Julia giggled.

"Are you a baseball fan?" Cassie asked.

"Yeah, I guess," Julia said. "You mean my jersey?"

"I *love* the Tigers," Cassie said.

Julia shrugged dismissively. "The girls in school keep calling me 'tomboy' because I wear it all the time."

"They're just jealous of your jersey," Nick put in, but Julia wasn't listening.

"You ever been to Comerica Park?" Cassie asked her.

Julia shook her head.

"Oh, it's amazing. You'd love it. We've got to go there some time."

"Really?" Julia said.

"Definitely. And listen—I got called 'tomboy' when I was a kid too," said Cassie. "Just 'cause I wasn't into Barbie."

"Really? I *hate* Barbie," Julia said.

"Barbie's kind of creepy," Cassie agreed. "I was never into dolls."

"Me neither."

"But I'll bet you have stuffed animals to keep you company, right?"

"Beanie Babies, mostly."

"Do you collect them?"

"Sort of." Julia was now looking at Cassie with interest. "They're very valuable, you know. But only if you don't use them and stuff."

"You mean like, never take the label off, and put them on the shelf?"

Julia nodded, this time more animatedly.

"I don't get that," Cassie said. "The whole point of Beanie Babies is to play with them, right? Do you have a lot, or just a couple of them?"

"I don't know. I guess a lot. You want to see my collection?"

"Really? I'd love to."

"Not now," said Nick. "Later. Right now it's supper-time, and we're having company."

"Okay," Julia said. Then she yelled, "Luke, supper! We have company."

As Nick took Cassie back to the front hall, she said, "She's a sweetie, isn't she?"

"A regular Ma Barker is what she is," Nick said. "For sweetness and light, we've got Lucas Conover." He took her upstairs, gestured toward the hallway. There was no need to specify which was Lucas's room. From beneath the closed door, thrash music pulsed, an avalanche of noise with someone shouting at the top of his lungs over a thudding bass beat. Something about *outta my mind,* something about *ashes to ashes,* something about *all pain, no gain.* A lot of incomprehensible screaming in between.

"As you can tell, he's a huge Lawrence Welk fan," Nick said. He decided against knocking on the door. Let Marta get him downstairs. Lucas responded better to her anyway.

"How do you know so much about Beanie Babies?" Nick asked.

"My knowledge of Beanie Babies is limited to what I read in *Newsweek.* Am I busted?"

"You sure got Julia believing you're a Beanie Babies expert."

"Hey, whatever works, right? Though I get a feeling your son isn't into Beanie Babies."

"He's a hard case, my son," Nick said, not wanting to dwell on it. "I'm going to change, meet you downstairs in a few."

When he came back down, Cassie and Julia were deep in conversation in the family room. "And there was blood everywhere," Julia was saying in a hushed, serious voice.

"Oh no," Cassie breathed.

"And it was Barney." Julia's eyes were moist.

"My God."

"And Daddy said he would protect us. He said he'd do whatever he had to do."

Nick cleared his throat; it wasn't a conversation he wanted to encourage. "Hey, girls," he called. "Suppertime."

"I've just been hearing about what happened to Barney," Cassie said, looking up. "Sounds horrible."

"It was rough," Nick said. "For all of us." He tried to sound a little brusque, to let Cassie know he didn't want the conversation to continue.

Luckily, Marta emerged from the kitchen just then and announced that dinner was ready.

"All right," Nick said. "Let's go, girls. Marta, would you go upstairs and ask Sid Vicious to join us?"

As Marta went upstairs, Julia asked, "Who's Sid Vicious?"

"*You* know the Sex Pistols?" Cassie said to Nick, smiling.

"I think I saw part of some movie about them before I walked out," Nick said. "I'm not a total geek, you know, no matter what my son thinks."

"But who's Sid Vicious?" Julia asked again.

Lucas's heavy footsteps thundered as if a crate of bowling balls had been upended at the top of the stairs. At the landing he looked around, taking in Cassie's presence with an unblinking stare.

"Luke, I'd like you to meet my friend Cassie Stadler," Nick said.

"Cassie *Stadler*?"

The way he said it made Nick's blood run cold.

"That's right," he said quietly. "She'll be joining us for dinner."

"I have to go out," Lucas said.

"You have to stay here."

"I have a homework project I need to do with some kids in class."

Nick refrained from rolling his eyes. A science experiment, no doubt, designed to study the effect of *Cannabis sativa* on the psychophysiology of the American sixteen-year-old. "It isn't up for discussion," he said. "Sit."

"I like your music," Cassie said to him.

Lucas looked at her with something just shy of hostility. "Yeah?" His tone of voice made it short for: *Yeah, what of it?*

"If you call that music," Nick said, feeling protective of Cassie. He gave her an apologetic shrug. "And when he isn't listening to this kind of noise, it's that gangsta rap stuff."

"Gangsta rap stuff." Cassie's mimicry was perfect, and devastating.

Lucas half snorted, half chortled.

"You'd prefer it if he listened to the Mamas and the Papas?" she asked. "Like some kind of Stepford son?"

Hey, no fair, Nick wanted to say. "*I* didn't even listen to the Mamas and the Papas," he said.

Cassie wasn't paying attention. She was focused on Lucas. "I'm curious. How long have you been into Slasher?"

"A few months," Lucas said, surprised.

"Not a lot of people your age even know about Slasher. I bet you have all their albums."

"Got downloads of some stuff they haven't released yet, and some bootleg demos, too."

"Slasher would be a rock band," Nick said, feeling obscurely excluded. "Tell me if I'm warm."

"'Slasher' is what they call Dad, you know," Lucas said, pleased.

"I've heard. Anyway, Slasher's cool, but John Horrigan's kind of a jerk, I gotta tell you," Cassie said, taking a step toward Lucas.

Lucas's eyes widened. "You *know* him? No fucking way." An entirely different Lucas was making an appearance.

She nodded. "You heard about how he fell off the stage in Saratoga, during the Sudden Death tour? Well, he had some problems with his neck and back after that. Nothing helped. So I used to teach this yoga class in Chicago, where he's based. One day he shows up, and it's the first thing that really helps. Then he's asking me for extra sessions. And then . . ." She walked closer to Lucas and put her hand on his arm as she murmured the rest.

Lucas giggled, blushing.

"I can't believe it," he said. "Horrigan *rocks*. So . . ." He glanced at Nick, at Julia, and lowered his voice. "What was he like?"

"Selfish," Cassie said. "First I thought, bad technique. But then I realized it was just selfishness. Finally I just stopped returning his phone calls. Great guitar player, though."

"Horrigan rocks."

"What do you mean 'selfish'?" Julia demanded, with a ten-year-old's unerring instinct for inappropriate subjects.

"We're just talking about who gets their guitar licks in," Cassie said.

Lucas began to quake with silent laughter.

Julia started to laugh, too, for no particular reason. Then Nick, too, began to laugh, and for the life of him he couldn't say why. Except that he couldn't remember when Lucas had last laughed.

Marta brought a platter of pork chops to the table, some sort of chili and cilantro thing on top. "More in the kitchen if anyone wants," she said, sounding slightly peevish, or maybe just a little out of sorts.

"Everything smells delicious, Marta," Nick said.

"And there's salad." She pointed to two covered ceramic bowls. "And there's rice and there's ratatouille."

"That's great, Marta," said Cassie. "I think we're going to be okay."

"I didn't make a dessert, but there's ice cream," Marta added darkly. "And some fruit. Some bananas."

"I make one hell of a banana flambé," said Cassie. "Any takers?"

"Knock yourself out," Lucas said, and grinned.

Perfect white teeth, clear blue eyes, almost perfect complexion. A beautiful kid. Nick felt a surge of paternal pride. *Three-day suspension.* They'd have to have The Talk. Just not now. It hung over him like a sword.

"All you need are bananas, some butter, brown sugar, and rum."

"We've got all that," Nick said.

"Oh, and a light. For a blaze of glory." Cassie turned to Lucas. "Got a lighter, kiddo?"

53

AFTER DRIVING CASSIE home, Nick returned to find Lucas in his room, lying back on his bed, earbuds in. Nick signaled to him to take them off. To his surprise, Lucas did without complaint, and he spoke first: "So, she's cool."

"Good. I'm glad you like her." Nick sat in the only chair in the room that wasn't piled with books and papers and discarded clothes. He took a breath, plunged in. The normal force field of hostility seemed to be down, or maybe just diminished. That was good; that would make it easier.

"Luke, buddy, you and I have to talk."

Lucas watched him, blinking, said nothing.

"I told you Mr. Sundquist called me in for a conference today."

"So?"

"You understand how serious this is, this suspension."

"It's a three-day vacation."

"That's what I was afraid I'd hear. No, Luke. It goes on your record. When you apply to colleges, they see that."

"Like you care?"

"Oh, now, come on. Of course I care."

"You don't even know what I'm studying in school, do you?"

"I didn't know you were studying anything," Nick cracked without thinking.

"That's a *big* help, Dad. You basically spend all your time at work, and now you're trying to pretend like you're interested in how I do in school?" It was amazing how Lucas could take those pure, innocent eyes and focus them like a laser beam into one cold, hard blue ray of hatred.

"Yeah, well, I'm worried about what's happening to you."

"What's happening to me," Lucas repeated mockingly.

"This is all about Mom, isn't it?" He regretted saying it as soon as it came out. That was way too blunt. But how else to say it?

"Excuse me?" Lucas said, incredulous.

"Look, ever since Mom's death, you've totally changed. I know it, and you know it."

"That's deep, Nick. Really deep. Coming from you, that's really great."

"What's that supposed to mean?"

"Well, look at you. You went right back to work, no problem."

"I have a job, Luke."

"Moving right on, huh, Nick?"

"Don't *ever* talk to me that way," Nick said.

"Get the hell out of my room. I don't need this shit from you."

"I'm not leaving until you hear me out," Nick said.

"Fine," Lucas said, getting up from the bed and walking out of his room. "Sit there and blab all you want."

Nick followed his son into the hall. "You come back here," he said.

"I don't need this shit."

"I said, get *back* here. We're not done talking."

"Hey, you've made your point, okay? I'm *sorry* I'm such a *disappointment* to you." Lucas raced down the stairs, taking them two steps at a time.

Nick ran after him. "You don't walk away from me when I'm talking to you," he shouted. He caught up with him just as Lucas reached the front door, put his hand on his son's shoulder.

Luke swiveled, swatted Nick's hand off. "Get your fucking hands off me!" he screamed, turning the big brass knob and shoving the door open.

"You get back here," Nick shouted after him, standing in the doorway. "This cannot go on!"

But Lucas was running down the stone path into the darkness. "I'm sick of this fucking house, and I'm sick of you!" came his son's voice, echoing.

"Where do you think you're going?" Nick yelled back. "You get back here right now!"

He thought about taking off after his son, but what would be the point, really? He was overcome with a sense of futility and desperation. He stood there on the threshold until the sound of Lucas's footsteps faded to silence.

Julia was there at the bottom of the stairs when he turned around. She was weeping.

He went up to her, gave her a tight squeeze, and said, "He'll be okay, baby. *We'll* be okay. Now you go to bed."

IN THE SHOWER a little later, Nick cursed himself for how badly he'd handled the whole thing, how ham-handed he'd been, how emotionally obtuse. There had to be ways of reaching Lucas, even if he didn't know them. It was like a foreign country where the language sounds nothing like your own, the street signs are unreadable, you're alone and lost. As the needles of water stung his neck and back, he looked at the row of shampoos and conditioners in the tiled inset: Laura's stuff, all of it. He hadn't bothered to remove it. Couldn't *bring* himself to remove it, really.

He soaped himself up, got soap in his eyes, which made them smart so that when they started stinging and watering, he couldn't tell if it was the soap or the tears.

He put on a T-shirt, pajama bottoms, and got into bed just as he heard the front door open, the alert tone go off. Luke had returned.

He switched off the bedside lamp. As always, he slept on the side of the bed that had always been his, wondered when, if ever, he'd start sleeping in the middle of the bed.

His bedroom door opened, and he thought for a split second that it might be Lucas, here to apologize. But it wasn't, of course.

Julia stood there, her lanky shape and curly hair silhouetted by the nightlight in the hall.

"I can't sleep," she said.

"Come here."

She ran to Nick, scrambled into the bed. "Daddy," she said very softly. "Can I sleep in your bed? Just for tonight."

He brushed back the curls, saw the tear-streaked face. "Sure, baby. But just for tonight."

54

LEON SLEPT LATE, of course, so it was no problem for Audrey to be up long before him Saturday morning. She enjoyed the quiet of the morning, the solitude, being in her own head. She made herself a pot of hazelnut coffee—the kind Leon hated, but she'd make regular coffee when he got up—and read the morning papers.

The weekends used to be their little island of intimacy, before—before he lost his job, before she started working overtime hours in order to be gone as much as possible. They'd sleep late on Saturday, snuggle, make love. They'd make brunch together, read the papers together, sometimes even make love again. Take a nap together. Then go out and enjoy the weekend, shopping or going for walks. Sundays he'd sleep until she returned from church, and then they'd maybe go out for brunch or make something at home, and they'd make love too.

Those days were like ancient Mesopotamia. She'd almost forgotten what they felt like, they'd receded so into the distant shrouded past.

This Saturday morning, after she'd had her coffee, she considered getting out her case files and working. But a glimmering of ancient Mesopotamia arose in her mind.

Someone had to break the gridlock, she told herself. They were both frozen. Neither wanted to make the first move to try to change things.

She debated internally, the way she debated most things large or small. *How many times are you going to keep trying?* she asked herself. *How often are you going to butt your head against a brick wall before you realize it feels better to stop?* The other voice—the wiser, more generous voice—said: *But he's the damaged one. He's the hurt one. You need to take the lead.*

This morning—maybe it was the still beauty of the morning, maybe it was the deliciousness of the coffee, maybe it was the time alone—she decided to take the lead.

She walked quietly through the dark bedroom, careful not to wake him. She slid open her bottom dresser drawer and pulled out the pale apricot silk teddy she'd bought from the Victoria's Secret catalog, never worn.

She closed the bedroom door and went down the hall to the bathroom, where she took a nice hot shower, using the loofah. She applied lotion all over—her skin tended to get ashy if she didn't—and then put on makeup, something she never did unless she was going out. She daubed perfume on in all the right secret places—Opium, the only perfume that Leon had ever complimented her on.

Wearing just her teddy, and feeling a bit silly at first, she went into the kitchen and made brunch. French toast, bacon, even some cantaloupe balls. His favorite breakfast: he liked French toast even more than eggs Benedict. A fresh pot of coffee, the kind he liked. A white porcelain creamer, in the shape of a cow, filled with half-and-half.

Then she arranged everything carefully on a bed tray—it took her a while to find it in the overhead storage in the little pantry, and then she'd had to wash off the accumulated dust—and went in to wake up Leon.

Since he'd been in a sour mood for most of the last year, she was pleasantly surprised at his sweet smile upon seeing her and the breakfast she'd placed on the bed.

"Hey, Shorty," he rasped. "What's all this?"

"Brunch, baby."

"French toast. It's not my birthday, is it?"

She climbed into the bed and kissed him. "I just felt like it, that's all."

He took a sip of coffee, made a contented noise. "I got to go take a whiz." The breakfast tray tottered dangerously as he tried to extricate himself from the bed.

She could hear the sound of his urine splashing noisily in the toilet bowl, the toilet flushing, then she could hear him brushing his teeth, something he didn't normally do before breakfast. A good sign. Even though he was getting as big as his sister, he remained a very sexy man.

He came back into the bed; she moved the tray to allow him to get in without upsetting it. He kissed her again, to her surprise. She shifted her body, angled it toward him, a hand on his upper arm, ready—but then he pulled away and took another sip of coffee.

"You forgot the syrup," he said.

She touched the white porcelain gravy boat.

He tipped it over the stack of French toast, dousing it liberally, then took the knife and fork and cut a tall wedge. She'd even dusted it with powdered sugar, which he liked.

"Mmm-mmm. You warmed it."

Audrey smiled, pleased. Didn't they always say the way to a man's heart is through his stomach? Maybe this was all it took to break through the ice floes that had accumulated in their marriage.

After he'd wolfed down half the stack of French toast and all but two of the bacon strips, he turned to her. "How come you're not eating?"

"I ate some in the kitchen."

He nodded, devoured another piece of bacon, took another swig of coffee. "I thought you were working today."

"I'm taking the day off."

"How come?"

"Well, I thought we could spend some time together."

He turned his attention back to the French toast. "Hmph."

"You feel like going for a walk later, maybe?" she asked.

After a moment, he said, "I thought we needed the money."

"One day's not going to send us to the poorhouse. We could go for a drive out in the country."

Another silence, and then he spoke through a mouthful of cantaloupe. "Just don't be telling me about getting a job as a night watchman."

She was annoyed but didn't let on. "We don't have to talk about that stuff now, honey."

"All right."

Her cell phone rang. She hesitated. Not just that it was a flow-breaker, but it was an unwelcome reminder of the job she had and he didn't. She knew it couldn't be a personal call. It rang again.

"I'll make it quick," she said, reaching for the cell phone on her nightstand.

Leon cast her a warning look.

It was Roy Bugbee. This was unusual, a call from Bugbee on a Saturday morning. He wasn't friendly, but neither was he as rude as usual. "The phone records," he said.

"One second." She walked out of the bedroom so as not to subject Leon to her conversation. "Rinaldi's cell phone records?"

"One of the numbers kept coming up a lot, no ID, so I looked it up in Bresser's." He was referring to one of the reverse phone directories. She was impressed at Bugbee's initiative, relieved that he'd finally agreed to take this job on. Maybe he wasn't completely beyond redemption.

Bugbee had paused, waiting for her to say something, or maybe for dramatic effect, so she said, "Great idea."

"Right. And three guesses who called Rinaldi at 2:07 in the morning, the day Stadler got plugged."

"Stadler," she ventured.

"No," Bugbee said. "Nicholas Conover."

"Two in the morning? The same morning when Stadler's body was found, you mean."

"Uh huh."

"But . . . but Conover told me he slept through the night."

"Hmph. Guess not, huh?"

"No," Audrey said, feeling a little tingle of excitement. "I guess not." Another awkward pause. "Is that it?"

"Is that *it*?" Bugbee scoffed. "You got something better on a Saturday morning?"

"No, I mean—nice job," she said. "Well done."

She ended the call and returned to the bedroom, but Leon was no longer in bed. He was sitting in the chair, dressed, tying his sneakers.

"What are you doing?" she said.

Leon stood up, and as he walked out of the bedroom, he passed the bed and flung out a hand at the breakfast tray, flipping it onto the floor. The cantaloupe balls went skittering across the carpet, the French toast flopping down in a neat pile, the maple syrup puddle sitting atop the gray wool. The coffee spill soaked right in, as did the half-and-half. Audrey couldn't keep from letting out a squawk of surprise.

She followed him out, crying, "Leon, baby, I'm sorry—I didn't . . ." But didn't *what*? The call was important, wasn't it?

"You'll make it quick, huh?" Leon said bitterly as he clomped down the hall. "Sure you will. You got business to do, you're gonna do it no matter what we're doing. You got your priorities straight, don't you?"

She felt sad and almost despondent. "No, Leon, that's not fair," she said. "I couldn't have been on the phone for more than a minute. I'm sorry—"

But the screen door slammed, and he was gone.

AUDREY WAS ALONE in the house now, feeling lonely and a tad anxious. She had no idea where Leon had stormed off to, just that he'd taken his car.

She called Bugbee back, reaching him on his cell.

He didn't sound happy to hear from her, but then, he never did. "You said Conover called Rinaldi at 2:07 on Wednesday morning. Was that the only call that night?"

"That morning," Bugbee corrected her. She could hear traffic noise in the background. He was probably in his car now.

"Were there any other calls that night or that morning between Conover and Rinaldi?"

"No."

"That means Rinaldi didn't call Conover first, wake him up or something. Conover wasn't calling Rinaldi back, in other words."

"Right. Put it this way: Rinaldi didn't call Conover from either his home phone or his cell phone. It's conceivable he called Conover from a payphone, but you'd have to get Conover's phone records for that."

"Yes. I think we should talk to both of these gentlemen again."

"I'd say so. Hold on, I'm losing you." A few seconds went by, a half a minute, and he was back on. "Yeah, put the squeeze on 'em both. I'd say we got 'em there with an inconsistency."

"I'd like to talk to them tomorrow."

"Tomorrow's Sunday—don't you have church or something?"

"Sunday afternoon."

"I'm golfing."

"Well, I'm going to see if I can't talk to Nicholas Conover tomorrow afternoon."

"On Sunday?"

"I figure he can't be too busy at work if it's a Sunday."

"But that's family time."

"Stadler had a family too. Now the thing is, Roy, I think we should talk to these gentlemen simultaneously. And we ought to call them at the last minute before we go over. I really don't want one calling the other to get their stories straight."

"Right, but like I said, I'm golfing tomorrow."

"I'm flexible as to the time tomorrow," she said. "You tell me what works best for you. I'm usually out of church by eleven."

"Christ. Well, I'd rather do Conover. I want to take down the fucker. You can talk to Rinaldi."

"My sense, talking to Rinaldi, is that he might respond better to a male detective."

"I don't really give a shit what makes him comfortable."

"It's not a matter of comfort," Audrey said. "It's a matter of what's going to work best, what will help us extract the information we want most effectively."

Bugbee raised his voice a few decibels. "You want

to get information out of Nicholas Conover, you gotta play him hard. And that calls for me. My style. Not yours. You're a pushover, and he can tell."

"Oh, I'm less of a pushover than you might think, Roy," she said.

55

CASSIE WAS ALREADY seated at a booth when Nick arrived at the Town Grounds, Fenwick's upscale coffee house. The national craze for good coffee had even come to Fenwick, a Maxwell-House-in-the-can kind of place if ever there was one, but Starbucks had stayed clear so far. The result was this small, sort of neo-hippy joint that roasted their own coffee, did a healthy take-out business in beans, and served coffee in little glass French presses.

She was drinking a cup of herbal tea—a Celestial Seasonings Cranberry Apple Zinger packet was crumpled next to the teapot—and looked tired, gloomy. The smudges under her eyes were back.

"Am I late?" Nick asked.

A quick shake of the head. "No, why?"

"You look pissed off."

"You obviously don't know me well enough yet," she said. "You'll learn to recognize pissed off. This isn't pissed off. This is tired."

"Well, that dinner wasn't so bad, was it?"

"Your kids are great."

"You really hit it off with them. I think Julia loved having another woman around."

"It's a pretty male household, with you two Conover men exuding all that testosterone."

"The thing is, you know, Julia's at this age where— well, I don't know who's going to talk to her about periods and tampons, all that girl stuff. She doesn't want to hear it from me. Like I know anything about it anyway."

"Her nanny, maybe? Marta, right?"

"I guess. But it's not the same thing as a mom. There's Laura's sister, Aunt Abby, but we barely see her anymore since Laura's death. And Luke spends most of his time hating me. One big happy family." He told her about the big fight, Lucas storming out of the house.

"You talk about him like he's the bad seed."

"Sometimes I think he is."

"Since Laura's death."

Nick nodded.

"How'd that happen?"

Nick shook his head. "I don't want to get into that, you mind?"

"Hey, fine. What do I care?"

Nick looked at her. "Come on, don't get offended. It's just a sort of heavy topic for a Sunday morning, okay?" He took a breath. "We were driving to a swim meet and we hit an icy path and skidded." He studied the tabletop. "And blah blah blah."

"You were driving," she said softly.

"Laura was, actually."

"So you don't blame yourself for it?"

"Oh, I do. I totally do."

"But you know it's not rational."

"Who's talking rational?"

"Whose swim meet?"

"Luke's. Can we talk about something else, please?"

"So he gets to blame you and also share in the guilt, right?"

"You got it. It's a mess."

"He's a good kid, deep down. Lot of attitude, like most sixteen-year-old boys. Hard shell, but soft nougat center."

"How come I never get to see the nougat center?"

"Because you're his dad, and you're safe."

"Well, maybe you can talk to him about the evils of smoking."

"Yeah, right," she said, chuckling. She took a pack of Marlboros from her jeans jacket and tapped one out. "I think I'm not the best person to do that. Kinda like your Sid Vicious giving 'Just Say No' lectures on heroin." She took out her orange plastic Bic lighter and lit the cigarette, pulling the saucer toward her to use as an ashtray.

"I thought people who do yoga don't smoke," Nick said.

She flicked him a glare.

"Isn't yoga all about breath?"

"Come on," she said.

"Sorry."

"Can I ask you something?" she said offhandedly.

"Sure."

"Julia told me about your dog." Nick felt his guts constrict, but he said nothing. "God," she went on. "That's so incredible. I mean, how did you feel when that happened?"

"How did I feel?" He didn't know how to respond. How would anyone feel? He shook his head, faltered for a bit. "I was frightened for my kids, I guess, most of all. I was terrified they might be next."

"But you must have been furious too. I mean, God, someone who'd do something like that to your family!" She tilted her head as she peered at him, her eyes keen. "I'd want to kill him."

Why was she asking this?

He felt a wave of cold wash over him. "No," he said, "it wasn't anger so much as—as this protective instinct. That's what I felt most of all."

She nodded. "Sure. That's right. The normal dad re-action. Gotta protect the kids."

"Right. Got a new alarm system, told all the kids to be extra careful. But there's only so much you can do." His cell phone rang.

He apologized, and picked it up. "Nick Conover," he said.

"Mr. Conover, this is Detective Rhimes?"

He paused for a few seconds. "Oh, yes. Hi—"

He wondered whether Cassie could hear the police detective's voice.

Cassie smoked, idly studying a hand-lettered "THIS IS A SMOKE-FREE ZONE!" sign on a little chalkboard, pink Day-Glo chalk.

"I'm terribly sorry to bother you on a Sunday, but if there's any way you could spare a little time, I'd like to come by and talk for a little bit."

"Well, sure, I suppose. What's up?"

"There's a couple of little details I'm confused about, I thought you might be able to clear up for me. I know Sunday is family time, but if you wouldn't mind . . ."

"Sure," Nick said. "What time do you have in mind?"

"Is half an hour from now convenient for you?"

Nick hesitated. "I think that would be okay," he said.

When he ended the call, he said, "Cassie, listen— I'm sorry, but—"

"Family calls," she said.

He nodded. "Afraid so. I'll make it up to you."

She put a hand on his forearm. "Hey, don't worry about it. Family's always number one."

As soon as he'd dropped her off, he dialed Eddie's cell.

56

DRIVING UP TO the fancy iron gate with the brass plaque that said FENWICKE ESTATES, Audrey was distinctly aware that she was entering another world. She had changed out of her church clothes into something more casual, and now she felt underdressed. Her Honda Accord was definitely underdressed. The guard at the gatehouse looked her over with disapproval as he took her name and picked up his phone to call Conover. She doubted it was the color of her skin. More likely the color of the rust on her front left quarter panel.

She noticed all the security cameras. One, mounted to the gatehouse, took her picture. Another was positioned to capture her license plate at the rear of her car. There was a proximity-card reader by the guard's window too: people who lived in Fenwicke Estates probably had to wave a card at the sensor to be admitted. The security was impressive. But what must it be like to live like this? she wondered. In a place like Fenwick, where the crimes were mostly localized in the bad part of town, why would you want to live this way? Then she remembered what Conover had said about his wife's concern that the family might be threatened by employees laid off from Stratton.

When she drove up to the house, she drew breath.

This was a mansion, there was no other word for it. The place was immense, made of stone and brick, beautiful. She'd never seen a house like this in real life. It sat in the middle of a huge green field of a lawn, with specimen trees and flowers everywhere. As she walked up the stone path to the house, she glanced again at the lawn and noticed that the blades of grass were small and slender and sparse. Up close she could see that the lawn had recently been seeded.

The lawn.

She pretended to trip on one of the paving stones, fell to her knees, breaking her fall with one hand. When she got back on her feet, she slipped a good healthy pinch of soil into her purse just as the front door opened and Nicholas Conover came out.

"You okay?" he said, walking down the front steps toward her.

"Just clumsy. My husband's always saying to me, 'Walk much?'"

"Well, you're not the first to trip on those stones. Gotta do something about that path."

He was wearing faded jeans, a navy blue polo shirt, white running shoes. She hadn't noticed before how tall he was and trim and powerful looking. He looked like an athlete, or a former athlete. She remembered reading that he'd been a hockey star at the high school.

"I'm so sorry to disturb you at home on a Sunday."

"Don't worry about it," Conover said. "It's probably just as well. My schedule during the week's pretty jammed. Plus, anything I can do to help you out, I want to do. You're doing important work."

"I appreciate it. This is such a beautiful home."

"Thanks. Come on in. Can I get you some coffee?"

"No, thanks."

"Lemonade? My daughter makes the best lemon-ade."

"That right?"

"Right from frozen concentrate. Yep."

"That sounds tempting, but I'll pass." Before they got to the front steps, she turned around and said, "That really has to be the most beautiful lawn I've ever seen."

"Now, that's what a guy likes to hear."

"Oh, right. Men and their lawns. But seriously, it looks like a putting green."

"And I don't even golf. My greatest failing as a CEO."

"Is it—do you mind if I ask, because my husband, Leon, is always complaining about the state of our lawn—did you put down sod?"

"No, just seed."

"Regular grass seed, or, what's that stuff called—where you spray it?"

"Hydroseed. Yep, that's what we did."

"Well, I've got to tell Leon. He's always calling it hydro*weeding* because he says you get way too many weeds in the grass, but this looks just perfect to me."

"That Leon sounds like a real card."

"Oh, he is," Audrey said, feeling a prickle. "That he is."

The front door looked like something out of Versailles, ornately carved wood in a honey color. A quiet high-pitched tone sounded when Conover opened the door: an alarm system. He led her through an enormous foyer, high vaulted ceilings, really breathtaking. So this is how rich people live, she thought. Imagine being able to afford a house like this. She tried not to gawk, but it was hard.

She heard the sound of someone playing a piano and thought of Camille. "Is that one of yours?" she asked.

"My daughter," he said. "Believe me, it doesn't happen often, her practicing. It's like a total eclipse of the sun."

They walked by the room where a young girl was practicing, a lanky dark-haired girl around Camille's age wearing a baseball shirt. The girl was playing the first prelude from Bach's *Well-Tempered Clavier,* one of Audrey's favorite pieces. She played it haltingly, mechanically, clearly not yet grasping how fluid it had to be. Audrey caught a quick flash of a baby grand piano, a Steinway. She remembered how long LaTonya and Paul had scrimped to buy the battered old upright, which never stayed in tune. Imagine owning a Steinway, she thought.

She was briefly tempted to stop and listen, but Conover kept going down the hall, and she kept up. As they entered an elegant sitting room with Persian rugs and big comfortable-looking easy chairs, she said, "Oh, they never like practicing."

"Tell me about it," Conover said, sinking into one of the chairs. "You pretty much have to put a—" he began, then started again. "They fight you on everything at this age. You have kids, Detective?"

She sat in the chair alongside his, not the one directly opposite, preferring to avoid the body language of confrontation. "No, I'm afraid we haven't been blessed with children," she said. What was he about to say—You have to put a gun to their heads? What was interesting was not the figure of speech but that he'd caught himself.

Interesting.

She casually glanced at an arrangement of family photographs in silver frames on a low table between them, and she felt a pang of jealousy. She saw Conover and his late wife, a son, and a daughter, Conover with his two children and the family dog. An extremely handsome family.

This house, these children—she was overcome by envy, which shamed her.

Envy and wrath shorten the life, it said in Ecclesiastes. Somewhere else it said that envy is the rottenness of the bones—was it Proverbs? Who is able to stand before envy? Who indeed? *Behold, these are the ungodly, who prosper in the world; they increase in riches.* That was in Psalms, she was quite sure. *Surely thou didst set them in slippery places: thou castedst them down into destruction.*

Her entire house could fit into a couple of these rooms.

She would never have children.

She was sitting next to the man who was responsible for laying Leon off.

She took out her notebook and said, "Well, I just wanted to clear up a few things from our last conversation."

"Sure." Conover leaned back in his chair, arms folded back, stretching. "How can I help you?"

"If we can go back to last Tuesday evening, ten days ago."

Conover looked puzzled.

"The night that Andrew Stadler was murdered."

He nodded his head. "Okay. Right."

She consulted her pad, as if she had the notes from their last interview right in front of her. She'd already transcribed them and put them into a folder in one of the Stadler file boxes. "We talked about where you were that night," she prompted, "when your memory was maybe a little fresher. You said you were at home, asleep by eleven or eleven thirty. You said you slept through the night."

"Okay."

"You don't remember getting up that night?"

He furrowed his brow. "I suppose it's possible I got up to pee."

"But you didn't make a phone call?"

"When?"

"In the middle of the night. After you went to sleep."

"Not that I recall," he said, smiling, leaning forward. "If I'm making calls in my sleep, I've got even bigger problems than I'm aware of."

She smiled too. "Mr. Conover, at 2:07 A.M. that night you placed a call to your security director, Edward Rinaldi. Do you remember that?"

Conover didn't seem to react. He seemed to be examining the pattern on the Oriental rug. "We're talking after midnight, early on Wednesday?"

"That's right."

"Then I must have my days wrong."

"I'm sorry?"

"One of those nights I remember the alarm went off. I've got it set to make a sound in my bedroom so it doesn't wake up the whole house."

"The alarm went off," Audrey said. That was checkable, of course.

"Something set it off, and I went downstairs to check it out. It was nothing, as far as I could see, but I was a little anxious. You can understand, I'm sure, with what had just happened."

She nodded, compressed her lips, jotted a note. Didn't meet his eyes.

"Eddie, Stratton's security director, had just had one of his guys put in this fancy new alarm system, and I wasn't sure if this was a false alarm or something I should be concerned about."

"You didn't call the alarm company?"

"My first thought was to call Eddie—I asked him to come out to the house and check it out."

She looked up. "You couldn't check it out yourself?"

"Oh, I did. But I wanted to make sure there wasn't something faulty in the system. I didn't want to call the cops for what was sure to be a false alarm. I wanted Eddie to check it out."

"At two in the morning?"

"He wasn't happy about it." Conover grinned again. "But given what I've been through, we both agreed it was better safe than sorry."

"Yet you told me you slept through the night."

"Obviously I got the days mixed up. My apologies." He didn't sound at all defensive. He sounded quite casual. Matter-of-fact. "Tell you something else, I've been taking this pill to help me sleep, and it kind of makes the nights sort of blurry for me."

"Amnesia?"

"No, nothing like that. I don't think Ambien causes amnesia like some of those other sleeping pills, Halcion or whatever. It's just that when I pass out, I'm zonked."

"I see."

He'd just altered his story significantly, but in a completely believable way. Or was she being too suspicious? Maybe he really had mixed up the days. People did it all the time. If that night hadn't been unusual or remarkable for him—if, that is, he hadn't witnessed Andrew Stadler's murder that night, or been aware of it whether before or after the fact—then there was no reason for him to have any special, fixed memory of what he'd done. Or not done.

"And did Mr. Rinaldi come over?"

Conover nodded. "Maybe half an hour later. He walked around the yard, didn't find anything. Checked the system. He thought maybe a large animal had set it off, like a deer or something."

"Not an intruder."

"Not that he could see. I mean, it's possible someone was out there, walking around on my property, near the house. But I didn't see anyone when I got up, and by the time Eddie got here, he didn't see anything either."

"You said you took Ambien to go to sleep that night?"

"Right."

"So you must have been pretty groggy when the alarm went off."

"I'll say."

"So there might have been someone, or something, that you just didn't notice. Being groggy and all."

"Definitely possible."

"Did anyone else in the house wake up at the time?"

"No. The kids were asleep, and Marta—she's the nanny and housekeeper—she didn't get up either. Like I said, the alarm was set to sound in my bedroom, and not too loud. And the house is pretty soundproof."

"Mr. Conover, you said your security director had 'just' put in the new alarm system. How long ago?"

"Two weeks ago. Not even."

"After the incident with the dog?"

"You got it. If I could have had Eddie put in a moat and a drawbridge, I'd have done that too. I don't ever want my kids to be endangered."

"Certainly." She'd noticed the cameras around the house when she'd arrived. "If you'd had a system like this earlier, you might have been able to prevent the break-ins."

"Maybe," Conover said.

"But you live in this gated community. There seems to be a lot of security when you come in—the guard, the access control, the cameras in front and all around the perimeter fence."

"Which does a pretty good job of keeping out unau-thorized vehicles. Problem is, there's nothing that stops someone from just climbing the fence out of sight of the guardhouse and getting in that way. The cameras'll pick them up, but there's no motion sensor around the fence—no alarm goes off."

"That's a serious security flaw."

"Tell me about it. That's why Eddie wanted to beef up the system at the house."

But now another thought appeared at the back of her thoughts, and she tugged at it like a stray thread.

The security system.

The cameras.

Nothing that stops someone from just climbing the fence.

If Stadler had climbed the fence that surrounded Fenwicke Estates and walked to Conover's house in the middle of the night, walked across the lawn, setting off the brand-new motion sensors, wouldn't that have been captured by Conover's own video cameras?

And if so, wouldn't there be a recording somewhere? Probably not videotape: no one used that anymore. Probably recorded onto a hard drive somewhere in the house, right? She wondered about that. She didn't really know much about how these newfangled security systems worked.

She'd have to take a closer look.

"You know, I've changed my mind about that coffee," Audrey said.

57

AUDREY DID NOT arrive home until a little after seven, feeling a knot in her stomach as she turned the key in the front door. She'd told him that she'd be home for dinner, though she hadn't said what time that would be. It took so little to set Leon off.

But he wasn't home.

Several nights in a row he hadn't been home until late, almost ten o'clock. What was he doing? Did he go out drinking? Yet recently he didn't seem to be drunk when he got home. She couldn't smell liquor on his breath.

She had another suspicion, though it made her sick to think about it. It explained why Leon was no longer interested in having sex with her.

He was getting it somewhere else. He was, she feared, having an affair, and lately he was being brazen about it, not even attempting to cover it up.

Leon was at home all day while she was at work, which gave him plenty of opportunity to cheat without her ever finding out. But going out, coming home at nine, ten o'clock without so much as an excuse—that was a thumb in her eye. That was blatant.

Sure enough, at a few minutes after ten she heard the jingling of the keys in the lock, and Leon walked in, went right to the kitchen, ran water into a glass. He didn't even say hello.

"Leon," she called out.

But he didn't answer.

And she knew. You didn't have to be a detective. It was that obvious. She knew, and it was like a punch to her solar plexus.

NICK SAT IN his study, trying to go over some paperwork. He'd been calling Eddie, at home and on his cell, but no answer. On his fourth try, Eddie answered with an annoyed "What?"

"Eddie, she was just here," Nick said.

"Fenwick's own Cleopatra Jones? She don't have no superpowers, Nick. She's just sweating you. They tried the same shit on me today—the other one came by, Bugbee, asked me a shitload of questions, but I could see they got nothing."

"She asked me about the call I made to you that night."

"What'd you tell her?"

"Well, I—see, I'd told her I slept through the night that night."

"*Shit.*"

"No, listen. That's what I said at first, but then when she said she knew I'd made a call to you on your cell phone, I told her I must have mixed up the nights. I said the alarm went off that night, so I called you to ask you to check it out." Nick waited for Eddie's response with rising dread. "My God, Eddie, did you tell the other cop something different? I mean, I figured the alarm going off, that's a matter of record—"

"No, you did the right thing. I said pretty much the same once I saw what he had. But man, I was shitting bricks you might try to wing it, say something else. Good job."

"We've got to coordinate a little more closely, Eddie. Make sure we don't say different things."

"Right."

"And something else. She was admiring the alarm system."

"She's got good taste." He lowered his voice. "And so does the superfreak who's naked in my bed. Who was just admiring my dick. Which is why I gotta go."

"Especially the cameras. Especially the *cameras,* Eddie."

"Yeah?"

"Are you *positive* there's no way to retrieve the part of the tape you erased?"

"It's not tape, it's digital," Eddie snapped. "Anyway, I told you, you have nothing to worry about. What's gone is gone. Why are we fucking *having* this conversation? I just spent ten minutes preheating the oven— now I got to stick in my French bread before it cools down, you get what I'm saying?"

"The hard drive is totally clean, right? They can't bring it back?"

An exasperated sigh. "Stop being such a *girl,* okay?"

Nick felt a surge of anger he knew better than to vent. "I sure as hell hope you know what you're doing," he said stonily.

"Nick, you're doing it again. You're peeing in my pool. Oh, by the way. That work you wanted me to do on Scott McNally?"

"Yeah?"

"Remember last month when he was away for a week?"

"I remember. Some sort of dude ranch in Arizona. Grapevine Canyon, was it? He said it was like *City Slickers* without the laughs."

"*City Slickers,* he said? *Crouching* fucking *Tiger*'s more like it. He's a sneak, but a cheapskate numbers guy like him can't pass up the corporate travel rates, right? So this pencil dick puts in for a Stratton discount when he buys his ticket to Hong Kong. I got the receipts from the girls in the travel office. Unfucking*believable.*"

"Hong Kong?"

Eddie nodded. "Hong Kong and then Shenzhen. Which is this huge industrial area near Hong Kong, shitload of factories, on the mainland."

"I know about Shenzhen."

"That mean anything to you?"

"It means he's lying to me," Nick replied. *It also means that all these rumors are right. Where there's smoke there's fire, as the GSA guy said.*

"Sounds to me like you got trouble everywhere you go," Eddie said. "Big trouble."

58

AUDREY WAS SURPRISED to find Bugbee in this early, sitting in his cubicle on the phone. She approached and heard him talking to a lawn company, asking about hydroseeding. Well, she thought, what do you know? He really is working this case.

He wore his customary sport coat, a pale green with a windowpane plaid, a pale blue shirt, red tie. In repose, he was not a bad-looking man, even if he dressed like a used-car salesman. He saw her standing nearby, kept talking without acknowledging her presence. She held up a finger. After a little while he gave her a brusque nod.

She waited until he got off the phone, then wordlessly showed him the little clear-plastic eye-cream vial.

He looked at the pinch of dirt, said suspiciously, "What's that?"

"I took it from Conover's lawn yesterday." She paused. "His lawn was recently hydroseeded."

Bugbee stared, the realization dawning. "That's not admissible," he said. "Poison fruit."

"I know. But worth taking a look at. To my eye it looks like the same stuff from under Stadler's fingernails."

"It's been, what, like two weeks since the murder? It's probably disintegrated a lot since then. The mulch pellets are supposed to break down."

"It's been a dry couple of weeks. The only water probably came from his irrigation system. More interesting, I managed to get a look at his security system while he was making coffee for me." She handed him a While You Were Out message slip on which she'd written some notes. "Pretty fancy. Sixteen cameras. Here's the name of the alarm monitoring company he uses. And the makes and models of the equipment, including the digital video recorder."

"You want me to talk to one of the techs," he said. She noticed that for the first time he didn't argue with her.

"I think we should go over there and take a look at the recorder. And while we're at it, check for blood and prints, inside and outside the house."

Bugbee nodded. "You're thinking the whole thing went down in or near Conover's house, and the surveillance cameras recorded it."

"We can't ignore the possibility."

"They'd be stupid to forget about that little detail."

"We've both seen a lot of stupidity. People forget. Also, it's not like the old days when you could just take out a videotape and get rid of it. It's got to be a lot harder to erase a digital surveillance recording. You've got to know what you're doing."

"Eddie Rinaldi knows what he's doing."

"Maybe."

"Of course he does," Bugbee said. "Are you thinking Conover did it?"

"I'm thinking Eddie did it." Now that he was a suspect, she noticed, he'd gone from Rinaldi to Eddie. "I think Conover saw or heard Stadler outside his house. Maybe the alarm went off, maybe not—"

"The alarm company would probably have a record of that."

"Okay, but either way, Conover calls Eddie, tells him this guy's trying to get into his house. Eddie comes over, confronts Stadler, then kills him."

"And gets rid of the body."

"He's an ex-cop. He's smart enough, or experienced enough, to make sure he doesn't leave any trace evidence on the body—"

"Except the fingernails."

"It's the middle of the night, two in the morning, it's late and it's dark and they're both panicking. They overlook some things. Subtleties like that."

"One of them moves the body down to Hastings."

"Eddie, I'm guessing."

Bugbee thought a moment. "The gatehouse at Fenwicke Estates probably has records of who left when. We can see if Conover drove out of there some time after Eddie drove in. Or if it was just Eddie."

"Which would tell you what?"

"If the shooting happened inside or outside Conover's house, they had to move the body down to the Dumpster on Hastings. Which they're going to do in a car. If both Conover and Rinaldi left Fenwicke Estates some time after two, then it could have been either one of them. But if only Eddie left, then it's Eddie who moved it."

"Exactly." A moment of silence passed. "There are cameras everywhere around the community."

Bugbee smiled. "If so, we got 'em."

"That's not what I'm saying. If we can get the surveillance tapes, we can confirm when Eddie entered and exited, sure."

"Or Eddie and Conover."

"Okay. But more important, we can see if *Stadler*

came over. If Andrew Stadler entered. Then we've got Stadler's whereabouts pinned down."

Bugbee nodded. "Yeah." Another pause. "Which means that Eddie has an unlicensed .380."

"Why unlicensed?"

"Because I went through the safety inspection certificate files at the county sheriff's department. He's got paperwork for a Ruger, a Glock, a hunting rifle, couple of shotguns. But no .380. So if he's got one, he doesn't have any paper on it."

"I've been pushing the state crime lab," Audrey said. "I want to see if they can use their database to match the rounds we found in Stadler's body with any other no-gun case anywhere."

Bugbee looked impressed, but he just nodded.

"In any case, we're going to need a search warrant to see what weapons Rinaldi has."

"Not going to be a problem getting one."

"Fine. If we find a .380 and we get a match . . ." She was starting to enjoy the genuine back-and-forth, even if Bugbee was still prickly and defensive.

"You're dreaming. He can't be that stupid."

"We can always hope. What did he say about the phone call?"

"He was pretty slick. Said, yeah, he got a call from Conover that night, the alarm went off at Conover's house and could he check it out. Said he was a little pissed off, but he went over there to check it out. You know, the shit you do to keep your boss happy. It was like no big deal. Did Conover put his foot in it?"

"No. He—well, it felt like he sort of evolved his story."

"Evolved?"

"He didn't revise his story right away. I reminded him that he'd said he slept through the night, and then I asked him about the phone call he made at two in the morning, and he owned right up to it. He said he must have got the days mixed up."

"Happens. You believe him?"

"I don't know."

"He sound rehearsed?"

"It was hard to tell. Either he was telling the truth, or he'd done his homework."

"Usually you can tell."

"Usually. But I couldn't."

"So maybe he's a good liar."

"Or he's telling the truth. The way I see it, he's telling *part* of the truth. He called Eddie, Eddie came over—and that's where the true part ends. Did Eddie say if he found anything when he looked around Conover's yard?"

"Yeah. He said he found nothing."

"That much they got straight," Audrey said.

"Maybe too straight."

"I don't know what that means. Straight is straight. You know what? I say we ought to move quickly on this. The gun, the tape recorder—this is all stuff that they could do something about if they haven't already. Toss the gun, delete the tape, whatever. Now that we've talked to them both separately, at the same time, they're both going to be suspicious. If they're going to destroy evidence, now is the time they're going to do it."

Bugbee nodded. "Talk to Noyce, put in for the warrants anyway in case we need them. I'll make a couple of calls. Can you clear your schedule today?"

"Happy to."

"Oh, I called that Stadler chick for a follow-up."

"And?"

"She doesn't know shit about what her father did on the night he was killed. Says he never said anything about Conover."

"You think she's telling you the truth?"

"I got no reason to think otherwise. My instinct tells me, yeah, she's on the level."

Audrey nodded. "Me too."

A few minutes later, Bugbee came up to Audrey's cubicle with a cat-that-ate-the-canary smile. "Wouldn't you just know Nicholas Conover would use a company called Elite Professional Lawn Care? Sixteen days ago they hydroseeded the property around a house belonging to the CEO of the Stratton Corporation. The guy remembered it well—the architect, guy named Claflin, specified Penn Mulch. Said they had to put in a new gas line or something, tore up the old grass, and his client decided to put in a whole new lawn, replace the crappy old one. Lawn guy, he said it's a waste of money to put stuff like that in the slurry, but he's not going to argue. Not with a customer who has the big bucks, you know?"

59

SCOTT MCNALLY TENDED to get into work around the same time as Nick did, around seven thirty. Normally, they and the other early arrivers sat at their desks working and doing e-mail, tended not to socialize, took advantage of the quiet time to get work done uninterrupted.

But this morning, Nick took a stroll across the floor to the other side and approached Scott's cubicle quietly. He felt a pulse of fury every time he thought about how Scott had lied to him about going to that dude ranch in Arizona, had instead made a secret trip to mainland China. That coupled with what he'd learned from the Atlas McKenzie and the Homeland Security guys— these goddamned rumors that Stratton was quietly negotiating to "move the company to China," whatever that meant exactly.

It was time to rattle Scott's cage, find out what he was doing.

"Got any interesting vacation ideas?" Nick asked abruptly.

Scott looked up, startled. "Me? Come on, my idea of a great vacation is a Trekkie convention." He caught the look on Nick's face and laughed nervously. "I mean, well, Eden loves Parrot Cay in the Turks and Caicos."

"Actually, I was thinking some place further east. Like Shenzhen, maybe? Where do you like to stay when you visit Shenzhen, Scott?"

Scott reddened. He looked down at his desk—it was almost a reflex, Nick noticed—and said, "I'll go anywhere for a good mu shu pork."

"Why, Scott?"

Scott didn't answer right away.

"We both know how hard Muldaur's been pushing for us to move manufacturing to Asia," Nick said. "That what you're doing for him? Checking out Chinese factories behind my back?"

Scott looked up from his desk, looking pained. "Look, Nick, right now Stratton is like a puppy with diarrhea, okay? Cute to look at, but no one wants to get too close. I'm not doing any of us any good if I don't scout out these possibilities."

"Possibilities?"

"I realize you find it upsetting. I can't blame you. But one day, when you look at the numbers and you finally say, 'Scott, what are our options here?' I've got to be able to tell you what they are."

"Let me get this straight," Nick said. "You made some sort of secret-agent trip to China to scout out factories, then *lied* about it to me?"

Scott closed his eyes and nodded, compressing his lips. "I'm sorry," he said very quietly. "It wasn't my idea. Todd insisted on it. He just felt it was too much of a sore point with you—that you'd do everything you could to block any kind of overtures to China."

"What kind of 'overtures' are you talking about? I want specifics."

"Nick, I really hate being caught in the middle like this."

"I asked you a question."

"I know. And it's really not my place to say any more than I have already. So let's just leave it right there, okay?"

Nick stared. Scott wasn't even feigning deference anymore. Nick felt his anger growing greater by the second. It was all he could do not to reach over and grab Scott by the scrawny neck, lift him up, and hurl him against the silver-mesh fabric panel.

Nick turned to leave without saying another word.

"Oh, and Nick?"

Nick turned back, looked at him blankly.

"The Nan Hai is the place."

"Huh?"

"The place to stay in Shenzhen. The Nan Hai Hotel. Great views, great restaurant—I think you'll like it."

A voice squawked out of Scott's intercom. "Scott, it's Marjorie?"

"Oh, hey, Marge. Looking for Nick? He's right here."

"Nick," Marge said. "Call for you."

Nick picked up Scott's handset to speak to her privately. "There a problem?"

"It's someone from the police."

"My burglar alarm again."

"No, it's . . . it's something else. Nothing urgent, and your kids are fine, but it sounds important."

Scott gave him a curious look as Nick hurried away.

60

"THIS IS NICK Conover."

Audrey was astonished, actually, when Nicholas Conover picked up the phone so quickly. She was expecting the usual runaround, the game of telephone tag that powerful men so often liked to play.

"Mr. Conover, this is Detective Rhimes. I'm sorry to bother you again."

The slightest beat of silence.

"No bother at all," he said. "What can I do for you?"

"Well, now, I was wondering if we might be able to look around your house."

"Look around . . . ?"

"We were thinking it would help us a great deal in establishing Andrew Stadler's whereabouts that night. That morning." She hoped the shift to "we" was subtle enough. "If indeed it was Andrew Stadler who went to your house that night, he might have been scared off by all the new security measures. The cameras and the lights and what have you."

"It's possible." Conover's voice sounded a bit less friendly now.

"So if we're able to nail down whether he did go to your house—whether it really was him who came by and not, say, a deer—that'll be a big help in mapping his last hours. Really narrow things down for us."

She could hear Conover inhale.

"When you're talking 'look around,' what do you mean, exactly?"

"A search. You know, the usual."

"Not sure I know what that means." Was there the slightest strain in his voice? Certainly something had shifted, changed. He was no longer putting out friendly vibes. He'd gone neutral.

"We come over with our techs, collect evidence, take pictures, whatever."

They both knew what she meant. No matter how she spun it, how she dressed it up, it was still a crime-scene search, and Conover surely understood that. It was a funny sort of dance now. A performance, almost.

"You talking about searching my yard?"

"Well, yes. That and your premises as well."

"My house."

"That's right."

"But—but no one entered my house."

She was ready for that. "Well, see, if Andrew Stadler really is the stalker who's repeatedly broken into your house over the last year, we might find evidence of that inside. Am I wrong in concluding that no one from the Fenwick police ever took fingerprints after the previous incidents?"

"That's right."

She shook her head, closed her eyes. "The less said about that, the better."

"When are you talking about doing this? This week some time?"

"Actually, given how things are progressing in this investigation," she said, "we'd like to do it today."

Another pause, this one even longer.

"Tell you what," Conover said at last. "Let me call

you right back. What's the best number to reach you at?"

She wondered what he was going to do now—consult an attorney? His security director? One way or the other, whether he gave permission or not, she was going to search his premises.

If he refused—if she needed to get a search warrant—she'd be able to get one in about an hour. She'd already talked to one of the prosecutors, woke him up at home this morning, in fact, which didn't endear her to him. Once the prosecutor's head cleared, he'd said that there were sufficient grounds to grant a warrant. A district court judge would sign it, no problem.

But Audrey didn't want to get a search warrant. She didn't want to play hardball. Not yet. That was escalation, and if and when she needed to step things up, she could always do it. Better to low-key things. Keep up the pretense—the *shared* pretense, she was quite sure—that Nicholas Conover was being cooperative just because he was a good citizen, wanted to see justice done, wanted to get to the bottom of this. Because the moment he shifted to opposition and antagonism, she'd be all over him.

If he refused, four patrol units would be on their way over to his house in a matter of minutes to secure the premises and the curtilage, or the surrounding area, make sure no one took anything out. Then she'd be there an hour later with a search warrant and a crime-scene team.

She didn't want to go down that road yet. But she always had to be aware of the legalities. The prosecutor had rendered his judgment that she *could* get a warrant if she wanted to, yes. Instead, Audrey wanted to conduct what they called a consent search. That meant that Conover would sign a standard Consent to Search form.

It was a little tricky, though. If Conover signed it and

his signature was witnessed, that established that he'd given his knowing, intelligent, and voluntary consent to a search. But there'd been cases, she knew, where a suspect with a clever lawyer had managed to get the results of a search thrown out at trial, insisting that they'd been coerced, or they didn't totally understand, or whatever. Audrey was determined not to commit that gaffe. So she was following the prosecutor's advice: Get Conover to sign the waiver, date it, get two witnesses, and you're fine. And if he refuses, we'll get you a warrant.

Half an hour later he called back, sounding confident once again. "Sure, Detective, I have no problem with that."

"Thank you, Mr. Conover. Now, I'm going to need you to sign a consent form allowing us to search your premises. You know, cross every *T* and so on."

"No problem."

"Would you like to be there for the search? It's up to you, certainly, but I know how busy you are."

"I think it's a good idea, don't you?"

"I think it's a good idea, yes."

"Listen, Detective. One thing. I don't mind you guys searching my property, looking for whatever you want, but I really don't want the neighborhood crawling with cops, you know? There going to be a bunch of patrol cars with lights and sirens and all that?"

Audrey chuckled. "It won't be as bad as all that."

"Can you do this using whatever you call them, unmarked vehicles?"

"For the most part, yes. There will be an evidence van and such, but we'll try to be subtle about it."

"As much as a police search can be subtle, right? Subtle as a brick to the head."

They shared a polite, uneasy laugh.

"One more thing," Conover said. "This is a small

town, and we both know how people talk. I really hope this is all kept discreet."

"Discreet?"

"Out of the public eye. I really can't afford to have people hearing about how the police have been talking to me and searching my house in connection with this terrible murder. You know, I'm just saying I want to make sure my name stays out of it."

"Your name stays out of it," she repeated, thinking: *What are you saying exactly?*

"Look, you know, I'm the CEO of a major corporation in a town where not everybody loves me, right? Last thing I want is for rumors to start spreading—for people to be making stuff up about how Nick Conover's being looked into. Right?"

"Sure." She felt that prickle again, like an eruption of goose bumps.

"I mean, hey, we both know I'm not a suspect. But you get rumors and all that."

"Right."

"You know, it's like they say. A lie's halfway around the world before the truth has a chance to get its pants on, right?"

"I like that," she said. Here was another thing that made her uneasy. When an innocent person is being investigated for a homicide, he almost always squawks about it to his friends, protests, gets indignant. An innocent person in the klieg lights wants the support of his friends, so he invariably tells everyone about the outrage of the police suspecting him.

Nick Conover didn't want people to know that the police were interested in him.

This was not the reaction of an innocent man.

— PART FOUR —

CRIME SCENE

61

EARLY THAT MORNING, the day after Detective Rhimes had come over to the house to talk, Nick had awakened damp with sweat.

The T-shirt he'd slept in was wet around the neck. His pillow, even, was soaked, the wet feathers and down giving off that barnyard smell. His pulse was racing the way it used to during a particularly fierce scrimmage.

He'd just been jolted out of a dream that was way too real. It was one of those movielike dreams that feel vivid and fully imagined, not like his normal fleeting fragments of scenes and images. This one had a plot to it, a terrible, inexorable story in which he felt trapped.

Everyone *knew.*

They knew what he'd done That Night. They knew about Stadler. It was common knowledge, everywhere he went, walking through the halls of Stratton, the factory floor, the supermarket, the kids' schools. Everyone knew he'd killed a man, but he continued to insist, to pretend—it made no sense, he didn't know why—that he was innocent. It was almost a ritual acted out between him and everyone else: they knew, and he knew they knew, and yet he continued to maintain his innocence.

Okay, but then the dream took a sharp left turn into the gothic, like one of those scary movies about teenagers and homicidal maniacs, but also like a story by Edgar Allan Poe he'd read in high school about a telltale heart.

He came home one day, found the house crawling with cops. Not the house he and the kids lived in now, not Laura's mansion in Fenwicke Estates, but the dark, little brown-shingled, split-level ranch in Steepletown he'd grown up in. The house was a lot bigger though. Lots of hallways and empty rooms, room for the police to spread out and search, and he was powerless to stop them.

Hey, he tried to say but he couldn't speak, you're not playing by the rules. I pretend I'm innocent, and so do you. Remember? That's how it works.

Detective Audrey Rhimes was there and a dozen other faceless police investigators, and they were fanning out across the eerily large house, searching for clues. Someone had tipped them off. He heard one of the cops say the tip came from Laura. Laura was there too, taking an afternoon nap, but he woke her up to yell at her and she looked wounded but then there was a shout and he went to find out what was up.

It was the basement. Not the basement of the Fenwicke Estates house, with its hardwood floors and all the systems, the Weil-McLain gas-fired boiler and water heater and all that, neatly enclosed behind slatted bifold doors. But the basement of his childhood house, dark and damp and musty, concrete-floored.

Someone had found a pool of bodily fluids.

Not blood, but something else. It reeked. A spill of decomposition that had somehow seeped out from the basement wall.

One of the cops summoned a bunch of the other guys, and they broke through the concrete walls, and they found it there, the curled-up, decomposed body of Andrew Stadler, and Nick saw it, an electric jolt running through his body. They'd found it, and the game of pretenses was over because they'd found the proof, a body walled up in his basement, decomposing, rotting, leaching telltale fluids. The body so carefully and artfully concealed had signaled its location by festering and decaying and putrefying, leaking the black gravy of death.

A GOOD TEN hours after he'd awakened in a puddle of his own flop sweat, Nick pulled into the driveway and saw a fleet of police vehicles, cruisers, and unmarked sedans and vans, and it was as if he'd never woken up. So much for low-key. They couldn't have been much more obvious if they'd arrived with sirens screaming. Luckily the neighbors couldn't see the cars from the road, but the police must have caused a commotion arriving at the gates.

It was just before five o'clock. He saw Detective Rhimes standing on the porch waiting for him, wearing a peach-colored business suit.

He switched off the Suburban's engine and sat there for a moment in silence. Once he got out of the car, he was sure, nothing would be the same. Before and after. The engine block ticked as it cooled off, and the late afternoon sun was the color of burnt umber, the trees casting long shadows, clouds beginning to gather.

He noticed activity on the green carpet of lawn around the side of the house where his study was. A couple of people, a man and a woman—police techs?— were grazing slowly like sheep, heads down, looking closely for something. The woman was a squat fireplug with a wide ass, wearing a denim shirt and brand-new-looking dark blue jeans. The other one was a tall gawky guy with thick glasses, a camera around his neck.

This was real now. Not a nightmare. He wondered how they knew to look in the area nearest his study.

He tried to slow his heartbeat. Breathe in, breathe out, think placid thoughts.

Think of the first time he and Laura had gone to Maui, seventeen years ago, pre-kids, a Pleistocene era of his life. That perfect crescent of white sand beach in the sheltered cove, the absurdly blue crystal-clear water, the coconut palms rustling. A time when he felt more than just relaxed; he'd felt a deep inner serenity, Laura's fingers interlaced with his, the Hawaiian sun beating down on him and warming him to his core.

Detective Rhimes cocked her head, saw him sitting in the car. Probably deciding whether to walk up to the Suburban or wait for him there.

They were looking for spent cartridges. He had a gut feeling.

But Eddie had retrieved them all, hadn't he?

Nick had been such a wreck that night, so dazed and so out of it. Eddie had asked him how many shots he'd fired, and Nick had answered two. That was right, wasn't it? The thing was such a blur that it was possible it was three. But Nick had said two, and Eddie had found two shell casings on the grass close to the French doors.

Had there been a third shot?

Had Eddie stopped when he found two, leaving one there that waited to be found by the gawky man and the fireplug woman, those experts in locating spent cartridge casings?

The lawn hadn't been mowed, of course, because the grass was too new. The fast-talking guy from the lawn company had told him to wait a good three weeks before he let his gardener mow.

So a chunk of metal that might otherwise have been thrown up into the blades of Hugo's wide walk-behind

Gravely could well be lying there, glinting in the late-afternoon sun, just waiting for the wide-ass chick to bend over and snatch it up in her gloved hand.

He took another breath, did his best to compose himself, and got out of the Suburban.

"I'M TERRIBLY SORRY to intrude on you this way," Detective Rhimes said. She looked genuinely apologetic. "You're very kind to let us look around. It's such a big help to our investigation."

"That's all right," Nick said. Strange, he thought, that she was keeping up the pretense. They both knew he was a suspect. He heard the rattling squawk of a crow circling overhead.

"I know you're a very busy man."

"You're busy too. We're all busy. I just want to do everything I can to help." His mouth went dry, choking off his last couple of words, and he wondered if she'd picked up on that. He swallowed, wondered if she noticed that too.

"Thank you so much," she said.

"Where's your charming partner?"

"He's busy on something else," she said.

Nick noticed the gawky guy walking across the lawn to them, holding something aloft.

He went light headed.

The guy was holding a large pair of forceps, and as he drew closer Nick could see a small brown something gripped at the end of the forceps. When the tech showed it to Detective Rhimes, without saying a word, Nick saw that it was a cigarette butt.

Detective Rhimes nodded as the man dropped the cigarette butt into a paper evidence bag, then turned back to Nick. She went on speaking as if they hadn't been interrupted.

Was Stadler smoking that night? Or had that been

dropped there by one of the contractor's guys, taking a cigarette break outside the house, knowing they weren't allowed to smoke inside? He'd found some discarded Marlboro butts out there not so long ago, just before the loam was hydroseeded, picked them up with annoyance, made a mental note to say something to the contractor about the guys tossing their smokes around his lawn. Back when he had the luxury to be annoyed about such trivialities.

"I hope you don't mind that we got started a little early," Detective Rhimes said. "Your housekeeper refused to let my team in until you arrived, and I wanted to respect her wishes."

Nick nodded. "That's kind of you." He noticed that the woman articulated her words too clearly, her enunciation almost exaggerated, hypercorrect. There was something formal and off-putting about her manner that contrasted jarringly with her shyness and reserve, a glimmering of uncertainty, a vein of sweetness. Nick prided himself on his ability to read people pretty well, but this woman he didn't quite get. He didn't know what to make of her. Yesterday he'd tried to charm her, but he knew that hadn't worked.

"We're going to need to get a set of your fingerprints," she said.

"Sure. Of course."

"Also, we're going to need to take prints from everyone who lives in the house—the housekeeper, your children."

"My children? Is that really necessary?"

"These are only what we call elimination prints."

"My kids will freak out."

"Oh, they might think it's fun," she said. A sweet smile. "Kids often find it a novelty."

Nick shrugged. They entered the house, the high alert tone sounding quietly. The place different now:

hushed, tense, like it was bracing itself for something. He heard the sound of running feet.

Julia.

"Daddy," his daughter said, face creased with concern, "what's going on?"

62

HE SAT DOWN with the kids in the family room, the two of them on the couch that faced the enormous TV, Nick in the big side chair that Lucas normally staked out, which Nick thought of as his Archie Bunker chair. The Dad chair. He couldn't remember when they'd all watched TV together last, but back when they did, Lucas always grabbed the Archie Bunker chair, to his silent annoyance.

On a trestle table next to the TV set Nick noticed the little shrine that Julia and Lucas had made to Barney: a collection of photographs of their beloved dog, his collar and tags. His favorite toys, including a bedraggled stuffed lamb—his own pet—that he slept with and carried everywhere in his slobbering mouth. There was a letter Julia had written to him in different colored markers, which began: "Barney—we miss you SO MUCH!!!" Julia had explained that the shrine was Cassie's idea.

Lucas sat on the couch in huge baggy jeans, his legs splayed wide. The waistband of his boxer shorts was showing. He wore a black T-shirt with the word AMERIKAN in white letters on the front. Nick had no idea what that referred to. The laces on his Timberland boots were untied. He was wearing that rag on his head again. My own in-house, upper-middle-class, gated-community gangsta, Nick thought.

Lucas, staring off into the distance, said, "You gonna tell us what's up with the five-oh?"

"The police, you mean."

Lucas was looking out the bay window, watching the cops on the lawn.

"The police are here because of that guy who we think kept coming by and writing things inside our house," Nick said.

"'No Hiding Place,'" recited Julia.

"Right. All that. He was a man who had something wrong with his head."

She said in a small voice, "Is he the man who killed Barney?"

"We're not sure, but we think so."

"Cassie's dad," Lucas said. "Andrew Stadler."

"Right." Cassie's dad.

"He was fucked up," Lucas said.

"Watch your mouth around your sister."

"I've heard that word before, Dad," said Julia.

"No doubt. I just don't want either one of you using language like that."

Lucas, smirking, shook his head with amused contempt.

"So this man, Andrew Stadler, he died a couple of weeks ago," Nick went on, "and the police think he might have tried to come by our house the night he was killed, on his way to wherever he was going."

"They think you did it," Lucas said. A triumphant smile.

Nick's insides seized. Maybe he *had* heard, that night when Eddie came over. Or did he just put two and two together?

"Hey!" said Julia, outraged.

"Actually, Luke, what they're doing here is trying to trace his whereabouts."

"Then how come they're gathering evidence? I can see 'em out my window. They dug up some dirt from the lawn and put it in a little container thing, and they keep walking back and forth on the lawn like they're scoping for something."

Nick nodded, breathing in and out. They were gathering dirt? What did that mean? Had they found dirt on Stadler's body? He remembered that Eddie had brushed Stadler's shoes clean.

Could they have found dirt on Stadler's body that connected him with the house? Could they even do something like that? This was the awful thing: Nick had no idea of what the police were actually capable of, how advanced their forensic science was, or how backward.

"Luke," he said calmly, "they're looking for anything that can tell them whether the guy came by here that night or not." Nick knew he was treading water here. His kids were too bright. They'd watched too many TV shows and movies. They knew about cops and murders and suspects.

"Why do they care?" asked Julia.

"Simple," he said. "They need to nail down what he did that night, see if he really was here instead of somewhere else, so they can figure out where he might have gone after that, when he was killed."

"Wouldn't that be on the cameras?" Lucas asked.

"Could be," Nick said. "I don't remember when the new security system was put in and when exactly the guy was killed."

"I do," Lucas said right back. "They put the cameras in the day before Stadler was killed." How the hell did he know that, *remember* that?

"Well, if you're right, then yes, they might find

something on the cameras. I have no idea. Anyway, the police want to get your fingerprints while they're here."

"Cool," said Lucas.

"How come? They don't think *we* killed the man, right?" said Julia, looking worried.

Nick laughed convincingly. "Don't worry about that. When they check for fingerprints inside and outside the house, they're going to find our fingerprints—yours and mine and Marta's—"

"And probably Emily's too," said Julia.

"Right."

"And probably that guy Digga, right, Luke?"

Luke rolled his eyes, looked away.

"Who's Digga?" Nick asked.

Lucas didn't answer, still shaking his head.

"He's this guy who wears a do-rag just like Luke and plays really loud music when you're not here and always smells like smoke. He stinks."

"When does he come over?" said Nick.

"Like once or twice," Lucas said. "Jesus Christ. This is totally wack. He's a friend of mine, all right? Am I allowed to have friends, or is this, like, a prison where you're not allowed to have visitors? You happy, Julia? Fuckin' tattletale."

"Hey!" Nick said.

Julia, so unused to being yelled at by her older brother, ran out of the room crying.

"Uh, Mr. Conover?"

Detective Rhimes, standing tentatively at the door to the family room.

"Yes?"

"Could I see you for a minute?"

63

"WE FOUND SOMETHING on your lawn," she said.

"Oh?"

She'd taken him out into the hall, far enough away from the kids that they couldn't hear.

"A mangled piece of metal."

Nick shrugged, as if to say, So? Is that supposed to mean something to me?

"It may be a bullet fragment, maybe a piece of shell casing."

"From a gun?" His breath stopped. Outwardly he tried to project an image of nonchalance, but interested, as someone in his position should be. Someone who was innocent, who wanted the cops to find the killer.

"It's hard to say. I'm no expert."

"Can I take a look?" he said, and he immediately regretted saying it. Mustn't betray too much interest. Must get the balance right.

She shook her head. "The techs have it. I just wanted to ask you—it may seem a silly question—but you've said you don't own a gun, right?"

"That's right."

"So obviously you've never fired a gun on your property, I'm sure. But has anyone you know fired a gun in your yard, to your knowledge?"

He attempted a dismissive laugh, though it sounded hollow. "No target practice allowed here," he said.

"So, no one's ever fired a gun outside your house, to your knowledge."

"Nope. Not as far as I know."

"Never."

"Never." A cool trickle of sweat traced a path along the back of one ear and down his neck, where it was absorbed by the collar of his shirt.

She nodded again, slowly. "Interesting."

"The techs—are they sure it's from a bullet or whatever?"

"Well, you know, I doubt *I* could tell the difference between a bottle cap and a—a Remington Golden Saber .380 cartridge," she said. Nick couldn't stop himself from flinching, and he hoped she hadn't noticed. "But the crime scene techs, they're awfully good at what they do, and I have to defer to them on that. They tell me it sure looks like a fragment from a projectile."

"Strange," Nick said. He tried to look puzzled in a sort of neutral, disinterested way, not letting the way he was really feeling leak out—terrified and trembling and nauseated.

Eddie had assured him he'd collected everything, all the shell casings, and checked for any other trace evidence that might be on the lawn. Then again, he could easily have missed a small piece of lead or brass or whatever it was, a flying piece of metal that had lodged itself into the earth, say. That would be easy to miss.

After all, Nick had noticed the smell of liquor on Eddie's breath that night. He'd probably been sleeping it off when Nick called. Didn't have all his faculties about him. Maybe he hadn't been so thorough.

Detective Rhimes seemed about to say something more when Nick noticed someone walking by, carrying a black rectangular metal object sealed in a clear plastic bag. The fireplug woman, the evidence tech with the wide ass in the new jeans, was holding what Nick recognized at once as the digital video recorder that was hooked up to the security cameras. They must have taken it from the closet where the installer had put the alarm system.

"Hey, what's that?" Nick called out. The woman, whose nametag on her denim shirt said Trento, stopped, looked at Detective Rhimes.

The detective said, "That's the recording unit from your security system."

"I need that," Nick said.

"I understand. We'll make sure this is turned around just as quickly as possible."

Nick shook his head in apparent frustration. He hoped, prayed that the little shimmy of terror moving through his body wasn't obvious. Eddie had wiped the disk clean, he'd said. Reformatted it. Nothing was there from that night.

Nick could only imagine what the camera image would look like. The lurching of a man in a too-big flapping overcoat suddenly illuminated by the outside lights. The flailing hands. The way the man had crumpled to the ground. Or did one of the cameras capture the act itself, Nick holding the pistol, his face contorted with fear and anger, pulling the trigger? The gun bucking up and back, the smoke cloud. The murder itself.

But that was all gone.

Eddie had assured him of that. Eddie, whose breath had stunk of booze. Who was always cocky but never thoughtful and thorough, certainly not in the rink. Who'd always acted hastily, impulsively.

Who might have missed something.

Done it wrong. Failed to reformat it properly.

Might have fucked up.

"Also, Mr. Conover, we're going to need the keys to both of your cars, if you don't mind."

"My cars?"

"The Chevy Suburban that you drive, and the minivan. We'll want to dust for prints and so on."

"How come?"

"In case Stadler tried to get in, steal one of the cars, whatever."

Nick nodded, logy and dazed, reached into his pants pocket for his key ring. As he did so, he noticed a swarm of activity in his study, straight down the hall. "I'm going to need to check my e-mail," he said.

Detective Rhimes cocked her head. "I'm sorry?"

"My study. I need to get in there. I have work to do."

"I'm sorry, Mr. Conover, but this might take a while."

"How long are we talking?"

"Hard to say. The evidence techs move in mysterious ways." She smiled, her face lighting up, really lovely. "Oh, one quick question, if you don't mind?"

"Sure."

"About your security director—Mr. Rinaldi?"

"What about him?"

"Oh," she said with a quiet laugh, "I suppose it's like 'Who will guard the guards?' or something, but I'm sure you did a background check on him before you hired him to be your security director."

"Of course," Nick said. A background check was precisely what he hadn't done. Eddie was an old friend. Well, a buddy, maybe. Whatever that meant.

"What do you know about his police career?" she asked.

THERE WAS A yellow tape across the entrance to his study. It said, "Crime Scene—Do Not Cross."

Crime scene, he thought.

You don't know.

Two evidence techs in there, wearing rubber gloves. One was dusting the doors, door frames, light switch plates, the desk, the wood frame and glass panes of the French doors, with fluorescent orange powder. The other was vacuuming the carpet with a strange-looking handheld vacuum cleaner, a black barrel, long straight nozzle.

Nick watched for a moment, cleared his throat to get their attention, and said, "You don't need to do that. We've got a housekeeper."

A lame joke, pathetic even. Offensive, probably. *They* didn't have housekeepers.

The tech with the vacuum cleaner gave him a hard look.

Nick let it slide. They were dusting for fingerprints, but there was no way they were going to find anything incriminating. Stadler wasn't inside the house on the night of his murder. He'd dropped to the ground, easily twenty feet from the French doors.

That wasn't what bothered him.

What bothered him was why they seemed to be focusing on the study. There were lots of other rooms in the house where Stadler might plausibly have gotten in. Why the study?

Did they *know* something?

"Mr. Conover, do you have a key to this drawer?"

A confident baritone. One of the techs was pointing at the locked drawer where he'd kept the gun Eddie had given him.

He felt his entire body seize up.

"Key's right in the top middle drawer," Nick said mildly. "Real high security."

He flashed on the box of cartridges in the drawer next to the gun. A green and gold cardboard box, the words R<small>EMINGTON</small> and G<small>OLDEN</small> S<small>ABER</small> in white lettering.

Eddie had taken them away, right?

When he took the gun?

Nick didn't remember anymore. That night was such a blur.

Please God oh please God let them be gone the bullets make them gone.

He waited. Holding his breath, while the tech opened the big middle desk drawer, located the key at once, knelt down to unlock the bottom drawer.

The back of his shirt collar was seriously damp now. Downright wet.

My life is in this anonymous guy's hands right now. He has the power to lock me away forever.

There's no death penalty in Michigan, he found himself thinking. He'd never thought about it before, never had a reason to think about it. No death penalty.

Life in prison, though.

That was in the balance.

The drawer slid open, the tech bent over.

A second went by, two, then three.

The vacuum cleaner was turned off.

Nick felt like vomiting. He stood there on the other side of the yellow crime-scene tape like some casual sightseer, a tourist, and he waited.

The tech got to his feet. Nothing in his hands.

Maybe the drawer was empty.

If one stray bullet had rolled to the back of the drawer . . .

No, the tech would have taken out his camera and taken a picture if he'd found something.

The drawer had to be empty.

Nick felt relief. Temporary, maybe. Momentary.

He stood there watching the tech, the one who'd been vacuuming, take out a plastic bottle with a pistol grip and begin spraying a section of the hand-plastered walls around the light switch.

Decora rocker switch, Nick thought. Laura had replaced all the light switches in the house with Decora rocker switches, which she insisted were much more elegant. Nick had no opinion on Decora rockers. He'd never really thought much about light switches before.

The guy started spraying the bottom of the French doors, then the carpet.

He heard the two techs murmuring, heard the one with the plastic bottle say something like, "Miss my Luminol."

The other one said something in a low voice, something about a daylight search, and then the first one said, "But Christ, this LCV shit is messy."

Nick didn't know what they were talking about. He felt stupid standing there on the threshold of his own study, gawking and eavesdropping.

The first one said, "stain's gonna be degraded."

The second one said something about "DNA match."

Nick swallowed hard. "Stain" had to mean blood. They were looking for bloodstains on the door handles, on the door, on the carpet. Bloodstains that weren't visible to the naked eye, which had maybe been wiped away but not well enough.

Well, at least I'm safe on that, Nick thought. Stadler never entered the house.

But his brain was not cooperating. It kicked up a thought that made the adrenaline surge, made him break out in sweat once again.

Stadler had bled, fairly profusely.

The black puddle of blood.

Nick had walked up to him, kicked at the body with his bare feet. Maybe even stood in the blood, who knows, he couldn't remember.

Then walked back into the house.

Onto the carpet. To call Eddie.

He'd never *noticed* any bloodstains on the carpet, and neither did Eddie, but how much did it take? What scintilla of evidence, carried into the study on the soles of his bare feet from the puddle beside Stadler's body? Mere droplets perhaps, invisible to the naked eye, smeared onto the wall-to-wall carpet unseen, soaking into the woolen fibers, waiting to announce their presence?

The tech who wasn't spraying the carpet turned around to look at Nick's desk, noticed Nick still standing there.

Quickly Nick said something, just so they wouldn't think he was watching in terrified fascination, as he was. "Is that stuff gonna come off my carpet?"

The tech who was spraying shrugged.

"And what about all that powder?" Nick went on, fake-indignant. "How the hell am I going to get that out?"

The tech with the spray bottle turned around, blinked a few times, a lazy, malevolent grin on his face. "You got a housekeeper," he said.

64

"EDDIE." NICK, CALLING from his study, scared out of his mind.

"What?" He sounded annoyed.

"They were here today."

"I know. Here too. It's bullshit. They're trying to put a scare into you."

"Yeah, well, it worked. They found something."

A pause. "Huh?"

"They found a metal fragment. They think it might be a piece of a shell casing."

"What? They recovered a shell casing?"

"No, a piece of one."

"I don't get it." Eddie's swaggering confidence had evaporated. "I recovered both shells, and I don't remember any fragmentation. You said you fired two rounds, right?"

"I think so."

"You *think* so? Now you *think* so?"

"I was freaked out, Eddie. Everything was a blur."

"You told me you fired two rounds, so when I found two shells, I stopped looking. I coulda spent all night on that fucking lawn walking around with the flashlight."

"You think they really might have a piece of ammu-
nition?" Nick said, a quaver in his voice.

"The *fuck* do I know?" Eddie said. "Shit. Tell you
this, I gotta start digging into this lady detective. See
what skeletons she has in her closet."

"I think she's a good Christian, Eddie."

"Great. Maybe I'll find something real good."

And he hung up the phone.

"WE GOT SHIT, is what we got," said Bugbee.

"The search warrant," Audrey began.

"Was as broad as I could make it. Not just .380s, but
any firearms of any description. On top of the usual.
No blood or fibers in Rinaldi's car anywhere."

"We didn't expect he took the body home with him."

"Obviously not."

"Any .380s?"

Bugbee shook his head. "But here's the weird thing.
Guy's got a couple of those wall-mounted locking
handgun racks, right? Found it in a closet behind some
clothes, bolted onto the wall. Each one holds three
guns, but two of them are missing."

"Missing, or not there? Maybe he only has four."

Bugbee smiled, held up a finger. "Ah, that's the
thing. There's two guns in one, two in the other, and
you can see from the dust patterns that there used to be
two more. They've been removed."

Audrey nodded. "Two."

"I'm saying one is the murder weapon."

"And the other?"

"Just a guess. But maybe there's a reason he didn't
want us to find that one too. Two unregistered hand-
guns."

Audrey turned to go back to her cubicle when a
thought occurred to her. "You didn't warn him you
were doing the search?"

"Come on."

"Then how'd he know you were coming? How'd he know to remove the guns?"

"Now you get it."

"Conover knew we were coming to search his house," Audrey said. "I'm sure he told Rinaldi, and Rinaldi knew it was only a matter of time before we searched his house too."

Bugbee considered for a few seconds.

"Maybe that's all it is," he conceded.

AN E-MAIL POPPED up on Audrey's computer from Kevin Lenehan in Forensic Services, asking her to come by.

The techs in the Forensic Services Unit all went to crime scenes, but some of them had their specialties, too. If you wanted to get a fingerprint off the sticky side of a piece of duct tape, you went to Koopmans. If you wanted a serial number restoration, you took it to Brian. If you wanted a court exhibit, an aerial map, a scene diagram rendered in a hurry, you went to Koopmans or Julie or Brigid.

Kevin Lenehan was the tech most often entrusted with, or perhaps saddled with, retrieving information from computers or video capture work. That meant that while his co-workers got jammed with all the street calls, he had to waste vast amounts of time watching shadowy, indistinct video images of robberies taken by store surveillance cameras. Or poring over the video from the in-car cameras that went on automatically when an officer flipped on his overheads and sirens.

He was scrawny, late twenties, had a wispy goatee and long greasy hair that was either light brown or dark blond, though it was hard to tell, because Audrey had never seen him with his hair recently washed.

The rectangular black metal box that housed the

digital video recorder from Conover's security sys-
tem was on his workbench, connected to a computer
monitor.

"Hey, Audrey," he said. "Heard about your little
bluff."

"Bluff?" Audrey said innocently.

"The bullet fragment thing. Brigid told me. Never
knew you had it in you."

She smiled modestly. "You do what it takes. How's
this coming?"

"I'm kinda not clear on what you wanted," Kevin
said. "You're looking for a homicide, right? But noth-
ing like that here."

It was too easy, Audrey thought. "So what is on there?"

"Like three weeks of the moon moving behind the
clouds. Lights going off and on. Coupla deer. Cars go-
ing in and out of the driveway. Dad, kids, whatever.
Am I looking for something in particular?"

"A murder would be nice," she said.

"Sorry to disappoint you."

"If the cameras recorded it, it's going to be on there,
right?" She pointed at the box.

"Right. This bad boy's a Maxtor hundred-and-
twenty gig drive connected to sixteen cameras, set to
record at seven-point-five frames per second."

"Could it be missing anything?"

"Missing how?"

"I don't know, erased or something?"

"Not far's I can tell."

"Isn't three weeks a long time to record on a hard
drive that size?"

Lenehan looked at her differently, with more re-
spect. "Yeah, in fact, it is. If this baby was in a twenty-
four-hour store, it would recycle after three days. But
it's residential, and it's got motion technology, so it
doesn't use up much disk space."

"Meaning that the camera starts when there's a movement that sets off the motion detector and gets the cameras rolling?"

"Sort of. It's all done by software here. Not external motion sensors. The software is continually sampling the picture, and whenever a certain number of pixels change, it starts the recording process."

"It recycles when the disk gets full?"

"Right. First in, first out."

"Could it have recycled over the part I'm interested in?"

"You're interested in the early morning hours of the sixteenth, you said, and that's all there."

"I'm interested in anything from the evening of the fifteenth to, say, five in the morning on the sixteenth. But the alarm went off at two in the morning, so I'm most interested in two in the morning. Well, 2:07, to be exact. An eleven-minute period."

Kevin swiveled around on his metal stool to look at the monitor. "Sorry. Just misses it. The recording starts Wednesday the sixteenth. Three-eighteen A.M."

"You mean Tuesday the fifteenth, right? That's when it was put in. Some time on the afternoon of the fifteenth."

"Hey, whatever, but the recording starts Wednesday the sixteenth. Three-eighteen in the morning. About an hour after the time you're interested in."

"Shoot. I don't get it."

He spun back around. "Can't help you there."

"You sure the eleven-minute segment couldn't have just been erased?"

Kevin paused. "No sign of that. It just started at—"

"Could someone have recycled it?"

"Manually? Sure. Have to be someone who knows the system, knows what he's doing, of course."

Eddie Rinaldi, she thought. "Then it would have recorded over the part I'm interested in?"

"Right. Records over the oldest part first."

"Do you have the ability to bring it back?"

"Like, unerase it? Maybe someone does. That's kind of beyond what I know how to do. The State, maybe?"

"The State would mean six months at least."

"At least. And who knows if they can do it? I don't even know if it can be done."

"Kevin, do you think it's worth looking at again?"

"For what, though?"

"See if you can figure anything else about it. Such as whether you can find any traces. Anything that proves the recording was recycled over or deleted or whatever."

Kevin waggled his head from one side to the other. "Take a fair amount of time."

"But you're good. And you're fast."

"And I'm also way behind on my other work. I've got a boatload of vid-caps to do for Sergeant Noyce and Detective Johnson."

"That serial robber case."

"Yeah. Plus Noyce wants me to watch like two days' worth of tape from a store robbery, looking for a guy in a black Raiders jacket with white Nike Air shoes."

"Sounds like fun."

"Eye-crossing fun. He wants it done—"

"Yesterday. Oh yes, I know Jack."

"I mean, you want to talk to Noyce, get him to move you up in the queue, go ahead. But I gotta do what they tell me to do, you know?"

65

THE NEXT MORNING was jam-packed with compli-
cated, if tedious, paperwork, which Nick was actually
grateful for. It kept his mind off what was happening,
kept him from obsessing over what the cops might
have found in the house. And that fragment of a shell
casing had ruined his sleep last night. He'd tossed and
turned, alternating between blank terror and a steady,
pulsing anxiety.

There was a bunch of stuff from the corporate coun-
sel's office outlining the patent lawsuit they wanted to
file against one of Stratton's chief competitors, Knoll.
Stephanie Alstrom's staff insisted that Knoll had basi-
cally ripped off a patented Stratton design for an ergo-
nomic keyboard tray.

Stratton filed dozens of these complaints every year;
Knoll probably did too. Kept the corporate attorneys
employed. The legal department salivated at the pros-
pect of litigation; Nick preferred arbitration, pretty
much down the line. It kept the out-of-pocket costs
down, and even if Stratton won the ruling, Knoll would
have already figured out a workaround that would pass
legal muster. Go after Knoll in a public courtroom, and

you blow all confidentiality—your secrets are laid out there for every other competitor to rip off. Then there'd be subpoenas all over the place; Stratton would have to hand over all sorts of secret design documents. Forget it. Plus, in Nick's experience, the awarded damages rarely added up to much once you subtracted your legal expenses. He scrawled *ARB* on the top sheet.

After an hour of sitting at his home base, going over this sort of crap, Nick's shoulders were already starting to ache. The truth was, home base wasn't feeling especially homey these days. His eyes settled on one of the family photographs. Laura, the kids, Barney. Two down, three to go, he thought. The curse of the House of Conover.

He remembered a line he'd seen quoted somewhere: Maybe this world is another planet's hell. There had to be a bunch of corollaries to that. He had made someone else's world a hell, and someone had made his world a hell. Supply-chain management for human suffering.

An instant-message from Marjorie popped up, even though she was sitting not ten feet away, on the other side of the panel. She didn't want to break his concentration—she knew how fragile it tended to be.

The usual for lunch today, right?

Oh, right. Nick remembered: the regular weekly lunch with Scott. Which was just about the last thing he felt like doing.

He wanted to confront Scott, tell him to get the fuck out and go back home to McKinsey. But he couldn't, not yet. Not until he got to the bottom of what exactly was going on. And the truth was, he no longer had the power to fire Scott if he wanted to. Which right now he very much did.

He typed:

OK, thanks.

He noticed that there was an e-mail in his in-box from Cassie; he could tell from the subject line.

He hadn't given her his e-mail address, hadn't gotten an e-mail from her before, and he hesitated before clicking on it:

From: ChakraGrrl@hotmail.com
To: Nconover@Strattoninc.com
Subject: From Cassie
Nick—Where's my grocery delivery boy been? Free for lunch today? Come over between 12:30 and 1? I'll supply the sandwiches.
C.

He felt his spirits lift at once, and he hit Reply:

I'm there.

"Marge," he said into the intercom, "change in plans. Tell Scott I'm not going to be able to make lunch today, okay?"

"Okay. Want me to give a reason?"

Nick paused. "No."

On the way to the elevator he passed Scott, who was coming out of the men's room. "Got your message," Scott said. "Everything okay?"

"Everything's fine. Just got really hectic all of a sudden."

"You'll do anything to avoid talking numbers," Scott said with a grin.

"You got me figured out," Nick said, grinning right

back as he headed for the elevator bank. A couple of women from Payroll got in on the floor below, smiled shyly at him. One of them said, "Hey, Mr. Conover."

He said, "Hey, Wanda. Hey, Barb." They both seemed surprised, and pleased, that he knew their names. But Nick made it a point to know as many Stratton employees by name as possible; he knew how good it was for morale. *And there's fewer and fewer of them all the time,* he thought mordantly. *Makes it easier.*

When the elevator stopped at the third floor, Eddie got in, said, "It's the big dog."

Something awfully disrespectful about that, especially in front of other employees. "Eddie," Nick said.

"Had a feeling you were headed out to, uh, 'lunch,'" Eddie said. The way he dropped little quotation marks around the word "lunch" was unnerving. *Does he know where I'm going? How could he?* And then Nick remembered that he'd asked Eddie to start looking closely at Scott's e-mail. He wondered whether Eddie had taken that as an opportunity to look at Nick's e-mail too. If true, that would be outrageous—but how the hell could he prevent Eddie from doing it? He was the goddamned security director.

Nick just gave him a stony look, which would be missed by Wanda and Barb from Payroll.

"I'll walk you to your car," Eddie said. He was carrying an umbrella.

Nick nodded.

They walked together, silently, through the main lobby, past the waterfall that some feng shui expert had insisted they put there to repair a "blocked energy feeling" at the entrance. Nick had thought that was complete and utter bullshit, but he went along with it anyway, the way he'd always avoided stepping on cracks in the sidewalk so as not to break his mother's back. Anyway, the waterfall looked good there, that was the main thing.

Nick could see through the big glass doors that it was raining. That explained the umbrella, but had Eddie planned to go out for lunch, or did he "happen" to run into Nick in the elevator—by design? Nick wondered but said nothing. He considered, too, asking Eddie about what Detective Rhimes had told him—that Eddie had left the Grand Rapids police force "under a cloud of suspicion." But he didn't know why she'd told him that. Was she trying to put a wedge between the two men? If so, that was a clever way to do it. If Eddie had lied to him about why he'd left police work, what else might he have lied about?

He'd ask Eddie. Not yet, though.

Outside, Eddie opened the big golf umbrella and held it up for Nick. When they'd walked a good distance away from the building, Eddie said, "Foxy Brown better watch her ass."

"I don't know what you're talking about."

"Come on, man. Cleopatra Jones. Sheba baby."

"I'm in a hurry, Eddie. It's been fun free-associating with you."

Eddie gripped Nick's shoulder. "Your black lady detective, man. The one who's trying to roast our nuts over the fire." The rain thrummed loudly on the umbrella. "The Negro lady who's got it in for you because you fucking *laid off her husband*," he said ferociously, drawing out the words.

"You're kidding me."

"Think I'd joke about something like that? About something that should get her fucking thrown off the case?"

"Who's her husband?"

"Some fucking nobody, man, worked on the shop floor spraying paint or whatever. Point is, Stratton laid him off, and now his wife's coming to collect your scalp." He shook his head. "And I say that ain't right."

"She shouldn't be investigating us," Nick said. "That's outrageous."

"That's what I say. Bitch gets disqualified."

"How do we do that?"

"Leave it to me." His smile was almost a leer. "Meanwhile, I got some interesting stuff on your man Scott."

Nick looked at him questioningly.

"You asked me to poke into his e-mail and shit."

"What'd you get?"

"You know what Scott's been doing just about every weekend for the last two months?"

"Burning hamburgers," Nick said. "I was just over there last Saturday."

"Not last Saturday, but almost every other weekend. He's been flying to Boston. Think he's visiting his sick Aunt Gertrude?"

"He's getting the corporate discount through the travel office," Nick said.

Eddie nodded. "I guess he figures you don't look at travel expenses—not your job."

"I do have a company to run. Run into the ground, some would say."

"Plus a shitload of phone calls back and forth between him and that guy Todd Muldaur at Fairfield Equity Partners. Kinda doubt it's all social chitchat, right?"

"Any idea what they're talking about?"

"Nah, that's just phone records. Voice mails I can hack into, but Scotty-boy's a good camper. Deletes all voice mails when he's done listening to them. Him and Todd-O e-mail each other, but it's all kinda generic stuff like you'd expect—you know, here's the monthly numbers, or shit like that. Scotty must know e-mails aren't safe. Maybe that's why, when he's got something he wants to keep quiet, he uses encryption."

"Encryption?"

"You got it. My techs intercepted a couple dozen encrypted documents coming and going between Scotty and Todd-O."

Nick couldn't think of any possible reason why Scott would be sending or receiving encrypted documents. Then again, he couldn't think of a reason why Scott would make a secret trip to China either.

"What are they about?"

"Don't know yet, seeing as how they're encrypted. But my guys are crackerjacks. They'll get 'em open for me. Let you know the second they do."

"Okay." They'd reached Nick's Suburban, and he pressed the remote to unlock it.

"Cool. Enjoy your"—Eddie cleared his throat—"lunch."

"You implying something, Eddie?"

"No umbrella or raincoat?" Eddie said. "Don't you have a nice view out of your office? You musta seen it was raining."

"I was too busy working."

"Well, you don't want to go out without protection," Eddie said with a wink. "Not where you're going."

And he walked off.

66

WHEN HE ARRIVED at Cassie's, the rain had turned into a full-fledged downpour. He parked in her driveway and raced to the front door, rang the bell, stood there getting soaked. No answer; he rang again.

No answer. He rang a third time, looked at his watch. It was 12:40, so he was on time. She'd said between 12:30 and 1:00. Of course, that was ambiguous; maybe she'd wanted him to specify a time.

Drenched, shivering from the cold rain, he knocked on the door and then rang again. He'd have to change his clothes back at the office, where he kept a spare set. It wasn't exactly cool for the CEO of Stratton to walk around headquarters looking like a drowned rat.

Finally he turned the knob and was surprised when it opened. He went in, called, "Cassie?"

No answer.

He walked into the kitchen. "Cassie, it's Nick. You here?"

Nothing.

He went to the living room, but she wasn't there either. In the back of his mind he worried. She seemed a little fragile, and her father had just died, and who the hell knew what she might do to herself?

"Cassie," he shouted, louder still. She wasn't downstairs. The blinds were drawn in the living room. He opened a slat and looked out, but she wasn't out there either.

Nervous, he went upstairs, calling her name. The second floor was even darker and dingier than the downstairs. No wonder she didn't want him going up here. Two doors on either side of a short hallway, and two at both ends. None of the doors was closed. He started at the room at the far end of the hall. It was a bedroom, furnished with not much more than a full-size bed and a dresser. The bed was made. The room had the look and smell of vacancy, as if no one had been in here for a long time. He assumed it was Andrew Stadler's room. He left and went into the room at the other end of the hall, where a sloppily unmade bed, a discarded pair of jeans turned inside out on the floor, and the odor of patchouli and cigarettes told him it was Cassie's.

"Cassie," he called again as he tried another room. It smelled strongly of paint, and he knew even before he entered that this was the room Cassie was using as her studio. Sure enough, there was a half-finished canvas on an easel, a weird-looking picture, a woman surrounded by bright strokes of orange and yellow. Other canvases leaned against the walls, and all of them seemed to be variations on the same bizarre image of a black-haired young woman, naked, her mouth contorted in a scream. It looked a little like that famous painting by Edvard Munch, *The Scream*. In each one, the woman was surrounded by concentric strokes of yellow and orange, like a sunset, or maybe fire. They were disturbing paintings, actually, but she was pretty good, Nick thought, even if he didn't know much about art.

Well, she wasn't here either, which meant that something really was wrong, or they'd somehow gotten their signals crossed in the couple of hours since he'd sent his e-mail. Maybe she'd changed her mind, or had to go out, and had e-mailed back to tell him that, and the e-mail never arrived. That happened.

He tried the last door, but this was a bathroom. He took a much-needed piss, then took a bath towel and began blotting his shirt and pants. He put the towel back on the rod, and then, before he left, he took a peek in the mirror-fronted medicine cabinet, hating himself for snooping.

Apart from the usual cosmetics and women's products, he found a couple of brown plastic pharmacy bottles labeled Zyprexa and lithium. He knew lithium was for manic-depressives, but he didn't know what the other one was. He saw Andrew Stadler's name printed on the labels.

Her dad's meds, he thought. Still hasn't thrown them out.

"They're not all his, you know."

Cassie's voice made him jump. He reddened instantly.

"That lithium—that's mine," she said. "I hate it. Makes me fat and gives me acne. It's like being a teenager all over again." She waved an unopened pack of cigarettes at him, and he realized at once where she'd been.

"Cassie—Jesus, I'm sorry." He didn't even try to pretend he was looking for an Advil or something. "I feel like such a shit. I didn't mean to snoop. I mean, I *was* snooping, but I shouldn't have—"

"Would you snoop around to find out whether it's raining? It's pretty much staring you in the face. I mean, when you meet a person who was valedictorian of her high school, eight hundreds on her SATs, got into every college she applied to, and she's basically doing fuck-all in the world, well, you've got to wonder. How come she isn't pulling down six figures at Corning or working on signal-transduction pathways at Albert Einstein College of Medicine?"

"Listen, Cassie . . ."

Cassie made a circular gesture at her temple with her forefinger, the sign for crazy. "You just got to assume that this girl is a few clowns short of a circus."

"Don't talk that way."

"Would you feel better if I put on a white coat and talked about catecholamine levels in the medial forebrain of the hypothalamus? Put my science education to work? Is that less offensive? It isn't any more informative."

"I don't think you're crazy."

"Crazy is as crazy does," Cassie said in a cornpone Forrest Gump voice.

"Come on, Cassie."

"Let's go downstairs."

Sitting together on the nubby brown couch in the living room, Cassie kept talking. "Full scholarship to Carnegie Mellon. I wanted to go to MIT, but my stepdad didn't want to spend a red cent on me, and even with financial aid it was going to be a stretch. Freshman year was tough. Not the course work so much as the classmates. My sorority house burns down freshman year, and half the girls are killed. Blew me away. I mean, I came back here and didn't want to leave my room. Never went back to college."

"You were traumatized."

"I also got addicted to cocaine and Valium, you name it. I was self-medicating, of course. Took me a few years before I figured out I had 'bipolar tendencies.' Was hospitalized for six months with depression. But the meds they put me on worked pretty well."

"Better living through chemistry, I guess."

"Yeah. By then, of course, I'd wandered off the Path."

"The Path? That some religious thing?"

"The Path, Nick. The Path. You went to Michigan State, studied business, got a job at the Vatican of Office Furniture, and you were pretty much set so long as you kept working hard and kept your nose clean and didn't piss too many people off."

"I get it. And you . . . ?"

"I got off the Path. Or I lost my way. Maybe I was in the woods and a big gust of wind came and blew leaves all over the Path and I just headed off in the wrong direction. Maybe birds ate the damn bread-crumb trail. I'm not saying my life lacks a purpose. It's just that maybe the purpose is to provide a cautionary tale for everyone else."

"I don't think the world is that unforgiving," Nick said.

"People like you never do," Cassie said.

"It's never too late."

Cassie stepped over to him, pressed herself against his chest. "Isn't it pretty to think so?" she murmured.

67

NOYCE CALLED AUDREY into his office and asked her to sit down.

"I got a call from the security director at Stratton," he said.

"He can't have been happy."

"He was ripshit, Audrey. About both him and Conover."

"I can't speak for Roy, but I know my team was as careful as can be. We didn't trash the place."

"I don't think Bugbee was as careful."

"That doesn't surprise me. Mine was a consent search. Roy had a warrant."

"And Roy is Roy. Listen." He leaned forward, rested his elbows on a bare patch of desk, rested his chin on his hands. "Rinaldi hit me with something we have to take seriously."

"They're threatening us with legal action," Audrey said, half-kidding.

"He knows about Leon."

"About Leon."

"I'm surprised, frankly, it took him this long. But he obviously did some looking into you, and Leon's name came up."

"You knew Leon was laid off from Stratton. I didn't keep that from you."

"Of course not. But I didn't really weigh that as carefully as I should have. It didn't occur to me, frankly."

"Everyone in this town's got someone in their family who's been laid off by Stratton."

"Just about."

"You start taking everyone off this case who has any connection to Stratton, and pretty soon there'd be no one left. I mean lab techs and crime scene—"

"This is always something we have to be hypersensitive about."

"Jack, I was assigned to this case randomly. My name came up on the board. I didn't request it."

"I know."

"And when I started it, there was no connection to the Stratton Corporation."

"Granted, but—"

"Let me finish. Leon's situation has nothing to do with this. I'm following the leads here. I'm not on any witch hunt. You know that."

"*I* know it, Aud. Of course I know that. But if and when this comes to trial, I don't want anything fucking it up. If I go to the prosecutor, he's going to say he doesn't want you involved—this has to be clean and pristine. And he'll be right. Any DA is going to worry that this'll look like payback on your part."

She sat up straight in the uncomfortable chair, looked at her boss directly. "Are you taking me off the case?"

He sighed. "I'm not taking you off the case. That's not it. I mean, maybe I should. The Stratton security guy is demanding it. But the fact is, you're one of our best."

"That's not true, and you know it. My clearance rate is pretty darned mediocre."

He laughed. "Your modesty is refreshing. I wish everyone around here had some of that. No, your clearance rate could be higher, but that's because you're still getting your chops. You tend to use a microscope when binoculars are what you want."

"Pardon me?"

"You do waste time, sometimes, looking superclose at evidence that doesn't lead anywhere. Going up blind alleys, barking up the wrong trees, all that. I think that gets better with experience. The more cases you do, the more developed your instinct gets. You learn what's worth following up and what isn't."

She nodded.

"You know I'm your biggest fan."

"I know it," she said, feeling a surge of affection toward the man that was almost love. Maybe it was love.

"I pushed you to apply for the job, and I pushed you through. You know how many hoops you had to jump through."

An abashed smile. She remembered how many interviews she'd had to do. Just when she thought she'd clinched it, someone else asked to interview her. Noyce had steered it all the way. "The race thing," she said.

"The woman thing. That was really it. But look, a lot of people are waiting for you to fail."

"I don't see it that way."

"I do, and believe me, I know. A good number of people around here are waiting for you to trip and fall flat on your face. And I don't want that to happen."

"I don't either."

"Go back to the Leon issue for a second. Whether you say it's an issue or not. We're all susceptible to being driven by unconscious biases. Protective instincts. I know you, and you have a lot of love in your heart, and you hate seeing what your husband's going through. You hate seeing him hurt in any way." Audrey started to object, but Noyce said, "Hear me out. My turn, okay?"

"Okay."

"You've got a forest of facts, of evidence and clues. You've got to find a path through that forest. I mean, the stuff about the hydroseed—that's damned good police work."

"Thank you."

"But we don't know, do we, what that means? Did Stadler walk around Nicholas Conover's premises? Sure. No one's disputing that. Did he crawl around the property on his hands and knees, get dirt under his fingernails? Sure, why not? But does that mean Conover did it?"

"It's a piece of the puzzle."

"But is the puzzle one of those easy twenty-piece wooden jigsaws that little kids do? Or is it one of those impossible thousand-piece jobs my wife likes to do? That's the thing. A hunch and some hydroseed isn't enough."

"The body was too clean," she said. "Most of the trace evidence was removed by someone who knew what he was doing."

"Maybe."

"Rinaldi's an ex-homicide detective."

"Don't have to be a cop to know about trace evidence."

"We caught Conover in a lie," she went on. "He said he slept through the night, the night Stadler was killed. But at two in the morning he called Rinaldi. That's in the phone records."

"They give different stories?"

"Well, when I asked Conover about it, he said maybe he got the day wrong, maybe that was the night his alarm went off and he called Rinaldi to check it out, since Rinaldi's staff put it in."

"Well, so maybe he did get the day wrong."

"The bottom line," Audrey said, exasperated, "is that they knew Stadler was stalking Conover. He butchered the family dog. Then he turns up dead. It just can't be a coincidence."

"You sound certain of it."

"It's my instinct."

"Your instinct, Aud?—don't take this the wrong way—but your instinct isn't exactly developed yet."

She nodded again, hoping her irritation didn't show in her face.

"The bullet fragments," he said. "At Conover's house. What was that all about?"

She hesitated. "We didn't find any bullet fragments."

"That's not what you told Conover. You said you found a piece of metal. You said it was a fragment from a projectile." Rinaldi must have told him this. How else could he know?

"I didn't say that."

"No, but you let him think that, didn't you?"

"Yes," she confessed.

"That was a little show you put on for Conover, wasn't it?" he said sadly. "That was all a bluff, designed to get Conover to break down and admit it. Am I right?"

She nodded, hotly embarrassed. "I hardly think I'm the first homicide detective to try a bluff."

"No, you're not. Far from it. I've done my share, believe me. But we're dealing with the CEO of the Stratton Corporation. That means we're under the klieg lights here. Everything you do, everything *we* do, is going to be scrutinized."

"I understand. But you know, if my little bluff pushes him closer to an admission, it'll be worth it."

Noyce sighed. "Audrey. Okay, so the crack on Stadler's body was really lemon drops. Whether the guy got swindled or the thing was a setup, we just don't know. But you got a schizo guy wandering around the dog pound in the middle of the night, it's not so surprising he gets shot, right?"

"None of the informants knew anything about it."

"Stuff goes on down there, our informants only know one little slice of it."

"But boss—"

"I don't want to be a backseat driver on this one, but before you go off trying to sweat the CEO and the security director of a major corporation for conspiracy to murder some crazy guy—two men who have an awful lot to lose—you want to make sure you're not being seduced by a great story. I mean, your theory is sure a heck of a lot sexier than some drug killing. But this case mustn't be about entertainment value. It's got to be about hardnosed police work. Right?"

"Right."

"For your own sake. And ours."

"I understand."

"I can't help you if you don't keep me fully informed, okay? From now on, I want you to keep me in the loop. Help me help you. I don't want you getting burned on this."

68

EDDIE LIVED IN a small condominium complex called Pebble Creek. It had been built about half a dozen years ago, and consisted of four five-story buildings— stained wood, red brick, big windows—set on a big square of grass and gravel. Each of the condos had its own white-trellised balcony, where residents had put out things like folding chairs and trees in pots. It was a look Nick had heard described as neo-Prairie. No creek anywhere, but plenty of pebbles around the parking lot. There were homey-looking office parks that looked like this—the Conovers' pediatric dentist was located in one—and some people might have found Pebble Creek a little officey-looking for a home. Eddie wouldn't have been one of them.

"Be it ever so humble," Eddie said as he let Nick in. He was wearing black jeans and a gray knit shirt that was furred from one too many tumbles in the dryer. "Welcome to the Edward J. Rinaldi fuck pad."

Nick had never visited Eddie at his home before, but he wasn't surprised at what he saw. A lot of glass, a lot of chrome. Blue-gray carpeting. Black lacquered furniture and booze cabinet, big mirrors on the wall behind it. The biggest things in the room were two big flat

Magnapan speakers, in silver, standing at either side of a black sofa like shoji screens. Everything more or less matched. In the bedroom, Eddie showed off an immense waterbed that he said got so much use he'd had to replace the liner three times already.

"So what do you know?" Eddie said, walking Nick into the area of his living room he no doubt called his "entertainment center," though maybe he had a more colorful name for it.

"Well," Nick said, "I know that 'J' was the last letter added to the alphabet."

"No shit? How did they get by without it? Jacking off. Jheri Curl. Jism. Jesus. Jock straps. You got all the basics of civilization right there." Eddie opened the drinks cabinet, twisted open a bottle of Scotch. "Not to mention J & B. And Jameson's. What'll you have?"

"I'm okay," Nick said.

"Yeah," Eddie said, settling into a chair covered in fake silver-gray suede, and putting his feet on the glass coffee table, next to a couple of books titled *Beyer on Speed* and *Play Poker Like the Pros*. "I think maybe you are."

"What makes you say that?" Nick sat on the adjoining sofa, which was covered in the same fake suede.

"'Cause, Nicky, I got something for you. Figured you wouldn't mind coming over to my place to look at a couple of e-mails our boy Scotty deleted a couple of weeks ago. I guess he figures if you delete something it's gone, poof. Doesn't realize all e-mail's archived on the server. So who's Martin Lai?"

"Martin Lai. He's our manager for Asia Pacific, out of Hong Kong. In charge of accounting. Truly the deadliest, most stultifyingly dull guy you're ever going to meet. Human ether."

"Well, check it out." He handed Nick a couple of pages.

To: SMcNally@Strattoninc.com
From: MLai@Strattoninc.com
Scott,

Can you please confirm for me that the USD $10 million that was wired out of Stratton Asia Ventures LLC this morning to a numbered account, no attached name, was done at your behest? The SWIFT code indicates that the funds went to the Seng Fung Bank-Macau. This entirely depletes the fund's assets. Please reply soonest.

Thank you,
Martin Lai
Managing Director, Accounting
Stratton Inc., Hong Kong.

And then, Scott's immediate reply:

To: MLai@Strattoninc.com
From: SMcNally@Strattoninc.com
This is fine — just part of the usual process of repatriation of funds in order to avoid tax payments. Thanks for keeping an eye out, but all is OK.
—Scott

When Nick looked up, he said, "Ten million bucks? What's it for?"

"I don't know, but it looks to me like Scotty-Boy's being a little reckless. Playing fast and loose, huh?"

"It does, doesn't it?"

"Not like you."

"Huh?"

"*You're* not being reckless at all, right?"

"What's that supposed to mean?"

"What *you're* doing, man, is a fuck of a lot stupider than whatever Scott McNally's up to. You better check yourself before you wreck yourself, bro, or we're both going to the slammer. And don't think I'm going to take the rap for you."

"What the hell are you talking about?"

Eddie's gaze bore down on him relentlessly. "You want to explain what the fuck you're doing layin' pipe with Stadler's daughter?"

Nick was speechless for a moment. "Are you *spying* on me, Eddie? That's how you knew where I was going that day, in the rain, isn't it? You have no business monitoring my e-mail or my phone lines—"

"It's like we're on a road trip together, Nick. We gotta be taking the same turns. You need to be watching the speed limit, observing all traffic signs. And right here, see, there's no Merge sign. Sign says DO NOT ENTER. Are you hearing me? Because it's real important that you do." Eddie locked eyes with him. "Do you realize how unbelievably fucking *reckless* you're being?"

"It's totally none of your business, Eddie."

Eddie stretched, raised his arms and put his hands behind his head. Under his arms, sweat stains blackened his gray shirt. "See, that's where you're wrong, buddy. It's very much my business. Because if this keeps up, we could both be making license plates in the shithouse, and I promise you, that's not going to happen."

"This is out of bounds. You lay off her."

"I wish you'd lay off her too. You tell me you're getting rim jobs from the local Brownie troop, I could give a shit. You tell me you're setting up a crystal-meth lab in your basement, I could give a flying fuck. But this thing involves the two of us. You let that piece of ass into your life—for whatever freaky, fucked-up reasons of your own—and you are jeopardizing both of us. What the fuck do you *think* she's after?"

"I don't know what you're talking about."

"News flash," Eddie said in a low voice. "You wasted her old man."

The blood left Nick's face. He was groping for words, but none came.

"You really don't get it, do you? Cops think you might've had something to do with it. Let's say the cops talk to her, maybe let on their suspicions, let it slip, see if she knows anything, right? So this little girl figures she gets close to you—I'm just spitballing here—and maybe she finds something out. Something that could help bring you down. Who the hell knows what? Maybe her thing isn't really getting into your pants. Maybe it's about getting into your *head*."

"That's bullshit. I don't believe it," Nick said. It felt as if his guts had furled into a small hard ball.

That time at Town Grounds.

God, someone who'd do something like that to your family.

I'd want to kill him.

"Believe it," Eddie said. "Entertain the goddamn possibility." He drained his glass, exhaled with a loud alcohol wheeze. "The ass you save could be your own."

"I'm not going to sit here and listen to this," Nick said, his face burning. He stood up, went to the door, but stopped halfway there and turned back around. "You know, Eddie, I'm not so sure you're in any position to be giving lectures about recklessness."

Eddie was staring at him defiantly, an ugly grin on his face.

Nick went on, "I don't think you really leveled with me about why you left the Grand Rapids police."

Eddie's eyes narrowed to slits. "I already told you about that bullshit charge."

"You didn't tell me you were drummed out for pilfering."

"Oh, Christ. Sounds like the kinda thing Cleopatra

Jones might have told you. You going to believe her, or me?"

Nick pursed his lips. "I don't know, Eddie. I'm beginning to think I believe her."

"Yeah," Eddie said acidly. "You would, wouldn't you?"

"You didn't say it wasn't true."

"Did I cut corners? Sure. But that's it. You can't believe everything you hear. People talk some crazy shit."

69

AUDREY'S DESK PHONE rang, and she checked the caller ID to make sure it wasn't poor Mrs. Dorsey again. But it was a 616 area code, which meant Grand Rapids, and so she picked it up.

A woman was calling from the Michigan State Police crime lab who identified herself as an IBIS technician named Susan Calloway. She was soft-spoken but authoritative-sounding, her voice arid, devoid of any warmth or personality. She gave the case number she was calling about—it was the Stadler homicide—and said, "The reason I'm calling, Detective, is that I believe you asked us to see if we could match the bullet in your case with any others, correct?"

"That's correct."

"Well, it seems we got a warm hit on IBIS."

Audrey knew a fair amount about the Integrated Ballistics Identification System. She knew it was a computerized database of archived digital images of fired bullets and cartridges that linked police and FBI crime labs across the country. It was sort of like AFIS, the fingerprint-matching network, only the fingerprints here were photographs of bullets and casings.

"A warm hit?" Audrey said. That term she hadn't heard before, though.

"I mean a possible hit," the woman said, her bland voice betraying the tiniest hint of annoyance. "To me, it looks quite similar to a bullet recovered in a no-gun case in Grand Rapids about five, six years ago. Six years ago, to be precise."

"What kind of case?"

"The file class is 0900-01."

That was the Michigan state police offense code for a homicide. So the gun used to kill Stadler had been used six years earlier in another homicide, in Grand Rapids. That could be significant—or it could mean almost nothing. Guns were bought and sold on the black market all the time.

"Really? What do we know about the case?"

"Not much, Detective, I'm sorry to say. I have only the submitting agency's case number, which won't do you much good. But I've already called over there and asked them to bring over the bullet in question so I can do the comparison."

"Thank you."

"And as to the question you're probably about to ask—how long will this take?—the answer is, as soon as I get the bullet from the GR PD."

"Well, I wasn't going to ask that," Audrey said. She thought: Only because it would rankle if I *did* ask. If you had no juice with these firearms examiners, you'd better be as sweet as pie. "But I appreciate the information."

Interesting, she thought. Very interesting.

She took a stroll across the squad room and over to Forensic Services, where she found Kevin Lenehan slumped over his desk, arms folded, a dim shadowy tape playing on a TV monitor, numbers racing across the top of the screen.

She put a hand on his shoulder, and he jolted awake.

"Hey," she said, "you don't want to miss the guy in the Nike Air sneakers and the Raiders jacket."

"I hate my life," he said.

"You're too good for this kind of work," she said.

"Tell that to my manager."

"Where is she?"

"Maternity leave. Noyce's my manager these days. Aren't you tight with him?"

"I wouldn't say that. Kevin, listen. Could you take another look at my recorder? I mean, unofficially and off the books and all that?"

"When? In my voluminous spare time?"

"I'll owe you one."

"No offense, but that doesn't really work on me."

"Then how about out of the goodness of your heart?"

"Not much there," he said.

"Kevin."

He blinked. "Let's say, hypothetically now, that I had ten minutes for a coffee break that I decided to spend chasing the great white whale out of a personal obsession. What would I be looking for anyway?"

70

"I JUST TRIED Fairfield," Marge said over the intercom, "but Todd's assistant said he's out of the office for the day, so I left a message."

"Can you try his cell? You have the number, right?"

"Of course."

Of course she did. She never lost a phone number, never misplaced an address, could pull up a name from her file in a matter of seconds without fail. God, she was the best.

There was a certain etiquette to making phone calls, which she appreciated. If she called Todd's office and he was there, she'd put Nick on before Todd picked up. That was how it worked. Nick had always hated the telephone brinksmanship, where someone's assistant would call Marge, be put through to Nick, and then the assistant would say, "I have Mr. Smith," and Nick would say, "Okay, thanks," and then Mr. Smith would get on, as if he were too busy even to suffer a few seconds of being on hold. It was demeaning. Nick had devised his own way around that. He'd instructed Marge to tell the assistant, "Put Mr. Smith on, please, and I'll get Mr. Conover." That usually worked. So when Marge placed calls for him, he didn't like to play Mr. Smith's

game. Todd picked up his own cell phone, of course—
who didn't?—so Nick dialed the call himself.

Todd answered right away.

"Todd, it's Nick Conover."

"Oh, hey, man." No background noise. Nick won-
dered whether Todd actually was in his office anyway.

"Todd, we've got some funny things going on around
here, and we need to talk."

"Hey, that's what I'm here for." Like he was a shrink
or something.

"Two massive deals just fell through because they
each, separately, heard that we're planning to shift all
manufacturing to China."

"Yeah?"

"Any truth to it?"

"I can't be responsible for gossip, Nick."

"Of course. But I'm asking you now, flat out—man
to man—if it's true." Man to toad, he thought. Man to
weasel. "If you guys are even exploring the idea."

"Well, you know how I feel about this, and I've let
you know. I think we're eroding our profit margins by
continuing to operate these old factories in Michigan
like it's nineteen fifty-nine or something. The world's
changed. It's a global economy."

"Right," Nick said. "We've been through all that,
and I've made it clear that the day Stratton stops mak-
ing its own stuff is the day we're no longer Stratton. I'm
not going to be the guy who shuts down our factories."

"I hear you," Todd said testily.

"I've already laid off half the company as you guys
asked me to. It was the most painful thing I've ever
done. But turning Stratton into some kind of virtual
company, a little sales office with all the manufactur-
ing done eight thousand miles away—that's not going
to happen on *my* watch."

"I hear you," Todd said again. "What are you calling for?"

"Let me repeat the question, because I don't think I heard your answer. Is there any truth to these reports that you guys are negotiating to move our manufacturing offshore, Todd?"

"No," he said quickly.

"Not even preliminary talks?"

"No."

Nick didn't know what else to say. Either he was telling the truth, or he was lying, and if he was willing to lie so baldly, well, what the hell could Nick do about it anyway? He thought about mentioning all the back-and-forth e-mail between Todd and Scott, the encrypted documents—but he didn't want Todd to know he was having his security director keep a close watch. He didn't want to shut one of the few windows he had into what was really going on.

"Then maybe you can explain to me why you've got Scott going to China on some secret mission, like Henry fucking *Kissinger*, without even telling me."

A few seconds of silence. "News to me," Todd finally said. "Ask him."

"Scott said he went to China to explore the options. He didn't do that for you? Because if he did, I want you to understand something. That's not the way it works around here, Todd."

"He doesn't report to me, Nick."

"Exactly. I don't want to be undermined."

"I don't want that either."

"The job's tough enough without having to worry about whether my chief financial officer's taking secret flights to the Orient on Cathay Pacific."

Todd chuckled politely. "It's a tough job, and it takes a lot out of you." The timbre of his voice suddenly changed, as if he'd just thought of something. "You know, I understand your family's been through some rough times, death of your wife, all that. If you need to spend more time with them, we're here to help. You want to take a little sabbatical, a little break, might be a good thing. You could probably *use* a vacation. Be good for you."

"I'm fine, Todd," Nick said. *Not so easy, Todd.* "Going to work every day—that's what keeps me going."

"Good to hear it," Todd said. "Good to hear it."

71

BUGBEE WAS GOBBLING Cheetos out of a small vending machine bag. His fingers—which Audrey had noticed were usually immaculate, the nails neatly clipped—were stained orange.

"Makes sense," he said through a mouthful of Cheetos. "Rinaldi picked up a piece in Grand Rapids when he was working there."

"Or here. Those guns travel."

"Maybe. So where'd he toss it?"

"Any of a million possibilities." She was hungry, and he wasn't offering her any, the jerk.

"I forget who the poor slobs were searched the Dumpster, but nothing there."

"There's probably hundreds of Dumpsters in town," Audrey pointed out. "And the dump. And sewer grates, and the lake and the ponds and the rivers. We're never going to find the gun."

"Sad but true," Bugbee said. He crumpled up the empty bag, tossed the wad at the metal trash can against the wall, but the bag unballed in the air and landed on the floor. "Shit."

"Did you have a chance to talk to the alarm company?"

He nodded. "Fenwick Alarm's just an office downtown. I don't know what the hell they do—they install, but not in this case. They don't even do the monitoring themselves. That's done by a joint called Central Michigan Monitoring, out of Lansing. They keep all the electronic records."

"And?"

"Nada. Just confirms what we already know. That Wednesday morning one of the perimeter alarms at Conover's house got triggered. Alert lasted eleven minutes. Big fucking deal. You got the hard drive—that ought to give up what the cameras recorded, right?"

She explained what she knew about Conover's digital video recording system. "I've asked Lenehan to look again. But Noyce has him doing all kinds of other things ahead of us."

"Why does that not surprise me?"

"Speaking of cameras, one of us should check out whatever they have at Fenwicke Estates security for that night."

Bugbee shook his head. "Did already. They use a central station downtown. Nothing special—Stadler climbs a perimeter fence, that's it."

"Too bad."

"I say we poly the guy. Both of those assholes."

"That's a tough one. It may be early. We may want to wait until we have more. I know that's what Noyce would say."

"Screw Noyce. This is our case, not his. You notice the way he's been breathing down our necks?"

"Some."

"He must smell something big about to pop."

She didn't know how much to say. "I think it's more that he wants to make sure we don't slip up."

"Slip up? Like we're rookies?"

Audrey shrugged. "It's a big case."

Bugbee said, with a crooked grin, "No shit."

Audrey responded with a rueful smile as she turned to go back to her cubicle.

"That thing about the shell casing or bullet fragment or whatever," Bugbee said.

She turned. "What shell casing?"

"That bluff?"

"Yes?"

"Not bad," Bugbee said.

72

NICK WAS BEYOND weary. All the shit that was going on with Todd and Scott, all the crap he didn't understand: it was draining. And that on top of Eddie and his warnings about Cassie: check yourself before you wreck yourself. And: What do you think she's after? Could there be something to what Eddie was saying?

Was it possible, he'd begun to wonder, that, on some subconscious level, he *wanted* to be found out?

And worst of all, so awful he couldn't stand to think about it, was this fragment of a shell casing the police had discovered on his lawn.

He'd always prided himself on his ability to endure pressure that would crush most other guys. Maybe it was the hockey training, the way you learned to find the serene place inside you and go there when things got tough. He never used to panic. Laura, always on the high-strung side, never got that. She thought he didn't care, didn't get it. And he'd just shrug and reply blandly, "What's the use in panicking? Not going to help."

But since the murder, everything had changed. His hard shell had cracked or turned porous. Or maybe all the stress of the last few weeks was additive, the worries heaped onto his back until his muscles trembled and spasmed. Any second now he'd collapse to the ground.

But he couldn't, not yet.

Because whatever Todd and Scott were up to—all this maneuvering, the secret trips and the phone calls and the encrypted document—it had ignited a fuse in him that crackled and sparked.

You want to take a little sabbatical, a little break, might be a good thing.

Like Todd gave a shit about his emotional well-being.

Todd wanted him to take time off. Not resign: that was interesting. If Todd and the boys at Fairfield wanted to get rid of him, they'd have fired him long ago. So why hadn't they? Was it really the huge payday, the five million bucks they'd have to pay to fire him without cause, that was stopping them? Given how many billions Fairfield had under management?

He tapped at his keyboard and pulled up the corporate directory, clicked on MARTIN LAI. A photo popped up—a fat-faced, phlegmatic-looking guy—along with his direct reports, his e-mail, his phone number.

He glanced at his watch. Thirteen-hour time difference in Hong Kong. Nine-thirty in the morning here meant ten-thirty at night there. He picked up the phone and dialed Martin Lai's home number. It rang and rang, and then a recorded message came on in Chinese, followed by a few perfunctory words in heavily accented English. "Martin," he said, "this is Nick Conover. I need to speak to you right away." He left the usual array of phone numbers.

Then he spoke into the intercom and asked Marge to locate Martin Lai's cell phone number, which wasn't on the Stratton intranet. A minute later, a long number popped up on his screen.

*   *   *

HE CALLED IT and got a recorded voice again, and he left the same message. He checked Lai's Meeting Maker, his online corporate schedule, and the man appeared not to be away from Stratton's Hong Kong office.

Todd's words kept coming back to him: *You want to take a little sabbatical, a little break, might be a good thing.*

What the hell were Todd Muldaur and Fairfield Equity Partners up to, really? Who, he wondered, might know?

The answer came to him so swiftly that he wondered why he hadn't thought of it before. A "cousin" in the extended Fairfield family, that was who.

He opened his middle desk drawer and found a dog-eared business card that said KENDALL RESTAURANT GROUP, and underneath it, RONNIE KENDALL, CEO.

Ronnie Kendall was a sharp entrepreneur, a quick-witted bantam with an impenetrable Texan accent. He'd started the Kendall Restaurant Group with a little Tex-Mex place in Dallas and turned it into a thriving chain and eventually a prosperous restaurant holding company. It was mostly a chain of Tex-Mex restaurants popular in the Southwest, but his company also owned a cheesecake chain, a barbecued-chicken chain that wasn't doing so well, a lousy Japanese-food chain where chefs dressed like samurai sliced and flipped your food right at your table, and a "good times" bar-and-grill chain known for its baby back ribs and gargantuan frozen margaritas. Ten years ago he'd sold to Willard Osgood.

Nick had met him at some business conference in Tokyo, and they'd hit it off. Ronnie Kendall turned out to be a big hockey fan and had followed Nick's college career at Michigan State, amazingly. Nick had confessed he'd eaten at the Japanese restaurant chain that Kendall's group owned and didn't much like it, and Kendall had shot right back, "You kidding? Every time I set foot in there I get diarrhea. Never eat there, but people *love* it. Go figure."

Nick was put on hold several times before Ronnie Kendall picked up, sounding exuberant as always, speaking a mile a minute. Nick made the mistake of asking how business was, and Ronnie launched into a manic monologue about how the barbecued-chicken chain was expanding in Georgia and South Carolina, and then he somehow shifted into a rant on the low-carb craze. "Man, am I glad that fad is over, huh? That was *killing* us! The low-carb cheesecake never went over, and the low-carb diet Margaritas—*forget* it! And then just when we signed up our new celebrity endorser"—he mentioned the name of a famous football player—"and we'd even taped a bunch of fifteen- and thirty-second spots, then out of the blue he gets hit with a *rape* charge!"

"Ronnie," Nick finally broke in, "how well do you know Todd Muldaur?"

Ronnie cackled. "I *hate* the slick bastard and he loves me just the same. But I stay out of his way, and he stays out of mine. He and his MBA buddies were trying to muck around in my business, got so bad I called Willard himself and said, you put a choke collar on your little poodles or I'm gone. I quit. I'm too old and too rich, I don't need it. Willard must have taken Todd to the woodshed, because he started backing off. 'Course, he had his hands full, what with the chip melt-down."

"Chip meltdown?"

"Isn't that what you call them things? Microchips or whatever? Semiconductors, right?"

"Yeah?"

"You read the *Journal,* right? The semiconductor

industry bubble, the way all those private-equity guys overinvested in chips, then the bubble burst?" He cackled again. "Gotta love it, the way all those guys took a bath."

"Hold on, Ronnie. Fairfield Equity Partners overinvested in microchips?"

"Not the whole of Fairfield, just the funds our boy Todd runs. He made a massive bet on the chip business. Put all his chips on chips, right?"

Nick didn't join Ronnie's laughter. "I thought there's some kind of limit to how much they can invest in one particular sector."

"Todd's an arrogant guy, you know that, right? You can smell it on him. He figured when the semiconductor stocks started sinking, he'd pick up a bunch of companies cheap, turn a big fat profit. Well, he's sure gettin' his. His funds are sucking wind. Willard Osgood has got to be madder 'n a wet hen. If Todd's funds collapse, the whole mother ship goes down."

"Really?"

"I imagine Todd Muldaur should be makin' nice to you these days. I know Stratton's going through some hard times, but at least you're solvent. Compared to some of his other investments, you're a cash cow. He could take you guys public, make some real money. Of course, given how long that takes, it might be too late for him."

"That would take a year at least."

"At least. Why, they talking about spinning you guys off?"

"No. Nothing about that."

"Well, Fairfield needs what they call a liquidity event, and real soon."

"Meaning they need cash."

"You got it."

"Yeah, well, they're up to something," Nick said. "Really pushing hard to cut costs."

"Forget that. You know what I always say, when your house is on fire, you don't hold a garage sale."

"Come again?"

"I mean, Todd's so deep in the shit that he's probably desperate to make a quick buck, sell Stratton quick-and-dirty just to save his ass. I were you, I'd watch Todd's moves *real* close." The instant he hung up, another call came in, this one from Eddie.

"The small conference room on your floor," Eddie said without preface. "Right now."

73

EVER SINCE THEY'D had it out at Eddie's condo, there had been an acute chill in their already frosty relationship. Eddie no longer joked around as much. He avoided Nick's eyes. He often seemed to be seething.

But when he entered the conference room, he looked as though he had a secret he couldn't wait to share. It was a look Nick hadn't seen in a while.

Eddie closed the conference room door and said, "The piece of shell casing?"

Nick's voice caught in his throat. He was unable to speak.

"It's bullshit," Eddie said.

"What?"

"The cops never found any fragment of a shell casing on your lawn."

"Are you sure?"

"Positive."

"What was it, then?"

"It was bullshit. A pressure tactic. There never was any metal scrap."

"They *lied* about it?"

"I wouldn't get on my high horse if I were you, Nick."

"You're certain? How do you know this for sure?"

"I told you. I got sources. It's a fake-out, dude. Don't you recognize a fake-out when you see one?"

Nick shrugged. "I don't know."

"Come on, man. Remember when we were playing Hillsdale in the finals, our senior year, and you made that great deke to your backhand at the blue line before you fired a rocket behind Mallory, sent the game into overtime?"

"Yeah, I remember," Nick said. "I also remember that we lost."

74

NICK PUT HIS briefcase down in the front hall. Its antique, reclaimed pumpkin-pine flooring—the strip oak that had been there didn't make the cut, as far as Laura was concerned—glowed in the amber light that spilled from soffits overhead. Without thinking about it, he expected to hear the *click click click* of Barney's dog toenails on the wood, the jangle of his collar, and the absence of that happy sound saddened him.

It was almost eight o'clock. The marketing strategy committee meeting had run almost two hours late; he'd called home during a break and told Marta to make dinner for the kids. She'd said that Julia was over at her friend Jessica's, so it would just be Lucas.

He heard voices from upstairs. Did Lucas have a friend over? Nick walked upstairs, and the murmur resolved into conversation.

It was Cassie's voice, he realized with surprise. Cassie and Lucas. What was she doing here? The staircase was solidly mortised, no squeaks and creaks like the old house, or like the house he'd grown up in. They hadn't heard him come up. He felt a prickling sensation as he paused at the top landing and listened. Lucas's door was open for a change.

"They should have assigned this in physics class," Lucas was complaining. "Why would a poet know how the world's going to end anyway?"

"You think the poem is really about how the world is going to end?" Cassie's husky voice.

He was relieved. Cassie was helping Lucas with his homework, that was all.

"Fire or ice. That's how the world will end. It's what he's saying."

"Desire and hate," Cassie said. "The human heart can be a molten thing, and it can be sheathed in ice. Don't think outer space. Think inner space. Don't think *the* world. Think *your* world. Frost can be an incredibly dark poet, but he's also a poet of intimacy. So what's he saying here?"

"Thin line between love and hate, basically."

"But love and desire aren't the same, are they? There's the love of family, but we don't call that desire. Because desire is about an absence, right? To desire something is to want it, and you always want the thing you don't have."

"I guess."

"Think about Silas, in the last poem they gave you. He's about to die, and he comes home."

"Except it's not his home."

"In that one, Warren says, 'Home is the place where, when you have to go there, / They have to take you in.' One of the most famous lines Frost ever wrote. Is that love or desire? How does *his* world end?"

Nick, feeling self-conscious, took a few steps down the hall toward his bedroom. Cassie's voice receded to a singsong murmur, asking something, and Lucas's adolescent baritone rose in impatience. "Some say this, some say that. You feel, like, Make up your friggin' mind already."

Nick stopped again to listen.

Cassie laughed. "What's the *rhythm* telling you? The

poem's lines mainly have four beats, right? But not the last lines, about hate: 'Is also great.' Two stressed syllables. 'And would suffice.' Clear and simple. Like it's funneling to a point. About the ice of hatred, how potent that is, right?"

"Mad props to my dawg Bobby Frost," Lucas said. "He could flow, no doubt. But he starts with fire."

"A lot of things start with fire, Luke. The crucial question is how they end."

Nick debated whether he should join them. He wouldn't have hesitated in the old days, but Lucas was different now. What was going on was a good thing, yet probably a fragile thing too. Lucas wouldn't let him help with his homework anymore, and now that he was in the eleventh grade, Nick wasn't much use anyway. But Cassie had somehow figured out a way to talk to him, and she knew that stuff—she was a natural. A goddamn valedictorian.

Finally, Nick walked past Lucas's bedroom, which let them know he was home, and made his way to his own room. Removed his clothes, brushed his teeth, took a quick shower. When he came out again, Lucas was alone in his room, sitting at his computer, working.

"Hey, Luke," he said.

Lucas glanced up with his usual look of annoyance.

Nick wanted to say something like, Did Cassie help? I'm glad you're focusing on work. But he held back. Any such comment might be resented, taken as intrusive. "Where's Cassie?" he said.

Lucas shrugged. "Downstairs, I guess."

He went downstairs to look for Cassie, but she wasn't in the family room or the kitchen, none of the usual places. He called her name, but there was no answer.

Well, she has the right to snoop around my house, he thought. After she caught me going through her medicine cabinet.

But she wouldn't do that, would she?

He passed through the kitchen to the back hallway, switched on the alabaster lamp, kept going to his study.

Unlikely she'd be in there.

The door to his study was open, as it almost always was, and the lights were on. Cassie was seated behind his desk.

His heart thumped. He walked faster, the carpet muffling his footsteps so his approach was silent. Not that he was intending to sneak up on her, though.

Several of the desk drawers were ajar, he saw.

All but the bottom one, which he kept locked. They were open just a bit, as if they'd been open and then shut hastily.

And he knew he hadn't done it. He rarely used the desk drawers, and when he did, he was meticulous about closing them all the way, otherwise the desk looked sloppy.

She was sitting back in his black leather Symbiosis chair, writing on a yellow legal pad.

"Cassie."

She jumped, let out a shriek. "Oh, my God! Don't ever do that!" She put a hand across her breasts.

"Sorry," he said.

"Oh—God. I was in my own world. No, I should apologize—I shouldn't be in here. I guess I'm just a low-boundaries gal."

"That's okay," he said, trying to sound as if he meant it.

She seemed instantly aware of the drawers that had been left slightly ajar and began pushing them all the way closed. "I was looking for a pad and a pen," she said. "I hope you don't mind."

"No," he said. "It's fine."

"I had this idea, and I had to write it down right away—that happens to me."

"Idea?"

"Just—just something I want to write. Someday, if I ever get my shit together."

"Fiction?"

"Oh, no. Nonfiction. Too much fiction in my life. I hope you don't mind my coming over tonight. I did call, you know, but Marta said you were at work, and Lucas and I got to talking, and he said he was busting his head over some poem. Which turns out to be one of the poems I actually know something about. So I . . ."

"Hey," Nick said. "You're doing God's work. I'm afraid my arrival broke things up."

"He's going to write the first few paragraphs of his poetry term paper. See where it's heading."

"You're good with him," Nick said. *You're amazing,* is what he thought.

Maybe that's all it was. She came over to help him figure out some Robert Frost poem.

"You ever teach?"

"I told you," Cassie said. "I've pretty much done everything." The pinpoint ceiling lights caught her hair, made it sparkle. She looked waiflike, still, but her skin wasn't so transparent. She looked healthier. The dark smudges beneath her eyes were gone. "'He thinks if he could teach him that, he'd be / Some good perhaps to some one in the world.'"

"Come again?"

Cassie shook her head. "It's just a line from *Death of the Hired Man.* It's a poem about home. About family, really."

"And the true meaning of Christmas?"

"You Conovers," she said. "What am I going to do with you?"

"I have a few ideas," Nick said, attempting a leer. "God, you're good at everything, aren't you?"

"Coming from *you*? The alpha male? Jock of all trades?"

"I wish. I may be the most math-challenged CEO in the country."

"Is there a sport you can't do?"

He thought a moment. "Never learned to ride a horse."

"Horseshoes?"

"That's not a sport."

"Archery, I bet."

"I'm okay."

"Shooting?"

He went dead inside. After a split second, he gave a small shake of his head, looking perplexed. For a second his eyes went out of focus.

"You know," she said. "Target shooting, whatever it's called. On the range."

"Nope," he said, hearing the studied casualness in his voice as if from a distance. He lowered himself onto a rush-seated Windsor chair that invariably threatened to leave splinters in his backside. Laura had banished his favorite old leather club chair when they moved. Frat house furniture, she called it. He rubbed his eyes, trying to conceal the flush of terror. "Sorry, I'm just wiped out. Long day."

"Want to talk about it?"

"Not now. Sorry. I mean, thanks, but another time. I'd rather talk about anything else than work."

"Can I make you dinner?"

"You cook?"

"No," she admitted with a quick laugh. "You've had one of my three specialties. But I'm sure Marta left something for you in that haunted kitchen of yours."

"Haunted?"

"Oh yeah. I met your contractor right when I got here, and I got the lowdown from him."

"Like why it's taking his guys forever to put in a kitchen counter?"

"Don't blame them. You're driving them crazy, is what I hear. He can't get signoffs when they need them. Things like that."

"Too many goddamn decisions. I don't really have the time for it. And I don't want to get it wrong."

"'Wrong' defined as what?"

Nick was quiet for a moment. "Laura had very definite ideas of what she wanted."

"And you want everything to be just the way she'd planned. Like it's your memorial to her."

"Please don't do the shrink thing."

"But maybe you're afraid to finish it too, because when it's over, something else is over too."

"Cassie, can we change the subject?"

"So it's like Penelope, in the *Odyssey*. She weaves a shroud during the day, and unravels it at night. That way it's never finished. She staves off the suitors, and honors the departed Odysseus."

"I don't even know what you're talking about." Nick took a deep breath.

"I think you do."

"Except, you know, it's reached a point where I really do want the damn thing finished already. It was her big project, and, okay, maybe as long as it was under way, it was like she was still at work. Which doesn't make any sense, but still. Thing is, now I just want the plastic draft sheets out of here, and I want the Dumpster gone, and the trucks, and all that. I want this to be a goddamn *home*. Not a project. Not a thing in process. Just a place where the Conovers live." A beat. "Whatever's left of them."

"I get it," she said. "So why don't you take me out to dinner somewhere?" A smile hovered around her lips. "A date."

75

THEY WALKED THROUGH the Grand Fenwick Hotel parking lot holding hands. It was a cool, cloudless night, and the stars twinkled. Cassie stopped for a moment before they reached the porte cochere and looked up.

"You know, when I was six or seven, my best friend, Marcy Stroup, told me that every star was really the soul of someone who'd died."

Nick grunted.

"I didn't believe it either. Then in school we learned that each star is actually a ball of fire, and some of them probably have solar systems of their own. I remember when they taught us in school about how stars die, how in just a few thousandths of a second a star's core would collapse and the whole star would blow up—a great supernova followed by nothingness. And I started to cry. Right there at my desk in sixth grade. Crazy, huh? That night I was talking to my daddy about it, and he said that was just the way of the universe. That people die, and stars die too—they have to, to make room for new ones."

"Huh."

"Daddy said if no one ever died, there'd be no room

on the planet for the babies being born. He said if nothing ever came to an end, nothing could ever begin. He said it was the same way in the heavens—that sometimes a world has to come to an end so that new ones can be born." She squeezed his hand. "Come on, I'm hungry."

The lobby of the Grand Fenwick was carpeted in what was meant to suggest an old-fashioned English broadloom, with lots of oversized leather furniture arranged in clubby "conversation pits," like a dozen living rooms stitched together. Velvet ropes on stanchions partitioned the restaurant from the lobby. The menu offered fifties favorites like duck à l'orange and salmon hollandaise, but mainly what it offered were steaks, for old-school types who knew the names for the different cuts: Delmonico, porterhouse, Kansas City strip. The place smelled like cigars, and not especially expensive ones; the smoke had seeped into everything like dressing on a salad.

"They have fish," Nick said, apologetically, as they were led to a corner table.

"Now why would you say that? You think girls don't eat red meat?"

"That's right, I forgot—you do. So long as it isn't actually red."

"Exactly."

Cassie ordered a rib steak well done, Nick a medium-rare sirloin. Both of them ordered salads.

After Nick ate his salad, he looked at Cassie. "Brainstorm. I always order a salad. But I just realized something: I don't particularly like salad."

"Not exactly the solution to Fermat's last theorem," Cassie said, "but we can work with this. You don't like salad. Same deal as with tea."

"Right. I drink tea. Laura would make it and I'd

drink it. Same deal. I order salads. But you know, I never liked tea, and I never liked salad."

"You just realized this."

"Yeah. It was always true. I just wasn't conscious of it, somehow. Like . . . Chinese food. I don't really like it. I don't hate it. I just don't have any liking for it."

"You're on a roll, now. What else."

"What else? Okay. Eggplants. Who the hell decided that eggplants were edible? Nontoxic, I get. But is everything that's nontoxic a food? If I were some cave man, and I weren't starving, and I bit into an egg-plant, cooked or not, I wouldn't say, wow, a new taste sensation—I've discovered a foodstuff. I'd say, well, this definitely won't kill you. Don't bother to dip your arrowhead in it. It's like—I don't know—maple leaves. You could probably eat them, but why would you?"

Cassie looked at him.

"You're the one who was complaining I was a stranger to myself," Nick said, tugging on the table linen absently.

"That wasn't really what I meant."

"Gotta start somewhere."

She laughed. He felt her hand stroking his thigh under the tablecloth. Affectionately, not sexually. "Forget eggplant. Give yourself credit—you know what's most precious to you. Not everyone does. Your kids. Your family. They're everything to you, aren't they?"

Nick nodded. There was a lump of sadness in his throat. "When I was playing hockey, I could convince myself that the harder I worked, the harder I trained, the harder I *played,* the better I'd do. It was true, or true enough. True of a lot of things. You work harder, and you do better. In hockey, they talk about playing with a lot of 'heart'—giving it your all. Not true of family, though. Not true of being a father. The harder I try to get through to Lucas, the harder he fights me. You got through the force field. I can't."

"That's because you always argue with him, Nick. You're always trying to make a case, and he doesn't want to hear it."

"The way he looks at me, I think he couldn't care less whether I lived or died."

"That's not what's going on here. Has Lucas ever talked to you about Laura's death?"

"Never. The Conover men don't really do *feelings,* okay?" Nick looked around the darkened room, and was surprised to see Scott McNally being seated a few tables away. Their eyes met, and Scott waved a hand. He was with a tall, gangly man with a narrow face and a prominent chin. Nick saw Scott talking to his dinner companion hurriedly, gesturing toward him. It looked like Scott was deciding whether to do the dessert visit, or to get it over with, and had decided that it would be better to get it over with. The two men stood up and came over to Nick's table.

"Fancy seeing you here," Scott said, patting Nick's shoulder. "I had no idea this was one of your hangouts."

"It's not," Nick said. "Scott, I'd like you to meet my friend Cassie."

"Pleasure to meet you, Cassie," Scott said. "And this is Randall Enright." He paused. "Randall's just helping me understand some of the legal aspects of financial restructuring. Boring technical stuff. Unless you're me, of course, in which case it's like *Conan the Barbarian* with spreadsheets."

"Nice to meet you, Randall," said Nick.

"Pleased to meet you," the tall man said pleasantly. His suit jacket was unbuttoned, and he put his glasses in his breast pocket before shaking hands.

"We get that contract with the Fisher Group analyzed?" Nick said.

"Not sure that's something we want to rush into, actually," said Scott.

"Sooner the better, I'd say."

"Well," said Scott, fidgeting with a lock of hair above his left ear, glancing away. "You're the boss."

"Enjoy Fenwick," Cassie said to the lawyer. "When are you heading back to Chicago?"

The tall man exchanged a glance with Scott. "Not until tomorrow," he said.

"Enjoy your dinner," Nick said, with a hint of dismissal.

Soon, heavy white plates arrived with their steaks, each accompanied by a scoop of pureed spinach and a potato. Nick looked at Cassie. "How did you know he was heading back to Chicago?"

"The Hart Schaffner and Marx label inside his jacket. The obvious fact that he's got to be some sort of hot-shot lawyer if he's having a working dinner with your CFO." She saw the question in his eyes and said, "He put his glasses away because they were reading glasses. And they hadn't been given their menus yet. We're definitely looking at a working dinner."

"I see."

"And Scott wasn't happy about introducing him. He did it strategically, but the fact is, he chose to have dinner here for the same reason you did. Because it's a perfectly okay place where you don't expect to see anyone you know."

Nick grinned, unable to deny it.

"And then there's the 'You're the boss' stuff. Resent-o-rama. A line like that always comes with an asterisk. 'You're the boss.' Asterisk says, 'For now.'"

"You're being a little melodramatic. Don't you think you might be over-interpreting?"

"Don't you think you might not be seeing what's right in front of your face?"

"You may have a point," Nick admitted. He told her about Scott's secret trip to China, the way he tried to cover it up with a lie about going to a dude ranch in Arizona.

"There you go," she said with a shrug. "He's fucking with you."

"Sure seems that way."

"But you like him, don't you?"

"Yeah. Or maybe it's more accurate to say, I did. He's funny, he's a whiz with numbers. We're friends."

"That's your problem—it's blinding you. Your alleged 'friendship' with Scott didn't exactly keep him from stabbing you in the back, did it?"

"True."

"He's not scared of you."

"Should he be?"

"Most definitely. Scared of you, not of what's-his-name, the Yale guy from Boston."

"Todd Muldaur. Todd's really calling the shots, and Scott knows it. Truth is, I'm surprised by him. I brought him in here, I would have expected a modicum of loyalty."

"You're a problem for Scott. A speed bump. An impediment. He's decided you're part of the problem, not part of the solution. His deal is all about Scott Incorporated."

"I'm not sure you're right, there—there's actually nothing greedy or materialistic about him."

"People like Scott McNally—it's not about making a life, or attaining a certain level of comfort. You told me he wears the same shirts he's probably worn since he was a student, right?"

"So whatever he's about, it's not exactly money. I get it."

"Wrong. You *don't* get it. He's a type. People like him don't care about enjoying the things money can buy. They're not into rare Bordeaux or Lamborghini muscle cars. At the same time, they're incredibly competitive. And here's the thing. *Money is how they keep score.*"

Nick thought about Michael Milken, Sam Walton, those other billionaire-next-door types. They lived in little split-level ranch houses and were completely fixated on adding to their Scrooge McDuck vaults, day after day. He remembered hearing about how Warren Buffett lived like a miser in the same little suburban house in Omaha he bought for thirty thousand bucks in 1958. He thought about Scott's nothing-special house and how much money he had. Maybe she was right.

"Scott McNally has his mind on winning this round, so he can play in the big-stakes games," Cassie went on.

"They teach this after the lotus position or before?"

"Okay, then let me just ask you this. What do you think Scott McNally wants to be when he grows up?"

"What do you mean?"

"Does he want to be selling chairs and filing cabinets, or does he want to be a financial engineer at Fairfield Partners? Which is more his style?"

"Point taken."

"In which case, it's fair to ask yourself, who's he really working for?"

Nick gave a crooked smile.

She stood up. "I'll be right back."

Nick watched as she made her way to the ladies' room, admiring the curve of her butt. She wasn't there long. On her way back, she walked past Scott's table, and stopped there briefly. She said something to the lawyer, then sat down next to him for a moment. She was laughing, as if he'd said something witty. A few moments later, he saw the lawyer hand her something. Cassie was laughing again as she stood up and returned to her seat.

"What was that about?" Nick asked.

Cassie handed him the lawyer's business card. "Just check him out, okay?"

"That was quick work." Nick glanced at the card and read, "Abbotsford Gruendig."

"Just being neighborly," Cassie said.

"By the way, I *can* see what's in front of my face," Nick said. "You're in front of my face. I see you quite well, and I like what I see."

"But as I said, we don't see things as they are. We see things as we are."

"Does the same go for you?"

"Goes for all of us. We lie to ourselves because it's the only way we can get through the day. Time comes, though, when the lies get tired and quit."

"What's that supposed to mean?"

Cassie looked at him steadily, searchingly. "Tell me the truth, Nick. What's the real reason the police were at your house?"

76

FOR A MOMENT, he was at a loss for words.

He hadn't told her about the police searching the house and yard, which was a pretty damn huge thing not to have told her about. Especially given the connection to her father. Both Lucas and Julia knew the police had been searching for traces of Andrew Stadler. They just didn't know the real reason.

"Lucas told you," Nick said neutrally. He tried to keep his pulse steady, his breathing regular. He took a forkful of steak for which he had no appetite.

"It freaked him out."

"Yeah, well, he seemed to think it was a hoot. Cassie, I should have said something to you about it, but I knew how it would upset you. I didn't want to bring up your dad—"

"I understand," she said. "I understand. And I appreciate it." She was toying with a spoon. "They actually think my *father* was the stalker?"

"It's just one possibility," Nick said. "I think they're really groping." He swallowed hard. "Hell, they probably even wonder if I had something to do with it." The last words came out in a rush, not the way he had heard himself say it in his mind.

"With his death," Cassie said carefully.

Nick grunted.

"And is it possible that you did?"

Nick couldn't speak right away. He didn't look at her, couldn't. "What do you mean?"

She set down the spoon, placed it carefully alongside the knife. "If you thought he might have been the one doing all that crazy stuff, maybe you could have intervened, somehow. Helped him to get help." She broke off. "But then, these are the questions I ask myself. Why didn't I *make* him get help? Why didn't I intervene? I keep asking myself whether there was something I could have done that would have changed things. Stratton's supposed to have all these great mental health programs, but suddenly he wasn't eligible for them anymore—that's a real Catch-22, isn't it? Because of a mental illness, you quit and lose your right to treatment for your mental illness. That isn't right."

Warily: "It's not right."

"And because of these decisions—decisions you and I and God knows how many other people made—my daddy's dead." Cassie was weeping now, tears spilling down both cheeks.

"Cassie," Nick said. He took her hand in his, and fell silent. Her hand looked pale and small in his. Then a thought came to him, and he felt as if he had swallowed ice. His hand, the hand with which he tried to comfort her, was the hand that had held the gun.

"But you want to know something?" Cassie said haltingly. "When I got the news about—you know—"

"I know."

"I felt like I'd run into a brick wall. But, Nick, I felt something else too. I felt *relieved*. Do you understand?"

"Relieved." He repeated the word numbly.

"All the hospitalizations, all the relapses, all the agony he'd endured. Pain that's not physical but every bit as real. He didn't like the place he was in—the world that, more and more, he *had* to live in. It wasn't your world or my world, it was his world, Nick, and it was a cold and scary place."

"It had to have been hell, for both of you."

"And then one day he disappears. Then he's dead. *Killed*—shot dead, God knows why. But it was almost like an act of mercy. Do you ever think that things happen for a reason?"

"I think some things happen for a reason," Nick said slowly. "But not everything. I don't think Laura died for any particular reason. It just happened. To her. To us. Like a piano that just falls out of the sky and flattens you."

"Shit happens, you're saying." Cassie palmed away the tears on her face. "But that's never the whole story. Shit happens, and it changes your life, and then what do you do? Do you just go on as if nothing happened? Or do you face it?"

"I choose option A."

"Yeah. I see that." Cassie rumpled her spiky hair with a hand. "There's a parable of Schopenhauer's, it's called *'Die Stachelschweine'*—the porcupines. You've got these porcupines, and it's winter, and so they huddle together for warmth—but when they get too close, of course, they hurt each other."

"Allegory alert," Nick said.

"You got it. Too far, and they freeze to death. Too near, and they bleed. We're all like that. Same with you and Lucas."

"Yeah, well, he's a porcupine, all right."

"Got to hand it to you Conover men," Cassie said. "You're as well defended as a medieval castle. Got your moat, got your boiling oil over the gate, got your castle keep. 'Bring it on,' right? Hope you got plenty of provisions in the larder."

"All right, babe. Since you see so much more clearly than I do, let me ask you something. How much do you think I have to worry about my son?"

"Well, some. He's a stoner, as you know. Probably gets high a couple of times a day. Which can do a number on your ability to concentrate."

"A *couple* of times a day? You sure?"

"Oh please. He's got two bottles of Visine on his dresser. He's got Febreze fabric spray in his closet."

Nick looked blank.

"Fabric freshener. You spritz it on your clothing to remove the smell of the herb. Then he's got these Dutch Master leavings in his wastebasket. For making a blunt, okay? This is all Pothead 101 stuff."

"Christ," said Nick. "He's sixteen years old."

"And he's going to be seventeen. And then eighteen. And that's going to be rough too."

"A year ago you wouldn't have recognized him. He was this totally straight, popular athlete."

"Just like his dad."

"Yeah, well. My mom didn't die when I was fifteen."

"What makes it worse is if you can't talk about it."

"He's a kid. It's hard for him to talk about stuff like that."

Cassie looked at him.

"What?"

"I wasn't just talking about Lucas," she said quietly. "I was talking about you."

A deep breath. "You like metaphors? Here's one. You know the cartoon coyote that's always racing off the edge of the cliff?"

"Yes, Nick. Wile E. Coyote. An odd role model for the CEO of Acme Industries, I'd have thought."

"And he's in midair, but his legs are still pumping and he's moving along fine. But then—he looks down, and he sinks like a stone. Moral of the story? *Never fucking look down.*"

"Beautiful," Cassie said, her voice as astringent as witch hazel. "Just beautiful." Her eyes flashed. "Have you noticed that Lucas can't even *look* at you? And you can barely look at him. Now why is that?"

"If you bring up those Black Forest porcupines again, I'm out of here."

"He's lost his mom, and he desperately needs to bond with his father. But you're not around, and when you are, you're not *there*. You're not exactly verbally expressive, right? He needs you to be the healer, but you can't do it—you don't know how. And the more isolated he feels, the more he turns on you, and the angrier you get."

"The armchair psychologist," Nick said. "Another one of your imaginative 'readings.' Nice guess, though."

"No," she said. "Not a guess. He pretty much told me."

"He *told* you? I can't even imagine that."

"He was stoned, Nick. He was stoned, and he started to cry, and it came out."

"He was *stoned*? In your presence?"

"Lit up a nice fat doobie," Cassie said, with a half-smile. "We shared it. And we had a long talk. I wish you could have heard him. He has a lot on his mind. A lot he hasn't been able to say to you. A lot you need to hear."

"You smoked marijuana with my *son*?"

"Yes."

"That is *incredibly* irresponsible. How could you do that?"

"Whoa, Daddy, you're missing the big picture here."

"Lucas has a problem with this shit. You were supposed to help him. Not encourage him, goddammit. He looks up to you!"

"I told him to lay off the weed, at least on school nights. I think he's going to."

"Goddammit! You haven't got a clue, have you? I don't care what kind of a fucked-up childhood you had. This is my *son* you're dealing with. A sixteen-year-old boy with a drug problem. What part of this isn't registering?"

"Nick, be careful," she said, in a low, husky voice. Her face was turning a deep red, but her expression remained oddly fixed, a stone mask. "We had a very open and honest conversation, Luke and I. He told me all kinds of things." Now she turned to look at him with hooded eyes.

Nick was torn between fury and fear, wanting to lay into her for what she'd done, getting high with Lucas— and yet frightened of what she might have found out from Lucas.

Lucas, who might—or might not—have heard shots one night.

Who might—or might not—have overheard his father and Eddie discussing what had really happened that night.

"Like what?" he managed to say.

"All *kinds* of things," she whispered darkly.

Nick closed his eyes, waited for his heart to stop hammering. When he opened them again, she was gone.

77

AUDREY'S E-MAIL ICON was bouncing, and she saw it was Kevin Lenehan, the electronics tech.

She walked right over there, almost ran.

"What's the best restaurant in town, would you say?" Kevin said.

"I don't know. Terra, maybe? I've never been there."

"How about Taco Gordito?"

"Why do you ask?"

"Because you owe me dinner. I told you the recording on this baby started at three-eighteen in the morning on Wednesday the sixteenth, right? After the sequence you're so interested in?"

"What'd you find?"

"The hard drive's partitioned into two sections, right? One for the digital images, the other for the software that drives the thing." He turned to his computer monitor, moved the mouse around and clicked on something. "Very cool system, by the way. Internet-based."

"Meaning?"

"Your guy had the ability to monitor his cameras from his office."

"What does that tell you?"

"Nothing. I'm just saying. Anyway, look at this."

"That doesn't mean anything to me. It's a long list of numbers."

"Not a techie, huh? Your husband has to program the VCR for you?"

"He can't either."

"Same with me. No one can. So, look. This is the log of all recorded content."

"Is that the fifteenth?"

"You got it. This log says that the recording actually started on Tuesday the fifteenth at four minutes after noon, right? Not like fifteen hours later."

"So you found more video?"

"I wish. No, you're not following me. Someone must have gone in and reformatted the section of the hard drive where the recordings are made, then started the whole machine over, recycled it, so it just *looked* like it started from scratch at three-whatever in the morning on Wednesday. But the log here tells us that the system was initiated fifteen hours earlier. I mean, it's saying there's recorded content going back to like noon that day. Only, when you click on the files, it says 'File not found.'"

"Deleted?"

"You got it."

Audrey stared at the screen. "You're sure of this."

"Am I sure the box started recording at noon the day before? Yeah, sure as shit."

"No. Sure you can't retrieve the recording."

"It's, like, so gone."

"That's too bad."

"Hey, you look, like, disappointed. I thought you'd be thrilled. You want proof part of the video was erased, you got it right here."

"You ever read the book *Fortunately* when you were a kid?"

"My mom plopped me down in front of *One Life to Live* and *General Hospital*. Everything I learned about life I learned from soap operas. That's why I'm single."

"I must have read it a thousand times. There's a boy named Ned, and he's invited to a surprise party, but unfortunately the party's a thousand miles away. Fortunately a friend lends him an airplane, but unfortunately the motor explodes."

"Ouch. I hate when that happens."

"Fortunately there's a parachute in the airplane."

"But unfortunately he's horribly burned over ninety percent of his body and he's unable to open the chute? See how my mind works."

"This case is like that. Fortunately, unfortunately."

"That pretty much describes my sex life," Kevin said. "Fortunately the girl goes home with Kevin. Unfortunately she turns out to be a radical feminist lesbian who only wants him to teach her how to use Photoshop."

"Thanks, Kevin," Audrey got up from the stool. "Lunch at Taco Gordito's on me."

"Dinner," Kevin said firmly. "That's the deal."

78

NICK'S CELL PHONE rang just as he was pulling into the parking lot, almost half an hour later than usual this morning.

It was Victoria Zander, the Senior Vice President for Workplace Research, calling from Milan. "Nick," she said, "I'm at the *Salone Internazionale del Mobile* in Milan, and I'm so upset I can barely speak."

"Okay, Victoria, take a deep breath and tell me what's up."

"Will you please explain to me what's going on with Dashboard?"

Dashboard was one of the big new projects Victoria was developing, a portfolio of flexible, modular glass walls and partitions—very cool, beautifully designed, and something Victoria was really high on. Nick was high on it for business reasons: there was nothing else like it out there, and it was sure to hit a sweet spot.

"What do you mean, 'What's going on'?"

"After all the time and money we've put in on this, and—it just makes no *sense*! 'All major capital expenditures on hold'—what do you *mean* by that? And not even giving me the courtesy of advance notice?"

"Victoria—"

"I don't see how I can continue working for Stratton. I really don't. You know, Herman Miller has been after me for two years, and frankly I think that's a far better home for—"

"Victoria, hold on. Cool your jets, will you? Now, who told you we're shelving Dashboard?"

"You guys did! I just got the e-mail from Scott."

What e-mail? Nick almost asked, but instead he said, "Victoria, there's some kind of glitch. I'll call you right back."

He clicked off, slammed the car door, and went to look for Scott.

"HE'S NOT HERE, Nick," Gloria said. "He had an appointment."

"An appointment where?" Nick demanded.

She hesitated. "He didn't say."

"Get him on his cell, please. Right now."

Gloria hesitated again. "I'm sorry, Nick, but his cell phone doesn't work inside the plant. That's where he is."

"The *plant*? Which one?"

"The chair factory. He's—well, he's giving someone a tour."

As far as Nick knew, Scott had been inside the factories maybe twice before. "Who?"

"Nick, I—please."

"He asked you not to say anything."

Gloria closed her eyes, nodded. "I'm really sorry. It's a difficult position."

Difficult position? I'm the goddamned CEO, he thought.

"Don't worry about it," he said kindly.

NICK HADN'T VISITED the chair plant in almost three months. There was a time when he'd visit monthly,

sometimes more, just to check out how things were
running, ask questions, listen to complaints, see how
much inventory backlog was on hand. He'd check the
quality boards at each station too, mostly to set an ex-
ample, figuring that if he paid attention to the quality
charts, the plant manager would too, and so would every-
one below him.

He made visits to the plant just like Old Man
Devries used to do, only when the old man did it, they
weren't called Gemba walks, as they were now. That
term had been introduced by Scott, along with Kaizen
and a bunch of other Japanese words that Nick didn't
remember, and that sounded to him like types of sushi.

It was the layoffs that made walking the plants an
unpleasant chore. He could sense the hostility when he
came through. It wasn't lost on him, or anybody else,
that Old Man Devries's job had been to build plants,
and Nick's was to tear them down.

But he knew it was something he should probably
start doing again, both here and in the other manufac-
turing complex about ten miles down the road. He'd go
back to the monthly walks, he vowed.

If he had the chance.

If the factories were still here.

He noticed the big white sign on the front of the red
brick building that said DAYS SINCE LAST ACCIDENT,
and next to it a black LED panel with the red digital
numerals 322. Someone had crossed out ACCIDENT and
scrawled over it, with a heavy black marker, LAYOFFS.

He went in the visitors' entrance and caught the old
familiar smell of welding and soldering, of hot metal. It
took him back to visits to his father at work, of dog-day
summers in high school and college spent working on
the line.

The plump girl who sat at the battered old desk and
handed out safety glasses, greeted visitors, and an-

swered the phone, did a double take. "Good *morning,* Mr. Conover."

"Morning, Beth." Beth-something-Italian. He signed the log, noticed Scott had signed in about twenty minutes earlier along with someone else whose signature was illegible.

"Boy, both you *and* Mr. McNally in the space of an hour. Something going on I should know about?"

"No, in fact, I'm looking for Mr. McNally—any idea where he is?"

"No, sir. He had a visitor with him, though."

"Catch the other guy's name?"

"No, sir." She looked ashamed, as if she hadn't been doing her job. But Nick couldn't blame her for not checking the ID of the CFO's guest too carefully.

"Did Scott say where they were going?"

"No, sir. Sounded like Mr. McNally was giving a tour."

"Brad take them around?" Brad Kennedy was the plant manager, who gave tours only to the VIPs.

"No, sir. Want me to call Brad for you?"

"That's okay, Beth." He put on a pair of dorky-looking safety glasses.

He'd forgotten how deafening the place was. A million square feet of clattering, pounding, thudding metal. As he entered the main floor, keeping to the "green mile," as it was called—the green-painted border where you'd be safe from the Hi-Lo electric lift trucks that barreled down the aisles at heedless speeds—he could feel the floor shake. That meant the thousand-ton press, which stamped out the bases of the Symbiosis chair control panel, was operating. The amazing thing was that the thousand-ton press was all the way across the factory floor, clear on the other end, and you could still feel it go.

The place filled him with pride. This was the real

heart of Stratton—not the glitzy headquarters building with its silver-fabric cubicles and flat-panel monitors and all the backstabbing. The company's heartbeat was the regular thud of the thousand-ton behemoth, which sent vibrations up your spine as you passed through. It was here, where you still found some of those antique, dangerous, hydraulic-powered machines that could bend steel three-quarters of an inch thick, the exact same one on which his father had worked, bending steel, a seething monster that could take your hand off if you weren't careful. His dad had in fact lost the tip of his ring finger to the old green workhorse once, which caused him more embarrassment than anger, because he knew it was his fault. He must have felt that the brake machine, after all those years of a close working relationship, had been disappointed in him.

As he walked, he looked for Scott, and the more he looked, the angrier he got. The idea that Scott, who worked for him, a guy he'd hired, would dare shelve projects, block funding, change vendors without consulting him—that was insubordination of the most egregious sort.

Four hundred hourly workers in this plant, and another hundred or so salaried employees, all turning out chairs for the Armani-clad butts of investment bankers and hedge-fund managers, the Prada-clad rumps of art directors.

He was always impressed by how clean the factory floor was kept, free of oil spills, each area clearly marked with hanging signs. Each section had its own safety board, marked green for a safe day, yellow for a day with a minor injury, red for an injury requiring hospitalization. Good thing, he thought grimly, he didn't have one of those hanging in his house. What was the color for death?

He was looking for two men in business suits. They

shouldn't be hard to find here, among the guys (and a few women) in jeans and T-shirts and hard hats.

Periodic messages flashed on the TV monitors, a steady stream of propaganda and morale-building. THE STRATTON FAMILY CARES ABOUT YOUR FAMILY— TALK TO YOUR BENEFITS ADVISER. And: THE NEXT INSPECTOR IS OUR CUSTOMER. And then: STRATTON SALUTES JIM VEENSTRA—FENWICK PLANT—25 YEARS OF SERVICE.

A radio was blasting out Fleetwood Mac's "Shadows" from the progressive-build station where the Symbiosis chairs were assembled. Nick had borrowed the process from Ford and pretty much forced it on the workers, who resisted any further dumbing-down of their jobs. They liked building the whole chair themselves, and who could blame them? They liked the old piecework incentives. Now, one chair was assembled every fifty-four seconds as a light cycled from green to amber to red, signaling the workers to finish up. This plant turned out ten thousand Symbiosis chairs a week.

He jogged past the in-line washer that cleaned the oil off the chair-control covers and then sent them clattering down into an orange supply tub. He couldn't help slowing a bit to admire the robotic machine, a recent acquisition, that took sized and straightened wire stock, made five perfect bends, and then cut it, all in twelve seconds. In front of a press that made tubes out of eight-foot steel coils for the stacking chairs, a guy wearing green earplugs was asleep, obviously on break.

The floor supervisor, Tommy Pratt, saw him, threw him a wave, came hurrying up. Nick couldn't politely avoid the guy.

"Hey! Mr. Conover!" Tommy Pratt was a small man who looked like he'd been compacted from a larger man: everything about him seemed *dense*. Even his hair was dense, a helmet of tight brown curls. "Haven't seen you down here in a while."

"Couldn't stay away," Nick said, raising his voice to be heard above the din. "You seen Scott McNally?"

Pratt nodded, pointed toward the far end of the floor.

"Thanks," Nick shouted back. He gestured with his chin at an orange tub stacked high with black chair casters. An unusual sight—Scott's new inventory-control system made sure there was never a backlog. Keeping too much inventory on hand was a cardinal sin against the religion of Lean Manufacturing. "What's this?" he said.

"Yeah, Mr. Conover—we've been having a problem with, like, every other lot of those casters. You know, they're vended parts—"

"Seriously? That's a first. I'll have someone call Lenny at Peerless—no, in fact, I'll call Lenny myself." Peerless, in St. Joseph, Michigan, had been manufacturing chair casters for Stratton since forever. Nick vaguely remembered getting a couple of phone messages from Lenny Bloch, the CEO of Peerless. "Uh, no, sir," Pratt said. "We switched to another vendor last month. Chinese company, I think."

"Huh?"

"The bitch of it is, sir, with Peerless, if we ever got a bad batch, which hardly ever happened by the way, he'd just truck us a new lot overnight. Now we gotta deal with container ships, you know, takes forever."

"Who switched vendors?"

"Well, I think Brad said it was Ted Hollander who insisted on it. Brad put up a fight, but you know, the word came down, we're cutting costs and all that."

Ted Hollander was vice president for control and procurement, and one of Scott McNally's direct reports. Nick clenched his jaw.

"I'll get back to you on that," he said in a voice of

corporate cordiality. "When I tell the guys to look at cost containment, some of them go a little overboard." Nick turned to go, but Pratt touched his elbow. "Uh, Mr. Conover, one more thing. I hope I'm not driving you away here—I don't want you to think all we're ever gonna do is bitch at you, you know?"

"What is it?"

"The damned Slear Line. We had to shut it down twice since the shift started this morning. It's really bottlenecking things."

"It's older than I am."

"That's just it. The service guy keeps telling us we gotta replace it. I know that's a load of dough, but I don't think we have a choice."

"I trust your judgment," Nick said blandly.

Pratt gave him a quizzical look; he'd been expecting an argument. "I'm not complaining. I'm just saying, we can't put it off that much longer."

"I'm sure you know what you're doing."

"Because we couldn't get the requisition approved," Pratt said. "Your people said it wasn't a good time right now. Something about putting major capital expenditures on hold."

"What do you mean, 'my people'?"

"We put the request through last month. Word came down from Hollander a couple of weeks ago."

"There's no freeze on major expenditures, okay? We're in this for the long haul." Nick shook his head. "Some people do tend to get a little overzealous. Excuse me."

Two men in suits and safety glasses were walking through the "supermarket," the area where parts were stored in aisles. They were walking quickly, and one of them—Scott—was waving a hand at something as they left the floor. Nick wondered what he was saying to the other man, whom he recognized from last night.

The attorney from Chicago who was supposedly advising Scott on structuring deals. The man whom Scott, who hadn't been on the shop floor in more than a year, was showing around in such a low-profile, almost secretive way.

There was, of course, no reason in the world for a financial engineer to tour one of Stratton's factories. Nick thought about trying to catch up with them, but he decided not to bother.

No need to be lied to again.

79

THERE WASN'T ANY e-mail from Cassie. Not that he expected any, but he was sort of hoping there'd be something. He realized he owed her an apology, so he typed:

Where'd my little porcupine go?
—N

Then he adjusted the angle on the flat-panel monitor, opened his browser and went to Google. He typed in Randall Enright's name, and the name of his law firm, from the card Cassie had gotten from him last night.

Abbotsford Gruendig had offices in London, Chicago, Los Angeles, Tokyo, and Hong Kong, among other places. "With over two thousand lawyers in 25 offices around the world, Abbotsford Gruendig provides worldwide service to national and multinational corporations, institutions and governments," the firm's home page boasted.

He typed in Randall Enright's name. It appeared, as part of a list of names, on a page headed with the rubric MERGERS & ACQUISITIONS and then more boilerplate:

Our corporate lawyers are leaders in M&A, focusing on multi-jurisdictional transactions. They can advise on licence requirements and regulatory compliance and provide local legal services in over twenty jurisdictions. Our clients include many larger corporations in the telecommunications, defence and manufacturing sectors.

Blah blah blah. More legal gobbledygook.

But it told him that Scott sure as hell wasn't getting up to speed on new accounting regulations.

He was up to something completely different.

STEPHANIE ALSTROM, STRATTON'S corporate counsel, wore a navy blue suit with a white blouse and a big heavy gold chain necklace that was probably intended to make her look more authoritative. Instead, the necklace and matching earrings diminished her, made her look tiny. Her gray hair was close-cropped, her mouth heavily lined, the bags under her eyes pronounced. She was in her fifties but looked twenty years older. Maybe that was what decades of practicing corporate law could do to you.

"Sit down," Nick said. "Thanks for dropping by."

"Sure." She looked worried, but then again, she always looked worried. "You wanted to know about Abbotsford Gruendig?"

Nick nodded.

"I'm not sure what you wanted to know, exactly, but it's a big international law firm, offices all over the world. A merger of an old-line British firm and a German one."

"And that guy Randall Enright?"

"M and A lawyer, speaks fluent Mandarin. A real hotshot. China law specialist, spent years in their Hong

Kong office until his wife forced them to move back to the States. Mind if I ask why the sudden interest?"

"The name came up, that's all. Now, what do you know about Stratton Asia Ventures?"

She wrinkled her brow. "Not much. A subsidiary corporation Scott set up. He never ran it by my office."

"Is that unusual?"

"We review all sorts of contracts, but we don't go after people and insist on it. I assumed he was using local counsel in Hong Kong."

"Check this out, would you?" Nick handed her the e-mail from Scott to Martin Lai in Hong Kong, which Scott had tried to delete.

"Ten million dollars wired to an account in Macau," Nick said as she looked it over. "What does that tell you?"

She looked at Nick, looked down quickly. "I don't know what you're asking me."

"Can you think of a circumstance in which ten million dollars would be wired to a numbered account in Macau?"

She flushed. "I don't want to be casting aspersions. I really don't want to guess."

"I'm asking you to, Steph."

"Between you and me?"

"Please. Not to be repeated to anyone."

After a moment's hesitation, she said, "One of two things. Macau is one of those money-laundering havens. The banks there are used for hidden accounts by the Chinese leaders, same way deposed third-world dictators use the Caymans."

"Interesting. Are you thinking what I'm thinking?"

She was clearly uncomfortable. "Embezzlement—or a bribe. But this is only speculation on my part, Nick."

"I understand."

"And not to be repeated."

"You're afraid of Scott, aren't you?"

Stephanie looked down at the table, her eyes darting back and forth, and she said nothing.

"He works for me," Nick said.

"On paper, I guess," she said.

"Excuse me?" Her remark felt to Nick like a blow to his solar plexus. It felt like the wind had been knocked out of him.

"The org chart says he's under you, Nick," she said hastily. "That's all I mean."

80

"GOT SOMETHING FOR you," Eddie said over the phone.

"I'll meet you in the small conference room on my floor in ten minutes," Nick said.

Eddie hesitated. "Actually, why don't you come down to my office?"

"How come?"

"Maybe I'm tired of taking the elevator up there."

The only thing worse than this kind of idiotic, petty game, Nick thought, was responding to it. "Fine," he said curtly, and hung up.

"YOU KNOW HOW much e-mail Scotty blasts out?" Eddie said, leaning back in his chair. It was a new chair, Nick noticed, one of a premium, super-limited run of Symbiosis chairs upholstered in butter-soft Gucci leather. "He's like a one-man spam generator or something."

"Sorry to put you out," Nick said. He also noticed that Eddie had a new computer with the largest flat-panel monitor he'd ever seen.

"Guy's a Levitra addict, first off. Gets it over the Internet. I guess he doesn't want his doc to know—small town and all that."

"I really don't care."

"He also buys sex tapes. Like *How to Be a Better Lover. Enhance Your Performance. Sex for Life.*"

"Goddammit," Nick said, "that's his business, and I don't want to hear about it. I'm only interested in *our* business."

"Our business," Eddie said. He sat upright, reached over for a thick manila folder, and set it down in front of Nick with a thud. "Here's something that's very much our business. Do you even know the first fucking thing about Cassie Stadler?"

"We're back to that?" Nick snapped. "You stay out of my goddamned e-mails, or—"

Eddie looked up suddenly, his eyes locked with Nick's. "Or what?"

Nick shook his head, didn't reply.

"That's right. We're joined at the hip now, big guy. I got job security, you understand?"

Nick's heart thrummed, and he bit his lower lip.

"Now," Eddie said, a lilt to his voice. "I'm not reading your fucking e-mails. I don't need to. You forget I can watch your house on my computer."

"Watch my *house*?" Nick shook his head. "Huh?"

Eddie shrugged. "Your security cameras transmit over the Internet to the company server, you know that. I can see who's coming and going. And I can see this babe coming and going a *lot*."

"You do not have permission to spy on me, you hear me?"

"Couple of weeks ago you were begging for my help. Someday soon you'll thank me. You know this chick spent eight months in a psycho ward?"

"Yeah," Nick said. "Only it was six months, and it wasn't a 'psycho ward.' She was hospitalized for depression after a bunch of college friends of hers were killed in an accident. So what?"

"You know that for the last six years, there's no record of any FICA payments on this broad? Meaning that she didn't have a job? Don't you think that's strange?"

"I'm not hiring her to be vice president of human resources. In fact, I'm not hiring her at all. She's been a yoga teacher. How many yoga teachers make regular Social Security payments, anyway?"

"I'm not done yet. Get this: 'Cassie' isn't even her real name."

Nick furrowed his brow.

Eddie smiled. "Helen. Her name is Helen Stadler. Cassie—that's not on her birth certificate. Not a legal name change. Totally made up."

"So what? What's your point?"

"I got a feeling about her," Eddie said. "Something about her ain't correct. We talked about this already, but let me say it again: I don't care how sweet the snatch. It ain't worth the risk."

"All I asked you to do was to find out what Scott McNally was up to."

After a few seconds of sullen silence, Eddie handed Nick another folder.

"So, those encrypted documents my guys found?"

"Yeah?"

"My guys cracked 'em all. It's really just one document, bunch of different drafts, went back and forth between Scotty and some lawyer in Chicago."

"Randall Enright."

Eddie cocked his head. "That's right."

"What is it?"

"Fuck if I know. Legal bullshit."

Nick started to page through the documents. Many of them were labeled DRAFT ONLY and REDLINE. The sheets were dense with legal jargon and stippled with numbers, the demon spawn of a lawyer and an accountant.

JOSEPH FINDER

"Maybe he's selling company secrets," Eddie said.

Nick shook his head. "Not our Scott. Huh-uh. He's not selling company secrets."

"No?"

"No," Nick said, once again short of breath. "He's selling the company."

81

"WHY DO YOU trust me?" said Stephanie Alstrom. They met in one of the smaller conference rooms on her floor. There was just no damned privacy in this company, Nick realized. Everyone knew who was meeting with whom; everyone could listen in.

"What do you mean?"

"Scott's stabbing you in the back, and you hired him too."

"Instinct, I guess. Why, are you working against me too?"

"No," she smiled. Nick had never seen her smile before, and it wrinkled her face strangely. "I just guess I should feel flattered."

"Well," Nick said, "my instinct has failed me before. But you can't be distrustful of everyone."

"Good point," she said, putting on a pair of half-glasses. "So, you know what you've got here, right?"

"A Definitive Purchase Agreement," Nick said. He'd looked over hundreds of contracts like this in his career, and even though the legalese froze his brain, he'd learned to hack his way through the dense underbrush to uncover the key points. "Fairfield Equity Partners is selling us to some Hong Kong–based firm called Pacific Rim Investors."

Stephanie shook her head slowly. "That's not what I pick up from this. It's strange. For one thing, there's not a single mention in the list of assets of any factories or plants or employees. Which, if they were planning to keep any of it, they'd have to list. And then, in the Representations and Warranties section, it says the buyer's on the hook for any costs, liabilities, et cetera, associated with shutting down U.S. facilities or firing all employees. So, it's pretty clear. Pacific Rim is buying only Stratton's name. And getting rid of everything else."

Nick stared. "They don't need our factories. They've got plenty in Shenzhen. But all this money for a *name*?"

"Stratton means class. An old reliable American name that's synonymous with elegance and solidity. Plus, they get our distribution channels. Think about it—they can make everything over there at a fraction of the price, slap a Stratton nameplate on it, sell it for a premium. No American firm would have made a deal like this."

"Who are they, this Pacific Rim Investors?"

"No idea, but I'll find out for you. Looks like Randall Enright wasn't working for Fairfield after all—he represents the buyer. Pacific Rim."

Nick nodded. Now he understood why Scott had given Enright the factory tour. Enright was in Fenwick to do due diligence on behalf of a Hong Kong–based firm that couldn't come to visit because they wanted to keep everything very quiet.

She said, "The least they could do is tell you."

"They knew I'd go ballistic."

"That must be why they put Scott on the board. Asians always demand to meet with the top brass. If Todd Muldaur thought firing you would help, he'd have done it already."

"Exactly."

"It freaks potential buyers out if a CEO gets fired right before a sale. Everyone's antennae go up. Plus, a lot of the key relationships are yours. The smarter move was to hermetically seal you off. As they did."

"I used to think Todd Muldaur was an idiot, but now I know better. He's just a prick. Can you explain this side agreement to me?"

Her pruned mouth turned down in a scowl. "I've never seen anything like it. It looks like some kind of deal-sweetener. From what I can tell, it's a way to speed up the deal, make it happen fast. But that's just a guess. You might want to talk to someone who knows."

"Like who? Scott's the only one I know who understands the really devious stuff."

"He's good, but he's not the only one," Stephanie said. "Does Hutch still speak to you?"

82

NICK HAD BEGUN to dread going out in public.

Not "public" as in going to work, though that still took a fair amount of effort, putting on his Nick Conover, CEO act, confident and friendly and outgoing, when a toxic spill of anxiety threatened to ooze out through his pores. But whether it was school functions or shopping or taking clients out to restaurants, it was getting harder and harder to keep the mask fastened securely.

What was once just uncomfortable, even painful— seeing people the company had laid off, exchanging polite if tense words with them, or just generally feeling like a pariah in this town—was now close to intolerable. Everywhere he went, everyone he ran into, he felt as if a neon sign was hanging around his neck, its gaudy orange tubes flashing the word MURDERER.

Even tonight, when he was just another spectator at Julia's piano recital. Her long-dreaded, long-awaited piano recital. It was being held in one of the old town performance theaters, Aftermath Hall, a mildew-smelling old place that had been built in the nineteen thirties, a Steinway grand on a yellow wooden stage, red velvet curtain, matching red velvet upholstered seats with uncomfortable wooden backs.

The kids in their little coats and ties or their dresses streaked across the lobby, propelled by nervous energy. A couple of little African-American boys in jackets and ties with their older sister, in a white dress with a bow: unusual in Fenwick, given how few blacks there were.

He was startled to find Laura's sister there. Abby was a couple of years older than Laura, had two kids as well, married a guy with a trust fund and no personality. He claimed to be a novelist, but mostly he played tennis and golf. Abby had the same clear blue eyes as Laura, had the same swan neck. Instead of Laura's corkscrew brown curls, though, her brown hair was straight and glossy and fell to her shoulders. She was more reserved, had a more regal bearing, was less approachable. Nick didn't especially like her. The feeling was probably mutual.

"Hey," he said, touching her elbow. "Nice of you to come. Julia's going to be thrilled."

"It was sweet of Julia to call me."

"She did?"

"You seem surprised. You didn't tell her to?"

"I can't tell her to do anything, you know that. How's the family?"

"We're fine. Kids doing okay?"

He shrugged. "Sometimes yes, sometimes no. They miss you a lot."

"Do they? Not you, though." Then she softened it a bit with a smile that didn't look very sincere.

"Come on. We all do. How come we haven't seen you?"

"Oh," she breathed, "it's been crazy."

"Crazy how?"

She blinked, looked uncomfortable. Finally she said, "Look, Nick, it's hard for me. Since . . ."

"Hey, it's okay," Nick put in hastily. "I'm just saying, don't be a stranger."

"No, Nick," Abby said, inclining her head, lowering her voice, her eyes gleaming with something bad. "It's just that—every time I look at you." She looked down, then back up at him. "Every time I look at you it makes me sick."

Nick felt as if he'd just been kicked in the throat.

Little kids, big kids running past, dressed up, taut with the preperformance jitters. Someone playing a swatch of complicated music on the Steinway, sounding like a professional you might hear at Carnegie Hall.

Laura's nude body on the folding wheeled table after the embalming, Nick weeping and slobbering as he dressed her, his request, honored by the funeral director with some reluctance. Nick unable to look at her waxen face, a plausible imitation of her once glowing skin, the neck and cheek he'd nuzzled against so many times.

"You think the accident was my fault, that it?"

"I really see no sense in talking about it," she said, looking at the floor. "Where's Julia?"

"Probably waiting her turn at the piano." Nick felt a hand on his shoulder, turned, and was stunned to see Cassie. His heart lifted.

She stood on her tiptoes, gave him a quick peck on the lips.

"Cass—Jesus, I had no idea—"

"Wouldn't miss it for the world."

"Did Julia order you to show up too?"

"She *told* me about it, which is a different thing. I'd say a daughter's piano recital falls in the category of a family obligation, don't you think?"

"I'm—wow."

"Come on, I'm practically family. Plus, I'm a big classical piano fan, don't you know that about me?"

"Why do I doubt that?"

She put her lips to his ear and whispered, her hot breath getting him excited: "I owe you an apology."

Then she was gone, before Nick had a chance to introduce her.

"Who's the new girlfriend?" Abby's voice, abrupt and harsh and brittle, an undertone of ridicule.

Nick froze. "Her name's . . . Cassie. I mean, she's—"

I mean, she's what? Not a girlfriend? Just a fuck? Oh, she's the daughter of the guy I murdered, ain't that a funny coincidence? Tell that to Craig, your alleged-writer husband. Give him something to write about.

"She's beautiful." Abby's arched brows, lowered lids, glimmering with contempt.

He nodded, supremely uncomfortable.

"She doesn't exactly seem like the Nick Conover type, though. Is she an . . . artist or something?"

"She does some painting. Teaches yoga."

"Glad you're dating again." Abby could not have sounded more inauthentic.

"Yeah, well . . ."

"Hey, it's been a year, right?" she said brightly, something cold and hard and lilting in her voice. "You're allowed to date." She smiled, victorious, not even bothering to hide it.

Nick couldn't think of anything to say.

LATONYA WAS LECTURING some poor soul as Audrey approached, wagging her forefinger, her long coral-colored nails—a self-adhesive French manicure kit she'd been hounding Audrey to try—looking like dangerous instruments. She was dressed in an avocado muumuu with big jangly earrings. "That's right," she was saying. "I can make a hundred and fifty dollars an hour easy, taking these online surveys. Sitting at home in my pajamas. I get paid for expressing my *opinions*!"

When she saw Audrey, she lit up. "And I figured you'd be working," she said, enfolding Audrey in an immense bosomy hug.

"Don't tell me Leon's here too." LaTonya seemed to have forgotten about her sales pitch, freeing the victim to drift off.

"I don't know where Leon is," Audrey confessed. "He wasn't at home when I stopped in."

"Mmm *hmm*," LaTonya hummed significantly. "The one thing I *know* he's not doing is working."

"Do you know something you're not telling me?" Audrey said, embarrassed by the desperation she'd let show.

"About Leon? You think he tells me anything?"

"LaTonya, sister," Audrey said, moving in close, "I'm worried about him."

"You do too much worrying about that man. He don't deserve it."

"That's not what I mean. He's—well, he's gone too much."

"Thank your lucky stars for that."

"We—we haven't had much of a private life in a very long time," Audrey forced herself to say.

LaTonya waggled her head. "I don't think I want to know the gory details about my brother, you know?"

"No, I'm . . . Something's going on, LaTonya, you understand what I'm saying, don't you?"

"His drinking getting even worse?"

"It isn't that, I don't think. He's just been disappearing a lot."

"Think that bastard is cheating on you, that it?"

Tears sprang to Audrey's eyes. She compressed her lips, nodded.

"You want me to have a talk with him? I'll slice his fucking balls off."

"I'll handle it, LaTonya."

"You don't hesitate to call me in, hear? Lazy bastard don't know what a good thing he has in you."

83

AUDREY'S HEART BROKE when Nicholas Conover's daughter played the first prelude from *The Well-Tempered Clavier*. It wasn't just that the girl hadn't played all that well—a number of note fumbles, her technique not very polished, her performance mechanical. Camille had all but stolen the show with the Brahms waltz, had played perfectly and with heart, making Audrey burst with pride. It was what was about to happen to Julia Conover. This little girl, awkward in her dress, had lost her mother, something that should never happen to a child. And now she was about to lose her father.

In just a couple of days her father would be arrested, charged with murder. The only time she'd ever see her remaining parent would be during supervised jail visits, her daddy wearing an orange jumpsuit, behind a bulletproof window. Her life would be upended by a public murder trial; she'd never stop hearing the vicious gossip, she'd cry herself to sleep, and who would tuck her in at night? A paid babysitter? It was too awful to think about.

And then her daddy would be sent away to prison. This beautiful little girl, who wasn't much of a pianist but radiated sweetness and naïveté: her life was about to change forever. Andrew Stadler may have been the murder victim, but this little girl was a victim too, and it filled Audrey with sorrow and foreboding.

As the teacher, Mrs. Guarini, thanked the audience for coming and invited everyone to stay for refreshments, Audrey turned around and saw Nicholas Conover.

He was holding up a video camera. Next to him sat a beautiful young woman, and next to her Conover's handsome son, Lucas. Audrey did a double take, recognizing the woman, who just then put her hand on Conover's neck, stroking it familiarly.

It was Cassie Stadler.

Andrew Stadler's daughter.

Her mind spun crazily. She didn't know what to think, what to make of it.

Nicholas Conover, having an affair with the daughter of the man he'd murdered.

She felt as if a whole row of doors had just been flung open.

84

IT HAD TO happen, since the two of them got into work at about the same time.

Nick and Scott had been avoiding each other studiously. Even at meetings where both of them were present, they were publicly cordial yet no longer exchanged small talk, before or after.

But they could hardly avoid each other right now. Nick stood at the elevator bank, waiting, just as Scott approached.

Nick was the first to speak: "'Morning, Scott."

"'Morning, Nick."

A long stretch of silence.

Fortunately, someone else came up to them, a woman who worked in Accounts Receivable. She greeted Scott, who was her boss, then shyly said, "Hi" in Nick's general direction.

The three of them rode up in silence, everyone watching the numbers change. The woman got off on three.

Nick turned to Scott. "So you've been busy," he said. It came out more fiercely than he intended.

Scott shrugged. "Just the usual."

"The usual include killing new projects like Dashboard?"

A beat, and then: "I tabled it, actually."

"I didn't know new product development was in your job description."

Scott looked momentarily uncertain, as if he were considering ducking the question, but then he said, "Any expenditures of that magnitude concern me."

The elevator dinged as it reached the executive floor.

"Well," Scott said with visible relief, "to be continued, I'm sure."

Nick reached over to the elevator control panel and pressed the emergency stop button, which immediately stopped the doors from opening and also set off an alarm bell that sounded distantly in the elevator shaft.

"What the hell are you—"

"Whose side are you on, Scott?" Nick asked with ferocious calm, crowding Scott into the corner of the elevator. "You think I don't know what's going on?"

Nick braced himself for the usual wisecracking evasions. Scott's face went a deep plum color, his eyes growing, but Nick saw anger in his face, not fear.

He's not scared of you, Cassie had observed.

"There aren't any sides here, Nick. It's not like shirts versus skins."

"I want you to listen to me closely. You are not to kill or 'table' projects, change vendors, or in fact make any changes whatsoever without consulting me, are we clear?"

"Not that simple," Scott replied levelly, a tic starting in his left eye. "I make decisions all day long—"

The elevator emergency alarm kept ringing.

Nick dropped his voice to a near-whisper. "Who do you think you're working for? Any decision you make, any order you give, that's not in your designated area of responsibility will be countermanded—by me. Publicly, if need be. You see, Scott, like it or not, you work for me," Nick said. "Not for Todd Muldaur, not for Willard Osgood, but for me. Understand?"

Scott stared, his left eye wincing madly. Finally he said, "The real question is, who do you think *you're* working for? We both work for our stakeholders. It's pretty simple. Your problem is that you've never really understood that. You talk about managing this company as if you own the place. But I've got news for you. You don't own the place, and neither do I. You think you're a better man than me because you got all teary-eyed when the layoffs came? You talk about the 'Stratton Family,' but guess what, Nick. It's not a family. It's a business. You're a great face to parade in front of the Wall Street analysts. But just because you look good in tights doesn't make you a superhero."

"That's enough, Scott."

"Fairfield gave you the car keys, Nick. They didn't give you the car."

Nick took a deep breath. "There's only one driver."

The tic in Scott's eye was coming more rapidly now. Nick could see a vein pulsing at his temple. "In case you haven't figured it out," Scott said, "things have changed around here. You can't fire me." He tried to reach around for the emergency stop button to get the elevator doors open. But Nick swiveled his body in one quick motion to block Scott's hand.

"You're right," he said. "I can't fire you. But let me be really clear: so long as I'm here, you are not to conduct any discussions regarding the sale of this company."

A thin smile crept across Scott's face as he kept staring. Several seconds ticked by. The only sound was the ring of the elevator alarm. "Fine," he said freezingly. "You're the boss." But his tone called to mind Cassie's interpretation of Scott's refrain: those unspoken words *for now*.

85

HE RETURNED TO his desk shaken and began to go through his e-mail. More Nigerians who sought to share their plundered millions. More offers to add inches, or borrow money, or acquire painkillers.

He called Henry Hutchens and made an appointment for coffee or an early lunch tomorrow. Then he tried Martin Lai in Hong Kong, at home, where it was around nine in the evening.

This time, Martin Lai answered. "Oh—Mr. Conover, yes, thank you, thank you," he said, a cataract of nerves. "I'm very sorry I didn't call you back—I was on a trip, sir."

Nick knew that wasn't true. Had Lai, surprised to get a call from the CEO, checked in with Scott, who told him not to reply? "Martin, I need your help with something important."

"Yes, sir. Of course, sir."

"What can you tell me about a ten-million-dollar transfer of funds out of Stratton Asia Ventures to a numbered account in Macau?"

"Sir, I don't know anything about that," Lai answered, too quickly.

"Meaning you don't know why the transfer was made?"

"No, sir, this is the first I hear of it."

He was covering up. Scott must have gotten to him.

"Martin, this financial irregularity has been called to my attention, and it's something I'm quite concerned about. I thought I'd see if you know anything before the formal investigation is launched by Compliance."

"No, sir," Lai said. "I never heard of it before."

AS HE STARED at the computer screen, Marjorie's voice came over the intercom, and at the same time an instant message popped up.

"Nick," she said, "it's the high school again."

Nick groaned.

The message was from Stephanie Alstrom:

Nick—info for you—talk soon?

"Is it Sundquist again?" he said to Marjorie, as he typed:

come by my office now.

"I'm afraid it is," Marjorie said. "And this time— well, it sounds awfully serious."

"Oh, God," he said. "Can you put me through?"

STEPHANIE ALSTROM WAS getting out of the elevator just as Nick was about to get in. He gestured for her to stay in the cabin, and once the doors closed, he said, "I'm in a rush. Personal business. What do you have, Steph?"

"Pacific Rim Investors," she said. "Apparently it's a consortium whose silent partner—their anonymous sugar daddy—is an arm of the P.L.A.—the People's Liberation Army of China."

"Why the hell would the Chinese *army* want to buy Stratton?"

"Capitalism, pure and simple. They've bought up thousands of foreign corporations, usually through shell companies to avoid the political backlash. I wonder if Willard Osgood knows it. He's somewhere to the right of Attila the Hun."

"I wonder," Nick said. "But no one's a bigger arch-conservative than Dorothy Devries. And you can bet *she* has no idea."

86

"NICK, I KNOW you're an extremely busy man," Jerome Sundquist said, leading him past the framed photos of multicultural tennis champs, "but if anyone owes you an apology, it's your son." He spoke loudly so Lucas could hear.

Lucas sat in one of the camel-upholstered side chairs, looking small, shoulders hunched, furled into himself. He was wearing a gray T-shirt under a plaid shirt and track pants that were zippered above the knee so you could turn them into shorts, not that Lucas ever did.

He didn't look up when Nick entered.

Nick stood there in his raincoat—this time he was prepared for the lousy weather, even brought an umbrella—and said, "You did it again, didn't you?"

Lucas didn't reply.

"Tell your father, Lucas," Sundquist said as he took a seat behind his overly large desk. Nick wondered, fleetingly, why it was that people with the biggest desks and the biggest offices were often not all that powerful, in the scheme of things.

Then he reminded himself that Jerry Sundquist might only run a high school in a small town in Michi-

gan, but right now he was as powerful in the lives of
the Conovers as Willard Osgood.

Lucas cast the principal a bloodshot glare and
looked back down at his feet. Had he been crying?

"Well, if he doesn't have the courage to tell you,
I will," Sundquist said, leaning back in his chair. He
actually seemed to be enjoying this moment, Nick
thought. "I told you that the second time he was caught
smoking he'd be expelled."

"Understood," Nick said.

"And I think I also told you that if we found drugs,
we'd let the police prosecute."

"Drugs?"

"The school board voted unanimously a few years
ago that any student using, distributing, or even pos-
sessing marijuana on school property will be sus-
pended, arrested, and face an expulsion hearing."

"Arrested," Nick said, suddenly feeling a chill, as if
he'd just stepped into a meat locker. Lucas wasn't cry-
ing. He was high.

"We notify the police and let them prosecute. And I
have to tell you, Michigan tends to be tough on minors
in possession of marijuana. The two-thousand-dollar
fine is probably insignificant to you, Nick, but I've seen
judges give minors anything from probation to forty-
five days in prison, as much as a year."

"Jerry—"

"Under Michigan law, we're required to notify the
local police, do you know that? MCL three-eighty,
thirteen oh eight. We don't have a choice about it."

Nick nodded, put a hand on his forehead and began
massaging away the headache. My God, he thought.
Expulsion? There wasn't another high school for forty
miles. And what private school would take Lucas,
given his record? How would Laura have handled this?
She was so much better at difficult situations than he

was. "Jerry, I'd like us to talk. You and me. Without Luke."

Sundquist didn't have to do anything more than raise his chin at Lucas, who quickly got up, as if shot from a cannon. "Wait in the faculty lounge," he said to Lucas's back.

"I'm sorry, Nick. I hate to do this to you."

"Jerry," Nick said, leaning forward in his chair. For a moment, he lost his train of thought. Suddenly he wasn't a prominent parent, the president and chief executive officer of the biggest company in town. He was a high school kid pleading with the principal. "I'm as angry about this as you are. More so, probably. And we've got to let him know it's totally unacceptable. But it's his first time."

"Somehow I doubt it's his first time using marijuana," Sundquist said with a sidelong glance. "But in any case, we have a zero-tolerance policy. Our options are severely limited here."

"It's not a gun, and he's not exactly a dealer. We're talking about one marijuana cigarette, right?"

Sundquist nodded. "That's all it takes these days."

"Jerry, you've got to consider what the kid has been going through in the last year, with Laura's death." There was a note of pleading in his voice that embarrassed Nick.

The principal looked unmoved. In fact, he looked almost pleased. Nick felt the anger in him rise, but he knew anger would be the worst response in this situation.

Nick took a deep breath. "Jerry, I'm asking for your mercy. If there's anything I can do for the high school, the school system. Anything Stratton can do."

"Are you offering a *payoff*?" Sundquist said, biting off the words.

"Of course not," Nick said, although both men knew

that was exactly what he was talking about. An extra deep discount on furniture could save the high school hundreds of thousands of dollars a year.

Sundquist closed his eyes, shook his head sadly. "That's beneath you, Nick. What kind of lesson do you think it's going to teach your son if he gets special treatment because of who his dad is?"

"What we talk about stays between us," Nick said. He couldn't believe that he'd just offered the high school principal a bribe. Was anything lower? Bribes—that was the coin of Scott McNally's realm, Todd Muldaur's realm. Not his.

Jerome Sundquist was looking at him with a new expression now, one of disappointment and maybe even contempt. "I'm going to pretend I didn't hear it, Nick. But I'm willing to show some leniency on the grounds of his mother's death. I do have to notify the police that we're willing to handle the incident ourselves, and generally they leave it to our discretion. I'm giving Lucas a five-day suspension and assigning him to crisis counseling during that time and for the rest of the school year. But the next time, I go right to the police."

Nick stood up, walked up to Sundquist's desk and put out his hand to shake. "Thanks, Jerry," he said. "I think it's the right decision, and I appreciate it."

But Sundquist wouldn't shake his hand.

TEN MINUTES LATER Nick and Lucas walked out together through the glass doors of the high school. The rain was really coming down now—it was monsoon season, had to be—and Nick held up his umbrella for Lucas, who shunned it, striding ahead through the rain, head up as if he wanted to get soaked.

Lucas seemed to hesitate before getting into the front seat, as if contemplating making a run for it. As the car nosed through the parking lot and onto Grand-view Avenue, the silence was electric with tension.

Lucas wasn't high anymore. He was low, and he was silent, but it wasn't a neutral silence. It was a defiant silence, like that of a prisoner of war determined to reveal nothing more than his name, rank, and serial number.

Nick's own silence was the silence of someone who had plenty to say but was afraid of what would happen if he began to speak.

Lucas's hand snaked around to the radio dial and turned on some alternative rock station, blasting it.

Nick immediately switched it off. "You proud of yourself?"

Lucas said nothing, just stared fixedly ahead as the windshield wipers flipped back and forth in a lulling rhythm.

"You know something? This would have broken your mother's heart. You should be relieved she isn't around to see this."

More silence. This time Nick waited for a reply. He was about to go on when Lucas said, in a hollow voice, "I guess you made sure of that."

"And what's that supposed to mean?"

Lucas didn't respond.

"What the *fuck* is that supposed to mean?" Nick realized he was shouting. He could see a spray of his own spittle on the windshield. He pulled the car over, braked to an abrupt stop, and turned to face Lucas.

"What do *you* think?" Lucas said in a low, wobbly voice, not meeting his eyes.

Nick stared, disbelieving. "What are you trying to say?" he whispered, summoning all the calm he could muster.

"Forget it," Lucas said, making a little buzz-off gesture with his left hand.

"What are you trying to say?"

"I wouldn't know, Dad. I wasn't there."

"What's gotten into you, Lucas?" The windshield wipers ticked back and forth, back and forth, and he could hear the regular clicking of the turn signal that hadn't gone off. He reached over, switched off the signal. The rain sheeted the car's windows, making it feel like the two of them were inside a cabin in a terrible storm, but it wasn't a safe place. "Look, Luke, you don't have Mom anymore. You just have me. You wish it were otherwise. So do I. But we've got to make the best of a bad situation."

"It wasn't me who made that situation."

"No one 'made' that situation," Nick said.

"You killed Mom," he said, so quietly that for a moment Nick wasn't sure Lucas had actually spoken the words.

Nick felt like someone had grabbed his heart and squeezed. "I can't deal with this right now. I can't deal with *you*."

You Conover men. Better defended than a medieval castle.

"Fine with me."

"No," Nick said. "No. Scratch that." He was breathing hard, as if he had just done an eight-hundred-meter sprint. "Okay, listen to me. What happened to your mother that night—God knows we've talked about it . . ."

"No, Dad." Lucas's voice was shaky but resolute. "We've never talked about it. You *refer* to it. You don't talk about it. That's the house rule. We don't talk about it. *You* don't. You talk about what a fuck-up I am. *That's* what you talk about."

The windows had begun to fog up. Nick closed his eyes. "About your mother. There isn't a day that goes by when I don't wonder whether there was anything

I could have done—anything at all—that might have made a difference."

"You never said . . ." Lucas's eyes were wet and his voice was thick, muffled.

"The truck came out of nowhere," Nick began, but then he stopped. It was too painful. "Luke, what happened happened. And it wasn't about me and it wasn't about you."

Lucas was quiet for a moment. "Fucking swim meet."

"Lucas, don't try to make sense of it. Don't try to connect the dots, as if there was some kind of logic to it all. It just *happened*."

"I didn't visit her." Lucas's words were slurred, whether from the pot or from emotion, Nick couldn't tell, and didn't care. "In the hospital. Afterward."

"She was in a coma. She was already gone, Luke."

"Maybe she could have heard me." His voice had gotten thin and reedy.

"She knew you loved her, Luke. She didn't need reminding. I don't think she wanted you to remember her like that, anyway. She wouldn't have been sore that you weren't there. She would have been glad. I really believe that. You were always attuned to her feelings. Like there was some radio frequency only the two of you could hear. You know something, Luke? I think maybe you were the only one of us who did what she would have wanted."

Lucas buried his face in his hands. When he spoke again, his voice sounded as if it were coming from a long way off. "Why do you hate me so much? Is it 'cause I look like her, and you can't deal with that?"

"Lucas," Nick said. He was determined to hold it together. "I want you to listen to me. I need you to hear this." He squeezed his eyes shut. "There is nothing in my life more precious to me than you are." His voice was hoarse, and he got the words out with difficulty, but he got them out. "I love you more than my life."

He put his arms around his son, who at first stiffened and squirmed, and then, suddenly, put his own arms around Nick and clasped him tightly, the way he did when Lucas was a little boy.

Nick felt the rhythmic convulsions of grief, the staccato expulsions of breath, and it took him a moment before he realized that Lucas wasn't the only one who was weeping.

87

THE PHONE RANG, and Audrey picked it up without thinking.

"Is this Detective Rhimes?" A sweet, female voice, the words slow and careful.

Her heart sank. "Yes it is," Audrey said, although she was sorely tempted to say, No, I'm afraid Detective Rhimes is on vacation.

"Detective, this is Ethel Dorsey."

"Yes, Mrs. Dorsey," she said, softening her voice. "How are you doing?"

"I'm doing as well as could be expected with my Tyrone gone and all. But I thank the good Lord I still have my three wonderful sons."

"There's so much we can't understand, Mrs. Dorsey," Audrey said. "But the Scriptures tell us that those who sow in tears will reap with songs of joy."

"I know he records our tears and collects them all in his bottle."

"He does. That he does."

"God is good."

"All the time," Audrey said, her response a reflex.

"Detective, I'm so sorry to disturb you, but I was

wondering if you've made any progress on my Tyrone's case."

"No, I'm sorry. Nothing yet. We keep plugging away, though." The lie made her ashamed.

"Please don't give up, Detective."

"Of course not, Mrs. Dorsey." She hadn't given the case more than a fleeting thought in the last several weeks. She was thankful that Mrs. Dorsey worshipped in another church, the next town over.

"I know you're doing your best."

"Yes, I am."

"May the Lord keep you strong, Detective."

"You too, Mrs. Dorsey. You too."

She hung up filled with sorrow, ashamed beyond ashamed, and the phone rang again immediately.

It was Susan Calloway, the bland-voiced woman from the state police lab in Grand Rapids. The firearms examiner in charge of the IBIS database. She sounded a little different, and Audrey realized that what she was hearing was excitement, in the woman's tamped-down, squelched way.

"Well, I do think we have something for you," the woman said.

"You have a match."

"I'm sorry this has taken so long—"

"Oh, not at all—"

"But the Grand Rapids PD certainly took their time. I mean, all I was asking them to do was to check the bullets out of Property and drive them all of seventeen blocks over to Fuller. You'd think I'd asked for a human sacrifice or something."

Audrey chuckled politely. "But you got a match," she prompted. The technician sounded positively giddy.

"Of course, the real problem was that it wasn't any-one's case anymore. I mean, it was from six years ago, and both detectives are gone, they tell me. There's always an excuse."

"Tell me about it," Audrey laughed.

"In any case, the bullets they brought over matched the ones in your case. They're copper-jacketed Rainiers, so the ammunition is different. But the striation markings are identical."

"So it's a positive match."

"It's a positive match, yes."

"The weapon—?"

"I can't tell you that for absolute certain. But I'd say it's a safe guess it's a Smith and Wesson .380. That's not legally admissible, though." The woman read off the Grand Rapids PD report number for the bullet.

"So Grand Rapids should have all the information I need," Audrey said.

"Well, I don't know how much more they'll have than I already told you. Both detectives on the case are off the force, as I say."

"Even so, those names would be a help."

"Oh, well, if that's all you want, I have *that*. The submitting detective, anyway. Right here in the comments box." The technician went silent, and Audrey was about to prompt her for the name, when the woman spoke again, and Audrey went cold.

"Says here it was submitted by a Detective Edward J. Rinaldi," the technician said. "But they say he's retired from the force, so that's probably not going to be much use to you. Sorry about that."

— PART FIVE —

NO HIDING PLACE

88

MULLIGANS—NEVER AN apostrophe—was a diner on Bainbridge Road in Fenwick famous for its Bolognese sauce, the subject of a yellowed framed article from the *Fenwick Free Press* on the wall as you entered. The headline was typical of the paper's dopey, punning style: "A Meaty Subject." This was the place Nick used to go at three in the morning, after the junior and senior proms. Frank Mulligan was long gone. It was now owned by a guy who'd been a few years ahead of Nick and Eddie in high school, Johnny Frechette, who'd done three years in Ionia for drug trafficking.

Nick hadn't been here in years, and he noticed that the place had a staleness to it. The Formica tables had a faint cloth pattern, faded to white in the areas where mugs and plates had banged and scraped against it. They were serving breakfast now, and the place smelled of coffee and maple syrup and bacon, all blended into a single aroma: Eau du Diner.

Eddie seemed to know the waitresses here. Probably he came here for breakfast a lot. They were seated in a corner, away from the window. Aside from a few people eating at the counter, the place was empty.

"You look like shit," Eddie said.

"Thanks," Nick said irritably. "You too."

"Well, you're not going to want to hear this."

Nick held his breath. "What is it?"

"They ID'd the gun."

The blood drained from Nick's face. "You said you tossed it."

"I did."

"Then how could that be?"

The two fell silent as an overperfumed waitress arrived with a Silex carafe, and sloshed coffee into their thick white mugs.

"They got all kinds of tricky ballistics shit these days," Eddie said.

"I don't get what you're telling me." Nick took a hurried sip of his black coffee, scalding his tongue. Maybe he didn't *want* to understand what Eddie seemed to be getting at.

"They matched the bullets with the gun."

"They matched the bullets with *what*?" Nick was aware that his voice was a bit too loud, and he lowered it at once. "There's *no gun,* right? You said it's *gone!*"

"Yeah, well, apparently they don't need a gun anymore." Eddie popped open a couple of little half-and-half containers and tipped them into his mug, stirring until it turned an unappealing gray. "All's they need is bullets, 'cause of the big new computer database, I forget what it's called. They must have matched up the bullets in Stadler's body with the ones from the scene years ago where I got the piece—how the hell do I know? My source didn't get into details."

"Who's your source?"

Eddie ducked his head to the side. "Forget it."

"You know this for a fact? You're one-hundred-percent certain?"

"It's a fact. Suck it up."

"Jesus Christ, Eddie, you said everything was cool!"

Nick's voice cracked. "You said the gun wasn't registered to you. You—you said you picked it up at a crime scene, and there was no record of it anywhere."

Eddie's normally confident expression had given way, disconcertingly, to a pallid, sweaty discomfort. "That's what I thought. Sometimes shit gets out of your control, buddy boy."

"I don't believe this," Nick said, his voice hoarse. "I don't fucking believe it. What the hell do we do now?"

Eddie set down his coffee mug and gave Nick a stone-cold look. "We do absolutely nothing. We say nothing, admit nothing, we don't say a fucking word. Are you getting this?"

"But if they—they know the gun I used was one you took—"

"They're going to try to connect the dots, but they don't have it nailed down. Maybe they can prove the ammo that killed Stadler came from that gun, but they can't prove I took it. Everything they got is circumstantial. They got *nada* when they searched your house—that whole thing was a scare tactic. They got no witnesses, and they got a lot of little forensic shit, and now they got this gun, but in the end it's all circumstantial. So all they can do now is scare you into talking, see. This is why I'm telling you about it. I want you to be prepared. I don't want those jokers springing this on you and having you crumble, okay? You got to be a rock." Eddie took a sip of coffee without moving his eyes from Nick's.

"They can't just arrest us? Maybe they don't need us to talk."

"No. If neither one of us says a damned thing, they're not going to arrest."

"*You* wouldn't say anything, would you?" Nick whispered. "*You're* not going to say anything, right?"

Eddie smiled a slow smile, and Nick got a shivery

feeling. There was something almost sociopathic about
Eddie, something dead in his eyes. "Now you're start-
ing to understand," he said. "See, at the end of the day,
Nick, they don't give a shit about me. I'm just some
small-time corporate security guy, a nobody. You're the
CEO everyone in this town despises. They're not inter-
ested in putting my puny antlers on the wall. You're
the monster buck they're hunting. You're the fucking
twelve-point rack, okay?"

Nick nodded slowly. The room was turning slowly
around him.

"The only way this thing unravels," Eddie said, "is
if you talk. Maybe you decide to play *Let's Make a
Deal* with the cops. Try to strike your own separate
deal—good for you, bad for me. This would be a huge,
huge fucking mistake, Nick. Because I will hear about
it. You have even the most preliminary, exploratory
conversation with those jokers, and I will hear about it
in a matter of *seconds,* Nick—count on it. Believe me,
I'm wired into that place. And my lawyer will be in the
DA's office so fast it'll make your head spin, with an
offer they will fucking jump at."

"Your . . . *lawyer*?" Nick croaked.

"See, Nick, let's be clear what they got me for. It's
called 'obstruction,' and it's no big deal. First offend-
ers get maybe six months, if any time at all, but not
me. Not when I agree to tell the whole story, testify
truthfully in the grand jury and at the trial. They get a
murderer, see. And what do *I* get out of it? A walk. Not
even probation. It's a sure thing, Nick."

"But you wouldn't do that, would you?" Nick said.
He heard his own voice, and it seemed to be coming
from very far away. "You'd never do that, right?"

"Only if you change the rules of the game, bud.
Only if you talk. Though I gotta tell you, I shoulda
done this on day one. Why I ever came over to help you

that night, I don't know. Goodness of my heart, I guess. Help an old buddy who's in deep shit. I shoulda said, Sorry, not me, amigo, and just stayed in bed. Look what I get for being a nice guy. Very least, I should have shopped you long ago. Rolled over, made a deal. I don't know why I didn't. Anyway, what's done is done, but let's be crystal clear, I am *not* going down for this. You try to make a deal, you talk, and at that point I'm gonna do what's in my own best interests."

Nick couldn't catch his breath. "I'm not going to talk," he said.

Eddie gave him a sidelong glance, and he smiled as if he were enjoying this. "All you gotta do, Nicky, is hold it together, and we're going to be just fine, you and me. Keep your fucking mouth shut, don't panic, and we'll ride this out."

The waitress was back, wielding her glass carafe. "Freshen your coffee?" she said.

Neither Eddie nor Nick responded at first, and then Nick said slowly, not looking at her, "I think we're okay."

"That's right," Eddie said. "We're okay. We're just fine."

89

THE FENWICK RACQUET Club wasn't a place where much tennis was played, as far as Nick could tell. But for Henry Hutchens—Hutch, as he was always known—it had evidently become a home away from home. Hutch had been Stratton's chief financial officer back when the position was called, less grandly, controller. He had served Old Man Devries for a quarter of a century, and when Nick took over, he helped prepare the financial statements for the sale to Fairfield. Did a good job of it too. His manner was unfailingly courtly, maybe a little formal. And when Nick had come to his office—that's how he did it, in Hutch's office, not his own—and told him that Fairfield wanted to replace him with one of their own, he didn't utter a word of protest.

Nick had told him the truth about Fairfield. Still, they both knew that if Nick had seriously objected, Fairfield would have backed down. Nick hadn't. Hutch was a highly competent old-school controller. But Fairfield was loaded up with high-powered financial engineers, ready to lecture you on the advantages of activity-based costing and economic-value-added accounting systems. They viewed Hutch as a green-eyeshades guy;

he didn't use words like "strategic." Scott McNally was someone the people at Fairfield were comfortable with, and he was someone who could help Nick take Stratton to the next level. *The next level*—there was a time when Nick couldn't get enough of that phrase; now the cliché had the stink of yesterday's breakfast.

"Long time between drinks, Nick," Hutch said as Nick joined him at a table inside the clubhouse. He lifted a martini glass, and smiled crookedly, but didn't stand. "Join me?"

Hutch had the kind of ruddy complexion that looked like good health from a distance. Up close, Nick could see the alcohol-inflamed capillaries. Even his sweat seemed juniper-scented.

"It's a little early for me," Nick said. Christ, it wasn't even noon yet.

"Well, of *course*," Hutch said, with his Thurston Howell III purr. "You're a working man. With an *office* to go to. And lots of employees who *depend* on you." He drained the last drops of his drink, and signaled to the waiter for another.

"For the moment, anyway."

Hutch clasped his hands together. "You must be riding high, though. Layoffs—everyone talks about the layoffs! They must be *ecstatic* in Boston. To think that my own humble self was to be the first of so many on the gallows. It's kind of an honor, really."

Nick blanched. "The company owes you a lot, Hutch. I've always been grateful to you, personally."

"Oh please. Not everyone has the privilege of selling the rope to one's own hangman." Another drink was placed before him. "Thank you, Vinnie," Hutch murmured. The waiter, a sixtyish man whose neck strained against the club-required red bowtie, nodded pleasantly.

"A tomato juice would be great," Nick told him.

"You surprised a great many people, you know," Hutch went on. He popped the cocktail olive into his mouth and chewed thoughtfully. "Have to keep my strength up," he added with a wink.

"What happened has been hard for everyone. A lot of good people have been hurt. I'm very aware of that."

"You misunderstand," Hutch said. "I didn't mean about the layoffs. I just meant that not everyone took you to be CEO material. A solid company man, absolutely. But not quite cut out for the corner office."

"Well." Nick looked around, taking in the fieldstone fireplace, the white tablecloths, the red patterned wall-to-wall carpet. "I guess Old Man Devries—"

"It had nothing to do with Milton," Hutch said sharply. "If he'd wanted to, Milton could have named you president, or chief operating officer. One of those next-in-line positions. That's the custom with a corporate heir apparent. He did not choose to do so."

"Fair enough," Nick said, trying not to bridle.

"He was *fond* of you. We all were. But when the issue came up, well . . ." Hutch peered into the watery depths of his cocktail. "Milton considered you a little callow. Too much of a big-man-on-campus type. Someone too concerned with being popular to be a real leader." He looked up. "Thought you didn't have the killer instinct. Now *there's* one heck of an irony."

Nick's face was hot. "Being that you're such a connoisseur of irony, you might enjoy this one." He unzipped his black leather portfolio and presented Hutch with the contract that Eddie had taken from Scott's e-mail.

"What is this?"

"You tell me." *If you're not too drunk to make sense of it,* Nick thought.

Hutch reached for his reading glasses, convex lenses with wire frames, and started paging through the document. A few times he tapped on the pages and gave a dry chuckle. "My, my," he finally said. "I take it this isn't your masterwork."

"Not mine."

"Milton! Thou shouldst be living at this hour: Stratton hath need of thee." Hutch put his reading glasses away, and made tsk-tsking sounds. "Pacific Rim Investors," he said, and then: "I can't even pronounce this name—is it Malaysian? Good Lord." He looked up, bleary-eyed. "So much for the match made in Heaven. Looks like your white knights came riding in from Boston only to sell Stratton down the Yangtze River."

Nick explained what Stephanie Alstrom had told him about the real owner being the Chinese P.L.A.

"Oh, that's rich," Hutch said happily. "That's really a thing of beauty. Though it's not exactly sporting to put one over on the Communists like that these days, is it?"

"Put one over?"

"If these balance sheets are authentic, then Stratton's doing marvelously well. But I have a suspicion they're as phony as a glass apple."

Lipstick on a pig, Nick thought.

"If I had access to your most recent P and L statements, *and* if I weren't three sheets to the wind, *and* if I actually *cared,* I could give you a breakdown of this document that was so clear even *you* could understand it." He took a swallow of his drink. "But even in my current condition, I can tell you that somebody's been coloring outside the lines. For one thing, you're taking your reserves against losses from your last profitable year and using it to cover over the new tide of red ink. That's 'cookie jar' accounting, and we both know about that company that got caught doing it not so long ago and had to pay three billion dollars in damages to make it all better. It's not nice to fool with your accrued liability."

"What good is that?" Nick said. "Once the new owners find out the truth, they'll hit Fairfield with a huge lawsuit."

"Ah, but you see, that's the beauty part, my boy. They can't sue."

"Why not?"

"There's a clever non-litigation clause here," Hutch said, tapping the paper. "Once the deal goes through, no lawsuits are permitted over any representations and warranties made herein, ya de ya de ya."

"Why in the world would the buyers agree to that?"

"I think the answer is manifest," Hutch said, looking up again. "It's in the side agreement. Guaranteeing a seven-figure payout to someone, no doubt a Chinese government official with the ability to speed through the acquisition."

"A bribe."

"You put it so *harshly,* son. The Chinese have a wonderful tradition of giving red envelopes of *hong bao*—good-luck money—to start off the lunar new year right."

"Ten million dollars is a lot of good-luck money for one man."

"Indeed. But to grease a deal like this through the Chinese bureaucracy without endless quibbling—well, that's quite a bargain, isn't it?"

"It's early for Chinese New Year, isn't it?"

"Now you're catching on. Unless you can think of some other reason why Stratton would be routing him his money to a numbered account in Macau. From where, I'll wager, it was immediately transferred to another account at the Bank of Commerce of Labuan."

"Labuan?"

"Labuan is an island off the coast of Malaysia. A speck of sand, and a great big offshore financial services industry. The bankers of Labuan make the Swiss seem *gabby*. Basically, it's where Chinese kleptocrats like to sock away their ill-gotten gains."

"I had no idea."

"I'm sure they were *counting* on that. Good boys and girls don't know about Labuan. And they certainly don't wire money there."

"Christ," Nick said. "How many people are in on this thing?"

"Impossible to say, though it only takes two counter-signers to execute it. One corporate officer—that would be your charming young CFO—and a managing partner from Fairfield. It does seem a little low-rent, the whole thing, but I suppose these are two young men in a hurry. There are a *lot* of people in a hurry these days. Sure you won't join me in a drink?"

"Still waiting for my tomato juice," Nick said. "Seems to be taking an awfully long time."

"Oh dear," Hutch said in a low voice. "I should have realized. Doubt it's ever going to come, Vinnie being your waiter and all. I guess you must be used to this sort of thing."

"What are you saying?"

Hutch glanced at the waiter and shrugged elaborately. "It's just that you laid off his brother."

90

AUDREY TRACKED DOWN Bugbee on his cell phone at the Burger Shack, the place he liked to go for lunch. He could barely hear her. In the background was a cacophony of laughter and clinking plates and bad rock music.

"When are you coming back?" she said several times.

"I'm on lunch."

"I can tell that. But this is important."

"What?"

"You'd better get over here."

"I said it can wait."

"No, it can't," she said.

"I'm at the Burger Shack for the next—"

"See you there," she said, and she hung up before he could object.

BUGBEE QUICKLY GOT over his pique at having his lunch with the guys—three uniformed officers, all around his age—interrupted.

He excused himself, and he and Audrey found an empty booth.

"That's it," he said when Audrey told him about the weapon match. "We got 'em."

"It's still tenuous," she said. "It's circumstantial."

He glared. There was a large splotch of ketchup on his hideous tie, which only improved its appearance. "The *fuck* are you waiting for—Nick Conover's diary with a special entry for that night saying, I plugged the guy, me and Eddie?"

"We're connecting dots that I don't know if the prosecutor's going to let us connect."

"Connecting *what* fucking dots?" he spat out.

She briefly considered asking him to cut out the potty-mouth stuff, but now was not the time. "We know this suggests that Eddie Rinaldi and Nick Conover were behind it."

"Tell me something I don't know—"

"Will you shut up for a second, please?" It was worth saying just to see Bugbee's stunned expression. "The gun that was used to kill Stadler was also used on a no-gun case that Eddie Rinaldi worked six years ago. But does that prove Rinaldi pocketed the gun back in Grand Rapids? The case is still full of holes."

"Yeah? I don't think so, and neither do you."

"Our opinion isn't the same thing as what's going to convince the DA to prosecute. Especially in a capital case involving the CEO of a huge corporation and one of his top officers."

"Tell you something—once we hook our boy Eddie up to a polygraph, he'll crack."

"He doesn't have to submit to a polygraph."

"If he's facing a first-degree murder charge and life without parole, believe me, he'll take it." He leaned back in the booth, savoring the moment. "This is beautiful. Shit, this is beautiful." He smiled, and she realized that this was the first time she'd seen him give a genuine smile of pleasure. It looked wrong on his face, didn't come naturally, looked like a disturbance in the natural order of things. His cheeks creased deeply, like heavily starched fabric.

"Conover won't take a polygraph," Audrey said. "Let's face it, we still don't know which one of them the shooter is," Audrey said.

"Fuck it. Charge 'em both with first-degree murder, and sort it out later. Whoever comes to the window first gets the deal, that's how it works."

"I don't know if we're even going to get to that point, if we'll get a prosecutor to write out a warrant."

"So you go prosecutor-shopping. Come on. You know how the game works."

"Noyce really frowns on that."

"Screw Noyce. This is our case, I told you. Not his."

"Still," she said. "I don't know. I don't want to mess this up."

Bugbee started counting on his left hand, starting with his thumb. "We got the soil match, we got the fucking erased surveillance tape, we got Conover's alarm going off at two A.M., followed by the desperate cell phone call, we got Schizo Man with a history of attacks on the suspect, and now we got a gun match." He held up five fingers triumphantly. "The fuck else you want? I say we run with it."

"I want to pass this by Noyce first."

"You want to run to Daddy?" He shook his head. "Haven't you figured out that Noyce isn't our friend?"

"Why do you say that?"

"Take a look. The closer we get to Stratton's CEO, the harder Noyce's been fighting us, right? He doesn't want us taking on the big kahuna. Wouldn't surprise me if he's in Stratton's pocket."

"Come on."

"I'm fucking serious. Something's off about the way that guy's taking their side."

"He's got to be cautious on a case this big."

"This is way beyond cautious. You notice how when I searched Rinaldi's condo, total surprise, and all of a sudden a couple of guns are missing from his rack, like someone gave him a heads-up?"

"Or maybe he dumped them after he or Conover murdered Stadler," Audrey said. "Or Conover called him, told him a team was coming to search Conover's house, and Eddie races home and disposes of the evidence."

"Yeah, any of those are possible. Theoretically. Then you notice how Noyce is trying to make life difficult for you, jam up your schedule with other shit so you don't have time to do this right? Look, Audrey, I don't trust the guy."

"He's my friend, Roy," she said softly.

"Oh, is he?" Bugbee said. "I wouldn't be so sure of that."

She didn't reply.

91

DOROTHY DEVRIES'S MANSION on Michigan Avenue in East Fenwick didn't seem quite as big as Nick remembered it, but was possibly even darker. Outside, the gables and peaked eaves stopped just shy of Addams Family gothic. Inside, wooden floors were stained to a chocolate hue and partly covered with blood red Orientals. The furniture was either a dark mahogany or covered in a dark damask. She kept the curtains drawn, and he remembered her once saying something about how sunlight could bleach the fabrics. The moon glow of her pale skin was the brightest thing in the house.

"Did you say you wanted tea?" she asked, squinting at him. She sat almost motionless in a burgundy-clad Queen Anne's chair. There was a chandelier above them, which she kept pointedly unlit.

"No thanks," he said.

"But I've interrupted you," she said. "Please go on."

"Well, the basic situation is what I've described. You and I worked hard on the sale to Fairfield, and we did that because we wanted to preserve your father's legacy. And your husband's."

"Legacy," she repeated. In the gloom, he wasn't sure

whether her dress was charcoal gray or navy. "That's a pretty word."

"And a pretty big accomplishment," he said. She seemed to brighten. "Harold Stratton created a company that did what it did as well as—or better than— any other, and he did it right here in Fenwick. And then your husband put Fenwick on the map, as far as corporate America was concerned." Dorothy had had a glossy vanity biography of her husband, Milton, privately printed, copies distributed widely. Nick knew she always responded to the most unctuous praise of her father's historical significance. "So the prospect of seeing Stratton bundled in brown paper and shipped to the Far East—well, I think he'd be appalled. I know I am. It isn't right. It's not right for Fenwick, and it's not right for Stratton."

Mrs. Devries blinked. "But you're telling me all this for a reason."

"Well, sure."

"I'm all ears, Nicholas." She used his full name as if he were a grade student, and a little small for all three syllables.

"You're part owner of the company. You sit on the board. I thought if I could enlist your support, we might be able to present the case together to the others. That way, they'd see it wasn't just about a manager trying to save his job. Because this deal—well, frankly, it would be a disaster. The Chinese aren't interested in our manufacturing facilities. They've got their own. They're going to gut Stratton, run a fire sale of the shop machines, and pass out walking papers to the remaining employees."

"That puts things rather starkly."

"It's a stark situation."

"Well, you do have a flair for the dramatic. That isn't

a criticism. But then you haven't come here to consult, have you?"

"Sure I have."

"Because I didn't hear you ask me my opinion. I heard you telling me yours."

"I just thought I should fill you in," Nick said, perplexed. "See what you thought." A pause. "I'm interested in getting your . . . help and guidance."

A watery smile. "Is that right?" she said.

Nick looked at her, and his face started to prickle. *Had she already known before I came here?*

"I must say I'm a little taken aback to hear you make an argument that's based on sentiment, as opposed to dollars and cents. Because, you see, I don't recall your seeking my help or guidance when you decided to discontinue the Stratton Ultra line. Which was, of course, one of my husband's proudest *legacies*." In a quiet voice, she added, "Pretty word."

Nick said nothing.

"And I don't recall your seeking my help or guidance when you decided to lay off five thousand workers, dragging the Stratton name through the mud," she went on. "And after Milton worked *so* hard to make it a byword for what was *best* about Fenwick. That was part of his legacy, too, Nicholas."

"Dorothy, you voted to approve the layoffs."

"Oh, as if I could stop that train in its tracks! But please don't misunderstand me. I'm not complaining. We sold the firm. Almost all of it belongs to Fairfield Partners. And so we must be *very* businesslike about the whole thing."

"With all respect, Dorothy, aren't you bothered by the idea of Stratton being owned by—by the Chinese government? The Communist Chinese?"

Dorothy Devries shot him a wintry look. "Please. Coming from *you*? Business is business. My family made good money when we sold to Fairfield, and we stand to make quite a bit more when they sell it to this consortium."

"But for God's sake—?" He saw something in her face. "You knew all about it, didn't you?"

She refused to reply. "Nicholas, I didn't give you Milton's job in order for you to dismantle his company, believe it or not. But you did. You cheesed it up with all that Office of the Future eyewash. You got rid of what was real, what was solid, and replaced it with gilt and papier mâchè. Milton would have been appalled. Though I suppose I really can't judge you without judging myself, can I? *I'm* the one who gave you the keys to the corner office."

"Yes," Nick said, finally. "And why did you?"

Dorothy sat silent for a while. "As you might imagine," she said with a drawn smile, "I've often asked myself the same thing."

92

AUDREY HAD PROMISED to keep Noyce in the loop, that was the thing. Strictly speaking, she knew she had the right to go right to the prosecutor's office and request an arrest warrant for Conover and Rinaldi without even telling Noyce. She knew that. But it wasn't right to exclude him. It was a matter of courtesy to keep Noyce updated. She'd told him about the gun match as soon as she found out, and there was no reason to start keeping him in the dark now. It would infuriate him, but worse, it would hurt his feelings, and she wasn't about to do that.

Music was playing softly in Noyce's office as she entered. Audrey recognized Duke Ellington's "Mood Indigo," a trumpet solo.

"Is that Louis?" she asked.

Noyce nodded, absorbed. "Ellington and Armstrong recorded this in one take. Unbelievable."

"Sure is."

"The Duke was great at composing under deadline pressure, you know. The night before a recording date, he's waiting for his mother to finish cooking dinner, and he goes to his piano, and in fifteen minutes he knocks off a piece he calls 'Dreamy Blues.' Next night his band plays it over the radio, broadcasting from the Cotton Club. Later he renames it 'Mood Indigo.'" Noyce shook his head, waited for the song to end, and then clicked off the CD player. "What can I do you for?"

"I think we've got enough to arrest Conover and Rinaldi."

Noyce's eyes widened as she explained, then just as quickly narrowed. "Audrey, let me take you out for ice cream."

"I'm trying not to eat—"

"Well, you can watch. I've been thinking about one of those chocolate-dipped strawberry sundaes at the Dairy Queen."

NOYCE TUCKED INTO a boat-sized dish of soft-serve vanilla ice cream smothered in syrupy strawberries, while Audrey tried to avert her eyes, because it looked too good, and her will was weak when it came to desserts, especially in the midafternoon.

"You don't want your butt out there for false arrest, Aud," he said, a strawberry smear at the side of his mouth. "You realize who you're dealing with, don't you?"

"You think Nicholas Conover's all that powerful?"

"He's a wealthy and powerful guy, but more to the point, he now works for a holding company in Boston that's going to be intent on protecting their investment. And if that means suing the police department in the town of Fenwick, Michigan, they've got the resources to do it. That means they sue you. And us."

"That could work the other way too," she pointed out. Her stomach was growling, and her mouth kept filling with saliva. "The holding company could get nervous about having a CEO charged with first-degree murder and jettison him."

Noyce didn't look up from his ice cream. "You willing to take that chance?"

"If I have a genuine belief that Conover and Rinaldi were involved in a homicide, and I got a prosecutor to back me up on it, how is that false arrest?"

"It just means more of us in the soup. Plus, I can tell you, you're not going to get a prosecutor to write a warrant unless he's sure he can win the case. And I worry that we're still thin on the ground here."

"But look at what we've got, Jack—"

He looked up. "Well, let's take a look at it, Aud. What's your most damaging lead? The gun? So you've got Rinaldi on some case in Grand Rapids, and the same gun in that one turns up here."

"Which is no coincidence. Rinaldi had a reputation as a bad cop."

"Now, you've got to be careful there. That's hearsay. Cops are always gossiping, stabbing each other in the back, you know that better than anyone." He sighed. "No one's going to let you run with that. If you want to say he took the gun, fine—but you don't have any proof of that."

"No, but—"

"Look at it through the eyes of a defense attorney. The same gun used in Grand Rapids turned up here? Well, you think that's the first time a gun was used in Grand Rapids and here? Where do you think our drug dealers get their guns? Flint, Lansing, Detroit, Grand Rapids. They've got to come from somewhere."

Audrey fell silent, watching him spoon the soft-serve, careful to catch a dollop of strawberry goo in each spoonful.

"Far more likely, in fact," Noyce went on, "is that some shitbird in Fenwick bought a piece from some other shitbird in GR. Pardon my French, Audrey."

"But the hydroseed stuff—the soil match—"

"That's an awfully slender reed to hang a first-degree murder on, don't you think?"

She felt increasingly desperate. "The cell phone call Conover lied about—"

"Again, maybe he really did get the day wrong. Audrey, I'm just being devil's advocate here, okay?"

"But Conover's own security system—the video for that night was erased, and we can *prove* it."

"You can prove it was erased, or you can prove the tape recycled? There's quite a difference."

Noyce had clearly been talking to Kevin Lenehan. "You have a point," she conceded.

"Then there's the fact that both you and Bugbee canvassed Conover's neighbors, and not one of them heard a shot that night."

"Jack, you know how far apart the houses are in Fenwicke Estates? Plus, a three-eighty isn't all that loud."

"Audrey. You've got no blood, no weapon, no footprints, no witnesses. What *do* you have?"

"Motive and opportunity. A stalker with a history of violence and a handgun who was stalking the CEO of Stratton—"

"Unarmed, as far as we know."

"Even worse for Conover if Stadler was unarmed."

"And you yourself told me the guy had no prior history of violence. 'Gentle as a lamb,' wasn't that the phrase you used? Audrey, listen. If you had a solid case against these guys, no one would be happier than me. I'd love to take 'em down for this murder, you kidding me? But I don't want us to fuck it up. I don't want us to go off half-cocked."

"I *know* we have a case here," she said.

"You know what you are? You're an optimist, down deep."

"I don't know about that."

"Anyone who loves God the way you do's got to

be an optimist. But you see, here's the sad truth. The longer you stay in this job, the harder it is to stay an optimist. Witnesses recant and the guilty go free and cases don't get solved. Pessimism, cynicism—that's the natural order. Audrey, did I ever tell you about the case I had when I was just starting out? Woman shot in the head standing in her front parlor, shifty cheating husband, we kept catching him lying about his alibis, which kept changing. The more we looked at him, the more we were convinced he was the shooter."

"He wasn't," she said, impatient.

"You know why he kept lying about his alibi? Turned out he was in the sack with his sister-in-law at the time. This guy wouldn't own up to the fact that he was cheating on his wife even when he was faced with a first-degree murder charge. He didn't crack until just before the trial was scheduled, the bastard. And you know what it was killed the wife? Just a random, stray bullet through her open window, a street shooting gone bad. Wasn't her lucky day. Or maybe that's what you get for living in a bad neighborhood. What seemed so obvious to us turned out not to be true when we really dug into it."

"I get it, Jack," she said, watching him scrape the boat clean, pleased to see that his last spoonful contained equal portions of ice cream and strawberry. "But we've dug into it."

"A crazy guy's found in a Dumpster in the dog pound, with fake crack on him—I'm sorry, but you've got to go with a crack murder as your central hypothesis. Not some white-collar CEO with so much to lose. You know the old saying—in Texas, when you hear approaching hoofbeats, you don't think zebra. You gotta think horses. And I think you're going after a zebra here."

"That's not—"

"Oh, I know it would be a hell of a lot more intriguing to spot a zebra than a horse, but you've always got to consider the likelihoods. Because ultimately your time is limited. Who's that woman who calls you every week?"

"Ethel Dorsey?"

"Tyrone's her son, probably killed in a drug deal, right? How much time have you been putting in on that case?"

"I haven't really had much time recently."

"No, you haven't. And if I know you, I'll bet you feel that you're letting Ethel Dorsey down."

"I—" she faltered.

"You're good, and you have the potential to be great. You can make a real difference. But think of how many other cases are clamoring for your attention. There's only so many hours in the day, right?"

"I understand." She was shaken; what he said made sense.

"There's another case I want you to get involved in. Not instead of this one, but in addition to it. One that will really, I think, give you an opportunity to shine. Instead of just getting bogged down in this dog-pound murder. Now, Jensen's got the Hernandez robbery trial on Monday, but he's going on vacation, so I'd like you to handle it."

"Isn't Phelps the secondary on that? I only did one follow-up interview."

"Phelps is on personal leave. I need you on this. And the prosecutor wants a pretrial conference on Friday."

"Friday? That's—that's in two days!"

"You can do it. I know you can."

She was befuddled and most of all depressed now. "You know," she said in a small voice, "that looks good, what you had. What do I ask for?"

93

MARTA CAME TO the front hall, holding a dish towel in wet hands. No doubt she'd heard the little double beep of the alarm system when he opened the door. Somewhere in the background were peals of girlish laughter.

"Something wrong?" Nick asked her.

Marta shook her head. "Everything's fine," she said huffily, her tone implying the exact opposite.

"Is it Luke?"

Marta stiffened. "Miss Stadler invited herself over."

"Oh," Nick said. "That's fine."

Marta shrugged unhappily. It wasn't fine with *her*.

"Is there a problem, then?" Nick asked. What was with this Mrs. Danvers act, anyway?

"It's just getting hard to keep track of who's in the family and who isn't, these days."

It was an invitation to a heavy conversation; Nick silently declined.

In the family room he found Cassie, in an oversized Stratton T-shirt and black jeans, sitting with Julia, who was wearing an outfit Nick hadn't seen before, a turquoise velour tracksuit. Very J. Lo. The word "Juicy" ran across her butt.

He stood at the threshold and watched, unnoticed.

"There's nothing dirty about it," Cassie was saying.

"Dirty pillows!" Julia said, in silly mode. "Dirty pillows!"

"You get older, your body changes. Boys seem less yucky. You start to feel more private about your body. Everyone goes through it. It's as natural as granola."

Julia giggled at that, somehow anxious and pleased at the same time. "I hate granola," she said.

"The main thing is, don't feel it's something you can't talk about. Don't feel it's some weird, shameful thing, okay? Tits aren't the end of the world. Zits, on the other hand . . .."

Another burst of giggles, less nervous and more high-spirited.

They were having The Talk. Relief washed over him, mixed with a little jealousy over the intimacy Cassie and Julia seemed to have developed. He'd mentioned to Cassie how much he was dreading the prospect of having the girl-stuff talk with his daughter: in his hands, it would probably have ended in some grisly level of mutual embarrassment. Marta, despite her tight jeans, was prim and embarrassed about talking about sex and had let Nick know that she most emphatically didn't consider it her place to tell Julia about things like periods.

Cassie, though, was talking about it as if it were no big deal, and somehow *making* it no big deal. Something about her low, commonsensical voice was keeping everything real, down-to-earth, and comfortable. Or at least as comfortable as it could be for a giddy, giggly ten-year-old.

"Lot of things change, lot of things don't," Cassie told Julia. "Just remember, whatever happens to you, you're always going to be your daddy's little girl."

Nick cleared his throat, then said to Julia, "Hey, baby."

"Daddy!" She got up and received his hug.

"Where's your brother?"

"He's upstairs working."

"Good to hear. And where'd you get this outfit?"

"Cassie bought it for me."

"She did, huh?" A velour tracksuit? It even exposed her tummy. She was ten years old, for Christ's sake.

Cassie looked up, shrugged sheepishly. "*All* the fifth-graders consider me their fashion guru," she said.

WHEN JULIA HAD left to go to her room, Nick looked at Cassie and shrugged. "Thanks, by the way. I gather you were talking about girl stuff with her. Not easy for her old man to do."

"She's a sweet pea, Nick. The main thing is that she knows you're always going to be her daddy, and you're always going to love her."

"Stay for dinner?"

"I can't," she said.

"Plans?"

"No. I just—you know, what's that they say about guests and fish? They start stinking after—I forget how many days."

"You think Julia considers you a guest? Or Luke?"

She couldn't hide her smile. "You understand, don't you?"

"Stay. Plus, I could use your take on what's going on at work."

"You've come to the right place," she said. "The wisdom tooth of Fenwick, Michigan."

He told her about his meeting with Dorothy Devries.

"Well, she's not calling the shots anymore," Cassie said. "You said Todd Muldaur is."

"That's the problem."

"The question I always like to ask is: Who's your daddy?"

"Yeah. You and Shaft."

"So who's Todd Muldaur's daddy?"

A shrug. "Willard Osgood is the chairman of Fairfield Partners. But it sounds like he's become an absentee father."

"Willard Osgood—the guy with the thick glasses and all that folksy investment advice, right? I read that profile in *Fortune* you showed me. He's the one you've got to go to."

"For what? I don't see the upside."

"Correct me if I'm wrong, but doesn't Osgood really think of himself as a father figure? What you're describing doesn't sound like his style."

"True," Nick said. "But times change. The face of the future is probably Todd Muldaur."

"See, that doesn't add up to me. The way it's all been kept under wraps—that's not just about keeping the details away from you. Is it possible they're trying to keep the details away from Daddy too?"

"Hmph. I hadn't thought of that."

"But it's possible, right?"

"It's possible, yes."

"So maybe you should go right to Osgood."

"And what if you're wrong? What if he knows everything that's going on?"

"Consider your options right now. The real question is, What if I'm right?"

94

AUDREY'S E-MAIL ICON was bouncing. It was a message from Kevin Lenehan. She opened it immediately, then practically ran to Forensic Services.

"Guess what?" he said.

"You got it. The video."

"No fucking way. I told you, that's so gone."

"Then what?"

"This is cool. I noticed this code on here. It backs up to an FTP server on a preset schedule."

"Can you explain that?"

"Sure. Certain archivable events, ranging from alarm inputs to motion-detector inputs, get automatically sent to an FTP server using the IP address that's preprogrammed in here."

"Kevin," she said, mildly exasperated, "that really wasn't much of an explanation, now, was it?"

"The eleven minutes of video you're looking for? That we thought got totally erased? Well, it got erased on the box, here. But it also got sent over the Internet to Stratton's LAN—sorry, the company's computers. There's a backup copy at Stratton. That clear enough?"

Audrey smiled. "Can you get into the Stratton computers from here—on the Internet or something?"

"If I was that good, do you think I'd have a job like this?"

She shrugged.

"But get me into Stratton and I'll know where to look."

95

IT WAS AN hour drive to the Gerald R. Ford International Airport, then a five-hour flight to Logan Airport, a bustling place that seemed as populous as all of Fenwick. Nick made his way past a Legal Sea Foods restaurant, a WHSmith bookstore, and a Brookstone gadget center before he reached the escalator to Ground Transportation. Among a flock of livery drivers, he caught the eye of an olive-skinned man in a blue blazer and gray slacks who was holding a card that read NICHOLAS CONVER. Close enough.

Fairfield Partners was the anchor tenant of a vast glass- and granite-faced building on Federal Street, in the heart of downtown Boston. Willard Osgood's offices were on the thirty-seventh and thirty-eighth floors. The reception area was all dove-gray velvet and tropical woods, and Nick expected he'd be given plenty of time to study its details, cooling his heels in preparation for his audience with the Great Man. To his surprise, though, the strawberry blond receptionist told him to go right in. Nick wondered whether he was late. His watch told him that he was a few minutes early if anything.

As he walked through the glass door, Nick was immediately met by another blond woman, this one with red plastic-framed glasses. "Mr. Conover," she said. "Your flight okay?"

"It was," Nick said.

"Can I get you anything? Water, a soda, coffee?"

"I'm fine," Nick said, striding to keep up with her power walk.

"I'm sorry Todd's on the road. I'm sure he would have loved to say hi if he knew you were coming in."

I'm sure he would have, Nick thought. "Well, you might want to check with Mr. Osgood before you tell Todd or anyone else that I was here."

"Yes, sir," she said quickly. "Of course."

The offices of Fairfield Equity Partners were soaring and glass-walled, two floors combined into one. Along the walls, he noticed framed magazine covers featuring Willard Osgood—holding a fishing reel on the cover of *Field & Stream,* wearing a blue suit and yellow tie on *Forbes.* Osgood's square, bespectacled face and pleased-yet-concerned expression were always identical, as if the head had been Photoshopped onto different models.

Finally, she gestured toward a tan leather sofa in what looked like a vast waiting area, and said, "Have a seat. I'll leave you here."

Nick craned his head around, took in the large glass desk and various fishing trophies on the wall. It took a moment before he figured out he was in Willard Osgood's own office. He looked out the windows on two sides and could see the Boston Harbor in the distance, then some scrubby little islands beyond that.

Moments later, Willard Osgood himself strode in: the square, weathered face, the Coke-bottle glasses—he could have been peeled off one of those magazine covers. Nick stood up and realized that Osgood probably had an inch or two on him.

"Nick Conover," Osgood said in a booming voice, giving him a friendly bump on the shoulder. "I hope you noticed what kind of chair I've got at my desk." He pointed to the Stratton Symbiosis chair.

Nick grinned. "You liked it so much you bought the company."

Osgood raised a shaggy eyebrow. "Did I make the right decision?"

"Hope you still like the chair. It's still a good company."

"Then what the hell are you doing here in Beantown?"

"I'm here to ask your help solving a problem."

Osgood's expression vacillated between amusement and perplexity. "Let me put that Stratton chair into service," he said after a moment, walking over to his desk. Nick took a chair in front of it. "I always think better on my butt."

Nick started right in. "As I recall, when you came to Fenwick, you told us that your favorite holding period is forever."

"Ah," Osgood said, seeming to understand. He blinked a few times, folded his hands on the desk, and then cleared his throat. "Nick, I think I also told you that my rule number one is, never lose money."

Osgood knew Todd was selling the company, Nick now realized. So maybe Cassie was wrong. Did he know *everything,* though? "Which is a lesson that Todd Muldaur seems to have forgotten, if he ever learned it," Nick said.

"Todd's had a rough year," Osgood came right back, sounding a little annoyed. "There are some mighty good explanations for that, though."

"Yeah, well, 'Explanations aren't excuses,' as you also like to say."

Osgood smiled, exposing a blinding row of porcelain veneers. "I see the gospel spreads."

"But I can't help but wonder whether one of the explanations is that no one's watching the shop. That's what Todd seems to indicate, anyway. He says you've taken to spending a lot of time away from the office. That maybe you've gotten more interested in fly-fishing than in profit margins."

Osgood's smile almost reached his eyes. "I hope you don't believe that."

"I don't know what to think."

"What my lieutenants really mean by that, of course, is that my day has passed. They like to think that, because it means their day has arrived." Osgood leaned back in his chair, but of course the Stratton Symbiosis chair, being ergonomic, wouldn't let him tip all the way back like the older chairs would. "Tell you a story, but don't repeat it, okay?"

Nick nodded.

"Couple years ago I took Todd down to Islamorada, Florida, for the annual migration of the tarpon. 'Course, he showed up with his brand-new Sage rod and his Abel reel, and he's got a leather belt on, with a bonefish on the buckle." He gave a hearty guffaw. "He's a confident fellow—told me he'd done a lot of fly-fishing at some fancy lodge in Alaska, kind of place with gourmet meals and a sauna and the guide does everything for you except wipe your ass. So I graciously allowed him the bow and watched him flail for hours. Poor guy missed shot after shot, got more and more frustrated, his line kept getting wrapped, the flies hitting him on the backside." He blinked a few times. "Finally I decided I'd had enough fun. I stood up, stripped out ninety feet of line. Soon as I spotted a school of fish approaching, I delivered the fly. The fish ate, and six and a half feet of silver king went airborne. You with me? One school of fish—one shot—one cast—and one fish brought to the side of the boat."

"Okay," Nick said, enjoying the tale but wondering what the point was.

"See, I don't think Todd realized that the secret isn't how pricey your equipment or how nice your Ex Officio slacks are. All that counts is *bow time*—just doing it over and over and over again. Takes years of practice. No substitute for it."

"How do you cook tarpon?"

"Oh, heavens, no, you don't eat it. That's the beauty part. You release it. It's all about the fight."

"Huh," Nick said. "Doesn't sound like my kind of sport."

"From what I understand, hockey's all about the fight too. And you don't even get a fish to show for it."

"I guess that's one way of looking at it."

"But anyway, you're right. Todd's made some mistakes. A couple of bold gambles."

"I believe the phrase 'sucking wind' might be more accurate."

Osgood wasn't amused. "I'm well aware of what's happening," he said brittlely.

"Are you? I wonder." Nick leaned over and removed a file folder from his briefcase, then slid the folder across the desk. Osgood opened it, tipped his glasses up onto his forehead, and examined the documents. Nick noticed that the horizontal creases on Osgood's forehead were equally spaced and straight, almost as if drawn with a ruler.

Osgood looked up for a moment. "I wish he hadn't done things this way."

"What way?"

"Keeping you out of the loop. It's not the way I prefer. I like to be a straight shooter. Now I see why you've come to talk to me. I understand why you're upset."

"Oh, no," Nick said quickly. "I totally understand why he didn't want me to know. Hell, he knew how opposed I was—am—to a sale like this. Even though I don't have the power to stop it, he was probably afraid I'd kick up a fuss, maybe even take it public. Better to just do the deal without me knowing, he figured, so that by the time I figured it out, it would be a fait accompli. It would be too late."

"Something like that. But as I say, that's not my way."

"Todd needed a quick infusion of cash to help bail out the firm, after all his bad bets on semiconductors. And an IPO takes forever. I get it."

"I told Todd you're a reasonable man, Nick. He should have just leveled with you."

"Maybe he should have leveled with *you*. Like telling you who the fairy godmother behind 'Pacific Rim Investors' really is. Though he probably figured that you, with your political beliefs, wouldn't want to hear where the money comes from." Nick paused. "The P.L.A."

Osgood blinked owlishly.

"That's the People's Liberation Army," Nick explained. "The Communist Chinese army."

"I know who they are," Osgood said curtly. "Wouldn't have gotten to where I am without doing my homework."

"You knew this?" Nick said.

"Good Lord, of *course* I knew it. There's nothing illegal about it, my friend."

"The Communist Chinese," Nick persisted, hoping the incantation might jangle the old right-winger.

"Oh, for heaven's sake, this is *office furniture*. Not

Patriot missiles or nuclear weapons or something. Desks and chairs and file cabinets. I hardly call that selling our enemy the rope they're going to hang us with."

"But have you actually looked at the numbers on Stratton that Todd provided Pacific Rim Investors?"

Osgood pushed the folder away from him. "I don't micromanage. I don't look over my partners' shoulders. Nick, we're both busy men—"

"You might want to. See, the balance sheet Todd gave them is a fraud. Prepared by my CFO, Scott McNally, who knows a thing or two about how to put lipstick on a pig."

Another flash of the porcelain Chiclets. "Nick, maybe you've been in the Midwest a bit too long, but that Jimmy Stewart, *Mr. Smith Goes to Washington* bit's not going to play here."

"I'm not talking morality, Willard. I'm talking illegality."

Osgood waved Nick away with an impatient hand. "There's all kinds of ways of doing the books. Anyway, we've got a no-litigate clause, even if they do get buyer's remorse."

"You know about that too," Nick said dully.

Osgood's stare seemed to drill right through him. "Conover, you're wasting your time and mine, trying to backtrack over everything. Horse is out of the barn. Gripe session's over. Now, this it? We done here?" Osgood rose, pressing a button on his intercom. "Rosemary, could you show Mr. Conover out, please?"

But Nick remained in his seat. "I'm not done yet," he said.

96

THE INFORMATION TECHNOLOGY Director at the Stratton Corporation didn't look like the computer type, Audrey thought. She was a tall, matronly woman named Carly Lindgren, who wore her beautiful and very long auburn hair knotted on top of her head. She wore a navy suit over an olive silk shell, a braided gold necklace and matching earrings.

Audrey had gotten an appointment with Mrs. Lindgren with a single phone call, telling her only it was "police business." But once Audrey had presented the search warrant, she could see Mrs. Lindgren rear up like a cornered tigress. She examined it as if searching for flaws, though very few people knew what to look for, and in any case the warrant had been written carefully. It was as broad as Audrey could get the prosecutor to sign off on, even though all she really wanted was any archived video images on the Stratton network that came from Nicholas Conover's home security system.

Mrs. Lindgren kept Audrey and Kevin Lenehan waiting in an outer office while she placed a flurry of panicked calls all the way up her reporting chain—the Chief Information Officer and the Chief Technology

Officer, and Audrey lost track of who all, but there really was nothing Mrs. Lindgren could do.

After twenty minutes or so, Kevin was given a chair and a computer in an empty office. Audrey had nothing to do but watch. She looked around, saw a blue poster with white letters that said something about "The Stratton Family," sort of a mission statement. The chairs they sat in were particularly comfortable; she noticed they were Stratton chairs. Nothing like this in Major Cases. Kevin put a CD in the computer and installed a program. He explained to her that it was viewer software he'd downloaded from the Web site of the company that made the digital video recorder in Conover's home. This would allow them to view, and capture, the video images.

"You know where to look?" Audrey asked, worried.

"It was in the settings in the DVR," replied Kevin. "The folder it was written to, the date and time and everything. No *problema*."

Audrey felt a little tremble of anticipation, which she tried to tamp down, tried to reason herself out of. She was sure that the murder of Andrew Stadler would be on this eleven minutes of camera footage. If indeed there was a backup here.

How often in any homicide detective's career could one hope to come across a piece of evidence like that? A digital image of a murder being committed? It was almost too much to hope for. She didn't want to allow herself to hope for it, because the disappointment would be crushing.

"Anything I can do to help, Detective?"

She looked up, saw Eddie Rinaldi standing in the doorway, felt her heart do a flip-flop. From where she sat, that angle, Rinaldi seemed tall and broad and powerful. He wore a dark blazer and a black collarless shirt. He was smiling, and his eyes glittered malevolently.

"Mr. Rinaldi," she said. Even when talking to murder suspects, she tended to be polite, but she refused to be cordial with this man. Something about him she really couldn't stand. Maybe it was his air of knowingness, his cockiness, the feeling she got that he was enjoying the games he was playing with her.

"So you have a search warrant for the company's network, that it?"

"You're welcome to examine it."

"No, no, no. I don't doubt you dotted every *i* and crossed every *t*. You're one thorough lady, I can tell."

"Thank you."

"Maybe thorough's a polite way to say it. Obsessed, maybe? Looks like you're still after my boss's home security tape."

"Oh, we have the recorder in our custody." She considered telling him they knew the tape had been erased, just to see his reaction, but that would be giving him information he shouldn't have.

Kevin muttered, "Almost there."

Rinaldi glanced at Kevin curiously, as if he'd only just noticed him. Then he looked back at Audrey. He couldn't have been more blasé.

"I still don't get what you're hoping to find," Rinaldi said.

"I have a feeling you know," Audrey said.

"You're right. I do."

"Oh?"

"Right. Couple of frames of some crazy old coot hobbling across my boss's lawn in the middle of the night. But what's that going to tell you, come right down to it?"

Audrey leaned over to the computer where Kevin was working. He tilted the monitor toward Audrey, who squinted, didn't see any picture, and then saw the words "ERASED HERE TOO" on a document on the screen.

"Excellent," Audrey said, nodding. "Good work."

She reached for the keyboard and typed out the words, "PLAY ALONG WITH ME." Then she said, "Beautiful, Kevin. Can you improve the resolution just a bit?"

"Oh yeah," he said. "Sure. I've got some great digital-imaging firmware that'll eliminate the motion artifacts and reduce the dot crawl. A comb filter oughta separate the chrominance from the luminance. A little line doubling and some deinterlacing, and we got a nice clean image. No problem at all on this guy."

Kevin tapped some more, and the document disappeared before Rinaldi had a chance to look for himself.

But that was the peculiar thing. Eddie Rinaldi never moved from where he stood, never bothered to peer at the monitor. He seemed utterly uninterested.

No, that wasn't it, Audrey realized.

He was utterly confident. He knew what Kevin had just discovered, that the backup video had been deleted on the Stratton LAN, just as it had been deleted from Conover's home security recorder.

And his confidence had just given him away.

97

NICK FELT A tiny tremble in his hands. He put them in his lap so Osgood wouldn't see. "Willard, don't get me wrong. I have no interest in taking you on. I'd much rather work together with you on this. You want to save the funds Todd's running, and I want to save the company. We both want to make money."

Osgood slid his glasses back into place and gave Nick a steely stare as he stood behind his desk. He grunted.

"Now, I don't know you," Nick said, "but I can tell you're not a gambler." Nick noticed that the blond woman with the red glasses had slipped into the office to usher him out and was hovering in the background, waiting for her cue. He lowered his voice so that the woman couldn't hear. "So when Scott McNally and Todd Muldaur funnel a ten-million-dollar bribe to a Chinese government official to make sure this deal happens, that's where I think they're crossing a line you don't want to cross."

"What the hell are you talking about?" Osgood put his hands flat on the glass of his desk and leaned forward, intimidatingly.

"They're putting your company at risk, doing that.

Word always leaks out. And then your entire firm will be jeopardized." Nick opened his arms wide. "All of this. Everything you've worked your whole life building. And I wonder whether you think it's really worth taking such an enormous risk, when there's another way to get what you want."

"Rosemary," Osgood barked. "Excuse us, please. We'll be another few minutes." When his secretary had left, he sat down again. "What the hell are you talking about, bribe?"

"Stratton Asia Ventures," Nick said.

"I don't know anything about that."

Was he being straight? Or was he being careful? "It's all right there in front of you—the last couple of pages in that pile. How do you think Todd was able to get this deal done in a month instead of a year? Call it a deal-sweetener or a kickback or a bribe—whatever you call it, it's a clear-cut violation of the Foreign Corrupt Practices Act. And it's the kind of legal exposure that you can't afford."

The way Osgood yanked the folder back toward him, Nick realized that this really was news to the man. Osgood shoved his glasses back up on his forehead and hunched over the papers.

A few minutes later, he looked back up. His leathery face seemed to color. He looked thunderstruck. "Jesus," he said. "Looks like you weren't the only one kept out of the loop."

"I had a feeling Todd wasn't telling you everything," Nick said.

"This is *stupid,* is what it is."

"Desperate men sometimes do stupid things. Frankly, on some level I resent it. My company's worth a hell of a lot more than what Pacific Rim Investors is paying for it. There's no need to pay anyone off."

"God*damn* it," Osgood said.

"You may be great with tarpons, Willard, but I think what we're dealing with here is a snakehead."

Osgood seemed to be doing a slow burn. "I think my Yale boy just got hisself in over his head."

"I guess he figured no one was watching the shop . . ."

Osgood's pearly Chiclets looked more like a snarl than a smile. "From time to time, someone thinks they can pull one over on the old man. Maybe they've been reading too many *Parade* magazine profiles of me. But they always realize the error of their ways."

Nick realized then how terrifying Willard Osgood could be once the cornpone mask fell away, a truly formidable opponent.

"A lot of people have been underestimating you too," Osgood said. "I think I may be one of them. So tell me: What do you have in mind?"

98

"DADDY!" JULIA RAN up to Nick as he entered the house. "You're back!"

"I'm back." He set down his garment bag, lifted her up, felt a slight twinge in his lower back around the lumbar. Yikes. Can't be picking her up anymore like she's an infant. "How's my baby?"

"Good." Julia never said anything else. She was always good. School was always good. Everything was good.

"Where's your brother?"

She shrugged. "Probably in his room? Do you know Marta just left a couple of hours ago for Barbados? She said she's going to visit her family."

"I know. I thought she needed some time off. Her trip to Barbados is a present from all of us. Where's Cassie?" Cassie had happily agreed to come over to watch the kids.

"She's here. She was just teaching me yoga."

"Where is she?"

"In your study, maybe?"

Nick hesitated a moment. That again. But there was nothing to find there. He had to stop being so suspicious.

"She has a surprise for you," Julia said with a mischievous smile, her big brown eyes wide. "But I can't tell you what it is."

"Can I guess?"

"No."

"Not even one guess?"

"No!" she scolded. "It's a *surprise*!"

"Okay. Don't tell me. But I have a surprise for *you*."

"What is it?"

"How would you like to go to Hawaii?"

"*What?* No *way*!"

"Way. We're leaving tomorrow night."

"But what about school?"

"I'm taking you and Luke out of school for a few days, that's all."

"Hawaii! I don't believe it! Maui?"

"Maui."

"The same place as last time?"

"Same place. I even got us the exact same villa on the beach."

Julia threw her arms around him, squeezing hard. "I want to do snorkeling again," she said, "and take those hula lessons, and I want to make a lei, and this time I want to learn how to windsurf. Aren't I old enough?"

"You're old enough, sure." Laura had been afraid to let her try, last time.

"Luke said he'd show me how. Are you going to scuba dive again?"

"I think I might have forgotten how."

"What about surfing? Can I learn how to surf too?"

Nick laughed. "Are you going to have time for all these lessons?"

"Remember when I found that gecko in our room, and its tail broke off? Oh, wow, this is so *awesome*."

* * *

NICK WENT TO the kitchen to take the shortcut to his study, but he stopped at the threshold.

In place of the usual plastic draft sheets hanging down was some kind of paper barrier. He looked closer. Wrapping paper had been taped across the entrance, floor to ceiling and jamb to jamb. A wide blue ribbon crisscrossed it like a gift. The paper, he noticed, had little pictures of Superman all over it, cape flying.

"Even though you look more like Clark Kent right now." Cassie's voice. Her arms slid around his waist; she kissed the back of his neck.

"What's this?"

He turned, gave her a hug and planted a big kiss on her mouth.

"You'll see. How was Boston?"

"Let's just say your instincts were right."

Cassie nodded. The dark smudges were visible beneath her eyes again. She looked drawn, exhausted. "Well, you'll get things back on track. You'll see. It's not too late."

"We'll see. Can I open my gift?"

She bowed her head, turned up an "After you" palm.

Nick punched a fist through the gift wrap. The kitchen was all lit up, every light on, dazzling. The granite-topped kitchen island was perfect, just as Laura had once sketched it for him.

"Jesus," Nick said. He went in slowly, taking it all in, awed. He ran a hand over the island top. There was an overhang, enabling the whole family to sit around it. Exactly what Laura had wanted.

He felt its edge. "Bullnose?"

"Half bullnose."

He turned to look at Cassie, saw the little pleased smile. "How the hell did you do this?"

"I didn't do it myself, Nick. I mean, I may have inherited my dad's mechanical ability, but I'm not *that* good. What I'm good at is getting what I want." She shrugged modestly. "It really only took them one full day of work. But it took me a lot of begging and pleading to get them here to do it and finish it by the end of the day."

"My God, you're a miracle worker," Nick said.

"Just like to finish what I start, that's all. Or what your wife started." She paused and then said in a small voice, "Nick, are you ever going to be able to talk about her death?"

He closed his eyes for a while before he spoke. He opened his eyes, took a breath. "I can try. Lucas had a swim meet. It was half past seven, but dark, you know? First week of December. It gets dark early. We were driving to Stratford, because the meet was in the high school there. We're on Stratford-Hillsdale Road, which is what truckers sometimes use to connect to the interstate."

Nick closed his eyes again. He was back in the car on that dark night, a nightmare he had relived only in dreams, and then in shards and fragments of time. He spoke in a low, expressionless monotone. "So there's a tractor trailer heading the opposite way, and the guy driving it had had a couple of beers, and the road surface was icy. Laura was driving—she hated to drive at night, but I asked her to, because I had some calls to make on the cell phone. That was me—company man, always working. We were bickering over something, and Laura was upset, and she wasn't paying attention to the road, see. She didn't see the truck drifting into our lane, across those double yellow lines, until it was too late. She—she tried to turn the wheel, but she didn't do it in time. The truck rammed into us."

He opened his eyes. "Funny thing is, it didn't seem like we were hit all that hard," Nick went on. "It wasn't like some horrible collision in the movies where everything goes black. It was a hard bump, like you might feel if you were playing bumper cars. Kind of a hollow crunch. I didn't get whiplash. Never blacked out. Nothing like that. I turn to Laura and I'm yelling, 'Can you believe that guy?' And she doesn't say anything. And I notice how the windshield is all spiderwebbed on her side. And there's some pebbles of glass on her forehead. Something glistening in her hair. But there's no blood, or hardly any. A fleck or two, maybe. She looked fine. Like she'd nodded off."

"There was nothing you could have done," Cassie breathed.

Nick only knew that his eyes were wet because his vision was blurred. "Except there were *hundreds* of things I could have done. Any one of them, and Laura would still be alive. You know, when we were leaving the house that night, Laura was about to make a phone call, and I made her hang up. I told her she was making us late. I told her it was ridiculous that she'd spent fifteen minutes putting on makeup and perfume for a goddamn *swim meet*. I told her that, for once, we weren't going to be late. I told her I wanted to get a good seat in the stands so I could see what the hell was going on. Now, thing is, if she had made that phone call, we wouldn't have been in an accident. If I hadn't been in such a hurry, we would actually have arrived. And I didn't have to make those goddamned phone calls in the car that night, for Christ's sake. Like they couldn't wait till the morning. I could have driven the car—I mean, look, I was the better driver, we both knew that, she *hated* driving. I shouldn't have been arguing with her while she was behind the wheel. Oh, and here's a sweet one. She wanted to take the Suburban. I said it would just be a pain to park. I insisted that we take the sedan. If we'd taken the Suburban, she might have survived the impact. And I'm just starting a long, long list.

All kinds of things I could have done differently. The weeks after she died, I became the world's leading expert on this subject. Had 'em all cross-tabulated in my mind. Should have been on *Jeopardy!* Thanks, Alex, I'll take Vehicular Fatalities for a hundred."

Cassie looked wan, ran her fingers through her hair. Nick wondered whether she was even listening to him. "Intracerebral hemorrhage," he went on. "She died in the hospital the next day."

"You're a good person."

"No," Nick said. "But I wish I were."

"You give so much."

"You don't know, Cassie. All right? You don't know what I've *taken,* what I've done. You don't know . . ."

"You've given me a family."

And I've taken yours away. He looked at her for a long time. He felt foolish about how he'd suspected her secret intentions and worried that she'd been trying to dig up the truth about what had happened to her father.

Then again, he obviously wasn't so good at sizing people up, he realized. He'd gotten Osgood wrong in all sorts of ways, and he'd gotten Scott wrong. Todd Muldaur—well, he had Todd's number from the start, so no surprise there. Eddie? He wasn't really surprised, when it came right down to it, that Eddie wouldn't hesitate to kick the skates out from under him.

But Cassie. He hadn't known just what to make of her, and maybe he still didn't know her all that well. Maybe his overpowering guilt and her overpowering seductiveness made it hard for him to see her clearly. She was a little emotionally unstable, that was obvious. Bipolar and having your dad murdered—that was a fairly lethal combination.

And he wondered how she'd react when he came clean.

It made no difference to him whether Eddie would

strike some kind of deal with the police or not. He'd leave Eddie to his own smarmy fate.

When he and the kids came back from Hawaii, he was going to tell her the truth. And then he'd tell Detective Rhimes the truth.

And there would be an arrest, he knew that. Because whether a DA decided it was self-defense or not, he had killed a man.

Back in Boston, after his meeting with Willard Osgood, he'd taken a cab over to Ropes & Gray, a big law firm where a friend of his worked as a criminal defense attorney. A really smart guy he knew from Michigan State. Nick had told him what had happened, the whole story.

The lawyer had blanched, of course. He told Nick he was in deep shit, there was no way around it. He said the best Nick could hope for was criminally negligent homicide, that if he were very lucky he might get only a couple of years in prison. But it might well be more—five, seven, even ten years, because there was also the matter of having moved the body—tampering with physical evidence. The lawyer said that if Nick wanted to go through with it, he'd get a local counsel and petition to try the case in Michigan *pro hoc vici,* whatever that meant. He'd arrange for Nick to surrender, and he'd try to negotiate a plea agreement with the DA in Fenwick. And he said he'd ask for a lot of money up front.

Whatever would happen to him, though, was the least of it. What was going to happen to his kids? Would Aunt Abby be willing to take care of them?

This was the worst thing of all, the thing that truly terrified him.

But he knew it was the right thing to do, at long last, however long it had taken him to come to his senses. It was like that dream he'd had recently, the one about the body in the basement wall that gave away its hiding place by oozing the fluids of decay. He couldn't hold the horrible secret inside anymore.

So in a week or so, after his last vacation with the kids, he was going to tell Cassie the truth. He'd already begun to rehearse, in his head, how he'd tell her.

"What is it?" she said.

"I've been doing a lot of thinking, and I've made some decisions."

"Decisions about the company?"

"Not that, no. My life is about other things."

An anxious look came over her. "Is this bad?"

"No," he said, shaking his head.

"Is it bad for us?"

"No. It's not about us, exactly."

"'Not about us, exactly'—what's that supposed to mean?"

"We'll talk when the time is right. Just not yet."

She placed her hand on his. He took it in his hand, holding it gently. Hers was small and trembling; his was big and steady.

The hand that killed her father.

"Cass, we're off tomorrow," he said. "We're going to Hawaii for a few days. I already got the tickets."

"Hawaii?"

"Maui. Laura loved that place most of all. There's this great resort Laura and I discovered before we had kids. We had our own villa, right on the beach, with its own pool—not that you needed it—and all you could see from it was the Pacific Ocean."

"Sounds amazing."

"Until Laura died, we used to take the family there every year. Our big splurge. Same villa every time, Laura made sure of it. I think of it as a time when we were completely happy, all of us. I remember last time we were there, Laura and I were in bed and she turned to me and she said she wanted to spray a fixative on the whole day and keep it forever."

"God, it sounds beautiful, Nick." A light seemed to flicker in her eyes. She looked almost serene.

"I called the travel agency we'd used, and—it felt like a miracle—they said that exact same villa's available."

"Are you sure you want to return to a place they associate so closely with Laura? It might be better to go somewhere new—you know, create new memories."

"You may be right. I know it won't be the same. It'll be sad in some ways. But it'll be a new start. A good thing—just going there as a family, being together again. And there isn't going to be any pressure to talk, or work through 'issues,' or anything else. We're just going to play on the beach and do stuff and eat pineapple and just *be*. It won't be the same, but it'll be *something*. And it'll be something we can all remember when things change, because they're going to change."

"The kids can miss school, right? No big deal."

"I already called the school, told them I'd be taking Julia and Lucas out of classes for a few days. Hell, I even picked up the tickets at the airport when I got in." He pulled an envelope from his breast pocket, took out the tickets and held them up, fanning them like a winning hand of cards.

Cassie's smile vanished. "Three tickets." She pulled her hand away.

"Just family. Me and the kids. I don't think we've ever done this. Just us three, heading off for a few days somewhere."

"Just family," Cassie repeated in a harsh whisper.

"I think it's important for me to try to reconnect with the kids. I mean, you get along with them better than I do, which is great. But I've let my part in it slip—I've sort of delegated that to you, like I'm CEO of the family or something, and that's not right. I'm their dad, whether I'm any good at it or not, and it's my job to work on making us a family again."

Cassie's face was transfigured, weirdly tight as if every muscle in her face were clenched.

"Oh God, Cassie, I'm sorry," Nick said, flushing, embarrassed by his own obliviousness. "You know how much you mean to us."

Cassie's eyelids fluttered oddly, and he could see the veins in her neck pulsing. It was as if she were struggling to contain herself—or maybe to contain something larger than herself.

He smiled ruefully. "Luke and Julia—they're my direct reports, you know. And I don't know when I'll have the chance again."

"Just family." The sound of one heavy stone scraping against another.

"I think it'll be really good for us, don't you?"

"You want to get away."

"Exactly."

"You want to escape." Her voice was an incantation.

"Pretty much."

"From me."

"What? Jesus, *no*! You're taking this the wrong way. It isn't about—"

"No." She shook her head slowly. "No. No hiding place. There's no hiding place down there."

Adrenaline surged through Nick's veins. "*What* did you say?"

An odd smile appeared on her face. "Isn't that what the stalker spray-painted in the house? That's what Julia told me."

"Yeah," Nick said. "Those very words."

"I can read the writing on the wall, Nick."

"Come on, Cassie, don't be silly."

"It's like the book of Daniel, isn't it? The king of

Babylon throws a big drunken party and all of a sudden he sees a mysterious hand appear and start writing something strange and cryptic on the plaster wall, right? And the king's scared out of his mind and he calls in the prophet Daniel who tells him the message means the king's days are over, Babylon's history, he's going to be killed." Her expression was glassy.

"Okay, you're starting to creep me out."

Suddenly her eyes focused, and she met his gaze. "Maybe I should be grateful. I was wrong, wrong about so many things. It's *humbling*. Humbling to be put right. Just like with the Stroups. But so necessary. Listen, you do what you think is best. You do what's best for family. There's nothing more important than that."

Nick held out his arms. "Cassie, come here."

"I think I'd better go," she said. "I think I've done enough, don't you think?"

"Cassie, please," Nick protested. "I don't get it."

"Because I can do a lot more." Noiselessly, she walked out of the kitchen, her steps so fluid she could have been gliding. "I can do a lot more."

"We'll talk, Cassie," said Nick. "When we get back."

A final glance over her shoulders. "A *lot* more."

99

EARLY SUNDAY MORNING, before church. Audrey sat in the kitchen with her coffee and her buttered toast while Leon slept. She was poring over the bills, wondering how they'd be able to keep up, now that Leon's unemployment benefits were running out. Usually she paid off the entire credit-card balance each month, but she was going to have to start paying only the minimum balance due. She wondered too, whether they should drop to basic cable. She thought they should, though Leon would not be happy about losing the sports channels.

Her cell phone rang. A 616 number: Grand Rapids.

It was a Lieutenant Lawrence Pettigrew of the Grand Rapids police. The man who'd first talked to her about Edward Rinaldi. She'd placed several calls to him over the last few days and had all but given up on him. Noyce had made it clear that he didn't want her asking around in GR about Rinaldi, but she had no choice in the matter.

"How can I help you, Detective?" Pettigrew said. "The kids are waiting for me to take them out for pancakes, so can we make this quick?"

The guy was no fan of Edward Rinaldi, so she knew

that asking about Rinaldi again would be like pushing a button and watching the vitriol spew out. But she had no reason to expect that he'd know the specifics of a long-forgotten and, in fact, quite minor, drug case.

He didn't. "Far as I'm concerned, Rinaldi's gone and good riddance," he said. "He wasn't exactly a credit to the uniform."

"Was he fired?"

"Squeezed out might be more accurate. But I were you, I wouldn't be bad-mouthing Eddie Rinaldi over there in Fenwick."

"He's the security director of Stratton, is that what you mean?"

"Yeah, yeah, but that's not what I'm talking about. Didn't you say you're in Major Cases?"

"That's right."

"Hell, you want to know chapter and verse on Eddie Rinaldi, you could ask Jack Noyce. But then again, maybe you shouldn't."

"I don't think Sergeant Noyce knows all that much about Rinaldi."

Pettigrew's laugh was abrupt and percussive. "Noyce knows him like a book, sweetheart. Guarantee it. Jack was Eddie's partner."

Audrey's scalp tightened.

"Sergeant Noyce?" she said, disbelieving.

"Partner in crime, I like to say. Don't take this the wrong way, Detective—what's your name again?"

"Rhimes." Audrey shuddered.

"Like LeAnn Rimes, the singer?" He warbled, off-key, 'How do I *live* . . . without you?'"

"Spelled differently, I believe."

"Quite the babe, though, no matter how you spell it."

"So I hear, yes. Noyce . . . Noyce was known to be dirty, is that what you're telling me?"

"Hell, there's a reason Jack got sent to Siberia, right?"

"Siberia?"

"No offense, sweetheart. But from where I sit, Fenwick is Siberia."

"Noyce was . . . squeezed out too?"

"Peas in a pod, those guys. I got no idea who did more pilfering, but I'd say they both did pretty good. Works better in a team, so they're each willing to look away. Eddie was more into the guns, and Jack was more into the home electronics and the stereo components and what have you, but they both loved the cash."

"They both . . ." she started to say, but she lost the heart to go on.

"Oh, and Detective LeAnn?"

"Audrey." She wanted to vomit, wanted to end the call and throw up and then wrap herself in a blanket and go back to sleep.

"Sweetheart, I were you, I wouldn't use my name with Noyce. Guy's a survivor, and he'll wanna let bygones be bygones, know what I'm saying?"

She thanked him, pushed End, and then did exactly what she knew she would. She rushed to the bathroom and heaved the contents of her stomach, the acid from the coffee scalding her throat. Then she washed her face. All she wanted to do right now was to enrobe herself in the old blue blanket on the living room couch, but it was time for church.

100

THE FIRST ABYSSINIAN Church of the New Covenant
was a once-grand stone building that had slowly, over
the years, gone to seed. The velvet pew cushions, badly
in need of replacing, had been repaired in far too many
places with duct tape. The place was always cold, sum-
mer or winter: something about the stone walls and
floor, that plus the fact that the building fund was suf-
fering, and it cost a fortune to heat the cavernous inte-
rior adequately.

Attendance was sparse this morning, as it was on
most Sundays except Easter and Christmas. There
were even a few white faces: a couple of regulars who
seemed to find the sustenance here they didn't get in
the white congregations. LaTonya's family wasn't here,
which was no surprise, since they came only a few
times a year. Early in their marriage, Leon used to ac-
company Audrey here, until he announced it wasn't for
him. She didn't even know whether he was sleeping
late this morning or doing something else, whatever
else he'd been doing.

Leon was only one of the reasons why her heart
was heavy today. There was also Noyce. That news
had punctured her. She felt betrayed by this man who'd

been her friend and supporter and who hid from her his true nature. It sickened her.

But this discovery, as much as it shook her to the core, liberated her at the same time. She no longer had to agonize about betraying him, going behind his back, end-running him. She knew there was no choice, really. Whether Jack Noyce was in the Stratton Corporation's pocket, had been leaking to his old partner details of the investigation—or was simply compromised, trapped, by what Rinaldi knew about him—he had been working to defeat her investigation. She thought back to the many talks she'd had with him about this case, the advice he'd dispensed so freely. The way he'd cautioned her to proceed carefully, telling her she didn't have enough to arrest Conover and Rinaldi. And who would ever know what else he'd done to slow things up, block her progress? What resources had he quietly blocked? Whatever the truth was, she couldn't tell Noyce that she and Bugbee were about to get an arrest warrant for the CEO and the security director of Stratton. Noyce had to be kept in the dark, or he'd surely notify Rinaldi and do everything in his power to halt the arrest.

But here, at least, here she felt at peace and welcome and loved. Everyone said good morning, even people whose names she didn't know, courtly gentlemen and polite young men and lovely young women and hovering mothers and sweet old white-haired women. Maxine Blake was dressed all in white, wearing an ornate hat that looked a little like an upside-down bucket with white tendrils coming out of it and encircling it like rings around a planet. She threw her arms around Audrey, pressing Audrey to her enormous bosom, bringing her into a cloud of perfume and warmth and love. "God is good," Maxine said.

"All the time," Audrey responded.

The service started a good twenty minutes late. "Colored people's time," the joke went. The choir, dressed in their magnificent red-and-white robes, marched down the aisle clapping and singing "It's a Highway to Heaven," and then they were joined by the electric organ and then the trumpet and drum and then Audrey joined in along with most everybody else. She'd always wanted to sing in the choir, but her voice was nothing special—though, as she'd noticed, some of the women in the choir had thin voices and tended to sing out of tune. Some had spectacular voices, it was true. The men mostly sang in a rumbling bass, but the tenor was more off-key than on.

Reverend Jamison started his sermon as he always did, by calling out, "God is good," to which everyone responded: "All the time." He said it again, and everyone responded again. His sermons were always heartfelt, usually inspired, and never went on too long. They weren't particularly original, though. Audrey had heard he got them off the Internet from Baptist Web sites that posted sample sermons and notes. Once, confronted on his lack of originality, Reverend Jamison had said, "I milk a lot of cows, but I churn my own butter." Audrey liked that.

Today he told the story of Joshua and the armies of Israel fighting the good fight, battling five of the kings of Canaan for the conquest of the promised land. About how the kings played right into Joshua's hands by joining the battle together. About how it wasn't the Lord who fought the battle, it was Israel. The five kings tried to hide in a cave, but Joshua ordered the cave sealed up. And after the battle had been won, Joshua brought the kings out of their cave, out of their hiding place, and humiliated them by ordering his princes to place their feet on the kings' necks. Reverend Jamison talked about how there's no hiding place. "We can't hide from

God," he declared. "The only hiding place from God is Hell."

That made her think, as it had so many times, about Nicholas Conover and the graffiti that had been repeatedly spray-painted on the interior walls of his house. No hiding place.

That could be frightening, as no doubt Conover found it to be. No hiding place: from what? From a faceless adversary, from a stalker? From his guilt, his sins?

But here in church, "no hiding place" was meant to be a stern yet hopeful admonition.

In his most orotund voice the reverend recited from Proverbs 28: "He that covereth his sins shall not prosper: but whoso confesseth and forsaketh them shall have mercy."

And she thought, because every single one of Reverend Jamison's sermons was devised to mean something to each and every one in the congregation, about Nicholas Conover. The king hiding in his cave.

But no hiding place. Andrew Stadler had been right, hadn't he?

Reverend Jamison cued the choir, which went right into a lively rendition of "No Hiding Place Down Here." The soloist was Mabel Darnell, a large woman who sang and swayed like Aretha Franklin and Mahalia Jackson put together. The organist, Ike Robinson, was right up front, on display, not hidden the way the organist usually was in the other churches she'd seen. He was a white-haired, dark-skinned man of near eighty with expressive eyes and an endearing smile. He wore a white suit and looked like Count Basie, Audrey had always thought.

"I went to the rock to hide my face," Mabel sang, clapping her hands, "but the rock cried out, 'No hiding place!'"

Count Basie's pudgy fingers ran up and down the keys, syncopating, making swinging jazz out of it, and the rest of the choir joined in at *the rock* and *my face* and *cried out* and *no hiding place no hiding place no hiding place.*

Audrey felt a thrill coursing through her body, a shiver that moved along her spine like an electric current.

And the instant the choir had finished, while the organ chords still resounded, Reverend Jamison's voice boomed out, "My friends, none of us can hide from the Lord. 'And the kings of the earth, and the great men, and the rich men, and the chief captains, and the mighty men, and every bondman, and every free man'"—his voice rose steadily until the sound system squealed with feedback—"'hid themselves in the dens and in the rocks of the mountains.'" Now he dropped to a stage whisper: "'And said to the mountains and rocks, fall on us, and hide us from the face of him that sitteth on the throne, and from the wrath of the Lamb. For the great day of his wrath is come; and who shall be able to stand?'"

He paused to let the congregation know that his sermon had concluded. Then he invited anyone in the congregation who wished to come up to the altar for a moment of personal prayer. Ike Robinson, no longer Count Basie, played softly as a dozen or so people got up from their pews and knelt at the altar rail, and all of a sudden Audrey felt moved to do it too, something she hadn't done since her mother's death. She went up there and knelt between Maxine Blake and her enormous rings-of-Saturn hat and another woman, Sylvia-something, whose husband had just died of complications from liver transplant surgery, leaving her with four small children.

Sylvia-something was going through a terrible, terrible time, and what did Audrey have to complain about, really? Her problems were small ones, but they filled her up, as small problems will until the big ones move in and elbow them aside.

She knew she had allowed her anger at Leon to fester inside her, and she recalled the words from Ephesians 4:26–27: "Let not the sun go down upon your anger: Neither give place to the devil." And she knew it was time to let go of that anger and confront him once and for all.

She knew that her hurt and disappointment over Jack Noyce might never heal, but it would not get in the way of her doing the right thing.

She thought of that poor little daughter of Nicholas Conover, fumbling at the piano, that beautiful needy face. That little girl who had just lost her mother and was about to lose her father too.

And that was the most wrenching thing of all, knowing that she was about to orphan that little girl.

She began weeping, her shoulders heaving, the hot tears running down her cheeks, and someone was rubbing her shoulder and consoling her, and she felt loved.

Outside the church, in the gloomy daylight, she took her cell phone out of her purse and called Roy Bugbee.

101

THE THROATY GROWL of a car coming up the driveway.

Leon? No, Leon's car didn't sound that way. Out cutting, Leon was. And on a Sunday. She felt a swell of resentment, of resolve.

She parted the sheer curtains in the front parlor. Bugbee.

His leering grin. "Finally decided to do it, eh?"

She invited him into the front parlor, where he took Leon's chair and Audrey sat facing him on the couch. Bugbee's foot jostled something, and a couple of brown glass bottles clattered.

He glanced down. "Hitting the sauce, Aud? Pressure getting too much for you?"

"I don't even like the taste of beer," she said, embarrassed. "So what's up?"

"One complication."

"Oh no."

"A good complication. Our friend Eddie's rolling over on Conover."

"What does that mean, exactly?"

"He wants to deal."

"How much did he tell you?"

"Not a fucking thing. Just that he might have some information of interest to us."

"He's got to show us the wares."

"He wants a deal first. I'm betting he's the coconspirator."

She thought a moment. "What if he's the shooter, not Conover?"

"Them's the breaks. If he gives up Conover for aiding and abetting, we got 'em both."

"He knows about the gun match." Another car engine, had to be Leon.

"You tell him? I sure as hell didn't."

She shook her head and told him about the call from Grand Rapids.

"Fucking Noyce," said Bugbee. "What'd I tell you?"

"What did you tell me?"

"I never liked him."

"That's because he doesn't like you."

"Touché. But not my point. Him and Eddie Rinaldi both have something on each other. Now looks like we have something on Noyce."

"I don't play that game," Audrey said firmly.

"Christ," said Bugbee. "The fuck is the point of being a church lady, time like this?"

"How about I put it in terms you might understand? You want to be up front and open with Noyce, I have no problem with that. But I'll bet you he knows that we know."

"You think?"

"He knows I've been talking to Grand Rapids. He knows I dig deep. Anyway, you want to play games with him later, I really don't care. My heart breaks for him, but right now I'm just thinking about this case and how we make it work. My way is to ignore him, work around him, put through this arrest paperwork on the down low so he doesn't have a chance to tell Rinaldi."

Bugbee shrugged, accepting defeat.

"And I'll tell you something else. I don't want to make a deal with Rinaldi."

"That's fucked up," Bugbee protested. "He's our way in."

"You're the one who kept saying we have this case nailed, right? Why do you want to give up so easily?"

"It's not giving up," Bugbee said.

"It's not, huh? I want to charge them both with open murder. That way we have maximum bargaining room. We sort it out later."

"So now *you* think we've got it nailed, that it?"

"Just about. Tomorrow morning first thing, I'm going to talk to Stadler's psychiatrist again."

"A little late for that, don't you think?"

"Not at all. It'll strengthen our hand considerably with the prosecutor's office if he'll agree to testify that Stadler could be deranged, even dangerous. If we get that, we'll get the arrest warrants for sure."

"I thought he already refused to talk to you."

"I'm not giving up."

"You can't force him."

"No, but I can persuade him. Or try, at least."

"You believe it?"

"Believe what?"

"Believe that Stadler was dangerous."

"I don't know what to believe. I think Conover and Rinaldi believed it. If we have the psychiatrist on board, we have motive. The slickest lawyer Nick Conover can find's going to have a steep hill to climb on that one. And then we sure don't need any deal with Eddie, understand?"

"Roll the dice, you mean?"

"Sometimes you have to," she said.

"You don't want to roast Noyce's balls over a camp-fire like I do, huh?"

She shook her head. "I'm not angry. I'm . . ." She thought. "I'm disappointed. I'm sad."

"You know something, I always thought you Jesus freaks were kidding, on some level. But I think you're serious about all that do-the-right-thing stuff. About being good. Aren't you?"

She laughed. "It's not about being good, Roy. It's about trying to be good. You think Jesus is some . . ." She searched for the word. "Some wimp? No. He was a real hard ass. He had to be."

Bugbee smiled, his eyes crinkling. She tried to read his expression, wasn't sure if she detected the tiniest glint of admiration. "Jesus the hard ass. I like that."

"So when was the last time *you* went to church, Roy?"

"Oh, no. Don't fucking start on me. Let's get one thing clear. That's not going to happen." He paused. "Besides, sounds to me like Jesus's got some work to do in your own household."

Stung, Audrey didn't reply.

"Sorry," Bugbee said after a few seconds. "That was out of bounds."

"That's okay," she said. "You may be right."

102

A CHILL WAS in the air, the fall days tinged with the coming winter. The sky was steel gray and ominous, threatening to rain at any moment.

In the living room, however, where Audrey sat reading, it was warm almost to the point of stifling. After Bugbee left, she'd made a fire in the fireplace, the first of the season. The fatwood had caught right away, which pleased her, and now the logs crackled loudly, making her jump from time to time as she lingered over a passage that wouldn't let go.

She opened the Bible to the book of Matthew and wept for the man who'd been her friend. She thought, too, about Leon, about how she'd have it out with him. Now she was all the more determined to somehow rise above anger and recrimination.

Noyce and Leon: they were nothing alike, but both were men with feet of clay. Leon was a lost man, but he was a man she loved. She knew how quick she was to judge others. Maybe it was time to learn forgiveness. That seemed to be the whole point of the parable of the unmerciful servant in the book of Matthew.

A king was owed a great sum of money by one of his servants and was about to sell the servant and his family in order to raise the money. But when the servant pleaded, his master took pity and forgave him his debt. Not long afterward, the servant met a fellow servant of the king's who owed *him* some money, and what did he do? He grabbed the man by the throat and demanded payment. The king summoned the ingrate and said, "You wicked servant! I forgave you all that debt because you besought me; and should not you have had mercy on your fellow servant, as I had mercy on you?"

A key jangled in the front door lock.

Leon. Back from wherever he went without telling her.

"Oh, hey, Shorty," he said as he entered. "You made a fire. That's nice."

She nodded. "You're out and about early."

"Looks like it's about to pour out there."

"Where'd you go, Leon?"

He immediately looked away. "Gotta get out of the house sometimes. Good for me."

"Come sit down in here. We need to talk."

"Uh oh," he said. "Those are words no guy ever wants to hear." But he sat down anyway, in his favorite chair, looking supremely uncomfortable.

"This is not going to continue," she said.

He nodded.

"Well?"

"Well what?" he said.

"I've been doing some reading in the Bible."

"I see that. Old Testament or New?"

"Hmm?"

"As I recall from my churchgoing days, the Old Testament God's a pretty judgmental sort."

"None of us is perfect, baby. And the Bible tells us about when Jesus refused to condemn an adulterer who was about to be stoned to death."

"Where's this going?" Leon said.

"You going to tell me what you're up to?"

"Ah," he said with a low chuckle that began to grow. "Oh, yeah," he said and his chuckle grew into an unrestrained guffaw. "My sister been putting crazy ideas in your head?"

"You going to explain yourself? Or is this going to be the last talk we ever have?"

"Oh, Shorty," Leon said. He got up from his chair and sat down on the couch next to her, snuggling close. She was astonished, but she didn't hug him back, just sat there, stiff and angry and confused. A bottle rolled around under the couch. She reached a hand down and grabbed it. A brown beer bottle. She held it up.

"Is it this, or is it a woman?" she said.

He was laughing, enjoying himself, and she grew steadily more furious. "It's funny to you?"

"You're some detective," he finally said. "That's root beer."

"Oh, so it is," she said, embarrassed.

"I haven't had a drink in seventeen days. You haven't noticed?"

"Is that true?"

"Forgiveness is Step Nine. I'm nowhere near that."

"Step Nine?"

"The Eighth Step is to make a list of everyone I ever harmed and be willing to make amends to them. I should do that too. You know I was never good about lists."

"You—how come you didn't tell me you're doing AA?"

Now it was his turn to look sheepish. "Maybe I wanted to make sure it would take."

"Oh, baby," she said, tears springing to her eyes. "I'm so proud of you."

"Hey, Shorty, don't go getting all proud yet. I still haven't gotten past step three."

"Which is what?"

"Hell if I know," Leon said. He put a big callused hand on her face, brushed away her tears, and leaned in to kiss her, and this time she kissed him back. She'd almost forgotten what it was like, kissing her husband, but she was remembering now, and it was nice.

The two of them got up and went to the bedroom.

Outside it began to rain, but it was warm in their bed.

In the morning she would get up early and arrange the arrest warrants for Eddie Rinaldi and Nicholas Conover.

103

ON HER WAY to the prosecutor's office, Audrey heard Noyce's voice calling to her.

He was standing in the door to his office, waving her in.

She stopped for just a moment.

"Audrey," he said, something different in his voice. "We need to talk."

"I'm in a rush, Jack. I'm sorry."

"What's up?"

"I—I'd rather not say."

His eyebrows shot up. "Audrey?"

"Excuse me, Jack. I'm sorry."

He put out a hand, touched her shoulder. "Audrey," he said, "I don't know exactly what they told you about me, but . . ."

He knew. Of course he knew. She fixed him with a level gaze. "I'm listening," she said.

Noyce took a breath, colored, and then said, "Fuck it. I don't want your pity." He turned and went into his office, and she hurried on.

DR. AARON LANDIS's habitual sneer had become an incredulous scowl. "We've been over this, Detective.

You've already asked me to breach Mr. Stadler's confidentiality. If you somehow imagine that your persistence is going to make me reconsider—"

"I'm sure you're aware what the *Principles of Medical Ethics,* published by the American Psychiatric Association, says about confidentiality."

"Oh, please."

"You're permitted to release relevant confidential information about a patient under legal compulsion."

"As I recall, it says 'proper' legal compulsion. Do you have a court order?"

"If that'll make a difference to you, I'll get one. But I'm appealing to you not as a law enforcement officer, but as a human being."

"Not the same thing, I take it."

She ignored this. "Ethically you have the right to testify about Andrew Stadler's history, especially if you have any interest in helping bring his killer to justice."

Landis's eyelids drooped as if he were deep in thought. "What does one have to do with the other?"

"Well, you see, Dr. Landis, we've found Andrew Stadler's killer."

"And who might that be?" His phlegmatic tone, carefully calibrated, didn't quite mask his natural curiosity.

"That I can't tell you until he's charged. But I'm going to ask you to take the stand and testify to the fact that Andrew Stadler was, at times, violent."

"I won't."

"Don't you understand what's at stake, Dr. Landis?"

"I will not testify to that," Landis said.

"If you refuse to speak for this man," Audrey said, "his killer may not find justice. Doesn't that make a difference to you?"

"You want me to testify that he had violent tendencies,

and I'm not going to do that. I can't. I can't say what you want me to say—because it's not true."

"What do you mean?"

"I saw no violent inclinations whatever."

"What makes you say that?"

"I didn't tell you a thing."

"Pardon me?"

"You didn't hear any of this from me." He scratched his chin. "Andrew Stadler was a sad, desperately afflicted man. A tormented man. But not a violent man."

"Dr. Landis, the man who killed him held him responsible for a particularly sadistic attack, an evisceration of a dog, a family pet. In fact, a whole series of attacks on the suspect's home. It's the reason, we're convinced, this man killed Stadler."

Landis nodded, a glint of recognition in his eyes. "Yes," he said. "That would make a certain sense."

"It would?"

"If it were true, yes. But I can tell you with a high degree of certainty that Andrew Stadler never did these things."

"Hold on a second. Last time we spoke, you talked about a pattern of sudden rages, brief psychotic episodes—"

"Indeed. I was describing a syndrome we call Borderline Personality Disorder."

"All right, but you said a schizophrenic like Stadler could have this borderline disorder."

"I've seen it, sure. But I wasn't talking about Andrew Stadler."

"Then who *were* you talking about, Doctor?"

He hesitated.

"Doctor, please!"

Ten minutes later, short of breath, Audrey raced out of County Medical, cell phone to her ear.

104

THE SPECIAL BOARD meeting was set to start at 2 P.M., and by a quarter to, most of the invited participants had arrived in the narrow anteroom. Scott had come first, and he didn't dance around the subject. Nick had a stack of unanswered phone messages from him, all from this morning. Marjorie had been instructed to keep him away from Nick's home base.

"Don't leave me in the dark here, Nick," Scott said. Nick noticed he was wearing a brand-new shirt: white, narrow-point collar, looked like Armani, completely different from the frayed Oxford-cloth button-downs he usually wore. "Come on, Nick, I can't read my lines if I don't have a script, okay?"

"I thought we'd be spontaneous."

"Spontaneous," Scott repeated. "Spontaneous combustion. Spontaneous abortion. Spontaneous aortic aneurysm." He shook his head. "I don't like that word 'spontaneous.'"

Nick cocked his head. "We're trying something new, here," he said, deliberately cryptic.

"I just want to help, Nick." There was a sullen look in his lilac-rimmed eyes.

"I'm counting on it," Nick said. "In fact, could you get me a Diet Coke? No ice if it's already cold."

Scott looked like he was about to say something when Davis Eilers—khakis and a white polo shirt beneath a blue blazer—slung an arm around Scott's shoulder and took him away.

"So where's the agenda?" Todd Muldaur asked Nick, as the anteroom started to grow crowded. "Dan, Davis, and I flew here on the Fairfield corporate jet together, and guess what—none of us got an agenda."

"Oh, there's an agenda," Nick said with a smile. "It's just not printed."

"I never heard of that. Special board meeting but no written agenda?" He exchanged glances with Dan Finegold. "Hope this isn't one of those panic moves," he said to Nick with what was meant to be a look of kindly concern in his too-blue eyes.

Finegold gave Nick an upper-bicep squeeze. "Slow and steady, right?"

"How's the brewery?" Nick asked him.

"Couldn't be better," Finegold said. "On the brewing end, at least. Micro's a crowded category right now."

Nick dropped his voice confidingly. "Truth is, Rolling Rock's more my speed. I like a beer I can see through." He scanned the room until he saw Scott McNally, huddled in a corner with Davis Eilers. Nick didn't need to hear them talk to work out that Eilers was trying to get the lowdown from Scott. Scott's response was evident from a series of nervous shrugs and headshakes.

Now Todd took Nick by the elbow, and spoke to him in a low, tense voice. "Pretty short notice, don't you think?"

"The chairman of the board has the power to convene an extraordinary session of the board," Nick said blandly.

"But what's the goddamned *agenda?*"

Nick grinned, didn't answer. "Funny, I was remembering what you said about turtles and turtle soup."

Todd shrugged. "Dan and I didn't mind canceling our other appointments, but, hey, there's a Yankees–Red Sox game tonight. We both had to give away our tickets. So I hope it's going to be worth our while, huh?"

"Definitely. Count on it. We weren't able to rustle up that good coffee, though. You'll have to overlook a few things."

"We're getting used to that," said Todd with a grin that snapped shut an instant later. "Just hope you know what you're doing." He craned his head and exchanged a long glance with Scott.

Nick noticed Dorothy Devries making her entrance. She was wearing a royal blue skirt suit, with big clown-suit buttons. Her mouth was pursed and she was fingering her silver brooch with a clawlike hand. Nick waved to her from across the room, a big hearty gesture that she returned with a refrigerator smile.

Nick continued to shake hands, and make welcoming noises, until he noticed that Eddie Rinaldi had entered the room. Eddie sidled up to him with a look of impatience. "Guess what? Your fucking alarm went off again."

Nick groaned. "I can't—can you handle it?"

Eddie nodded. "Gas leak."

"*Gas* leak?"

"Alarm company called, then they called back, said a 'Mrs. Conover' told them she's handling it, but I think I should check it out. Unless you got married without telling me."

Nick, distracted, shook his head. "And Marta's out of the country."

"Your girlfriend?"

"She's not there. The kids should be home by now, though."

Eddie put a hand on Nick's shoulder. "I'll head over

there. You don't fuck around with a gas leak." He took an amused look around the room before sidling off.

"Well, why don't we go sit down?" Nick said. His words were addressed to Todd but were loud enough to count as instructions to the room.

A couple of minutes later, everyone had taken a seat around the oversized mahogany table in the boardroom. Scott was playing with his plasma screen, raising it and lowering it nervously, like a kid with a Transformer Action Figure.

Nick didn't sit at his usual spot at the head of the table. He left that chair empty and took the seat next to it. He nodded at Stephanie Alstrom, who wore her usual look of arid unease. She rested her hands on a thick file folder.

"I want to start with some very good news," Nick said. "Atlas McKenzie is in. They signed this morning."

"Why, that's *tremendous,* Nick," Todd said. "Good going! You talk them off the ledge yourself?"

"Wish I could take the credit," Nick said. "Willard Osgood had to get on the horn himself."

"Really," Todd said, coolly. "That's an unusual tactic."

"He volunteered," Nick said. "I didn't twist his arm."

"Did he? I guess he likes to show that he can land a big one from time to time." Todd's expression hovered between amusement and condescension. "They don't make 'em like that anymore."

"I'll say." Nick pressed an intercom button and spoke to Marjorie. "Marjorie, I think we're all ready here. Could you let our visitor know?" Looking up, he went on, "Now, I didn't convene this extraordinary session to crow about good news. There are some serious issues we've got in front of us, which have to do with the future of this company." He paused for a moment. "A number of you have urged me to take a hard look at manufacturing costs. I've been resistant, and maybe I've been too resistant. Looking forward, now, we have decided to start diversifying our manufacturing base. Stratton is going to contract out the manufacturing for our low-cost Stratton/Basics lines. We're currently in negotiation with a number of overseas manufacturers, including some strong candidates in China. It's a move that will ensure we'll continue to be competitive in the most price-sensitive part of our market."

Dorothy Devries's expression was almost a smirk. Todd and Scott both looked confused, as if they were on a train that had gone one stop past their destination.

"We've reached a different decision about the higher-end lines, which are at the core of our brand identity," Nick went on. "These we'll continue to manufacture right here in Fenwick."

"I'm sorry to step in," Todd said, clearing his throat. "But you're referring to 'we,' and I don't know who you mean by that. Are you talking about your full management team? Because a lot of us are inclined to think that it's too late in the day for half measures."

"I'm aware of this." In a louder voice, he said, "As some of you here know and some of you don't know—and until recently, I was among those who didn't know—certain parties representing Fairfield have been negotiating to sell the Stratton brand to a consortium called Pacific Rim Investors, which controls a large Shenzhen-based manufacturer of office furniture, Shenyang Industries."

Nick didn't know whether he had been expecting gasps or cries of astonishment, but there weren't any. Just the sound of shuffling papers and cleared throats.

Todd looked smug. "May I say a few words?"

"Absolutely," Nick said.

Todd turned slightly, addressing the other members of the board. "First, I want to apologize to the CEO of this company for keeping him out of the loop on the deal. We at Fairfield have been taking a long, hard look at the numbers, and, frankly, we see an opportunity here, one we cannot afford to pass up. Stratton has entered into a crisis phase. Nick Conover—and I want to commend him for his candor—has made it very clear, every step of the way, that there are certain options he just can't accept. Well, we respect his views. And we certainly respect his excellent work on behalf of the company. But this is a case where management cannot be given the final word." A beat. "The greatest praise I can give any manager is to say that he does his work with passion." He turned to face Nick. "That's certainly true of you, Nick. But when a firm reaches a critical inflection point, there are hard choices to be made—and they need to be made with *dis*passion."

He leaned back in his black Stratton chair, looking sleeker by the moment. "That's the thing about being in a crisis zone," he said, hardly bothering to conceal his self-satisfaction. "It's what everyone at McKinsey gets drummed into their heads from day one. The Chinese word for 'crisis' combines the characters for 'danger' and 'opportunity.'"

"No doubt," Nick said breezily. "And the Chinese word for 'outsourcing' combines the characters for 'lost' and 'jobs.'"

"We owe you a lot," Todd said in a lordly tone. "Don't think we're not grateful. I'm sure I speak for *everyone* when I say that we appreciate all you've given to Stratton. It's just that the time has come to move on."

"I know you'd *like* to speak for everyone. But maybe some of us prefer to speak for themselves." Nick stood up, nodding at the tall bespectacled man who had just let himself into the room.

Willard Osgood.

105

THE CENTRAL MONITORING station for Fenwicke Estates also serviced three other gated communities in and around Fenwick, including Safe Harbor, White-wood Farms, and Catamount Acres. It was a low-slung windowless building located in an anonymous area of strip malls and fast-food restaurants. It could have been a warehouse. It was surrounded by chain-link fencing and was unmarked except for a street number. Audrey knew this was for security reasons. Out back were two hulking emergency diesel generators.

When in doubt, get a warrant. You couldn't count on people to be cooperative, even in an emergency, so she'd called in for a search warrant, had it faxed over to the central monitoring station, to the attention of the facility's general manager. Police headquarters had all that information on file.

The assistant operations manager, Bryan Mundy, was a man in a wheelchair who was as cooperative as could be, as it turned out. He was also extremely vol-uble, which was annoying, but she nodded and smiled pleasantly, silently urging him to hurry. She pretended to be interested, but not too interested.

As he led her through a maze of cubicles where

women, mostly, sat in front of computers wearing head-sets, he maneuvered his chair deftly and boasted about how they also monitored fire alarms for quite a few businesses and residences in the area. He talked about how they were connected via secure Internet protocol to the many cameras and guard booths they monitored. About how they did live remote viewing of all cameras via a Web browser. Rolling through another area where other people, mostly men, were watching video feed on computer monitors, he talked proudly, and in endless detail, about the digital watermark on the video files that provided authentication using something called an MD5 algorithm that ensured the image had not been altered.

Audrey didn't understand but stored away the fact that Bryan Mundy would be a good resource when the case went to trial.

He told her that he'd considered a job in law enforcement too, but preferred the pay of the private sector.

"Events up to thirty days ago are stored right here," he said as they entered another area, which was crowded with large racks of computer servers and storage media. "You're in luck. Anything older than that gets sent off to secure storage."

She gave him the date she was interested in viewing, and he hooked up the black disk-array box, inside of which were several hard drives containing digital video backups. He located for her the video file from between noon and 6 P.M. on the day that Nicholas Conover's family dog had been killed. She'd gotten the date and time from the uniform division. He showed her how to identify the files by camera number, but she told him she didn't know what camera it was she was looking for. Any camera located along Fenwicke Estates' perimeter fencing whose motion sensing might have been triggered during that time period.

Anyone, she thought, who had slipped into, or out of, Fenwicke Estates in the time surrounding the slaughter of Conover's dog.

"Lot of interest in this disk, huh?" Bryan Mundy said. "Log says that the security director of the Stratton Corporation came in here a while back and made some video caps off of it."

"Do you have a record of which video frames he copied?

Mundy shook his head and poked at his teeth absently with an orange wooden plaque stick. "He said he worked for Nicholas Conover, the CEO of Stratton. Wanted to know if we had any perimeter video near the Conover house, but no dice. Conover's house is apparently a good ways from the fence."

It didn't take her long to find a tall, gawky figure in a flapping coat, wearing heavy-framed glasses, approaching the fence, captured on camera 17.

"That's what he wanted too, the security director."

Yes. That's how he and Conover came to believe it was Stadler who had eviscerated the dog.

But she could see from the way Stadler was craning his neck and squinting, his body language, that he was following someone. He wasn't looking behind, not afraid that he might have been followed. He was definitely *following* someone.

She knew who he was following. Dr. Landis's speculations made a terrible and clear sense.

"Can this rewind slowly?" she asked.

"Doesn't really rewind per se," he said, smacking his lips around the plaque stick.

"How do I view earlier images, then?"

"Like this," he said, and he pointed and double-clicked the mouse.

"Let's go back, I don't know, fifteen minutes and go from there."

"You know which cameras you want?"

"No, unfortunately. Any one of them for fifteen minutes before this guy appears."

He set it up for her and sat back as she moved through the images. His curiosity had gotten the better of his politeness; he sat there and watched as if he had nothing better to do.

Fortunately there weren't too many images to go through, since the recording was triggered by motion.

Seven minutes before Andrew Stadler had climbed the fence around Fenwicke Estates, scrambling like he was in hot pursuit, she found another figure. This one was smaller, wearing a leather jacket, moving nimbly and with great purpose.

Dr. Landis's words: *Stadler would go off his meds periodically. His wife was unable to stay married to the man, understandably, and she abandoned her child, then took her away from her father a few years later—a psychic wound from which the child might have recovered had she not had an inherited genetic predisposition.*

As the leather-jacketed figure approached the wrought-iron fence, it turned its face to the camera, almost as if posing. A smile.

The figure's face was now distinct.

Cassie Stadler.

Helen Stadler, Dr. Landis had corrected Audrey.

She changed her name to Cassie some time in adolescence. She thought it was a more interesting name. Maybe she liked the association with Cassandra, the Greek heroine endowed with the gift of prophecy whom no one heeded.

She had been the one who had repeatedly broken into Nicholas Conover's house to spray ominous and threatening graffiti. The timing now made it clear that Cassie had been the one who had killed the Conovers' dog.

Not her father, who had followed her to Conover's house, just as he'd probably followed her many times before.

Knowing that his daughter was disturbed.

Andrew Stadler knew Cassie was afflicted with this disorder, talked about it with Dr. Landis obsessively, blamed himself.

With unsteady hands she picked up her cell phone and called Dr. Landis. His answering machine came on. After the beep, she began speaking.

"Dr. Landis, it's Detective Rhimes, and it's urgent that I speak with you at once."

Dr. Landis picked up the phone.

"You told me Helen Stadler was obsessed with the notion of the family she never had," Audrey said without giving her name. "Families she could never be a part of, families that excluded her."

"Yes, yes," the psychiatrist cut in, "what of it?"

"Dr. Landis, you mentioned a family that lived across the street from the Stadlers where Cass—Helen used to play all the time when she was growing up. A little girl she considered her best friend—she used to spend all of her time over there until they became annoyed and asked her to leave?"

"Yes." Dr. Landis's voice was grave.

"Andrew Stadler was questioned years ago in connection with a tragic house fire across the street in which an entire family, the Stroups, died. He apparently did some repair work for them. Was this—?"

"Yes. Andrew said his daughter had his mechanical ability, and he'd taught her how to fix all sorts of things, and one night after they'd asked her to stop coming over she slipped into their house through the bulkhead doors, opened the gas line, and lit a match on her way out."

"Dear God. She was never charged."

"I was quite sure this was simply a fantasy of Andrew's, a manifestation of his paranoid fixation on his daughter. In any case, who would suspect a twelve-year-old girl? The authorities thought it was Andrew, but his alibi apparently held up under questioning. Something similar happened, you know, at Carnegie Mellon University during Helen's freshman year there. Andrew told me that his daughter belonged to a sorority, and she was quite obsessed with them as a surrogate family of sorts. Much later, he said, he heard about the terrible gas explosion in the sorority house in which eighteen women perished. This was the same night that Helen drove home from Pittsburgh, quite upset that one of her sorority sisters had said something to make her feel rejected."

"I—I have to go, Doctor," she said, ending the call.

Bryan Mundy had rolled up to her in his wheelchair and was signaling to her. "Talk about coincidences," he said. "We were talking about Conover's house, and what do you know? We just got an alert on that system, maybe ten, fifteen minutes ago."

"An alert?"

"No, not a burglar alarm or anything. Combustible gas detector. Probably a gas leak. But the homeowner said she's got it under control."

"She?"

"Mrs. Conover."

"There is no Mrs. Conover," Audrey said, heart knocking.

Mundy shrugged. "That's how she identified herself," he said, but Audrey was already running toward the door.

106

TODD IMMEDIATELY SPRANG to his feet, followed by Eilers and Finegold. Their faces were wreathed in anxious cordiality.

"Mind if I join you?" Osgood asked gruffly.

"Willard," Todd said, "I had no idea you were coming." He turned to Nick. "You see? The personal touch—some people never lose it."

Osgood ignored him as he took the empty seat at the head of the board table.

"There isn't going to be any sale," Nick said. "The sale is wrong for Stratton, and wrong for Fairfield. We too have looked at the numbers—and by 'we,' I mean Willard and I—and that's our considered assessment."

"May I speak?" Todd said.

"We're talking about an opportunity here," Scott said. "Not something that's going to knock twice."

"An opportunity?" Nick asked. "Or a danger?" He paused, and turned to Stephanie Alstrom. "Stephanie, a few words? I know I haven't given you enough time to prepare a PowerPoint presentation, but maybe you can do it the old-fashioned way."

Stephanie Alstrom started sorting through the stapled

sheaths in her file, making three separate stacks next to her. "Here's the principal tort and criminal case law governing the salient issues, starting with federal statutes," she began in her most juiceless tone. "There's the Bribery of Foreign Officials Act of 1999, part No. 43, and the International Anti-Bribery and Fair Competition Act of 1998, and—oh heavens—the antifraud provisions of the securities laws, Section 10(b) of the Securities Exchange Act of 1934 and Rule 10b-5. And, though I haven't read through the case law properly yet, there's Section 13(b)(5) of the Exchange Act and Rule 13b2-1, to deal with." She was sounding increasingly flustered. "And, of course, Sections 13(a) and 13(b)(2)(A) of the Exchange Act, and Rules 12b-20 and 13a too. But also there's—"

"I think we get the picture," Nick said smoothly.

"Pretty much what Dino Panetta told me back in Boston," Osgood rumbled.

"That is ridiculous," Todd said. Blood was returning to his face. Too much blood. "These are completely unfounded allegations that I dispute—"

"Todd?" Osgood's craggy face formed a scowl. "It's one thing if *you* want to go fly-fishing with your private parts for bait, but you do *not* put the partnership at risk. Question I was asking myself last night was, Where did I go wrong? Then this morning, I had the answer. I didn't go wrong. You went wrong. You ignored company policy and made a huge bet on microchips, way more than you should have, and the entire firm almost went belly-up as a result. Then you figured you could save your ass, and ours, by doing a quick-and-dirty sale. A nice big pile of dough, and who cares how you got it. Well, not like this." He struck the table, stressing each word. "Not. Like. This." His eyes flashed behind his Coke-bottle glasses. "Because you've put Fairfield Equity Partners in a potentially ruinous legal situation.

We could have brown-suited lawyers from the SEC camped out on Federal Street for the next five years, combing through our files with a jeweler's loupe. You wanted to land a big fish—and you didn't care if you rammed the boat through a goddamned barrier reef to do it."

"I think you're blowing this out of proportion," Todd said, wheedling. "Fairfield is in no danger."

"Damned right," Osgood replied. "Fairfield Equity Partners is completely in the clear."

"Good," Todd said uncertainly.

"That's right," Osgood said. "Because the partnership did the responsible thing. Demonstrated it wasn't party to the misdeeds. As soon as the errant behavior came to our attention, we severed our relations with the principals—*former* principals, not to put too fine a point on it, and took all possible measures to separate ourselves from the malefactors. Including the commencement of legal action against Todd Erickson Muldaur. You violated the gross misconduct clause of your agreement with the Partnership, which means, as I'm sure you know, that your share reverts to the general equity fund."

"You're joking," Todd said, blinking as if there was a bit of grit lodged behind one of his blue contact lenses. "I've got all my money invested in Fairfield. You can't just declare—"

"You signed the same agreement we all did. Now we're activating the provision. Only way to show the feds we're serious. You can contest it—I'm sure you will. But I think you'll find most high-powered lawyers are going to want to see a hefty chunk of their fee up front. And we've already filed for a separate tort claim against you and your coconspirator, Mr. McNally, for a hundred and ten million dollars. We've requested that the judge place the funds we're trying to recover in escrow, pending legal resolution, and we've received indications that he intends to do so."

Scott's face looked like a plaster death mask. He tugged robotically at a lock of hair at his temple. As Nick listened to Osgood, he found himself staring out the window at the charred buffalo grass. It no longer looked like a lifeless black carpet anymore, he noticed. The new grass had begun to grow back. Tiny green blades were now peeking through the black.

"That's insane!" Todd spoke with a squeaky groan, a crowbar pulling out a long nail. "You can't do that. I will *not* be treated this way, Willard. I'm owed some basic respect. I am a full-fledged partner at Fairfield, of eight years' standing. I'm not some . . . some goddamn *catfish* you can play catch-and-release with."

Osgood turned to Nick. "He's got a point. You wouldn't want to mix him up with a catfish. You see, one's a bottom-feeding, scum-sucking scavenger . . ."

"And the other's a fish," Nick said. "Got it. And one more bit of business." He looked around the table. "Now that Stratton's future is secure, I'm hereby submitting my resignation."

Osgood turned to face him, stunned. "*What?* Oh, Christ."

"I'm about to face a legal . . . situation . . . which I don't want to drag my company through."

The men and women around the boardroom table seemed as astonished as Osgood was. Stephanie Alstrom began shaking her head.

But Nick stood up and shook Osgood's hand firmly. "Stratton's been through enough. When we make the announcement, we'll just say that Mr. Conover resigned 'in order to spend more time with his family.'" He gave a little wink. "Which has the added virtue of being true. Now, if you'll excuse me."

He got up and strode confidently out of the room,

and for the first time in a long while he felt a palpable sense of relief.

MARJORIE WAS CRYING as she watched him gather up his framed family pictures. Her phone was ringing nonstop, but she was ignoring it.

"I don't understand," she said. "I think you owe me an explanation."

"You're right. I do." He reached down to the bottom drawer of his desk and pulled out the rubber-banded stack of Post-it notes in Laura's handwriting. "But first, could you find me a box?"

She turned and, as she passed her desk, she picked up the phone. A few seconds later, Marge looked around the partition, looking grim. "Nick, there's some kind of emergency at your house."

"Eddie's handling it."

"Well, the thing is—that was a woman named Cathy or Cassie, calling from your house. I didn't get the name—she was speaking fast, sounding panicked. She said you've got to get over there as fast as you can. I don't have a good feeling about this."

Nick dropped the picture frames onto his desk and broke into a run.

107

ON HIS WAY to the parking lot he called home, let it ring.

No answer, which was strange. Cassie had just called from there—and what the hell was she doing there anyway? Plus, both kids should have gotten home from school by now to do their last-minute packing, both of them excited about the trip. Even, in his grudging way, Lucas, or so Nick thought.

But the phone rang and rang and the voice mail kept coming on.

Okay, so Lucas often didn't answer the home phone, let the voice mail get it, but Julia always answered. She loved the phone. And Cassie—she'd just called. Weird.

No answer.

Lucas's cell? He didn't remember the number, too many numbers in his head and this one he didn't call all that often. He hit the green call button on his phone, which pulled up the last ten or whatever calls he'd dialed.

There it was, LUCAS CELL. Had Marjorie programmed that in? Probably. He hit SEND as he ran through the parking lot, a couple of employees waving hello, but he didn't have time for niceties.

Come on, damn it, answer the fucking phone. Told

you if you don't answer the cell, I take it away, that's the deal.

A couple of rings and then his son's recorded voice, adolescent-buzzy in timbre, curt and full of attitude in just a few words.

Hey, it's Luke, what up? Leave a message.

A beep, then a female voice: *Please leave your message after the tone. Press One to send a numeric page—*

Nick ended the call, heart drumming and not from the run. He fumbled for the Suburban's key-fob thing, pressed it to unlock just as he reached the car door.

Roaring out of the parking lot, he tried Eddie's cell.

No answer.

"SHE'S NOT HERE," Bugbee said. The cellular signal began to fade . . . "Patrol units, but no Cassie Stadler at her house."

"She's at Conover's," Audrey said. "Gas leak."

"Huh?"

"I'm heading over there now. You too. Right away. Notify the fire department."

"You know she's there?"

"She answered the phone when the alarm monitoring service called. Get over there, Roy. Right now."

"Why?" Bugbee said.

"Just do it. And bring backup." She ended the call so he didn't have a chance to argue.

Gas leak. The Stroups, her neighbors when she was twelve.

She lit a match on the way out.

Her sorority house at Carnegie Mellon when she was a freshman.

Eighteen young women perished.

The families she desperately wanted to be part of. Who all rejected her.

Then Audrey called Nicholas Conover's office at the Stratton Corporation, but she was told he wasn't there.

Tell him it's urgent, she said. It's a matter of safety. His house.

The secretary's voice lost its hard edge. "He's on his way over there, officer."

THE ALARM COMPANY?

Nick didn't even remember the name.

A gas leak? He tried to imagine what that was all about—something goes wrong in the house, the kids smell gas, maybe they're smart about it and get the hell out of the house, that's why the house phone line went unanswered—but what about Lucas's cell?

Say he left it inside in the rush to get out. Sure, that was all.

But Eddie?

Guy lived with a cell phone planted to his ear. Why the hell would he not answer either?

Twelve minutes he could be at the gates of Fenwicke Estates. Assuming he caught the lights right. He gunned it, then slowed just a bit, keeping it no more then ten miles an hour over the speed limit. An overzealous cop could pull him over, slow things way down even if Nick told him it was an emergency. Ask for my license and registration, maybe decide to take his fucking time about it once he caught the name.

He drove the whole way in a mental tunnel of concentration, barely aware of the traffic around him, thinking only of getting to the house. Kept hitting REDIAL for Eddie's cell, but no answer.

A moment of relief as he pulled up to the gatehouse. No emergency vehicles here, no fire trucks or whatever, probably no big deal.

A gas leak is not the same thing as a fire, of course.

Could the kids and Eddie and Cassie all have been overcome by gas fumes, maybe that's why they couldn't answer? He had no idea if natural gas did that.

"Hi, Mr. Conover," said Jorge, behind the bullet-proof glass in the booth.

"Emergency, Jorge," Nick called out.

"Your security director, Mr. Rinaldi, he came through here already."

"How long ago?"

"Let me check the log—"

"Forget it. Open the gate, Jorge."

"It's opening, Mr. Conover."

And so it was, glacially slow. Inching open.

"Can you speed it up?" Nick said.

Jorge smiled apologetically, shrugged. "You know this gate, I'm sorry. Also your friend came by."

"My friend?"

"Miss Stadler? She came by too. Hour ago, I think."

Did the kids call Cassie to come over? he wondered. Why didn't they call me? They know how to reach me. More comfortable calling Cassie, that it?

"Goddammit," Nick shouted in frustration. "Speed this fucking thing up."

"I can't do that, Mr. Conover, I'm sorry."

Nick floored it, the Suburban lurching forward, hitting the solid iron bars of the gate, a crunch of metal that he knew wasn't the gate. Even the goddamned Suburban is a fucking tin can, crumples like a wad of aluminum foil. Front-end work. Fuck it.

It didn't budge the gate, which continued its stately pace, oblivious, arrogant, taking its goddamned fucking time.

Jorge's eyes widened. Finally the gate was open just enough, Nick calculated, to get through. He gunned it again, the squeal of metal against metal as the car scraped against the gate but got through, just barely.

SPEED LIMIT 20, the sign said.

Fuck it.

NO FIRE TRUCKS on the street or along the driveway. No police cars either.

Maybe this was nothing. He was overreacting, no emergency at all, no gas leak at all, a false alarm.

No. A false alarm, there would have been an answer, one of the calls he'd made.

Gas leak for real. Eddie came by, got the kids out of there and Cassie too, saved them all, thank God for that traitorous bastard, a bastard but *my* bastard, maybe turned out to be a real friend after all, maybe I owe him an apology.

Eddie's GTO in the driveway, parked behind the van. Cassie's red VW convertible too. It didn't compute. Cassie came over, Eddie too, both of their cars here, the van here too. That meant no one drove the kids away, thus the kids are still here and Eddie and Cassie too, so what the hell, then?

He raced up the stone path to the house, noticed all the windows were closed, the house sealed tight as if they were already out of there, on vacation, and as he approached the front door he smelled rotten eggs.

The gas smell.

It was for real. It was strong too, if he could smell it out here. Very strong. That odorant they add to natural gas so you know if there's a leak.

Front door was locked, which was a little strange if everyone had just run out of there, but he didn't linger on that, totally single-minded. He grabbed his key ring, got the door open.

Dark in here.

He yelled out, "Hello? Anyone here?"

No answer.

The rotten-egg smell was overpowering. More like skunk, maybe. A wall of odor, sharp as a knife, nauseating.

"Hello?"

Faint noises now. Thumping? From upstairs? He couldn't tell, the house was so solid. He entered the kitchen, but no one there either.

Distant bumping sounds, but then footsteps nearby, and Cassie appeared, walking slowly, looking worn out, a wreck.

"Cass," he said. "Thank God you're here. Where are the kids?"

She kept approaching, one hand behind her back, slowly, almost hesitant. Her eyes sleepy, not looking at him, her stare distant.

"Cass?"

"Yeah," she said at last. "Thank God I'm here." Flat, almost affectless.

He heard a high-pitched mechanical beeping coming from somewhere. What the hell was that?

"Where is everyone?"

"They're safe," she said, but something in her tone seemed off, as if she wasn't sure.

"Where's Eddie?"

A beat. "He's . . . safe too." She drew out the words.

He stepped toward her to give her a hug, but she stepped backward, shook her head.

"No," she said.

"Cassie?"

He felt the twang of fear even before his brain could make sense of it.

"You've got to get out of here. We've got to open some windows, call the fire department. Jesus, this is incredibly dangerous, this stuff is unbelievably combustible. Where are Luke and Julia?"

The high beeping was getting faster, higher in pitch, and Nick realized the source was a device on the kitchen counter he'd seen before, a small yellow box with flexible metal tubing coming out of it. What was it, and what was it doing there?

"I'm glad you came home, Nick." Her eyes were smudged, looking like black holes. They darted from side to side. "I knew you would, though. Daddy protects his family. You're a good daddy. Not like my daddy. He never protected me."

"Cassie," he said, "what *is* it? You look so frightened."

She nodded. "I'm terrified."

He felt his skin go cold and goosefleshy. He saw it in her eyes, that same absent look he'd seen before, as if she'd gone somewhere else where no one could reach her. "Cassie," he said in a gentle and firm tone, hollow inside, "where are my children?"

"I'm terrified of *me,* Nick. And you should be too."

With her left hand she reached into the pocket of her denim shirt and pulled out an object that he recognized as Lucas's Zippo lighter. The lighter decorated with a skull crawling with spiders and surrounded by spider webs, a real stoner lighter. She flipped the top off, one-handed, and her thumb touched the flint wheel.

"*No!*" Nick shouted. "What are you doing, are you *crazy*?"

"Come on, Nick, you *know* I am. Can't you read the writing on the wall?" She began singing softly, "Oh, I ran to the rock to hide my face, the rock cried out 'No hiding place.'"

"Where *are* they, Cassie?"

The electronic beeping, rising all the while in pitch, had now become a steady high squeal, almost ear-piercing. He realized where he'd seen that yellow box before: in the basement, placed there by the gas com-

pany serviceman. A combustible gas detector. Sup-
posed to warn you about gas leaks. Beeping got higher
and faster as the concentration of gas in the air in-
creased. A steady squeal meant dangerous amounts of
gas. Combustible levels. Someone had taken the device
upstairs from the basement, and he now knew who.

"I told you, they're safe," she said in a flat voice, and
her other hand, the one she'd been keeping behind her
back, came around to the front now, gripping the huge
carbon-steel Henckels carving knife from the kitchen
knife rack.

Heart thumping a million miles a minute now. Oh
sweet Jesus, she's out of her mind. Dear God, help me.

"Cassie," he said, moving closer, his arms outspread
to give her a hug, but she raised the knife and pointed
it at him, and with her left hand she held up the lighter,
thumb on the wheel, and said, "Not another step, Nick."

THE GUARD'S FACE appeared behind the tempered glass
of the security booth at the entrance to the Fenwicke
Estates.

His voice squawked through the intercom. "Yes?"

She flashed her police badge. "Police emergency,"
she said.

The guard looked at it through the glass and imme-
diately activated the security gate.

"JESUS, CASSIE, PLEASE *don't*—"

"Oh, I really don't like this part," she said, and at
that instant he noticed the red slick on the knife blade,
still wet.

108

THE HIGH WROUGHT-IRON gate began to open, but so slowly, so agonizingly slowly. She drummed her fingers on the steering wheel and finally she said, "Please, speed this up. There's no time to waste."

"Sorry, I can't make it go any faster," the guard said. "That's as fast as it goes. I'm sorry."

"PUT THE KNIFE down, Cassie," Nick said, all forced calm, voice soft and wheedling.

"When I'm done with my work, Nick. I'm very tired. I just want to finish. It has to end."

"Your work," Nick said numbly. "Please, Cassie. What have you done with them?" Fear rose in him like a flood tide.

Please God no not the kids no oh Jesus Christ no.

"Who?" she said.

No please not that dear God not the kids.

"My . . . family."

"Oh, they're safe, Nick. Like a family should be. Safe. Protected."

"Please, Cassie," he whispered, a catch in his throat, hot tears in his eyes. "Where are my kids?"

"Safe, Nick."

"Cassie, please tell me they're . . ." He stopped, couldn't say *alive,* couldn't allow himself to think the word, even, because its opposite was unendurable.

She cocked her head. "You can't hear them? Banging away? They're locked up nice and safe in the basement. You can hear it, I know you can."

And he could, now that she pointed it out, hear a distant thumping. The basement door? He almost gasped in relief, his knees buckling. She'd locked them in the basement. They were alive down there.

Where the gas was coming from.

"Where's Eddie?" he managed to say.

Oh God please if Eddie's down there he'll get them out, he'll figure out a way, he can bust through a locked door, pick it. Fucking windowless basement. Vent grates are too small to climb out of. But he'll figure it out.

She shook her head. "He's not down there. I never trusted him either." She waggled the lighter, the skull leering at him.

"Don't do it, Cassie. You'll kill us all. Please don't do it, Cassie."

She kept waggling the lighter back and forth, back and forth, her thumb at the flint wheel. "I didn't ask him to come. I told *you* to come. Eddie's not family."

His eyes frantically scanned the kitchen, then stopped when he saw a shape on the lawn outside the kitchen doors. Through the glass of the French doors he recognized Eddie's body.

He saw the blood-darkened front of Eddie's pale shirt.

The contorted position. The unnatural splay of the limbs.

He knew, and it was all he could do to keep from screaming.

AUDREY COULDN'T STAND how slowly the gate was opening, almost deliberately so, as if the residents of the Fenwicke Estates were never in a hurry, because haste was unseemly.

Move it! she screamed in her mind.

She gripped the steering wheel, tapping at the gas pedal.

Faster!

She knew what was going to happen, what the poor demented soul was doing, as she'd done before. Somehow Cassie Stadler had gotten into the Conover house—well, that couldn't have been too hard, right? She and Conover had become intimate; maybe she had a key—and something had happened to set her off, make her feel rejected. Cassie Stadler was a border-line personality, Dr. Landis had said, with a danger-ous psychotic component. An obsession with family, with inclusion, and rejection always propelled her into a towering irrational rage.

Cassie Stadler was going to incinerate the Conover home.

Audrey prayed that the children weren't home. It was early in the afternoon—maybe they were still in school. Maybe the house was empty. The worst that could happen, then, was that the house would be de-stroyed.

Maybe no one was home. She prayed that was so.

"PUT DOWN THE lighter, baby," Nick said, voice silky, all the fake affection he could summon. "Is this about Maui? Because I didn't invite you?"

Fuck the knife. He'd lunge at her, grab it.

The lighter? All that took was a flick of her Bic. Could happen by accident. That he'd have to be care-ful of.

"Why should you invite me on a family trip, Nick? I mean, it's just for family, right? I'm not family."

He understood. He realized that he didn't know her,

had never known her, that he'd seen in her only what he wanted to see.

She'd said as much, hadn't she? "We don't see things as they are," she'd said once, quoting someone. "We see things as *we* are."

But he knew enough about her to understand what she was saying now.

AUDREY COULD SMELL the natural gas as soon as she got out of the car.

She saw all the other vehicles in the driveway, two of them belonging to Nicholas Conover, the other she didn't recognize. Not Bugbee's. He was all the way across town. It would take him a while. She hoped he knew to get here fast, sirens and lights on.

Her instinct told her not to go in the front door. She had to obey her instinct, times like this.

She took out the pistol from her shoulder holster under her jacket and began walking across the wide expanse of lawn, so very green, heading toward the back of the house where she could enter unnoticed.

She chose the right side of the house, where she remembered the kitchen was. As she rounded the house she noticed a figure standing in the kitchen, a small slender figure, and she knew it was Cassie Stadler.

And then she saw the body sprawled on the lawn.

Running now, low to the ground, she approached the body.

A terrible bloody mess. Sweet Jesus. It was Edward Rinaldi, and it looked as if he'd been disemboweled.

His eyes open, staring, one hand curled by his abdomen, the other outstretched toward the kitchen. Blood-soaked beige knit shirt crisscrossed with slashes as if from a knife.

Most of his shirt front dark with blood, which pooled on the green lawn.

She dropped to her knees to feel for a pulse.

She wasn't sure.

If there was a pulse, it was so slow she couldn't detect it. Maybe there was a pulse. Maybe not.

She touched his jugular vein and felt nothing, and she knew for certain the man was dead.

Nothing she could do for him. She set down her pistol, took out her cell phone, got Bugbee on the first ring.

"Alert the ME," she said. "And body conveyance."

She was frightened as she'd never been frightened before, and she'd been through some horrific crime scenes. She got up and ran around to the back of the house.

"GOD, I WASN'T even thinking," Nick said, shaking his head. "I was in such a rush to just get the kids out of town, get us on a vacation, I really fucked that up. I mean, I really blew it."

"Don't, Nick," she said, but he saw something flicker in her eyes, as if maybe she wanted to believe.

"No, seriously, I mean, how could it be a true family vacation without you? You've become such an important part of the family, babe, you know that? If I hadn't been so distracted with everything that's been going on at work, I—"

"*Don't,* Nick," she said a little louder, her voice still petulant. "Please."

"We can still be a family, Cass. I'd like that. Wouldn't you like that?"

Her eyes glistened with tears. "Oh, Nick, I've been through this before, you know. I recognize the pattern."

"The pattern?" Heart thwacking, because he saw that faint glint of hopefulness in her eyes go dark like the last winking of a dying fire.

"The first signs. It's always the same. They take you

in and make you feel like a part of everything and then something always happens. There's like a line you can never cross. A brick wall. It's like the Stroups."

"The Stroups?"

"One day, no reason, they say I can't keep coming over, I'm spending too much time over there. Lines are drawn. They're family, you're not. Maybe that's the way it has to be. But I know I can't go through it again. It's too much."

"That's where you're wrong, baby," Nick said. "It's not too late. We can still be a family."

"Sometimes a world has to come to an end. So new ones can come into being."

The electronic squeal, steady, earsplitting.

AUDREY CONSIDERED, THEN rejected, entering through the French doors that led into the kitchen. No. She'd have to approach with some stealth. She raced to the next set of French doors, but they were locked too. Was there no basement entrance, bulkhead doors or whatever?

There didn't seem to be.

A hissing sound drew her to the far side of the house near the pool fence. She saw pipes—gas pipes, she realized. Some kind of metal objects were lying on the ground next to the pipe stand, and a crescent wrench. Valves or something. They'd been removed, and maybe that was why the hissing was so loud, like the flow had been turned up full, maybe.

The gas pipes had to lead into the basement, she knew, because that was always where they went.

Over the hissing she could hear a shout. It was coming from a grate about twenty feet away.

She ran to the grate, put her face against it, the skunky, metallic smell of gas nauseating her. "Hello?" she called out.

"Down here! We're down here!" An adolescent male voice. Conover's son?

"Who is it?" Audrey said.

"Lucas. And my sister. She's got us locked in here."

"Who does?"

"That crazy bitch. Cassie."

"Where's your dad?"

"I don't know—just, shit, will you *help* us? We're going to fucking *die* down here!"

"Stay calm," Audrey said, though calm was the one thing she didn't feel. "Listen, Lucas. Help me out. You can help me, okay?"

"Who're *you*?"

"I'm Detective Rhimes. Listen to me. How's your sister doing?"

"She's—she's scared, what the fuck do you think?"

"Julia, right? Julia, can you hear me?"

A small, frightened voice. "Yes."

"Are you getting enough oxygen?"

"What?"

"Stand over here by this grate, sweetheart. Make sure you get enough air from the outside. You'll be okay."

"Okay," the girl said.

"Now, Lucas, is there a pilot light down there?"

"A pilot light?"

"Are you near the water heater? There's usually a pilot light going on the water heater, and if that ignites the cloud of gas, the whole house is going to blow. You've got to turn it off."

"There's no pilot light." His voice was faint, distant, as if he'd gone to check. "No pilot light. She must have put it out so the gas wouldn't ignite too early."

Smart kid, she thought. "All right. Is there a shutoff for the gas line? It would be on the wall where the gas pipes enter."

"I see it."

"You see the shutoff?"

Footsteps. "No. I don't see a shutoff."

She sighed, tried to think. "Are any of the doors to the house open?"

"I—I don't know, how would I know?" the boy replied.

"I think they're all locked. Is there a key hidden somewhere outside, like under a rock or something?"

She heard a jingling, and a small steel key ring poked up through the slats in the grate. "Use mine," the boy said.

THUMPING FROM THE basement, frantic, the noises reassuring because they were alive. Now in the few seconds of stillness Nick could faintly hear Lucas's voice yelling. They were alive. And desperate to get out of there.

"I'm going to call United right now," Nick said. "I'll get you on our flight no matter what it costs. First class if you want it, but you probably want to sit with us in business class." He thought, *Don't pick up the phone, even as a pretense. The phone could ignite the gas.* He remembered reading somewhere about a woman who had a gas leak and she picked up the phone and called 911, and an electric arc from the phone circuit sparked and the house exploded. "The kids would love that. You know they would, baby."

"Please, Nick." She toyed with the lighter, and in her other hand the knife dangled at her side.

He could leap at her, hurl her to the ground, if he did it carefully, chose the right moment.

"I know you now," she said in a monotone. "I can see right through you."

QUIETLY, QUIETLY, AUDREY turned the key in the back-door lock, and then pushed the door open.

A tone sounded. The alarm system's entry alert.

It had just announced her arrival.

The skunk stench was overpowering in here.

SHE WALKED SLOWLY, orienting herself. She didn't remember the layout of the house well, but then she could hear voices, female and male, and she knew which way to go.

Was the unhinged woman holding Conover hostage? If she was, then the sound of Audrey entering might attract her attention, unnerve her, maybe make her do something rash. The wrench, the gas pipes—it told Audrey that Cassie Stadler, it had to be her, had opened the pipes in order to fill the house with gas just as she'd done in other houses before.

All she'd have to do would be to strike a match and the house would explode, killing herself and the children in the basement and Audrey too. But why hadn't she done it yet?

Audrey had an idea now.

Cassie Stadler was filling the house with gas, had been for a while. Maybe she was just waiting for the entire house to fill up. So she could get the biggest bang possible.

Yes. That's what she was waiting for.

The children. That was the first thing. She had to free them.

A pounding on a door somewhere nearby told her where to go. A door in the hall. She heard the kids, or maybe it was just Lucas, pounding and pounding.

Swiftly she turned the deadbolt with a loud, satisfying click, and she pulled the door open. The boy tumbled out, sprawled to the floor.

"Hush," Audrey whispered. "Where's your sister?"

"Right here," said Lucas, and the girl came streaking out, weeping, her face red.

"Go!" Audrey whispered. "Both of you." She pointed to the open door. "Run!"

"Where's Dad?" Julia cried. "Where is he?"

"He's all right," Audrey said, not knowing what else to say. She had to get them out of here. "Go!"

Julia took right off, pushed open the screen door and began running across the lawn, but Lucas didn't move. He looked at her.

"Don't fire that gun," he said. "That'll set it off."

"I know," she said.

"WHAT WAS THAT?" said Cassie.

"What?"

"That sound. The alarm. Someone just came in the house."

"I didn't hear it."

Cassie turned slowly, looked from one entrance to the other, all the while flicking her eyes back to Nick, making sure he didn't advance toward her.

"You know," she said, her eyes trained on him, "it's funny, the way I went through stages of thinking about you. First I saw you as the destroyer of families. You sure destroyed my dad's life when you fired him, so I had to let you know you weren't any safer than anyone else."

"The graffiti," Nick said, realizing. "'No hiding place.'"

"But then I got to know you a little better, and I thought I'd been wrong, I decided you were a good man. But I know better now. Sometimes you gotta trust your first impressions."

"Put the lighter down, Cassie. You don't want to do this. Let's talk, let's figure things out."

"You know what fooled me? When I saw what a good daddy you were."

"Please, Cassie."

Behind her was the entrance that led to the back hallway. He became aware of a slight change in the light, a shadow. A movement.

A figure slowly approaching.

Nick knew enough not to break eye contact with Cassie. He looked into her red-rimmed eyes, while in his peripheral vision he could make out a woman moving stealthily along the wall, advancing toward the kitchen.

It was the police detective, Audrey Rhimes.

Don't break eye contact. He forced himself to look into Cassie's desperate heavy-lidded eyes, bottomless pools of anguish and madness.

"Not like my daddy. He was scared of me, he followed me everywhere, wouldn't leave me alone, but he'd never do for me what you did for your kids."

"He loved you, Cass, you know that." His voice was shaking a little.

Keep your eyes on Cassie.

Detective Rhimes was advancing ever so slowly.

"You were so scared that night. I could see it from where I was standing, in the woods. I could hear it. The way you told him, 'Freeze,' and, 'One more step, and I shoot!'" She shook her head. "I don't know what they told you about him, but I can just imagine. Schizophrenic, right? You thought *he* was the one who killed your dog. You didn't know he was just trying to hand you a note saying he was innocent, right? You thought he was pulling out a gun. So you did the right thing, the brave thing. You protected your family. You protected your kids. You squeezed the trigger and you shot him down, and you did what a dad should do. You protected your family."

Oh, Christ. I took her father away from her and she knew it all along. Before we met, she knew it.

I took her family, and now she's going to take mine.

A terrible chill ran through his body.

She nodded, raised her left hand, the lighter hand, and Nick flinched, but she only rubbed her left forearm against her nose, sniffling. "Yeah, I was there that night, Nick. I was there first. He was following me, always following me. He knew I was paying another visit to your house. I *saw* you, Nick."

Out of the corner of his eye he saw Detective Rhimes inch ahead, closer, closer, but he didn't dare shift his eyes even a millimeter.

"He just kept coming at you and coming at you, didn't he? And no matter how much you told him to stop he kept coming because he really didn't understand." Her voice deepened, in an eerie imitation of her father's voice: "Never—safe! Never—safe!" She shook her head. "I'll never forget the look on your face afterward. I've never seen a man look so frightened. And so sad."

"Cassie, I—God, I'm so, *so* sorry, I don't know what else to say. I'm going to face up to what I've done. I'm going to answer for it."

"Sorry? Oh, don't get me wrong, I'm not *mad*. Don't apologize. It was beautiful, what you did. You were protecting your family."

"Cassie, please . . ."

"Of course you had to do it. Oh, don't I know it. Don't get me wrong, I'm grateful. It was a liberation, you know. It freed me. My daddy was in a prison of his own mind, but I was a prisoner, too, until you freed me. And then I met you and I saw what a strong man you were. A good man, I thought. You needed a wife, and your kids needed a mommy, and we could all be a family."

"We can still be a family."

She shook her head, knife dangling at one side, toying with the lighter in the other. A rueful smile. "No,

Nick. I know how these things work. I've been through it time and time again, and I just"—her voice cracked, her face got small and wrinkled, and she began to really cry now—"I just can't go through it again. I'm tired. I can't do it again. Once the door slams shut you can't open it again. It's never the same. Do you understand?"

"I understand," Nick said, moving closer, wearing an expression of gentle empathy.

"Stop, Nick," she said, holding up the lighter warningly as she stepped back. "No closer."

"Things can change, Cassie. In a good way."

Tears were streaming down her face now from her smudged eyes. "No," she said. "It's time," and Nick could hear the rasp of her thumb on the flint wheel.

109

AUDREY LISTENED CLOSELY as she advanced toward the kitchen. She could hear everything the two said, and it was strange how insignificant, all of a sudden, it was to have Nicholas Conover's guilt confirmed from his own mouth.

She thought of that passage from Matthew, the parable of the unmerciful servant. She thought of the sign taped to her computer monitor that said, "Remember: We work for God."

She understood what she had to do about Nicholas Conover. The weapon that had killed Andrew Stadler had been stolen years earlier by Eddie Rinaldi, who now lay dead on the lawn.

You can't convict a dead man.

Things would be sorted out later.

But for now she had to stop Cassie Stadler.

The problem was that this situation fit no pattern she had ever trained for. She slid along the wall, felt it cold against her cheek. Gripped the smooth paint of the doorframe molding.

Did Conover know she was there?

She thought he did.

She could hear the steady high-pitched tone, and she

saw where it was coming from. It was a combustible gas detector, which measured the concentration of gas in the air. The steady tone meant that the gas in the air had reached optimal combustibility—she forgot the exact percentages, but she knew it was a range on either side of ten percent. Cassie Stadler was waiting until the air up here had reached the most dangerous concentration of propane gas, no less and no more.

You must always think several steps ahead, she told herself. What if, as she stole up on Cassie, relying on the element of surprise to take her down barehanded, she startled the woman, causing her to strike the lighter?

That had to be avoided at all costs.

She slid past the hall table, careful not to jar it and thus knock the alabaster lamp to the floor. Finally, she entered the room, and she didn't know what she was going to do next.

She listened hard, and she thought.

THE FLINT DIDN'T spark on her first try. Cassie frowned, tears coursing down her cheeks.

The gas detector shrilled, and meanwhile she sang softly in her lovely, lilting voice: "Oh, the rock cried out, I'm burning too—I want to go to Heaven the same as you."

"Cassie, don't do it."

"This was your decision. You made this happen."

"I made a mistake."

She looked above Nick's shoulder, saw something. "Luke?" she said.

"Cassie," Lucas said, walking across the kitchen straight toward her.

"Luke," Nick said. "Get out of here."

"What are you doing here, Luke?" Cassie said. "I told you and Julia to stay in the basement."

Audrey Rhimes had somehow gotten into the house

through the back door; that was the alert tone sounding, she knew to unlock the basement, let the kids out. But where was Julia?

Lucas must have taken the back corridor around, through the family room to the kitchen's other entrance.

"You locked us in," Lucas said, coming right up to her, standing to one side of her. "I know you didn't mean to. But I found the spare key."

What the hell was he doing? "Luke, please," Nick said.

But Lucas was ignoring his father. "Cassie," he said, touching her shoulder, "remember that poem you helped me with—that guy Robert Frost?" He smiled, warm and winning and appealing. "'Hired Hand' or 'Hired Man' or whatever it was called."

Cassie didn't move Lucas's hand off her shoulder, Nick noticed. She turned to look at him, her expression seeming to soften just a bit, he thought.

"Home is the place where, when you have to go there, they have to take you in," Cassie said, her voice hollow.

Lucas nodded.

His eyes slid toward Nick's for just a fraction of a second.

Nick saw it.

Lucas wasn't ignoring him at all. He was *signaling* to his father.

"Remember what you told me?" Lucas said. His luminous blue eyes held hers. "There's nothing more important than family. You said that's what it's all about, finally, in the end. That's what makes us human."

"Lucas," Cassie said, and there was a slight shift in her tone, and at that instant Nick dove at her to knock her to the ground—

—but Cassie spun, snakelike, off to one side, the

speed of a jungle animal, all lithe arms and legs. He slammed against her, knocking the knife out of her hand, but she managed to sidestep him. The knife went clattering across the tile.

She sprang to her feet and held the lighter aloft, displaying it for both men to admire, and she said, "You Conover men. What am I going to do with you?" She made a strange grimace. "I think it's time. We have to go now. A world must come to an end."

A sudden movement from behind Cassie.

Must hold her attention.

"Cassie," Nick said. "Look at me."

Her opaque eyes locked with his.

"I'm not hiding anymore, Cass. Look in my eyes and you can see it. I'm not hiding."

Her face was radiant, flushed and gleaming, more beautiful at that moment than Nick had ever seen her before. She was transfigured. A remarkable serenity had settled over her features as she thumbed the flint wheel.

And something flew out of the background and smashed down upon her head, the white alabaster lamp, and as the stone cracked into her skull, Cassie crumpled to the floor with an *Unnnnh* sound as the lighter skittered under the refrigerator.

An eerie burbling sound escaped her lips.

Audrey Rhimes's face was streaked with sweat. She looked down at the lamp still in her hand, apparently stunned by what she'd just done.

Nick stared in shock. Mixed with the powerful gas smell he could detect the faint scent of Cassie's patchouli perfume.

"Run!" she shouted. "Get out of here *now*!"

"Where's Julia?" Nick said as he started toward the exit.

"She's outside somewhere," Lucas said.

"Go!" Audrey screamed. "Anything—the slightest spark—can set this gas off. We've all got to get out of here immediately and let the fire department clear the house. *Now!"*

Lucas vaulted ahead of Nick, crashing against the front screen door before he managed to get it open, then held it open for Audrey and his father.

Julia was standing on the front lawn alongside the driveway, a good distance away.

Nick raced to her, grabbed her and hoisted her up to his shoulder, and kept on running, Lucas and Audrey close behind. They all stopped at the edge of the property just as Nick heard the loud wail of sirens.

"Look!" said Lucas, pointing back toward the house, and Nick immediately saw what he was indicating. It was Cassie, standing unsteadily at the window, watching them, a cigarette dangling out of her mouth.

"No!" Nick shouted, but he knew she couldn't hear him and wasn't listening anyway.

There was a blinding flash, and in the next instant, the house erupted in a massive brilliant fireball.

The ground shook, and fire engulfed the house almost instantly, entirely, throwing up a great column of sparks and billowing gray smoke, and seconds later the windows popped and the glass in the French doors shattered as the door frames and the window frames flew into the air, and then the flames began to plume out of every orifice, blackening the stone walls and chimneys, lighting up the clouded sky a terrible orange, and waves of heat came after them, searing their faces as they ran. Julia shrieked, and Nick held her tight, as they all ran down the long driveway.

Nick didn't stop until they had reached the road, when, winded by carrying his daughter, he had to stop. He turned back to look at the house, but all he could see now were the plumes of fire and smoke. The sirens of the fire trucks had gotten no louder, no closer. Nick knew they'd been halted at the security gate.

There would be very little left for the fire department to salvage.

He squeezed Julia harder as he said to Audrey Rhimes, "Before I come in to . . . face charges . . . I'd like to take a little vacation with my kids. Just a few days together. Is that possible, you think?"

Detective Rhimes stared at him. Their eyes locked. Her face was impassive, unreadable.

After what seemed an endless pause, she nodded. "That should be okay."

Nick looked at the blaze for a moment, and then turned to thank her, but she had already started walking down the driveway toward the police car that was just pulling in ahead of a convoy of fire trucks. The blond detective was behind the wheel.

He felt something clutch his elbow, a trembling needy grip, and he saw it was Lucas. Together, dazed and speechless, they watched the inferno for another few minutes. Though the afternoon was overcast and gray, the fire blazed so brightly that it illuminated the sky a dusky orange, the color of sunrise.

EPILOGUE

THE FIRST COUPLE of days, Nick did little besides sleep. He went to bed early, got up late, took naps on the beach.

Their "villa," as the resort called it, was right on Ka'anapali Beach. You stepped out the door and onto the sand. At night you could hear the lulling sound of the waves lapping against the shore. Lucas, normally the late sleeper, got up early with Julia to swim or snorkel. He even taught her to surf. By the time the kids returned to the bungalow in the late morning, Nick would just be getting up, drinking his coffee on the lanai. They'd all share a meal, a late breakfast or early lunch, and then the kids would go snorkeling at Pu'u Keka'a, a volcanic reef that the ancient Hawaiians revered as a sacred place where the spirits of the dead leaped from this world to the next.

He and the kids talked some, but rarely about anything serious. They'd lost just about all of their earthly possessions, which seemed not to have sunk in yet. It was funny how they never mentioned it.

Several times he tried to bring himself to talk with them about the legal nightmare he'd face when he got home: the likelihood of a trial and the near-certainty of his going to prison. But he couldn't do it, maybe for the same reason nobody wanted to talk about the day the house burned down. He didn't want to spoil what was sure to be their last vacation together for many years.

It was as if they were all surfing, riding the perfect wave, and for the moment it didn't matter that deep in the water beneath them were big, scary creatures with big, sharp teeth. Because the Conovers were up here, in the sun, and they all seemed to know without articulating it that the key to staying afloat was not thinking about what might lurk down below.

So they swam and snorkeled, surfed and ate. Nick fell asleep on the beach too long on the second day and got a painful sunburn on his ears and forehead.

Nick brought no work—he had no work—and he left his cell phone on his bedside table, switched off. He lay on the beach reading and thinking and dozing, wriggling his toes in the powdery gray sand and watching the sun shimmer over the water.

On the third day, he finally turned his cell phone back on, only to find dozens of messages from friends and Stratton colleagues who'd heard or read about what had happened to their house and wanted to make sure Nick and the kids were okay. Nick listened but answered none of them.

One was from his former assistant, Marge Dykstra, who reported that the Fenwick newspaper had run several front-page stories about how Fairfield Equity Partners had been on the verge of selling the Stratton Corporation to China, shutting down all U.S. operations, and laying off all employees—until the deal had been blocked by "ex-CEO Nicholas Conover," who'd just announced his resignation "in order to spend more time with his family."

It was the first good press he, and Stratton, had gotten in a long time. Marge pointed out that it was the first time in almost three years that his name had appeared in a headline without the word "slash" next to it.

On the fourth day, Nick was lying on a lounge chair on the lanai, reading a book about D-Day that he'd been trying to read for months and was determined to finish now, when he heard the distant ring tone of his cell phone. He didn't get up.

A minute later, Lucas came out from the bungalow holding the phone and brought it over to him. "It's for you, Dad."

Nick looked up, marked a place in his book with his forefinger, reluctantly took the phone.

"Mr. Conover?"

He recognized the voice immediately, and he felt the old tension clutch his abdomen again. "Detective Rhimes," he said.

"I'm sorry to interrupt your family vacation."

"That's quite all right."

"Mr. Conover, this call is completely off the record, okay?"

"Okay."

"I think you should have your attorney contact the district attorney's office and arrange a plea bargain."

"Excuse me?"

"If you're willing to plead guilty to criminally negligent homicide—or maybe even just attempted tampering with evidence—the DA's willing to recommend probation with no time served."

"*What?* I don't get it."

"I don't imagine you've been reading the *Fenwick Free Press*."

"Delivery out here's kind of spotty."

"Well, Mr. Conover, we both know that the DA is a very political animal—again, this is purely between you and me, you understand?"

"Yes, of course."

"And it seems the climate around here has changed. The news about what you did for your company—well, the DA's just not optimistic that a jury will convict. Then there's the death of one of our chief suspects, Mr. Rinaldi. The district attorney's reluctant to go to trial." She paused. "Hello? Hello?"

"I'm here."

"And—well, there was another article in the paper, this morning. Raising questions about how the police handled the Andrew Stadler case."

"Such as?"

"Oh, I'm sure you know some of it. How nothing was done to stop the stalker at your house or follow up on . . . her. I think it's become obvious that if the police hadn't been so negligent, the situation wouldn't have escalated the way it did. I had to let the DA know that my testimony would inevitably make even more of this negligence public. Which no one in this department wants."

For a long time, Nick was unable to speak. Finally, he said: "I—and how do *you* feel about this?"

"That's not for me to say. You mean, do I feel justice is being served?"

"Something like that, yeah."

"I think we both recognize that the DA's decision to drop most of the charges is motivated by political expedience. But as for justice?" Audrey Rhimes sighed. "I don't know that there's any justice to be done here, Mr. Conover. I certainly don't think it would serve justice to cause your children to suffer anymore. But that's just my personal opinion."

"Am I allowed to thank you?"

"There's nothing to thank me for, Mr. Conover. I'm just trying to do the right thing." She was silent for a moment. "But maybe there *is* no right thing to do here.

Maybe it's not so much a matter of doing the right thing as trying not to do the wrong thing."

Nick set down the cell phone and for a long while watched the sunlight dance on the blue water.

He watched the seagulls caw and swoop, the waves surge and recede, the froth dissolve into the sand.

A few minutes later, Lucas and Julia emerged from the bungalow together and announced that they wanted to go for a hike, explore the nearby tropical forest and waterfalls.

"All right," Nick said, "but listen, Luke—I want you to keep a close watch on your sister."

"Dad, she's almost eleven," Lucas said. His voice seemed to be getting even deeper.

"Dad, I'm not a baby," said Julia.

"I don't want you doing anything crazy like jumping off the waterfalls," Nick said.

"Don't give me any ideas," Lucas said.

"And stay on the trail. It's supposed to be muddy and slippery in some places, so be careful."

"Dad." Lucas rolled his eyes as the two of them started down the palm-lined path. A few seconds later he turned around. "Hey, can you give me twenty bucks?"

"What for?"

"In case we stop to get something to eat on the way."

"All right." Nick pulled a couple of twenties out of his wallet and handed them to Lucas.

He watched them walking away. They were both bronzed already. Julia's curly hair was flying wildly in the breeze. Her legs were lanky, coltish; she was neither a girl nor a woman. Lucas, taller and broader all the time, wore long surfer shorts and a white T-shirt, dazzling in the sun, that was still creased from the suitcase.

As Nick stared after his kids, Lucas suddenly turned around. "Dad?"

"What?"

A gull cawed as it spotted a fish, then dove to the water.

Lucas looked at him for a moment. "You come too."

ACKNOWLEDGMENTS

NO, THE STRATTON Corporation is *not* a thinly disguised fictional version of Steelcase or Herman Miller—as anyone who works there knows. But I'm grateful to several key people at those great companies who understood the difference between fiction and reality and were willing to let me poke around, tour their offices and factories, and ask rude, provocative, and irrelevant-seeming questions. At Steelcase, Inc., in Grand Rapids, Michigan, I was helped immeasurably by Debra Bailey, director of corporate communications, and Jeanine Hill, public relations manager. I've visited a lot of corporations by now, but I've never encountered a PR staff as open and honest and welcoming and just damned *friendly*. Deb Bailey also gave me the consummate insider's tour of Grand Rapids that made me want to move there . . . almost. I was particularly impressed by the president and CEO of Steelcase, Jim Hackett, who was generous with his time and insights into the challenges (personal and professional) of running a major corporation, modernizing it, and getting it through some really tough times. Frank Merlotti Jr., president of Steelcase North America, told me about being a hometown kid who makes it to the top of the biggest company in town. At Herman Miller in Zeeland, Michigan, Bruce Buursma gave me a fascinating introduction to that company's very cool headquarters. Rob Kirkbride of *The Grand Rapids Press* gave me an interesting journalistic perspective on those companies. Unfortunately, in neither place did I meet anyone who remotely resembled Scott McNally.

Most of the CEOs and CFOs I talked to during the research for *Company Man* prefer to remain anonymous. They know who they are, and I thank them for setting aside precious time for this fictional enterprise. My friend Bill Teuber, chief financial officer of the EMC Corporation, contributed in innumerable ways, including explaining what the hell a CFO does. My Yale classmate Scott Schoen, senior managing director of Thomas H. Lee Partners in Boston, kindly took time away from some very high-powered deal-making to help me flesh out the fictional Fairfield Partners and its machinations. No Todd Muldaurs there either, by the way.

Once again, my old buddy Giles McNamee, managing director of McNamee Lawrence & Co., was a key unindicted coconspirator in devising creatively evil financial plots; I appreciate his complicity and generosity. Mike Bingle of Silver Lake Partners was an immense help in solving all sorts of tricky plot problems. (Thanks to Roger McNamee of Elevation Partners for introducing us.) Nell Minow, founder of the Corporate Library, clarified how corporate boards of directors work (or don't).

Many thanks to my corporate security experts, none of whom bore any resemblance to Eddie Rinaldi, including George Campbell, former chief security officer at Fidelity Investments; and the brilliant Jon Chorey, chief engineer, Fidelity Security Services, Inc. Bob McCarthy of Dedicated Micros illuminated the intricacies of digital video surveillance systems, as did Jason Lefort of Skyway Security, and particularly Tom Brigham of Brigham Scully. Thanks, too, to Rick Boucher of Seaside Alarms in South Yarmouth, Massachusetts. Skip Brandon, formerly deputy assistant director of the FBI and founding partner of the international security consulting firm Smith Brandon—a valued source, and friend, since *The Zero Hour*—provided some intriguing background on money laundering and shell corporations. And again, the attorney Jay Shapiro, of Katten Muchin Zavis Rosenman, was my main man on criminal law. If I got in trouble like Nick, I'd hire Jay in a second.

Even an ordinary homicide investigation can be complicated, but in trying to make Audrey Rhimes's job as hard as possible, I surely drove my two homicide experts half-crazy. My deepest thanks to Dean Garrison of the Grand Rapids Police Department's Forensic Services Unit—writer, firearms specialist, and mordantly funny observer of the foibles of police work—and Detective Kenneth Kooistra, legendary homicide investigator recently retired from the GRPD Major Case Unit, whose war stories are spellbinding and whose generosity was boundless. Trooper Ryan Larrison, firearms examiner with the Michigan State Police, patiently took me through the intricacies of the Integrated Bullet Identification System. I thank, also, Gene Gietzen of Forensic Consulting in Springfield, Missouri; George Schiro of Acadiana Criminalistics Laboratory in New Iberia, Louisiana; Sergeant Kathy Murphy of the Cambridge Police Department; and Detective Lisa Holmes of the Boston Police Department. Stanton Kessler, M.D., was again my chief source on autopsy procedures and pathology. Mike Hanzlick was quite instructive on the perils of natural gas.

It's been a while since I've been a sixteen-year-old—I

seem to have repressed all memories—so when it came to Lucas, I was fortunate to draw upon the trenchant observations of Eric Beam and Stefan Pappius-Lefebvre, who are both charismatic and articulate (though, alas, nowhere *near* as angry and alienated as I wanted them to be, for my purposes). Nick's family life, and particularly his relationship with Luke, owes much to Michael Gurian, therapist and bestselling author of *The Wonder of Boys*.

On the esoterica of fly-fishing, my friend Allen Smith was a great source; on hockey, I'm indebted to Steve Counihan, tennis pro and hockey star. Thanks again to my gifted researcher on this and several other of my books, Kevin Biehl, and to my wonderful former assistant, Rachel Pomerantz. And to a few good friends for chipping in, too: Joe Teig and Rick Weissbourd. My brother Dr. Jonathan Finder, contributed medical advice; my younger sister, Lisa Finder, a research librarian at Hunter College, assisted with research; and my older sister, Susan Finder, an attorney in Hong Kong, fact-checked the China stuff. I'm grateful, as always, to my terrific agent, Molly Friedrich, and her assistant, Paul Cirone, of the Aaron Priest Agency for their constant support as well as some very useful editorial contributions.

Now, as to my publisher, St. Martin's Press—man, am I lucky to have joined such an excellent and enthusiastic publishing team, and I thank them all, particularly CEO John Sargent, publisher Sally Richardson, Matthew Shear, John Cunningham, George Witte, Matt Baldacci, Christina Harcar, Nancy Trypuc, Jim DiMiero, Alison Lazarus, Jeff Capshew, Brian Heller, Ken Holland, Andy LeCount, Tom Siino, Rob Renzler, John Murphy, Gregg Sullivan, Peter Nasaw, Steve Eichinger, and at Audio Renaissance, Mary Beth Roche, Joe McNeely, and Laura Wilson.

And to my amazing editor, Keith Kahla—well, you're the best.

My daughter, Emma, was my chief source on the lives of ten-year-old girls, from baseball to The Sims. In the frenzied last months of my work on *Company Man,* she had to suffer my long absences; but she cheerfully brought lemonade down the hill to my writing studio in Truro and always kept my spirits up. She and my wife, Michele Souda, were my great sources of support during the writing of this book.

And once again I thank, above all, my brother Henry Finder, editorial director at *The New Yorker*: perpetual-motion idea generator, tireless brainstormer, peerless editor of first and last resort. I could not have done it without you.

Read on for an excerpt from

KILLER INSTINCT

BY JOSEPH FINDER

Available from
St. Martin's Paperbacks!

PROLOGUE

I'D NEVER FIRED a gun before.

In fact, before this evening, I'd never even held one.

It was a Colt .45 semiautomatic pistol, and it felt heavy and awkward in my hand. Its grip was rough. I couldn't steady the weapon. Still, I was close enough to him now to put a bullet in the center of his chest. If I didn't—if I didn't kill him now—there was no question he'd kill me. I was no match for him, and we both knew it.

It was the middle of the night, and we were the only ones on the twentieth floor, probably in the entire building. Outside my office, the maze of cubicles was dark. All those people who worked with me and for me, I'd probably never see again.

My hand was trembling, but I squeezed the trigger.

JUST A FEW days ago, if you looked at me you'd see a successful corporate executive. A guy with a high-powered job married to a beautiful woman. A man for whom everything seemed to be going perfectly.

My idea of danger had been going to bed without brushing my teeth.

Now I didn't think I was going to live to see the morning.

So where did I go wrong? How far back did it go? First grade, when I hit that kid Sean Herlihy with a snowball? Fourth grade, when I was picked third to last for the kickball team?

No, I can tell you exactly when it began.

It was ten months ago.

1

OKAY, SO I'M an idiot.

The Acura went into a ditch because I was trying to do too many things at once. Radiohead's "The Bends" was playing, loud, while I was driving home, too fast, since I was late as usual. Left hand on the wheel, while with my right hand I was thumbing my BlackBerry for e-mails, hoping I'd finally nailed a deal with a huge new customer. Most of the e-mails were blowback from the departure of our divisional vice president, Crawford, who'd just jumped ship to Sony. Then my cell phone rang. I dropped the BlackBerry on the car seat and grabbed the cell.

I knew from the ring that it was my wife, Kate, so I didn't bother to turn down the music—I figured she was just calling to find out when I'd be home from work so she could get dinner ready. She'd been on a tofu kick the last few months—tofu and brown rice and kale, stuff like that. It had to be really good for you, since it tasted so bad. But I'd never tell her so.

That wasn't why she was calling, though. I could tell right away from Kate's voice that she'd been crying, and even before she said anything I knew why.

"DiMarco called," she said. DiMarco was our doctor

at Boston IVF, who'd been trying to get Kate pregnant for the last two years or so. I didn't have high hopes, plus I didn't personally know anyone who'd ever made a baby in a test tube, so I was dubious about the whole process. I figured high tech should be for flat-screen plasma monitors, not making babies. Even so, it felt like I'd been punched in the stomach.

But the worst thing was what it would do to Kate. She was crazy enough these days from the hormone injections. This would send her over the edge.

"I'm really sorry," I said.

"They're not going to let us keep trying forever, you know," she said. "All they care about is their numbers, and we're bringing them down."

"Katie, it's only our third try with the IVF stuff. It's like a ten percent chance or something per cycle anyway, right? We'll keep at it, babe. That's all."

"The point is, what are we going to do if this doesn't work?" Kate's voice got all high and choked, made my heart squeeze. "Go to California, do the donor egg thing? I can't go through that. Adopt? Jason, I can barely hear you."

Adoption was fine with me. Or not. But I'm not totally clueless, so instead I focused on turning down the music. There's some little button on the steering wheel that I've never figured out how to use, so with the thumb of my driving hand I started pushing buttons, but instead the volume increased until Radiohead was blaring.

"Kate," I said, but just then I realized that the car had veered onto the shoulder and then off the road. I dropped the phone, grabbed the wheel with both hands, cut it hard, but too late.

There was a loud *ka-chunk*. I spun the steering wheel, slammed on the brakes.

A sickening metallic crunch. I was jolted forward,

thrown against the wheel, then backwards. Suddenly the car was canting all the way down to one side. The engine was racing, the wheels spinning in midair.

I knew right away I wasn't hurt seriously, but I might have bruised a couple of ribs slightly. It's funny: I immediately started thinking of those old black-and-white driver-ed shock movies they used to show in the fifties and sixties with lurid titles like *The Last Prom* and *Mechanized Death*, from the days when all cops had crew cuts and wore huge-brimmed Canadian Mountie hats. A guy in my college frat had a videotape of these educational snuff flicks. Watching them could scare the bejeezus out of you. I couldn't believe anyone learning to drive back then could see *The Last Prom* and still be willing to get behind the wheel.

I turned the key, shut off the music, and sat there for a couple of seconds in silence before I picked the cell phone off the floor of the car to call Triple A.

But the line was still open, and I could hear Kate screaming.

"Hey," I said.

"Jason, are you all right?" She was freaking out. "What *happened*?"

"I'm fine, babe."

"Jason, my God, did you get in an *accident*?"

"Don't worry about it, sweetheart. I'm totally—I'm fine. Everything's cool. Don't worry about it."

FORTY-FIVE MINUTES LATER a tow truck pulled up, a bright red truck, M.E. WALSH TOW painted on the side panel. The driver walked over to me, holding a metal clipboard. He was a tall, broad-shouldered guy with a scruffy goatee, wearing a bandana on his head knotted at the back and long gray-flecked brown hair in a kind of mullet. He was wearing a black leather Harley-Davidson jacket.

"Well, that sucks," the dude said.

"Thanks for coming," I said.

"No worries," Harley said. "Let me guess. You were talking on your cell phone."

I blinked, hesitated for a microsecond before I said sheepishly, "Yeah."

"Damn things are a menace."

"Yeah, totally," I said. Like I could survive without my cell phone. But he didn't exactly seem to be a cell phone kind of guy. He drove a tow truck and a motorcycle. Probably had a CB radio in there along with his Red Man chewing tobacco and Allman Brothers CDs. And a roll of toilet paper in the glove compartment. Kind of guy who mows his lawn and finds a car. Who thinks the last four words of the national anthem are "Gentlemen, start your engines."

"You okay?" he said.

"Yeah, I'm good."

He backed the truck around to my car, lowered the bed, hooked the winch up to the Acura. He switched on the electric pulley thing and started hauling my car out of the ditch. Fortunately, we were on a fairly deserted stretch of road—I always take this shortcut from the office in Framingham to the Mass Pike—so there weren't too many cars whizzing by. I noticed the truck had a yellow "Support Our Troops" ribbon sticker on one side and one of those black-and-white POW/MIA stickers on the windshield. I made a mental note to myself not to criticize the war in Iraq unless I wanted to get my larynx crushed by the guy's bare hands.

"Climb in," he said.

The cab of the truck smelled like stale cigar smoke and gasoline. A Special Forces decal on the dashboard. I was starting to get real warm and fuzzy feelings about the war.

"You got a body shop you like?" he said. I could

barely hear him over the hydraulic whine of the truck bed mechanism.

I had a serious gearhead friend who'd know, but I couldn't tell a carburetor from a caribou. "I don't get into accidents too often," I said.

"Well, you don't look like the kinda guy gets under the hood and changes the oil himself," Harley said. "There's a body shop I know," he said. "Not too far from here. We're good to go."

WE MOSTLY SAT there in silence while he drove. I made a couple of attempts to get a conversation started with Harley, but it was like striking a wet match.

Normally I could talk to anyone about anything— you name it, sports, kids, dogs, TV shows, whatever. I was a sales manager for one of the biggest electronics companies in the world, up there with Sony and Panasonic. The division I work for makes those big beautiful flat-panel LCD and plasma TVs and monitors that so many people lust after. Very cool products. And I've found that the really good sales reps, the ones who have the juice, can start a conversation with anybody. That's me.

But this guy didn't want to talk, and after a while I gave up. I was kind of uncomfortable sitting there in the front seat of a tow truck being chauffeured around by a Hells Angel, me in my expensive charcoal suit, trying to avoid the chewing gum, or tar, or whatever the hell it was stuck on the vinyl upholstery. I felt my rib cage, satisfied myself that nothing had broken. Not even all that painful, actually.

I found myself staring at the collection of stickers on the dashboard—the Special Forces decal, a "These Colors Don't Run" flag decal, another one that said "Special Forces—I'm the Man Your Mother Warned You About." After a while, I said, "This your truck?"

"Nah, my buddy owns the towing company and I help out sometimes."

Guy was getting chatty. I said, "He Special Forces?"

A long silence. I didn't know, were you not supposed to ask somebody if they were in the Special Forces or something? Like, he could tell me, but then he'd have to kill me?

I was about to repeat the question when he said, "We both were."

"Huh," I said, and we both went quiet again. He switched on the ball game. The Red Sox were playing the Seattle Mariners at Fenway Park, and it was a tight, hard-fought, low-scoring game, pretty exciting. I love listening to baseball on the radio. I have a huge flat-panel TV at home, which I got on the friends-and-family discount at work, and baseball in high-definition is awesome. But there's nothing like a ball game on the radio—the crack of the bat, the rustling crowd, even the stupid ads for auto glass. It's classic. The announcers sound exactly the way they did when I was a kid, and probably sound the same as when my late father was a kid. Their flat, nasal voices are like an old pair of sneakers, comfortable and familiar and broken-in. They use all the well-worn phrases like *"high—fly—ball!"* and "runners at the corners" and "swing and a miss." I like the way they suddenly get loud and frenzied, shouting things like, "Way back! *Way back!*"

One of the announcers was commenting about the Sox pitcher, saying, ". . . but even at the top of his game, he's never going to come close to the fastest recorded pitch speed of one hundred point nine miles an hour, thrown by . . . ? Jerry, you must know that one."

And the other guy said, "Nolan Ryan."

"Nolan Ryan," the first guy said, "very good. Clocked at Anaheim Stadium, August the twentieth, nineteen-seventy-four." Probably reading off the prompter, some research fed him by a producer.

I said, "Wrong."

The driver turned to me. "Huh?"

I said, "These guys don't know what they're talking about. The fastest recorded pitch was Mark Wohlers."

"Very good," Harley said, nodding. "Mark Wohlers. Hundred and three."

"Right," I said, surprised. "Hundred and three miles per hour, in nineteen-ninety-five."

"Atlanta Braves spring training." Then he smiled, an easy grin, his teeth even and white. "Didn't think anyone else knew that," he said.

"Of course, the fastest pitcher ever, not in the major leagues—"

"Steve Dalkowski," said Harley. "Hundred and ten miles an hour."

"Shattered an umpire's mask," I said, nodding. "So were you a baseball geek when you were a kid, too? Collection of thousands of baseball cards?"

He smiled again. "You got it. Those Topps gum packs with that crappy stale bubble gum inside."

"That always stained one of the cards in the pack, right?"

He chuckled.

"Your dad take you to Fenway a lot?" I said.

"I didn't grow up around here," he said. "Michigan. And my dad wasn't around. Plus we couldn't afford to go to games."

"We couldn't either," I said. "So I listened to games on the radio a lot."

"Same here."

"Played baseball in the backyard?" I said. "Break a lot of windows?"

"We didn't have a backyard."

"Me neither. My friends and I played in a park down the street."

He nodded, smiled.

I felt like I knew the guy. We came from the same background, probably—no money, no backyard, the whole deal. Only I went to college and was sitting here in a suit, and he'd gone into the army like a lot of my high school buddies did.

We listened to the game for a bit. Seattle's designated hitter was up. He swung at the first pitch. You could hear the crack of the bat. "And there's a *high* fly ball hit *deep* to left field!" one of the announcers crowed. It was headed right for the glove of a great Red Sox slugger, who also happened to be a famously clumsy outfielder. And a space cadet who did things like disappear from left field, right in the middle of a game, to take a leak. When he wasn't bobbling the ball.

"He's got it," said the announcer. "It's headed right for his glove."

"He's going to drop it," I said.

Harley laughed. "You said it."

"Here it comes," I said.

Harley laughed even louder. "This is painful," he said.

A roar of disappointment in the ballpark. "The ball hit the *back* of the glove," said the announcer, "as he tried to slide to make the play. This is a *major*-league error right here."

We groaned simultaneously.

Harley switched it off. "I can't take it anymore," he said.

"Thank you," I said, as we pulled into the auto body shop parking lot.

IT WAS A kind of scuzzy place that looked like a converted gas station. WILLKIE AUTO BODY, the sign said.

The manager on duty was named Abdul and probably wouldn't have an easy time getting through airport security these days. I thought Harley would start off-loading the carcass of my poor Acura, but instead he came into the waiting room and watched Abdul take down my insurance information. I noticed another "Support Our Troops" sticker on the wall in here, too, and a Special Forces decal.

Harley said, "Jeremiah at home?"

"Oh, yeah," said Abdul. "Sure. Home with the kids."

"This is a friend of mine," he said. "Make sure you guys take care of him."

I looked around and realized the tow truck driver was talking about me.

"Of course, Kurt," Abdul said.

"Tell Jerry I was here," Harley said.

I read an old copy of *Maxim* while the tow truck driver and Abdul walked back to the shop. They returned a couple of minutes later.

"Abdul's going to put his best master tech on your car," Harley said. "They do good work here. Computerized paint-mixing system. Nice clean shop. Why don't you guys finish up the paperwork, and I'll get the car in the service bay?"

"Thanks, man," I said.

"Okay, Kurt, see you," said Abdul.

I came out a few minutes later and saw Harley sitting in his tow truck, engine idling, listening to the game.

"Hey," he said, "where do you live? I'll drop you off."

"It's pretty far. Belmont."

"Grab your stuff out of the car and jump in."

"You don't mind?"

"I get paid by the hour, buddy. Not by the job."

I got my CDs off the floor of the car and my briefcase and baseball glove off the backseat.

"You used to work in a body shop?" I said when I'd gotten back into the truck.

The walkie-talkie started blaring, and he switched it off. "I've done everything."

"How do you like towing?"

He turned and gave me an *Are you out of your mind?* look. "I take whatever work I can get."

"People don't like to hire soldiers anymore?"

"People love to hire soldiers," he said. "Just not ones with DDs."

"What's a DD?"

"Dishonorable discharge. You gotta put it down on the application, and as soon as they see that, you're out the door."

"Oh," I said. "Sorry I asked. None of my business."

"No big deal. It just pisses me off. You get a DD, you don't get any VA benefits or pension. Sucks big-time."

"How'd it happen?" I said. "If you don't mind my asking."

Another long silence. He hit the turn signal, changed lanes. "Nah, I don't mind." He paused again, and I wasn't sure he was going to answer. Then he said: "The CO of my Special Forces A-Team ordered half of us to go on this suicide mission, this broke-dick reconnaissance mission in Tikrit. I told the CO there was a ninety-nine percent chance they'd get ambushed, and guess what? The guys got ambushed. Attacked with rocket-propelled grenades. And my buddy Jimmy Donadio was killed."

He fell silent. Stared straight ahead at the road as he drove. Then: "A good kid, just about finished with his tour, had a baby he'd never even seen. I loved that guy. So I just lost it. Went after the CO—head-butted the bastard. Broke his nose."

"Wow," I said. "Jesus. I can't blame you. So you got court-martialed or something?"

He shrugged. "I'm lucky they didn't send me to Leavenworth. But nobody in the command wanted to draw any attention to what went down that night, and they sure as hell didn't want CID looking into it. Bad for army morale. More important, bad PR. So the deal was, dishonorable discharge, no time."

"Wow," I said again. I wasn't sure what CID was, but I wasn't going to ask.

"So are you, like, a lawyer or something?"

"Salesman."

"Where?"

"Entronics. In Framingham."

"Cool. Can you get me a deal on a plasma TV?"

I hesitated. "I don't sell the consumer line, but I might be able to do something."

He smiled. "I'm kidding. I couldn't afford one of those anyway, even wholesale. So, I noticed the glove you got back there. Sweet. Rawlings Gold Glove, Heart of the Hide. Same as the pros use. Looks brand-new. Right out of the box. Just get it?"

"Um, about two years," I said. "Gift from my wife."

"Oh. You play?"

"Not much. Mostly on my company's team. Softball, not baseball, but my wife didn't know the difference." Our team sucked. We were on a losing streak that resembled the Baltimore Orioles' historically pathetic 1988 season. "You play?"

He shrugged. "Used to."

A long beat of silence.

"In school or something?" I said.

"Got drafted by the Detroit Tigers, but never signed."

"Seriously?"

"My pitch speed was clocked at ninety-four, ninety-five miles an hour."

"No way. Jesus!" I turned to look at him.

"But that wasn't where my head was, at that point.

Enlisted instead. I'm Kurt, by the way." He took his right hand off the wheel and gave me a firm handshake. "Kurt Semko."

"Jason Steadman."

There was another long silence, and then I had an idea.

"We could use a pitcher," I said.

"Who?"

"My company's team. We've got a game tomorrow night, and we sure could use a decent pitcher. How would you like to play on our team tomorrow?"

Another long pause. Then: "Don't you have to work for the company?"

"Guys we play have no idea who works for us and who doesn't."

Kurt went quiet again.

After a minute, I said, "So what do you think?"

He shrugged. "I don't know." He was staring at the road, a half smile on his face.

At the time it seemed like a fun idea.

2

I LOVE MY wife.

Sometimes I can't believe that a woman as intelligent and sophisticated and, oh yeah, unbelievably beautiful, settled for a guy like me. She likes to joke that our courtship was the greatest job of salesmanship I ever pulled off. I don't disagree. I did close the deal, after all.

When I walked in, Kate was sitting on the couch watching TV. There was a bowl of popcorn in her lap and a glass of white wine on the coffee table in front of her. She was wearing faded old gym shorts from her prep school, which nicely set off her long, toned legs. As soon as she saw me come in, she got up from the couch, ran over to hug me. I winced, but she didn't notice. "Oh, my God," she said. "I've been so worried."

"I'm fine, I told you. The only thing that got hurt was my pride. Though the tow truck driver thought I was an idiot."

"You're totally okay, Jase? Were you wearing a seat belt and everything?" She pulled back to look at me. Her eyes were a great shade of hazel green, and her hair was full and black, and she had a sharp jawline and high cheekbones. She reminded me of a young, dark-haired Katharine Hepburn. Endearingly enough, she considered herself plain, her features too sharp and exaggerated. Tonight, though, her eyes were bloodshot and puffy. She'd obviously been crying a lot.

"The car just went off the side of the road," I said. "I'm fine, but the car got messed up."

"The car," she said with an airy wave, as if my Acura TL were a wad of toilet paper. I assume she inherited these aristocratic gestures from her parents. You see, Kate comes from money, sort of. That is, her family was once very rich, but the money never made it to her generation. The Spencer fortune took a big hit in 1929, when her great-grandfather made some really dumb investment decisions around the time of the Crash, and finally got finished off by her father, who was an alcoholic and only knew how to spend money, not manage it.

All Kate got was part of an expensive education, a cultivated voice, a lot of rich family friends who now felt sorry for her, and a houseful of antiques. Many of which she'd jammed into our three-bedroom colonial house on a quarter acre in Belmont.

"How'd you get back?" she said.

"Tow truck driver. Interesting guy—ex–Special Forces."

"Hmm," she said, that not-interested-but-trying-to-fake-it noise I knew so well.

"Is that dinner?" I said, pointing to the bowl of popcorn on the coffee table.

"Sweetie, I'm sorry. I just didn't feel like cooking tonight. You want me to make you something?"

I could visualize the brick of tofu lurking in the refrigerator, and I almost shuddered. "Don't worry about it. I'll just grab something. Come here." I hugged her again. Braved the pain without wincing this time. "Forget about the car. I'm worried about you."

All of a sudden she started crying as I held her. She kind of crumpled. I felt her chest heave and her hot tears dampen my shirt. I squeezed her tight. "It's just that I really thought . . . this one was going to work," she said.

"Next time, maybe. We just have to be patient, huh?"

"Do you not worry about *anything*?"

"Just stuff I can do something about," I said.

AFTER A WHILE, we sat down together on the couch, which was an uncomfortable but no doubt really valuable English antique as hard as a church pew, and watched some documentary on the Discovery Channel about bonobos, which are apparently a species of monkey smarter and more highly evolved than us. Seems the bonobos are a female-dominated society. They showed footage of the female bonobo trying to seduce a male, spreading her legs and putting her butt up to the male's face. The announcer called that "presenting." I suppressed a remark about our own conjugal relations, which had become just about nonexistent. I don't know if it was the fertility treatments or what, but our sex life lately had turned into a kind of bed death. I couldn't remember the last time Kate had "presented."

I took a handful of popcorn. It was air-popped and lightly spritzed with I Can't Believe It's Not Butter. It tasted like Styrofoam peanuts. I couldn't politely spit it out, so I finished chewing and swallowed it.

The female bonobo didn't seem to be scoring, but she kept at it. She stretched out an arm and beckoned at the male with upstretched fingers like a silent film star playing a harlot. But the guy was a dud. So she went up to him and grabbed his balls, hard.

"Ouch," I said. "I don't think she's read *He's Just Not That Into You*."

Kate shook her head and tried not to smile.

I got up and went to the bathroom and swallowed a couple of Advil. Then I went to the kitchen and served myself a big bowl of ice cream, Brigham's Oreo. I didn't bother to ask Kate if she wanted any, because she never ate ice cream. She never ate anything remotely fattening.

I sat back down and dug into the ice cream while the narrator said, "The females kiss and hug and rub their genitals together with their special friends."

"So where are the male bonobos, anyway?" I said. "Sitting on the couch with the remote control?"

She watched me tuck into the ice cream. "What's that, babe?"

"This?" I said. "Fat-free tofu ice-milk substitute."

"Sweetheart, you know, you might want to lay off the ice cream at night."

"I never feel like it at breakfast."

"You know what I'm saying," she said, and touched her perfectly flat belly. I, on the other hand, was already developing a potbelly at thirty. Kate could eat anything she wanted and not gain weight. She just had this incredible metabolism. Women hated her for that. I found it a little annoying myself. If I had her metabolism, I wouldn't be eating bulgur and tempeh.

"Can we watch something else?" I said. "This is getting me too horny."

"Jason, that's disgusting." She grabbed the remote and began flipping through the hundreds of channels until she stopped at a show that looked familiar. I recognized the actors who played the beautiful high-school-age brother and sister and their divorced father, himself a divorce lawyer. This was that Fox show *S.B.*, about beautiful rich high-school kids and their broken families in Santa Barbara—proms, car crashes, divorce cases, drugs, cheating moms. It had become the hottest TV show of the season.

And it was created by my brother-in-law, Craig Glazer, the hotshot TV producer who was married to Kate's older sister, Susie. Craig and I pretended to get along.

"How can you watch that crap?" I said, grabbing the remote and switching the channel to some old *National Geographic*-style show about a primitive Amazonian tribe called the Yanomami.

"You'd better deal with that hostility before Craig and Susie come next week."

"Without my hostility, what's left? Anyway, they have no idea how I feel about him."

"Oh, Susie knows."

"She probably feels the same way about him."

Kate cocked a brow provocatively but said nothing.

We watched some more of the nature show, sort of listlessly. The narrator said in a plummy British accent that the Yanomami were the most violent, aggressive society in the world. They were known as the Fierce People. They were always breaking out into wars, usually over women, who were scarce.

"I'll bet you like that, huh?" I said. "Fighting over women?"

She shook her head. "I studied the Fierce People in one of my feminism classes. The men beat their wives too. The women think the more machete scars they have, the more their husbands must love them." There was always some book about feminism on Kate's bedside table. The latest was called something like *This Sex Which Is Not One*. I didn't get the title, but luckily there wasn't going to be a quiz.

Kate had gotten interested in obscure African and South American cultures in the last few years because of her job, I think. She worked for the Meyer Foundation for Folk and Outsider Art in Boston. They gave money to poor and homeless people who made paintings and sculptures that looked like they could have been done by my eight-year-old nephew. But they didn't give much money to their employees. The foundation paid Kate eight thousand dollars a year and apparently believed she should be paying them for the privilege of working there. I think she spent more in gas and parking than she earned.

We watched the show some more. Kate ate popcorn and I ate Oreo ice cream. The narrator said that Yanomami boys proved their manhood by "blooding their spear," or killing someone. They used axes and spears and bows and arrows. And blowguns carved from bamboo that shot poison darts.

"Cool," I said.

The Yanomamo tribe cremated their dead and mixed the ashes into plantain soup and then drank it.

Maybe not so cool.

When the show was over I gave her the latest news about how the divisional vice president, Crawford, had just left the company for Sony and taken six of his top guys with him. Which left a huge, gaping hole in my department. "It sucks," I said. "Huge mess."

"What are you talking about?" Kate said, suddenly interested. "It's terrific."

"You don't get it. Entronics just announced they're acquiring the U.S. business of this Dutch company called Meister."

"I've *heard* of Meister," she said, sounding a little annoyed. "So?"

Royal Meister Electronics N.V. is an immense electronics conglomerate, one of our biggest competitors. They had a unit based in Dallas that sold the same things we did—the LCDs and the plasma screens and the projectors and all that.

"So Crawford's getting the hell out of Dodge. He must know something."

Kate sat up, drew her knees to her chest. "Listen, Jase, don't you realize what this means? This is your *chance*."

"My chance?"

"You've been stuck at the level of district sales manager for *years*. It's like you're frozen in amber."

I wondered whether she was dealing with the bad pregnancy news by throwing herself into my career. "Nothing's opened up."

"Come *on*, Jase, think about it. If Crawford's gone, along with six of his top guys, the sales division has no choice but to backfill some of those slots from inside, right? This is your chance to get into management. To really start climbing the ladder."

"Greasy pole, more like it. Katie, I like my job. I don't want to be a VP."

"But your salary's basically capped out right now, right? You're never going to make much more than you do now."

"What do you mean? I'm doing pretty good. Remember how much I made three years ago?"

She nodded, her eyes fixed on mine, like she was weighing whether to say more. Then she said, "Honey, three years ago was a freak. Plasma screens were just coming out, and Entronics owned the market, right? That's never going to happen again."

"See, Kate, here's the thing. There's this corporate egg-sorting machine for guys around my age, okay? It starts dropping the eggs into the Large and Extra Large and Jumbo cartons, right?"

"So what are you?"

"I'm not going into Jumbo. I'm just a sales guy. I am what I am."

"But if you get into management, baby, that's when you start making the real money."

A couple of years ago, Kate used to talk to me about

how I should focus on climbing the corporate ladder, but I thought she'd given that up. "Those guys in upper management never leave the office," I said. "They have to put a LoJack on their ankles. They turn fishbelly white from being in meetings all the time. Too much sucking up, too much politics. It's not for me. Why are we talking about this?"

"Look. You become the area manager and then a DVP and then a VP and general manager and pretty soon you could be *running* a company. In a couple of years, you could be making a *fortune*."

I took a deep breath, wanting to argue with her, but there was no point. When she got like this, she was like a terrier that wouldn't let go of its Nylabone.

The fact was, Kate and I had very different ideas of what a "fortune" was. My dad was a sheet-metal worker at a plant in Worcester that made ducts and pipes for air-conditioning and ventilation systems. He rose as high as shop foreman, and he was pretty active in the Sheet Metal Workers Local 63. He wasn't a very ambitious guy—I think he took the first job that came along, got good at it, stuck with it. But he worked really hard, did overtime and extra shifts whenever possible, and he arrived home at the end of the day wiped out, unable to do anything more than sit in front of the TV like a zombie and drink Budweiser. Dad was missing the tips of two of the fingers on his right hand, which was always a silent reminder to me of how nasty his job was. When he told me he wanted me to go to college so I didn't have to do what he did, he really meant it.

We lived on one floor of a three-decker on Providence Street in Worcester that had asbestos siding and a chain-link fence around the concrete backyard. To go from that to owning my own colonial house in Belmont—well, that was pretty damned good, I thought.

Whereas the house Kate had grown up in, in Wellesley, was bigger than her entire Harvard dorm building. We'd once driven by the house. It was an immense stone mansion with a high wrought-iron fence and endless land. Even after her boozer father had finally killed off what remained of the family fortune with some lame-brained investment, and they'd had to sell their summer house in Osterville, on Cape Cod, and then their house in Wellesley, the place they moved to was about twice as big as the house she and I lived in now.

She paused, then pouted. "Jason, you don't want to end up like Cal Taylor, do you?"

"That's a low blow." Cal Taylor was around sixty and had been a salesman with Entronics forever, since the days when they sold transistor radios and second-rate color TV sets and tried to compete with Emerson and Kenwood. He was a human cautionary tale. The sight of him creeped me out, because he represented everything I secretly knew I was in danger of becoming. With his white hair and his nicotine-yellowed mustache, his Jack Daniel's breath and his smoker's hack and his never-ending stock of stale jokes, he was my own personal nightmare. He was a dead-ender, a timeserver who somehow managed to hang on because of a few tenuous relationships he'd built over the years, those he hadn't neglected anyway. He was divorced, lived alone on TV dinners, and spent almost every night at a neighborhood bar.

Then her face softened and she tipped her head. "Honey," she said softly, almost wheedling, "look at this house."

"What about it?"

"We don't want to bring up kids in a place like this," she said. There was a catch in her breath. She suddenly looked sad. "There's no room to play. There's barely a yard."

"I hate mowing the lawn. Anyway, I didn't have a yard growing up."

She paused, looked away. I wondered what she was thinking. If she was expecting a return to Manderley, she sure married the wrong guy.

"Come on, Jason, what happened to your ambition? When I met you, you were this totally fired-up, sky's-the-limit kind of guy. Remember?"

"That was just to get you to marry me."

"I know you're kidding. You've got the drive, you *know* you do. You've just gotten"—she was about to say "fat and happy," I'll bet, but instead she said, "too comfortable. This is it. This is the time to go for it."

I kept thinking about that documentary about the Fierce People. When Kate married me, she must have thought I was some Yanomami warrior she could groom into a chieftain.

But I said, "I'll talk to Gordy." Kent Gordon was the senior VP who ran the entire sales division.

"Good," she said. "Tell him you demand to be interviewed for a promotion."

" 'Demand' isn't exactly my style."

"Well, surprise him. Show him some aggression. He'll love it. It's kill or be killed. You've got to show him you're a killer."

"Yeah, right," I said. "You think I can get one of those Yanomami blowguns on eBay?"